Darker Water

Once and Forever, Book 1

LAUREN STEWART

Cover Design by www.PixelMischiefDesign.com
Edited by Jen Blood www.AdianEditing.com
Formatted by IRONHORSE Formatting

Other Titles by Lauren Stewart
Unseen, The Heights Vol. 1
Hyde, an Urban Fantasy
Jekyll, Hyde Book II
Strange Case, Hyde Book III
The Complete Hyde Series Box Set
No Experience Required, a Summer Rains Novel
Second Bite

ReadLaurenS@gmail.com
www.ReadLaurenS.com

ISBN-13: 978-0-9903340-2-6

DEDICATION

For everyone who doesn't yet know they're strong enough to
ask for help, and for those who want to help them

Once Upon a Time...*there was a young woman who lived in a tall glass tower in the middle of a city. She wasn't incredibly beautiful but she was attractive, probably somewhere around the eighty-fifth percentile. She was smart, kind, honest, and good with animals.*

But the most beautiful thing about her was her heart, for it was made of the purest of golds. Unfortunately, she wasn't very good at taking care of it, and over the years, it lost its shine. Because every time she met a prince, she believed him to be perfect—strong but gentle, brave, and caring. So, she would show him her heart and give it to him to hold, thinking he would take care of it.

What she hadn't yet realized was that there was a curse put on her...at some time...by someone. And the curse was this: The moment the woman gave her heart away and kissed the prince—believing it to be true love—the prince would begin to change. Sometimes slowly, other times quickly. But he always turned into a frog. And although the frog would give her heart back to her, each time it was a little more worn, a little less brilliant.

But the woman didn't give up trying to find a prince who would remain a prince, knowing that somewhere out there was someone who could heal her heart and break the curse by

remaining a prince after she kissed him.
Then one day, she finally understood the curse's power.
No one could heal her, she would never find a prince, and the
curse would never be broken.

And so, clutching what was left of her heart, she gave up
her search.

CHAPTER 1 - LANEY

My laugh cut off as soon as I realized he might not be kidding. "Wait. What are you talking about?"

"I'm getting married." Yeah, he'd mentioned that. But that was impossible. "I've been seeing her for about a month." Kevin sighed. "Sometimes you just know it's right."

It was right. He knew it was 'right.' After a month. So all the excuses about why he couldn't see me or why he was running late were lies. But why did he keep lying to me if he knew it was 'right' with another woman? How could he have slept with me less than twenty-four hours ago if he'd known it was 'right' with someone else?

I set my coffee cup down but kept my hands wrapped around it. Just so they wouldn't shake or reach out and prove how desperate I was.

He ducked his head to meet my eyes. "Laney, did you hear me?"

"Um..." I struggled to find a word. It didn't have to be the *right* word, but I couldn't find even one to use. Because I didn't know how to feel. I hadn't seen any of this coming— our relationship was the best one I'd ever had. At least, I'd thought it was.

There had to have been signs, clues. How could I have missed them? Again.

"I need to go," Kevin said. "But if you want to talk more we can— Actually, I'm not sure that's a good idea."

I blinked and looked at him. "Where are you going?"

"How far back did you tune out?"

"I'm not sure." The moment my world dropped out from under me. How long ago was that?

"I'm meeting Brittany downtown. Since the hotel room was already booked, we're going away for the weekend. But if I have a second, how about I call you and fill you in on the last ten minutes of our conversation?"

If he had a break from fucking Brittney—the woman he'd proposed to after a month—in the hotel room he'd invited me—the woman he'd been cheating on—to go to a week ago, he'd give me a call to rub it in. Well, that was thoughtful of him.

"No, don't do that," I whispered, lowering my eyes and picking apart the paper napkin, hiding behind my bangs. "I just don't get what happened. I thought things were good." Which was why I couldn't stop wondering if this was some kind of truly torturous joke, or nightmare. But I knew it wasn't. Kevin was leaving me because I'd screwed up somehow. Because I always seemed to screw up somehow.

"What did I do wrong?"

"It's not about you, Laney. You need to understand that."

Then who the fuck was it about? No. This was Kevin, not some jerk. He was doing his residency so he could help people, for shit's sake. He would never want to hurt me. So maybe *he* was the one who didn't understand. Maybe he'd change his mind if he understood how I felt about him. If I told him.

"Kevin, I—"

A little voice in my head screamed, "*Don't say it. It's too late!*"

It was right. Because even though Kevin and I had never

said the actual words to each other, he'd used a lot of others: 'falling in love,' 'care so much,' and the ones that got me on my back the fastest: 'for the rest of my life.' Yeah, that was a good one. I'd used some of the same and some different, but he knew how I felt—that I was in love with him. And evidently, he didn't care.

If he cared he wouldn't be saying what he was saying, and we wouldn't be sitting here—him with his brow furrowed and his head tilted in pity and me with tears welling in my eyes, the feeling of something crushing my chest and the heat of humiliation spreading throughout my body. If he cared, none of that would be happening.

"You what?" His tone was impatient but even with that, his voice was one of the sexiest parts about him. He was attractive, smart, made good money, and was ambitious enough to be sure that amount would quadruple when he opened his own practice in a few years. Years I had thought I'd be sharing with him.

Oh my god, I'd told my roommate I would be moving out by the end of next month. I'd been so excited when Kevin asked me to move in with him that I was already packing up my stuff.

Wait a minute. Back up a sec. When did he ask me? Right after getting out of this other woman's bed?

What a prick.

"You what?" he repeated.

I flipped my hair out of my face and glared at him. "I was just wondering how many times you slept with me after you realized it was 'right' with whatever her name is." Every word was stronger than the last because I was sick of being quiet. "How many of those times were after you proposed to her?" Quiet got me nothing but footprints on my back. Man-sized footprints that felt like they were made with metal cleats.

"Come on, Laney, it doesn't have to end like this."

"Really?" My laugh was flat even to my own ears. "How *does* it have to end? You're so smart, Kevin. Shit, you coasted through med school, right? Top of your class ever since kindergarten. So *please*, use all those years of fancy private school and tell me how it should end." I paused, not expecting or wanting an answer. "Maybe it could end with a parade or a sky banner or, hey, here's an idea—how 'bout it ends with you showing a little respect for *both* the women you're fucking? Or honesty or integrity or honor. Would any of those be a good way to end this?"

Shushing me, he glanced around the restaurant uncomfortably. Because he cared about twenty strangers more than he cared about me.

"*They* aren't asking you—I am. And after eight months of what evidently was total bullshit, I deserve a fucking answer."

He didn't offer one. Maybe he was preparing another lie or a way to turn it around on me. Did it matter? No. It didn't change anything—not the situation, not my feelings, not how successfully he'd lied, used, and hurt me.

"Good luck with whatever her name is, Kevin. I hope you treat her better than you treated me." Better than I treated myself, for that matter. I'd spent the last eight months desperately trying to do what it had only taken Brittany a month to pull off. Shit, I'd spent the last eight *years* trying.

Different guys, same unhappy ending.

I know exactly the moment it all began: fifteen-year-old me finding out that my first boyfriend cheated on me with a girl on the softball team. The softball team. I still don't understand that. Flash forward eight years, and it's some woman named Brittany. She probably knows how to play with soft balls, too.

I couldn't take a deep-enough breath until I was on the street and didn't have to look at Kevin's face anymore. The face of a guy who was everything I'd always wanted. Nope, that wasn't true. If it *was*, I wouldn't be crying on the sidewalk, looking for a cab to take me home so I could tell my roommate my plans had changed and I needed to keep living with her instead of moving in with Kevin.

There were always cabs in this part of San Francisco. Always except for now. I stopped looking so I could concentrate on walking home without bumping into anyone. The bright side of living in a huge city was that no one would notice my tears or whimpering. Even if they did, they wouldn't care.

I watched the elevator numbers go up to nine before I realized I hadn't pressed the button for my floor. So whoever had called this elevator, whoever was expecting it, would get what they wanted really soon. And I would have to wait. I punched the sixth floor button and leaned against the back wall so I could close my eyes and imagine I was somewhere else, some*one* else. Someone who wasn't cursed.

"Is this you?"

"Huh?" I opened my eyes and saw a woman looking at me with impatience, gesturing to the open elevator door. I hadn't even noticed when she got on.

"Six?"

"Yeah. Sorry."

I was glad my roommate Hillary wasn't home, because I didn't want to talk to anyone right now. I went into my room, curled up in bed, and closed my eyes so they would stop spraying idiot-tears all over me.

When I woke up it was nineteen hours later. It had taken nineteen hours of unconsciousness to figure out the obvious.

Nothing was worth this. Nothing was good enough to keep trying and failing as many times as I had. Eight years, five guys, and I was used up. I didn't have any more to give and, if I did, I needed to hold onto it or I'd have nothing left for myself.

All I'd wanted was for someone to love me, to be someone I could love. A friend and a lover who respected me and didn't lie, manipulate, or use me. But evidently, that wasn't something I could have. Evidently, my judgment was so off, the only men I wanted were the ones who would treat me like shit. So my only choice was to stop looking—for a man, for heartbreak, for someone to love.

Lesson learned at the ripe old age of twenty-three. No matter how many times a man says he cares, he doesn't. He only cares about the pieces he can use, picking the parts he wants and leaving the rest behind. A woman wouldn't do that, *couldn't* do that. A woman wouldn't want to tear someone apart and throw away the leftovers.

Because women were just stupid enough to believe we could have it all—the knight in shining armor and all that bullshit. I'd spent a lot of nights with knights, and when I finally woke up, when there was enough light to see who he truly was, he was already on his way out the door. Off to sweep the next idiot off her feet, to promise her everything and leave her with nothing.

But ultimately it wasn't the guys' faults. It was mine, for trusting them, for believing in something that wasn't true or possible. For handing them all the weapons necessary to beat me.

I give up.

'Don't worry, sweetie,' my parents would say every time I called them sobbing over a guy. *'You'll find someone. Someone who deserves you.'* I'd bought into that crap for my entire dating life. But who the fuck *deserves* a spineless idiot? Someone who doesn't even remember what she wants or likes because she's always been told what those things were by whoever she was dating at the time. Too afraid to actually have an opinion, let alone share it.

I didn't want to be like this anymore. I wasn't always. I was a real person at one point. A strong one. That's who I needed to be again, to turn back into.

'You have to kiss a lot of frogs to find your prince.' My mother's favorite expression was completely fucking wrong. If you kiss a lot of frogs, all you end up with is sore lips and a bunch of frogs. And if you kiss a lot of *princes*, hoping at least *one* of them will stay that way, all you get is a horrific amount of disappointment and even *more* frogs.

Thanks, but I was done lying to myself. Princes didn't exist, happy endings never happened, love was all make-believe.

I took a long, cleansing shower and got ready for the day. A new day, new start, new Laney. And all the frogs could go fuck themselves.

Hillary was in the kitchen pouring cereal. "Have you been in your room this whole time?"

I nodded, taking another bowl down. "Had to figure some stuff out. The deep emotional shit you don't have to think about." Because Hillary was happily deluded and had been for almost two years, minus about a week and a half six months ago. A moment of clarity that she called a mistake. But her boyfriend was nice and treated her well, so I hoped it lasted even while I knew it wouldn't.

"Did you figure it out?"

"Think so."

"And the verdict?"

"I'm done."

"With your business or the art?"

"Neither. I'm done with men. Relationships. Love. It's not real. Except for you and Eric," I added because it wasn't my place to ruin Hillary's fantasy. "I think most"—*all*—"people only pretend they're in love. Or are deluded." It couldn't just be me—I'd have to be a lot more narcissistic to think that the whole world was against me and only me. There had to be others who'd figured it out. I hadn't met any of them, though. We realists needed to set up a support group. No frogs or fairy tales allowed.

"Well, I think you're wrong." Of course she did. Because Hillary hadn't met as many frogs as I had.

CHAPTER 2 - LANEY

Five months later...

Even though it was Saturday and I'd taken most of the day off—a big perk of working for myself—I couldn't go home yet. I'd heard Hillary and Eric yelling at each other from out in the hallway and did an about-face to avoid getting involved. I'm sure the fight was truly important, like why he never took her out anymore or something equally vital to the well-being of the planet.

By my estimation, twenty minutes later, they were either *still* fighting or they were already making up. Either way, there'd be screaming I didn't want to hear. So, I decided to stay at my favorite coffee shop for at least another half hour.

I took one of the comfy chairs in the corner, put my coffee and my feet up on the large ottoman in front of me, and opened the Angry Birds app on my phone. About fifteen minutes later, I saw jean-clad legs in my peripheral vision. His shoes were pointed towards me, but he didn't say anything.

"Listen, I'm sure you're a wonderful person, but I need to focus." I pointed to my phone without raising my head. "Or I'm going to break my winning streak."

"I'm not sure if you know this"—the legs moved a step closer—"but when you win, you don't actually get any candy. Yeah," he grumbled. "The day I found that out was one of the worst days of my life."

I wiped my mouth to cover my smile—he'd probably take it as a sign I wanted to keep talking to him. "As much as I appreciate the tip, I'm not interested."

"Me neither. Wait, what aren't we interested in again? Oh, did you mean you and me...being interesting *together*? Then yeah, actually, I *am* interested in that."

I looked up at him briefly. Well, no one could ever mistake him for average looking, that was for sure. Full lips that looked very comfortable wearing a smirk. The tattoos covering most of both forearms would've made my mom shake her head and say something witty like, '*Maybe his parents didn't give him enough coloring books when he was little.*' Light-brown hair tossed in a hot, I-have-more-important-things-to-take-care-of-than-my-hair way. One of those more important things might be his body. If I wasn't completely cured of men, I'd thank him for making it a priority. Not that I didn't find men attractive anymore—I couldn't control that. And sure, I'd love to take a few more looks at the guy. But that wouldn't bring me anything but frustration. And frustration didn't bring me anything but the need for more batteries.

Three months ago, I would've been blushing, stuttering, making a fool of myself, and planning our wedding. Now I had more important things to take care of, like my sanity. And some very unhappy birds.

So I slumped into the chair and went back to my game. "Trust me, you don't want me to get to know you, not if you like who you are right now. I'm cursed. I could turn you into a frog with barely any effort at all. Go find someone else to pretend to be in love with. I wish you luck."

He picked up my coffee from the ottoman and sat down. "Congratulations. You've just made yourself twice as intriguing. You have to know that all men enjoy a good chase every once in a while."

"I'm not running—I'm telling *you* to run. Go hunt down someone else."

"I'm Carson."

"Okay, go hunt down someone else, Carson."

"Maybe three times as intriguing." After a second, he stood. "Nice to meet you, Lane."

"It's Laney, but how did you—?"

He glanced down at my coffee cup, which he was still holding. My name was written in big letters on the side, the 'Y' an illegible scribble. I should've gone the more environmentally friendly route and skipped the paper cup. But not a big deal. All he knew was most of my name and my drink order. Thankfully they didn't write my phone number on there, too. Not that he would remember it three minutes from now, because frankly, I'm not worth that much of his effort.

He handed my coffee back but didn't go away, seemingly content to keep staring at me with a cocky grin. Okay, he was really far from average looking. But guaranteed, he was as much a liar as they all are. Maybe worse because the more attractive a guy is, the more he thinks he can get away with. I take that back—the more he *can* get away with. Because women are idiots.

"Let me guess," I said. "You're different from every other guy, searching for the one woman who will complete you. You're considerate, caring, and really want a chance to know who I truly am."

"Not at all," he said, ticking the points off with his fingers and grimacing. "Definitely not. Dear god no. That's not even *close* to what I want from you. And…was that all of them? I got distracted by your breasts for a little while there, so I may have missed one."

I coughed, covering my mouth before I spit my coffee out. "Seriously?" In the last few months I'd had a lot of similar conversations with moderately similar guys. But not a single one had an answer even remotely like that.

"Seriously. I'm a complete asshole who only cares about what he can get from someone. Take you, for example. I saw you sitting here alone, no ring, great body. And thought, 'I want to fuck her.' And yeah, those were the exact words that went through my head. On the way over here I tried to figure out the fastest and most efficient way to get you into my bed—which isn't far from here, by the way—hoping you weren't the type who needed a couple dinners out first. So, Lane"—he popped an eyebrow—"are you?"

I didn't know how to respond. Was I? I used to be. Except it had taken more than a *couple* dinners before I slept with someone. It had taken a commitment of some kind. And now? Even though I was done with relationships and love, I didn't want to be celibate for the rest of my life. I wasn't sure I was ready, but there was only one way to find out. And, as far as guinea pigs went, I couldn't have found a more attractive one. So...

Fuck it. For some unknown reason, I'd shaved my legs this morning. Maybe it was a sign from the universe that today was the day to do some experimenting.

Oh my god, I can't believe I'm about to do this. I stood, grabbed my bag, and pushed past him on my way to the door. Then I turned around. "I think that was an exceptionally efficient way to get me into your bed."

"Wow, great. Can you remind me what I said?" He winked as he came towards me and put his hand on the small of my back to nudge me outside. "So I know how to do it the next time I meet another fantastic-looking woman I can't wait to see naked."

"Hang on," I said. "Give me your wallet."

"My what?"

"Wallet."

He handed it over, an amused and curious look on his face. I peeked through it—some cash I didn't care about, a condom.

"I see you come prepared." Hadn't meant to make the pun, but both of us laughed anyway.

"I consider it a public service. You never know when a beautiful woman might need one to have sex with a guy who will do everything in his power to make sure she never regrets her decision. But if you're worried that there's only one, I have more back at my place."

He was ten times more wicked than anyone I'd ever dated, the complete opposite of everything I used to look for in a man. Untamed, irreverent, demanding. Exactly what I needed. I wouldn't fall in fake-love with a guy like this in a million years.

"You know that 'Ribbed for her Pleasure' doesn't actually mean she's all taken care of and you don't have to do anything, right?" I asked.

"No one has put anything in my complaint box since I was fifteen. And I can explain that one—it was just a simple misunderstanding."

"Uh huh. And now you are..." I pulled out his driver's license. "Twenty-five. A decade of good behavior. Well done, Carson Bennett."

"I didn't say anything about good behavior." He looked even better when he smiled.

After a deep, calming breath, I took a picture of his license with my cell phone, followed by a picture of him. Then I handed the wallet back and attached both photos to a text message that read, 'I'm going home with this guy. If he's a psycho, avenge my death. Thx,' and showed it to him before I pressed send. "I sent it to a friend. He's a cop." It wasn't true, but it sounded good.

"I didn't mean *that* kind of bad behavior."

"It's just a warning—if you turn out to be more than just a selfish bastard, you should expect to be castrated."

"Duly noted, painfully imagined, and will never be necessary. I'm only a selfish bastard. Promise."

"Okay, then." I started walking in the direction he pointed.

Because I was going home with him. *Oh my god, I'm really going to do this.* Big breath. "One thing you should know about me is that I hate small talk. So don't ask me what I do or where I'm from originally."

He gave a small nod. "I don't open doors or pull out chairs. And I rarely apologize."

"Interesting." Definitely selfish-bastard behavior. Cool. "I won't lie and tell you how incredible you are if you aren't." I'd done that with every guy I'd ever been with and all I got in return was resentment and the need to sneak into the bathroom to finish myself off after he fell asleep.

"I can't sleep with someone else in my bed," he said.

"If you push my head down, expect to feel my teeth. Sharp teeth."

"Ouch." He grimaced, laughing. "Okay, my turn." He paused for only a second. "Got one. I like to switch things up a lot because I see sex as a team sport—there are a lot of different positions on the field and we should have a chance to try all of them."

"Good one. I really, really hate it when a guy thinks he knows what I like better than I do."

"I love when a woman tells me exactly what she wants." He slipped his finger through the belt loop of my jeans and pulled me along. "I also love it when she lets me do whatever I want to do."

"There is a time and a place for a quickie, but not *every* time and not *every* place."

"Well said. If I tell a woman she's beautiful, I'm not lying. Seriously, why can't women take a compliment?"

"Not enough practice, I guess."

He stopped, keeping hold of my pants so I had to stop as well. Then he looked me in the eyes. "You're beautiful."

I felt the blush smack me in the face. I know I'm moderately attractive, but beautiful...? "I already agreed to sleep with you."

"And *that,* ladies and gentlemen, is exactly what I'm

talking about." He ran his thumb across my skin, along the thin space between my jeans and my shirt, his eyes never leaving my mouth. "Say thank you."

I swallowed. "Thank you."

He cocked his head to the side. "Better, but you'll need more practice. If there's not an app for it, there should be." He started walking again. "Now say, 'Carson, I'm going to let you do whatever you want to me for as long as you want to do it.'"

I laughed. "Nice try."

"It was worth a shot."

I couldn't remember ever being this comfortable with someone I'd just met. Obviously a good thing, seeing as how I'd be having sex with him really soon. But—

"Do you do this a lot?" Oh my god. Even *I* heard the fear and insecurity in my voice. Please, make it stop. Please?

"That's a vague and serious-sounding question." He led me towards a liquor store. Awesome idea—I was going to need a few drinks. But instead of going in, he leaned up against the glass and crossed his arms. "If you mean do I pick up a lot of women in coffee shops, then no. If you're asking me if I have a lot of sex? You'd have to define 'a lot' and I would probably still say 'not enough.' But I'm always safe, and I get regular check-ups. If you're asking me if I'm having a hard time deciding how fast I want to walk because part of me can't wait to get you naked and the other part is actually having a great time hearing your do's and don'ts, then I'd definitely say yes."

"What would you say if I asked if you were honest?"

"I'd say, 'Always'." His eyes didn't leave mine. "And then I'd tell you I *really* want to sleep with you, but you need to understand upfront that I don't date or get involved. With anybody, not just you. If that's not the same thing you want, then I will very happily continue this conversation all the way to your place where I will *keep* being honest and tell you that it was great to meet you but I have to say goodnight. So…"

His eyebrows went up expectantly.

He was so far from being the perfect guy, and that was what made him so perfect for me. No expectations, no emotional crap, no frog.

"So..." I started walking again, not checking to see if he followed. "While I think it's really hot when a guy talks dirty, certain terms must be agreed upon beforehand."

Carson started speaking when he was a step behind me. "Oral sex is never obligatory, just very, very appreciated. That also means when I go down on a woman, it's because I *want* to be there, and she better not get all shy about it. I hate that."

"Nice."

"Wait, there's more to that one. A woman should love her body at *least* as much as I do."

I liked that one a lot.

"Okay, your turn now," he said with the most honest smile I'd seen in a really long time.

It took me a minute to think of another. And then I did— one that I'd never have admitted to anyone I knew. "A guy shouldn't make a face or laugh when he hears a woman's deepest, darkest fantasies."

"What do you mean? Like what kind of fantasy?"

"I don't know. Like that I want to try fooling around with another woman and be tied up and—"

"Fuck," he groaned, then I did but for a different reason. I could tell from his expression that he'd deliberately set me up for that. And I'd completely fallen for it.

"That wasn't nice."

"True, but it was highly enlightening, don't you think?"

"I can't believe I just told you that." Although, honestly, putting it out there was freeing. And horribly embarrassing.

"Me neither, but I'm really glad you did. Now walk faster."

"I hope you're not this hurried in *all* things."

He stopped and turned to me, cupping my chin and leaning close. "I plan on exploring every curve of your body until you're begging me to be inside you. Then I'm going to make you wait while I make absolutely sure I've been everywhere. When I'm ready, I'm going to take you. Slowly. I'll set the pace, not you—not the first time, anyway." He took a breath but, at some point, I'd forgotten how. "So should we keep power-walking to my place or would you rather take a casual stroll around the neighborhood?"

"Walking. I'm walking," I said quickly. "Come on, we're walking!"

His building had a doorman, the lobby was gorgeous, and I couldn't wait to see what his apartment looked like. He didn't seem like someone who could afford a place like this.

He flipped around as soon as we saw a middle-aged couple waiting for the elevator and arguing loudly. "Mood killer, for sure. Let's take the stairs."

He pulled me up three flights of stairs. I slammed into his back before the door to the stairwell had even closed behind me, and he dropped my hand as if it burned.

"What are you doing here?" he asked someone in front of him. I peeked around and saw an incredibly beautiful blonde standing next to what I assumed was the door to Carson's apartment.

"I need to talk to you."

"Shit, Anna. Now's... You can't just drop by whenever you want. We talked about this."

All lust quelled, I stepped away from him. "I'll see you around."

"No, wait. Anna was—"

"Going to tell you about the call I just got from—"

"Enough, Anna," he snapped. "I get it." He ran a hand through his hair and came a step closer to me. "Can I get your number?"

"Jesus, Carson," she grumbled. "Where do you find these women?" She leaned around him to look down her nose at me. "Do you charge by the hour or by the night, honey?"

"By the orgasm. I make a lot more that way." I heard Carson laugh but kept my attention on the snob. "His name is

Carson?" I asked dramatically. "Thanks. I wasn't sure what to scream when I come. 'Oh god' is so impersonal, don't you think?"

Anna's look of offense was hysterical—*she* was the one who threw the stone. I wasn't going to let anyone knock me down again—man, woman, or bitchy blonde.

"I don't know about you," I said, "but I usually stick to 'baby' because it's a lot safer to go generic. *Sooo* awkward when you call out the wrong name, right? Wait, I should test it out." I cleared my throat. "Carson, that's so good," I screamed. "Yes, yes, right there, Carson!" And then smiled. "It sounds good, don't you think? You have a nice name, Carson. I like it."

"Good, 'cause I like *you*." He stared at me, his eyes traveling from my eyes to my lips and back again. "And I'm really looking forward to hearing you do that again."

"There's a first." Anna chuckled. "Carson actually said something nice to a woman he's fucking."

"We're not fucking," I said. "Because you're blocking the door."

He wrapped his hand around the nape of my neck, pulled me close, and whispered, "I might be tempted to step in to defend your honor…if you weren't so fucking good at doing it for yourself. But while it's one of the hottest things I've ever seen and that name thing was *definitely* the hottest thing I've ever heard, it's not going to make her leave."

"Then what will?" I mumbled.

Anna tapped her foot on the floor but didn't move away from the door. "Are you going to make me wait in the hallway until you're done with her, Carson?"

"Are you seriously giving me shit about how I live my life?"

"I'm not allowed to care?"

They started speaking over each other—stuff about bad timing, there not *being* a good time, priorities, and other things I couldn't follow. They sounded an awful lot like the middle-aged couple arguing near the elevators, actually.

"I'm gonna go now," I said, not knowing if either of them heard me. I didn't run to the stairway, but it was tough, humiliated in a situation that should have meant nothing to me. The opinion of his ex or his fuck buddy or whatever Anna was shouldn't matter. It wasn't a competition. Thankfully, because if it was at all based on looks, I'd lose in the first three seconds. I'm the girl who has long hair just so it looks okay stuck up in a clip right out of the shower. Anna was the kind of girl who spent three hours drying and straightening her hair before she put it up in a clip.

Carson hadn't promised me anything but a good time. And this wasn't one. But it wasn't the end of the world or even close to the worst thing that had happened to me this year, either. So, comparatively speaking, I'd get over it in no time at all.

He chased me, calling my name, but didn't catch up until I'd reached the first-floor landing. He grabbed my arm and turned me towards him. "Anna is famous for saying shit she shouldn't."

"She can say whatever she wants to other people—I don't care. But I dislike it when people call me a whore." I shrugged. "I didn't actually know I disliked it until today because Anna's the first who's ever called me one, but now I know I should add it to the list of names I don't want to be called."

"I'm sorry," he said, even though it wasn't his fault.

"I thought you didn't apologize."

"Rarely. I *rarely* apologize."

"It was nice to almost fuck you, Carson."

"It was nice to almost fuck you, too." He stepped closer, pushing me backwards with his hands on my hips. I stopped moving when I hit the wall but he didn't, not until his body was flush to mine. "But I'm not letting you go until I get something out of it."

"In the stairwell?"

"I'll take you wherever, whenever." He kissed me, slowly at first, giving us a chance to learn each other's lips. Then it got deeper and I learned that he tasted incredible and masculine and was very possibly the best kisser I'd ever met. Because I could feel his passion, understand exactly what he'd be like in everything else—commanding, experienced, patient but only up to a point. I wanted to see him lose control, to be with him when it happened.

He ran his hand up my side and cupped my breast. I think I whimpered when the pressure disappeared. Thankfully, it showed up again, this time to grab hold of my hair and tilt my head back so he could get to my neck.

Everything moved in slow motion: his lips brushing my neck, his hands holding me right where he wanted me, his hips grinding against mine. It had been a few months since I'd been this close to an erection, but I didn't remember them being *that* hard. He took my mouth again, pressing me tighter to the wall, a few too many layers of clothing separating us.

"Damn," he said after breaking the kiss and putting his hands on the wall to either side of me, his eyes still closed. I couldn't help staring at his lips, watching the way they moved, remembering the way they tasted. But the rest of him was just as gorgeous, so I wanted to taste all of that, too. "When I call you and invite you over, what are you going to say?"

"Um…" I swallowed and took a breath. "I think I'll start with something like, 'Is Anna still there?'"

"And when I say, 'No?'" He held back a second longer before leaning down to my neck and running his lips across my skin. I tilted my head farther back to give him more room to maneuver.

"I'll say, 'Are you actually going to let me into your apartment or are you planning to do me in the stairwell?'"

"Then I'll say, 'I have a very big, very empty bed to do you in and—'" Groaning, he pushed himself backwards and adjusted his cock. "Shit. We need to stop talking or I'm going to carry you upstairs over my shoulder. Which, as much as I want to do, is something I can't. I wish Anna hadn't been such a bitch but I need to—"

"You need to do whatever you need to do."

"No, I need to do *one* of the things I need to do. I'm praying that the *other* thing I need to do with the person I need to do it with will still be available to me when I can do it. Because I'm not sure I've ever needed to do anything this badly before."

"Then I guess you should ask that person very, very nicely."

"Oh, I intend to be nicer to her than any man has ever been."

"God, I hope you can do better than that," I said, typing my number into his phone.

"Ouch." He grimaced, then kissed me lightly. "Believe me, I can. You are a beautiful and complicated woman, Lane." His next kiss was harder. "Say thank you."

"Thank you." It was more moaned than said. I couldn't remember ever wanting someone this much either, and I knew next to nothing about him. But what I did know, I really, really liked. He was blistering hot, funny, smart—

No! My body tightened when I felt the unwanted warmth of emotion go through me. I couldn't let my curse ruin another man.

"You're not a nice guy, right?" I asked, pushing him away. "I mean you seem nice, but that's only because you want to get in my pants. Once you've done that, you'll stop being nice, right?" My voice sounded frantic, desperate.

"Umm… I'm not sure how nice I am, but I *am* sure that I'm one-hundred percent screwed up and without a doubt the worst possible man a woman could ever have a relationship with. If I *did* relationships, which I don't. And I've never broken anyone's heart because I don't stick around long enough to create any of those feelings. Does that make you feel better?"

I blew out a breath. "Yeah. Thanks. Just make sure you

stay that way, okay?"

"Four times more intriguing," he said, cocking his head slightly. "At least."

Oh shit. I needed to get out of here before I said something stupid like...any of the things that were flying through my head at the moment.

"Okay, bye." That was embarrassingly lame, but at least it got me moving.

The rest of the way downstairs and the whole way home, I played a mental recording of what he'd said: He was no good. He wouldn't stick around. He was there for one reason and one reason only. But even all that wasn't working.

I wasn't cut out for this. I'd never had a one-night stand before and, evidently, there was a very good reason for that. I couldn't separate the physical from the emotional, sex from love. Talking dirty and kissing in the stairwell, and I was already feeling butterflies. Stupid, toxic butterflies. I couldn't let myself turn into a weak doormat again. After months of feeling okay with myself and being alone, it should've taken at least an hour for me to turn into mush. Definitely longer than fifteen minutes.

When he called, *if* he called, I'd tell him I changed my mind. He'd probably be disappointed for three whole minutes until he found somebody else. Someone who wasn't such an idiot.

CHAPTER 3 - CARSON

Jesus. What the hell just happened? I'd kissed, touched, fucked a lot of women. But I'd never been that desperate for more. Probably a shift in the weather, or I was coming down with something. Maybe she'd just given me the flu...in two minutes. *Sure.* My body aches were all in my cock and abs and I didn't have a fever, but, sure, it could be the flu. Actually, there'd been more heat than I remembered feeling in a long time, and I'd felt a slight shortness of breath near the end of the kiss. So yeah, I should probably relax, drink a lot of liquids—obviously the alcoholic kind—take a cold shower, and go to bed. Alone.

I didn't want to go to bed alone. But she was already gone.

I stopped staring in the direction she'd gone and walked back upstairs. Something was definitely wrong with me. It wasn't overtaking the lust because that was never going to happen, but it seemed to hook itself onto it. I didn't know what the feeling was but I knew what it *wasn't.* I didn't do relationships. I didn't want to cuddle or share or find out why she was the way she was.

Except I really, really did. *Fuck.*

What I'd said to her was completely true: She was beautiful and complicated, normally not a good combination. But I wasn't looking for long term—I was looking for one, maybe two, nights. That wasn't overly complicated. Lane was funny. Something about her... What the hell was wrong with me?

My wicked stepsister huffed when I pushed by her to unlock the door to my place.

"Nice attitude on that girl," she said.

"You called her a whore, Anna. What did you expect?" I didn't invite her in, but I left the door open. "I thought she was too polite."

She tossed her bag onto a side table and went into the kitchen to get something to drink. "You used to stand up for me."

I laughed, unamused. Not gonna touch that one. "You look nice."

"I have a new boyfriend."

The words instantly made me sick. "Who is he?" Someone rich—that was a requirement. Attractive. Possibly married. Make that *probably* married, because there's nothing Anna enjoyed more than competition and misogynists.

"No one you know."

"That's not surprising considering I don't know anyone you know."

"Except your mom."

"Okay, then I don't *talk* to anyone you know," I grumbled.

"Renee wants you to call her." She set two wine glasses onto the counter and took out a bottle, grimacing at a 2006 Pinot Noir and putting it back before taking out another. And another. And another. Until she found one to her liking. The bottles were for guests, and as far as I knew, guests were wanted. So Anna wasn't a guest.

Not that I wanted the *wine* either—I'd been doing the prohibition thing for two whole weeks. And not going out meant I'd been doing the abstinence thing for two weeks, too.

Which was why I was so incredibly happy to meet Lane and so incredibly unhappy to see Anna.

"I send her a check every month so I don't have to do that." One for her and one, occasionally two, for Anna—despite my financial consultants advising against writing such fat checks to two women who were such talented shoppers.

"You know I'd be more than happy to send the check to you directly from the bank like everyone else in the world does, right?" I asked. "Then you wouldn't have to come over here." Even a year after moving out, Anna still made the trip over here twice a month if I was lucky, more frequently if I wasn't.

"But then I would never see you." She handed me a glass of wine I didn't want. "I miss you, Carson."

"Why? Doesn't your new boyfriend buy you things?"

"Did that woman find you amusing? No wonder you ran after her—you finally found someone who thinks you have a sense of humor."

"Yeah, I figured someone laughing at my jokes would be a nice change. You know, since I already have someone using me for my wallet." I nodded to her. She'd only officially been my stepsister for two years, eight years ago, and was only a few months younger than me, but I'd always felt responsible for her. And would probably always give her money.

"Speaking of..." I said. "If you aren't a fan of the postal service, I could leave the check at the lawyer's office. I'm sure they miss you, too."

"Sure they do." She sat on my couch and set her wine down. "We only have each other, Carson. You know that. From the day we met, you've known that."

Had I? Did I owe her more than I was already giving? No. Would I give her more? Absolutely. Unfortunately, Anna was my biggest weakness, and that was saying a lot considering how many weaknesses I had.

"Remember when you brought Adrienne Mackey over?" she asked. "And I snuck her out when my dad heard you guys going at it? It must have been a few months before he and your mom split up, so we were about..." She looked up at the ceiling for the answer.

"We were seventeen. And I've always considered that move a grade-A cock-block. There was never any proof your dad knew she was there."

"Oh my god, that was so *not* a cock-block! Adrienne was practically screaming two minutes after you closed the door—the entire neighborhood knew she was there." She leaned back and took a sip of wine. "I've always wondered what you did to make her scream like that, but I don't want to know. If I did, I'd never be able to get that visual out of my head." She grimaced. "Plus, I don't get your taste in women at all. Adrienne was such a skank."

"She was your best friend!"

"Duh, that's how I know she was a skank." She laughed and damn her, I did too. It was nice to see her smile—rare, and nice. And she was one-hundred percent right about Adrienne, which was exactly why I'd snuck her into the house.

"What's your point here, Anna?"

"I saved you from getting whatever horrible disease you would've gotten back then. And I saved you again tonight."

"Lane's not like that. She's—"

"Oh god! I'm gonna vomit in my mouth if you say she's 'different'."

I wasn't. I was going to say she's smart and the kind of person neither Anna nor I would ever really understand. "I get to decide who I sleep with. You get to decide who *you* sleep with. I think that's how we should keep things."

She talked for a while, as if she thought I was actually listening. I may have even nodded off, but when I opened my eyes again, she was still sitting next to me.

I cut her off mid-sentence. "Why are you here?"

"Since you never answered your phone when Scott called," she said, annoyed, "he called your mom. Since you never answered your phone when *she* called, she called me. Since you—"

"Yeah, I get it. Can you tell me what Scott wants or is his message going to be warped from going through so many dysfunctional people?" I already knew what Scott wanted. Only three reasons your family lawyer calls: money or trouble or both. And in this case, both were completely my fault. My own stupidity, a horrible conversation with my mother, and my terrible judgment about when I'd had too much to drink. Thus my new and incredibly inconvenient just-say-no attitude.

"Something about you needing to sign a check and the nondisclosure agreement. Or... The guy you tried to kill signs that, not you, right?"

"I didn't—" I didn't know what I'd tried to do. I still didn't remember how the fight started or what happened after that. But evidently it was over a woman, not a big surprise considering all men test the limits of our stupidity whenever a woman's involved. Supposedly, I didn't start the fight and tried to talk the guy down, but once it was on, it was on. I woke up without a scratch and he woke up in the hospital. So I guess I won.

"Relax," Anna said. "Sign the papers, write a check, and it's done."

It would never be done. I just didn't know what to do about it except stay farther away from trouble. Since my friends were the fuckers who always goaded me into getting wasted and stupid with them, I'd stopped going out completely. Unfortunately, that limited my opportunities to get laid.

Which reminded me... I had a very beautiful, very complicated woman to call.

"Anna?" I waited until she looked up and smiled. "You need to fuck off now."

"Always the gentleman, aren't you?" She stood and got her bag. "You'll call Scott and your mom?"

"No."

"Carson, you really—"

"Good seeing you, Anna," I said. As soon as I'd slammed the door, I called Lane. She picked up on the third ring.

"Hey, it's Carson."

"Oh, hi." Her voice wasn't as excited as it had been. What'd I expect after some foreplay up against a concrete wall in a cold stairwell before telling her I had to go talk to the crazy woman who'd just called her a whore? Fortunately, I'm persistent when I want something.

"Anna is gone. And... What was the other thing?" Right.

"I have a big bed. It's empty. Needs you in it."

She laughed, but didn't sound happy.

"What's going on?" I asked.

"I don't think I can do the casual thing. Sorry. Take—"

"Wait! Don't hang up." What was I doing? Take her obvious hint and hang up the fucking phone. But I didn't. "We don't have to have sex. We could just hang out." Oh shit, I really just said that.

"Have you ever just hung out with a woman before? Without having sex with her?"

"No, but I don't see a reason it couldn't happen."

"I'm not sure it's a good idea."

"We can meet in public. You'll be perfectly safe as long as we stay away from sex shops and mattress stores." Probably.

She didn't respond right away. "I'm not sure."

"One time. Test run. If it's too weird or I can't control myself, we can shake hands and part ways." Who was I kidding? I wouldn't be able to control myself. In public or not. There was no way I could be within three feet of her and not touch her. Just to see if the jolt I'd felt when we kissed was real. If it was, I'd get hard just imagining what everything beyond a kiss would feel like.

She sighed. "I get a cup of coffee at Bella everyday on my way home from work."

"I'll buy you tonight's."

"I'm already home and it's ten o'clock."

Damn. Had Anna been here that long? "Tomorrow."
"Just to be clear—we're not going to sleep together."
"Right." I hung up and spent the rest of the evening
thinking of a way to make her change her mind.

CHAPTER 4 - LANEY

I spun my head towards Carson when I heard him yell, "Don't let her pay for that," to the barista.

"If you buy a woman coffee," I said as soon as I didn't have to yell, "she might think it's a date."

"I take it back!" He pulled back, hands at two and ten. "That was a close one. Thanks."

"Since that's something neither of us are interested in, I think I'll get my own."

"Cool, would you pay for mine, too?" He laughed at the shock on my face. "Relax, Lane. I was kidding."

"Once we've established the rules and are settled into things, feel free to offer again." What was I doing establishing rules for anything? Or settling into anything? I walked over to the counter that held the cream and sugar. After he paid for his own cup, he followed and watched me while I doctored up my coffee.

"Wow. So the coffee is just a vehicle for the cream and sugar?"

"They don't have a Grande Cream and Sugar on their menu, so I have to improvise."

He picked the same spot I'd been in yesterday. "I meant to

get here earlier so I could put up a big 'We're not going to sleep together' sign. But it was so crazy at work, I forgot to pick it up."

"What do you do?" I asked as I sat down across from him. "I thought you didn't like small talk."

"We're trying to get to know each other. That's what friends do."

"I have friends. We meet, get drunk, and watch each other make fools of ourselves. There's a fair amount of pointing and laughing involved, too."

"That's what friends do when all of them are boys. When one of them is a woman, there's more talking involved. So tell me what you did today."

He paused.

I wiped a drop of coffee from my lip. "Would you be more comfortable if I pointed and laughed while you answer?"

"Um…" His eyes came back up to mine. "I went to the…place I work. Then I worked. Ate lunch. Worked some more. Went somewhere else to help someone with a problem they were having. And then came here."

"Well done, but next time try being more vague." I laughed. "It's fine if you don't want to tell me. But just in case you do but don't know how to talk to a woman who's clothed, I'll show you how it's done. I have a small furniture business. I know: it's a weird profession for a girl and it must be so boring, right? Well yeah, not too many women do it, but it's definitely not boring. I like it a lot. It's the business part of it I hate, and that's the part that could be going a lot better.

"Today I got up, took a shower, and went to work. I had lunch and kept working. Then I stopped working and came here. Just like I do every night, because I need to get out and I think interaction with people is important." I shook my head dismissively. "Even though I don't really interact anymore. And *that* is my current life. Wanna give yours another shot?"

"I run the fundraising for the Bennett Foundation."

My mouth dropped open. The Bennett Foundation raised

money for families of hospitalized kids. "You're such a liar! You said you weren't nice."

"I'm not."

"Anyone who works for a charity *has* to be nice."

"I thought you were referring to me in my private life, not my professional one."

"So you're a saint during the day and a sinner by night?"

"Besides saint going a *big* step too far, I sometimes work at night." He shrugged. "And I'd be happy to sin during the day if you ask really nicely, but only when I'm not working because the two should never, ever mix." He paused. "You now know my horrible secret. So how'd I do?"

"It was great. You should be really proud of yourself—you didn't stutter or explode or anything."

He leaned forward and spoke conspiratorially. "I'm new to this being-friends-with-someone-I-want–to-sleep-with thing, so you'll have to help me out. What happens now?"

"I'm not sure. I'm new to the being-friends-with-someone-who-wants–to-sleep-with-me thing."

"You've never had a heterosexual male friend?"

"Of course I have."

"Then you're not new to it. He just didn't tell you."

I touched my cheek as I felt it redden. "Do you think eventually I'll stop blushing every time you say something?"

"I hope not. Would a friend tell you that your blush shows him what you'll look like after sex? Minus the I-just-got-fucked hair."

"No. A friend wouldn't say that."

"Then I think you're going to have to do most of the talking."

Refocusing, I asked, "So you work for the Bennett Foun—?" I squinted at him. "Bennett." Carson… I'd seen his ID yesterday, knew his last name. What were the chances?

He slumped back in his chair unhappily as he watched me figure it out.

"Give me your wallet again," I said.

"No."

"Give it to me."

"Only if you're looking for a condom—yes, it's still there—and plan on going home with me right now—yes, I'll let you take advantage of our friendship...*this* time."

"I couldn't do that to you...this time." I waited with my palm out. "Fine, then remind me what your last name is, friend."

"It's a common name. In fact, it's used as a first name *and* a last name because it's so damn common."

"True, although I can't imagine everyone named Bennett would look as uncomfortable as you do right now. So you fundraise for your family's foundation? You should be proud, not embarrassed. Your dad started it, right?"

His brow tightened briefly. "No, it was setup after he died. But it was his money."

"Isn't it depressing to think about sick kids all day?"

"A lot of them get better."

"I didn't mean... I just mean it must be so stressful."

"The families have to live it 24/7. I only have to think about it for around 10/7. Doesn't seem as stressful when you look at it like that. Plus, I enjoy various methods of stress relief as often as I can. Not tonight, though, because I have a rule about not sleeping with my friends. Granted, until now they've all been men, so I've never even been tempted to break the rule before."

I could tell he changed the subject because he didn't want to talk about his family's foundation or the kids. Probably needing the division between his work and the rest of his life—saint and sinner. It explained both, actually.

"Does my job make the fantasies you had about me last night less exciting?"

"I didn't fantasize about you, Carson." Complete lie.

"Really? That's too bad. I fantasized about you twice last night and once in the shower this morning."

"Friends don't say that kind of stuff."

"Shit, you mean we're not past that yet?"

We talked for a while, and the number of innuendos he used dropped slightly. Eventually, I could look at him without thinking about how attractive he was and focus on the fact that he was completely at ease with himself and who he was, what he wanted and didn't want.

He said things so matter-of-factly that nothing came off as cheesy or slimy. As if other people would have the balls to say even *half* the things he did. As if he had no desire to be charming or seductive, even when he was directly propositioning me. I knew that when I said no, he didn't take it personally and if I said yes, he'd be one-hundred percent involved in the sex and be able to walk away right afterward. Then, if we saw each other again, he'd be exactly the same, no awkwardness or embarrassment. Because he wouldn't have anything invested—not emotionally, anyway. He gave none of his power or control away. He gave none of *himself* away.

That's how I needed to be. Someone else shouldn't be able to change who I was or what I thought about myself. Love wasn't real, but sex sure was. Logically, I understood sex didn't equal love and that, just because I was done with romantic relationships, I wouldn't have to spend the rest of my life with a plastic lover instead of a flesh-and-blood one. But I didn't know how to translate the intellectual to the psychological. And Carson did.

It wasn't something you could learn from a book. If there was a way to learn from him without regressing, I may have found a hysterical new friend *and* a hot new teacher. And if I did it slowly enough, I'd see the cliff before I stepped off it.

Of course, that was giving myself a lot of credit for doing something I'd never shown any skill at. If I was smart and just a tiny bit less curious, I would've walked out. But it was easy to convince myself to stay. I'd never had a friend I was so attracted to, and the men I'd been with never started out as friends. So it wasn't as if I'd gotten myself into another unhealthy relationship. This might be a good test to see how much I'd changed. First step would be hanging out with someone I was incredibly attracted to without letting myself start reading into everything he said or didn't say and did or didn't do.

I wasn't even close to being ready for sex yet—the rush of emotional adrenaline in the stairwell was proof of that. There was a big chance Carson wouldn't stick around until I was, but I had nothing to lose. If I was honest with him.

"I'm not ready to sleep with anyone right now," I blurted. Smooth.

He sat back in his seat. "You already mentioned that. Is this your way of telling me to fuck off?"

"Not at all. I just don't want you to think I'm leading you on. I'm not sure when I'll be ready. It might not be for a while. A really long while. Like, reeeeaaally long."

"Good thing I didn't show up naked then." He clicked his tongue against the roof of his mouth. "If you want me to go, I'm gone. But if you want me to stay or don't give a shit whether I stay or not, then I'm okay where I am.

"I don't do things I don't want to do or stay somewhere I don't want to be or behave the way someone else wants me to. On their deathbed, I doubt anybody says, 'I wish I'd let more people control my life and force me to be someone I'm not.' Do you?"

"Probably not."

"We already agreed to be friends, right?"

"Yeah."

"And, currently, neither of us sleep with our friends, right? No matter how badly we want to."

"Right."

"Then as long as you're honest with me, I'll be honest with you. Actually, I'll be honest with you even if you're not. Like if you lied about say…fantasizing about me, I would still tell you I did." He knew I had. Damn him. "I might even tell you that fantasy-you is fucking wild and if we ever do have sex, you have a lot to live up to."

"If we ever have sex, I'll show you how much you underestimated real-me when you compared me to that fantasy bitch."

"Damn, I hope you're not lying about that."

Me, too. We'd both have to wait and see.

CHAPTER 5 - CARSON

The beginning of hour two marked the longest continuous conversation I'd ever had with a woman I wanted to fuck. It passed without any balloons or lightning bolts. I decided to stick around just until I got bored. I didn't get bored. I didn't even notice how long we'd been talking until an hour later, when the café staff kicked us out.

I'd never had to wait for sex—fortunately, women seemed to like the way I looked and there were more than enough of them whose goals aligned with mine. I knew that because I made sure things were clear from the get-go. I was offering one night. If they wanted to take me up on it, fantastic. If not, both of us walked away with no hard feelings.

And Lane was the exception because *why* exactly? Because I'd been so close, had a small taste of who she'd be in bed, and I wanted more. Shit, I wanted all of it. Maybe it was her damage that made her so interesting, I didn't know. That I enjoyed talking to her was an unexpected perk. But my rules were my rules, and I wouldn't—*couldn't*—break them for anyone.

Outside the café, she paused before deciding which way to go. I already knew she would choose the opposite direction of my place. She figured it out a few seconds later.

The whole time we'd been talking, I could tell she was battling herself, trying to decide if she could have what she wanted. An easy answer for me, but Lane was different. Supposedly, a woman worries a guy will think she's a slut if she fucks him before a certain day or something. That makes no sense. The guy isn't thinking anything other than, 'Hallelujah, I'm getting laid.'

People are people and everybody is fucked up. Including Lane. But she was also unusual. What she'd said to Anna showed she had claws, and she wasn't into casual sex or being in a relationship. Which meant some asshole had done a thorough job of fucking with her head. Too bad. For all kinds of reasons.

"Why no relationships?" I asked.

She looked at me and laughed. "Kettle meet pot."

"I'm not judging, just curious. I know why *I* don't do them, but I don't know why you don't."

"You first this time. Did you have your heart broken?"

"I don't have a heart. Okay, technically I have one but I... It wasn't fair of me to ask. Sorry."

"That's twice you've apologized. I'm starting to think you were lying about that."

"What can I say?" I shrugged. "You bring the pitiful out in me."

"You're not going to tell me, are you?"

I shoved my hands into my pockets. "Nope, and that's why it was unfair of me to ask."

"Unfair, but honest." She kept walking. "I'm not good in relationships. I meant it when I told you I was cursed. It's like the Frog Prince but in reverse. I can take a really great guy and transform him into a nightmare. A cheater, a liar, an asshole, a deadbeat. Once I even turned a guy into a drug addict."

"Come on. You can't seriously claim credit for that."

"You know that saying, about how if the same thing keeps

happening and you're the only constant, chances are *you're* the problem? That's me. I'm the constant. I'm the problem."

I liked that she didn't get emotional. Her tone was serious without being whiny or melodramatic, as if she'd thought about it a lot and was satisfied with the conclusion she came to.

"Every relationship I've ever had ended when I thought things were great and *he* thought things were done. It sucks and it hurts and it involves a lot of self-pity, tears, and fried food. Way too much fried food. No offense, but men aren't worth it."

"I'd have to disagree with you to be offended. You're pretty young to be completely done with men, though, don't you think?"

She took a moment before she answered. "I'm old enough to be done being lied to and manipulated and used. I haven't spent a lot of time thinking about what comes next. It never occurred to me until my last breakup, but I've been part of a couple since I was fifteen. Eight years with only minor breaks in between. That's kind of sad, don't you think?"

I didn't answer because I'd be sad being part of a couple for eight *minutes*.

"Now I like being single," she said. "At least I know I'm not going to fuck *myself* over." She smiled. "And I guess... I guess if I decide to start something, I want to go into it knowing exactly what it is and isn't. Instead of being blindsided. But, like I said, I haven't actually thought about it a lot, which is why I think I jumped the gun with you." She made a face. "I need to work up to sex with strangers. Baby steps, right?"

Would I take her in baby steps? That would require patience—something I didn't have much of—and incredible care, something I'd never tried. Because if I wasn't careful with her, I'd add to her damage, and I already liked her too much to do that.

Fuck. What a waste of something that would've been

really, really fun.

"You've never had sex with someone you didn't love?" I asked, just to make absolutely sure it couldn't work.

She shook her head. "No one I didn't *think* I loved. But just because I know that love is bullshit and all relationships are doomed doesn't mean I want to be celibate for the rest of my life. So eventually I'm going to have to do something about it. I'm just afraid I'll revert, turn someone else into a frog, and get sex confused with love."

"I might be able to help with that. We can go as slow as you want. Baby steps, right?" *You idiot.* But once the words hit the air, I realized I was okay with the idea. Maybe better than okay. It wasn't often you were handed a situation where sex was the only way to help someone. Hell, if it was, I'd be starting another foundation tomorrow.

"It could take a lot of tiny baby steps. Do you really want to get in my pants that badly?"

"Yes. Yes, I do," I said, smiling. "Provided there are no actual babies involved, I believe it's my civic duty to help my fellow man. Make that *woman,* because I'm not into men. This is me giving back."

"I'm not sure there's a way to take that as a compliment."

"Then I'll clarify—I like you and your body and would love to spend more time with both of you, preferably with less clothing on." I stopped her and turned her by the shoulders so she faced me. "Sex without strings is something I'm good at. Whether you want to dip your toe in the water or jump in, it might be better to do it with someone who isn't going to fuck with your head. Someone who will tell you to your face that he wants to use you because he thinks you're incredibly hot, and in return you can use him."

"*That* I can take as a compliment."

"You should." I had to concentrate to keep my hands on her shoulders instead of wandering. "What I'm proposing is that you use me for anything you want—anything non-emotional. No overthinking needed, desired, or allowed."

Her smile was gone, probably because she was gnawing on her lip. "I'm not sure I can control it yet."

"You need practice separating the physical from the emotional. So practice on me. I promise you: I'm not emotional, and I'm not interested in your emotions—the girlie ones, at least. We can go as slow as you want and stop whenever you need to." All things I'd never wanted, let alone offered anyone. But I liked her, wanted her, and was currently going through a self-imposed dry spell. Strangely, the challenge was a huge turn-on. My cock was ready to jump out of my pants as soon as she gave the word. How long could it possibly take?

Even if the sex never happened, what was I out? Nothing. Of course, you can bet your ass I'd do everything I could to make it happen. As long as we both kept everything out in the open. After all, the poor girl needed my help.

She sighed, stopping in front of one of the newer apartment buildings in the city. "This is me."

One of two things would happen—she would invite me up to her place or she'd say goodnight. Lots of things *wouldn't* happen. I wouldn't kiss her goodnight, because this wasn't a date. This was a meeting to negotiate an arrangement that would suit us both. I wouldn't tell her I had a nice or a good or, god forbid, a great time. Another indicator that this was a date, which it wasn't. I wouldn't tell her I'd call at a certain time—*biiiig* no-no. The promise of a time-specific call sets up expectations, and expectations set up a huge amount of trouble and the possibility of hurt feelings.

Unfortunately, by offering her an open invite, I'd already broken my number-one rule—don't stay long enough for them to develop *any* feelings. Because aww-sweet feelings turn into hurt feelings really, really rapidly. That wasn't what I did. Two people make each other feel good and then walk away feeling good. Very simple and straightforward. As long as I was upfront and avoided potential triggers, everybody left satisfied and with a smile on their faces.

I didn't kiss her goodnight. I didn't tell her I had a great time. "I'll call you tomorrow." F*uck!* The words I never said, not ever, slipped out so easily. Twice in the last twenty-four hours. I must have put on someone else's mouth and brain this morning. Because *mine* knew better.

"I'm not sure that's a good idea."

Thank the heavens. I'd never been as happy to be rejected as I was right now. "Why not?" *Are you fucking kidding me?* Maybe I could go by the butcher's on my way home and get them to cut out my tongue.

"I think you're great," she said, "and I'm sure you're something to behold in bed. But after I left your place yesterday, I started actually thinking. A few hours later, I realized that I don't work that way. I wish I did and maybe someday I will. But not now. If we had sex now I think my head would get all jumbled up, and I would start seeing things that weren't there or think you had feelings you didn't have."

"Honesty seriously appreciated." Problem averted. Moving on and away. But first... "What if I told you with absolute certainty that it could never work out and I'll never feel that way about you?"

"Then I'd probably wonder what was wrong with me that you couldn't care about me."

"There's nothing wrong with you." Nothing at all. And knowing that could very possibly make this the biggest mistake of my life.

CHAPTER 6 - LANEY

He called. We met for a drink after he got off work. He ordered a beer but didn't touch it. I refused the second drink, because even a buzz might have me ending up somewhere I wasn't ready to end up. We talked and then I went to my home and he went to his.

Two days later, he called again. We met for coffee. We talked. He propositioned me in a completely non-subtle way and was totally nonplussed when I refused. Then I went to my home, and he went to his.

That weekend, he called again. I worried about how happy I was but was even happier it wasn't a butterfly kind of happy. It was because I had a great time when we hung out, and I wasn't feeling as guilty when I turned him down. Of course, that was mostly because he never seemed angry and his frustration didn't affect his attitude. In fact, it made him more amusing. I think he was pretty used to always getting what he wanted, at least when it came to women.

"What do you want?" I put him on speaker while I cut some veneer to use on an Edwardian writing desk that was in terrible shape.

"I ran out of cash, and I need a drink."

"Liar." But in a non-hurtful way, which was a nice change from all the other liars I'd met.

"I'm not lying. I need a drink. A big one. Or multiple smaller ones."

"I'm at work, Carson."

"Great. Do you have liquor there?"

"You don't even drink, do you?"

"I drink all the time, but not in public. I stick to closet drinking—it's easier to hide my shame that way."

I laughed. "Fine, I'll take you out for a drink." It would take me at least twenty minutes to clean up. "But I'm a mess."

"Then we should probably go to my place instead. You can take off your clothes and get cleaned up."

I groaned when he so obviously forgot to mention me putting my clothes back *on*. I gave him the address of my shop. "There's a pub down the street. They won't care how dirty I am."

"But I care very much how dirty you are."

"Twenty minutes, Carson. Think you can handle it?"

"I think I'm already halfway there."

I'd just finished rinsing the last brush when I heard an impatient knock on the metal door.

"Lane! Are you alright in there? Should I call the police?"

What was he talking about? "I'm coming!"

He was leaning against the doorframe looking around the area, grimacing. "This is not at all what I was expecting."

"When I said I work in the Warehouse District, you didn't know there would be warehouses?"

"I thought you were joking. Only Dexter works in a place like this. You're not a serial killer, are you?"

I ignored him, going back to put my tools away and make sure all the jars and cans were tightly closed.

"Hey, Lane? You know all your furniture's broken, right?" He opened and shut the drawer of the writing desk.

"Be careful with that! *Really* careful."

"Did you make it?"

"It's over one-hundred years old."

"Wow. I figured you for your early twenties. You're holding up really well for an old lady. I'm down with the cougar thing, though, don't worry."

"I'm fixing it. That's how I make a living—repairing and selling antique furniture." I nodded towards a coffee table I'd built from debris and reclaimed wood. "I made that one. It's about three years old."

"When you told me you sold furniture, I pictured a store full of cheap mattresses and bedroom sets imported from China."

"Nope. That's what I'm working up to." I held up my crossed fingers. "Every girl needs a dream."

"I want it." He looked up from the coffee table and reached for his wallet. "Do you take credit cards?"

"You don't even know how much it costs."

"Okay, how much does it cost?"

"Sticker price on my website is fifteen-hundred dollars."

"Great. Do you take credit cards?"

I expected him to at least pause, if not completely reconsider. I was so used to everyone thinking my art was 'sweet' or 'interesting,' I wasn't sure how to react to someone taking it seriously. Taking *me* seriously. Even my parents didn't think I could do it. They hadn't said anything outright, but I could tell they still thought it was my 'little hobby.' That's why I left San Diego and came up north—well, that and to be with Kevin, my last frog. I wanted to be around more people who understood. Unfortunately, there were about twenty artists to every art buyer and fifty to every gallery owner, so I still wasn't even close to proving my parents wrong.

Carson didn't seem like an art collector, other than his tats. And somehow, buying one of my pieces to humor me seemed even worse than if he'd just ignored it. But I wasn't in a position to refuse money, either.

"Do you really want it?" I asked. "Because I have no qualms about taking your money."

"Then you should answer my question."

"Yes, I take credit cards."

"Do you deliver? If so, can you do it naked?"

I took his card. "That would be an additional charge, and it would be way over your limit."

"What's a limit?"

I knew he was joking, but I also knew his family had gobs of money, so it wasn't that big a joke.

"Honestly, I don't think it's right for your place," I said, pretending to hand him back his card. "I mean, it's not made to withstand strippers dancing on it."

"No problem. I already have enough that are. Anyway, it's way too nice for my place—stripper-strong or not. I'm going to donate it to the auction."

"The auction for your foundation?" I held out his card. "Take this back."

"Why?"

"Because I'm not going to charge you fifteen-hundred dollars for something that will raise money for sick kids."

"But you were okay with price gouging if I was going to put it in my living room?"

"Just take it."

"That's what I'm trying to do." He walked away without his credit card. "Right after I compensate you for your time and I'm assuming a fair amount of nails and wood and things. Hopefully under fifteen-hundred dollars' worth or you're a terrible business woman." He knelt down and ran his hand across the top.

"I made it years ago and nobody wants to buy it. If you don't auction it off, it's just going to sit there."

"Gorgeous." He wasn't looking at the table. "Anyone who can't see that is an idiot."

I suddenly felt very exposed, my arms wrapping around

myself to stop a shiver not brought on by the cold. "Yeah, well, it's art. And art doesn't sell. Especially by unknown artists with lame websites."

"Take my money and use it to get a better website. It's really beautiful, Lane."

"It's okay. If I could do—"

"I said it's beautiful." He looked at me with a raised brow.

"Thank you." I leaned back on my worktable. "I have a lot more pieces sitting around here getting dusty, so if you take it, at least I'd know this one is sitting around *not* getting dusty in some rich person's house instead."

"Thank you, Lane," he said with a small bow. "So why didn't you ever tell me you were an artist?"

I shrugged. "I don't feel like one most of the time." Uncomfortable with the way he was staring at me, I started sweeping.

"I'll have someone pick up the table and get some pictures taken for the auction catalogue."

"Eric!"

"Huh?"

"Eric's my roommate's boyfriend. He's a photographer, a really good one. He could take some pictures and send them to whoever you want." It only seemed right—Eric would do it for free and would love the exposure. I was paying it forward and helping a good cause.

"Great." He stood and wiped his hands on his pants. "You don't fix broken drawers by any chance, do you? On young furniture? My dresser—"

"Yes, Carson. I'll fix your drawer." I grabbed my bag and put the basics in it. "And it will only cost you $999."

"That seems totally fair," he said, following me out. "Do you take credit cards?"

Ten minutes later we were in front of his apartment, somewhere that, thus far, I'd been able to avoid. "This was just a ploy to get me up to your place, wasn't it?"

"Furniture! Damn it, of course! What better way to get a woman up here? That drawer has been broken for months. So many wasted opportunities. I wouldn't have had to resort to picking up women in cafés if only I'd thought of it earlier."

"You're kidding," I said as soon as we went inside. It was unbelievable. "It's like a Barbie Dreamhouse, but not pink and with way more electronics." It also screamed Danger Zone, but I would ignore that.

"That's a terrifying description and, thankfully, not one I've ever heard before."

"I just mean it's so..." Perfect. Beautiful. "Spacious."

After a quick, male tour—meaning he told me where the bed, the beer, and the bathroom were—he showed me the dresser that needed my help.

Shaking the drawer pull, he said, "It doesn't do the forward and backward thing. Not sure why."

It took me about three minutes and four finishing nails to fix. "You've got to be the least handy man I've ever met."

"And that's why I need you, Lane. Well, that's *one* of the reasons I need you. The others are because I really enjoy staring at your breasts and after you finish laughing, you get this breathiness in your voice that's a big turn-on, and I can't stop imagining how your—"

I held up my hammer. "Stop before I accidentally hurt you."

CHAPTER 7 - LANEY

Almost every day, I would find Carson in what I now, sadly, referred to as 'our corner' of the café. I would slide into the chair opposite him and pick up the cup of coffee in front of me. Since he didn't want me to get the wrong idea, he never bought it for me. Instead he insisted he'd bought both of them for himself but just this once, I could have it. Then we'd sit and drink and talk comfortably for a really long time, except for all the moments that were uncomfortable because the images of us wrapped around each other never seemed to leave my mind for longer than a few minutes.

After my first sip of coffee, I smacked my lips together. "Hmm…"

"Hmm, what?" he asked.

"It's almost perfect. I like a *lot* of cream."

"Stop teasing, Lane."

I gasped. "I meant the—" He knew exactly what I meant.

He still hadn't mastered the exact proportions of cream to sugar to coffee, but he was getting pretty damn close. Somehow that seemed more significant than I would've imagined it would be. A sign of the amount of time we were spending together or the amount of effort he was putting in to getting to know me.

Coffee was not a symbol of intimacy, for god's sake. Get a grip. Grow up. Stop emoting all over yourself. Damn it, I was still a love struck fool, even when I wasn't in love. When the realization it was happening slugged me in the gut, I jumped up. I couldn't control it. I couldn't be around him and still be who I wanted to be. It was stupid to think I could. Stupid to think I wouldn't screw this up.

"I need to go."

"What's wrong?" he asked, dumbfounded by my obvious loss of sanity.

"It's... I was feeling very girlie for a second there." Was that a big enough hint? Enough to scare him off? "Emotionally girlie."

"Girlie." He nodded slowly. "Would it stop you from ever feeling girlie again if I told you the only reason I'm still hanging out with you is because I want to put my tongue in your"—his eyes darted to the two little girls sitting with their mom two tables away—"belly button?"

"Yes, but I'd also know you were lying."

Only one corner of his mouth curled. "There may be a couple other reasons, but I promise, none of them are anything to get girlie over." He stood, gathering his stuff. "You stay, I'll go." His voice dropped to a whisper when he got close enough. "Was that the first time?"

"That I felt girlie about you? I think so."

"Good. I like you, Lane. But that needs to be the first and last time you get girlie on me, because that would fuck everything up. Know what I mean?"

I nodded. "Do you ever think us spending time with each other is one big, drawn out lapse of good judgment?"

"All the fucking time," he muttered, his lips grazing my forehead before he walked away. "By the way, you're in charge of making your own coffee from now on. Evidently it touches on some weird emotional erogenous zone for you."

I smiled for about a second before panic set in. Carson had

stopped in front of Eric, Hillary's boyfriend, who was standing in front of the door. His eyes were about two sizes larger than normal.

"Hey. Can I—?" Carson glanced towards me, then to Eric, then back to me. When he smirked, I stopped breathing, knowing whatever he said next would be horribly inappropriate. "Do you think I slept with his wife?" he asked me, but it was loud enough for Eric to hear.

"Oh my god, who says stuff like that?" I stepped forward just as Eric stopped gaping and started laughing.

"Apparently, *he* does," Eric said. "Of course, I wouldn't have found it so amusing if it were true. Or if I was married." When he pointed backwards, I knew I was in trouble—any second now Hillary would walk through that door and want to be introduced to Carson. "Are you two…?"

"No, Eric!" I shouted. "No. He…um…he's a guy…" I'd deliberately not told Hillary anything about Carson because I knew what her reaction would've been. I didn't want to deal with it, now or ever. "He's a guy who was just leaving. Where's Hillary?"

"Hillary, your roommate?" Carson asked. "That means you're Hillary's…"

"Boyfriend," Eric said.

"Right. And Lane's photographer friend. So the"—he imitated the wide-eyed silent stare Eric had done—"makes sense then. But I swear, anything bad Lane told you about me is completely accurate."

"She didn't actually tell me—"

"You were leaving, right?" I asked Carson. "Right?"

He looked so amused, he probably wanted to stay, which was exactly why I wanted him to leave. I pushed him towards the exit on the other end of the café.

"Bye, Carson." I shoved him in the chest.

He grabbed one of my hands and pulled me towards him until his lips grazed my ear. "I think little Lane is hiding things—meaning me—from her friends. How badly would he freak out if I kissed your beautiful little mouth right now?"

"Not nearly as badly as *I* would," I whispered back.

"As if I needed more temptation."

"Please, Carson. Just go."

After one more, slow inhalation and a slow exhalation that came with a quiet groan of disappointment, he stepped back. "Thanks for the coffee..." He smiled wickedly as I pushed him out the door. "What was your name again?" he mimicked. "It's so awkward when you call someone by the wrong name, isn't it?" Lucky for him, I didn't have enough time to hurt him.

Less than a half second later, Hillary came in, her smile quickly morphing into a mask of confusion, her gaze darting back and forth from Eric to me to the door Carson had just walked out of.

"What did I miss?" Hillary said slowly. I shook my head, silently begging Eric not to say anything. Hillary would throw a party if she thought I was dating again.

"Laney's date."

"Traitor," I grumbled. "He's not my date."

"I thought you were done with love and relationships," Hillary said.

"I am. He's a friend."

"*Sure* he is."

"We're not dating, Hillary."

"Okay."

"We're not. We just hang out and drink lots of coffee."

Hillary turned towards Eric. "Why'd you think it was a date, honey?"

"Because when a guy who seemed pretty cool and was— not that I noticed—really attractive, looked like he would've sold a kidney to kiss a very cool, single woman who is—not that I've ever noticed—really attractive, it usually involves more than just drinking lots of coffee." Curse Eric and his honesty. "But if Laney says he's just a friend, I guess he's just a friend."

"He is."

"You don't actually believe her, do you?" Hillary asked him.

"I'm telling the truth!"

"Uh huh," she said, rolling her eyes. "I'm going to ignore the fact that people don't usually hide relationships with people they are just friends with, especially from their so-called *best* friend." She held up her hand when I opened my mouth to explain. "I said I'm going to ignore it. Because I know you've been through a lot of crap this year. I'm just glad you're done with that whole 'all men are frogs' thing."

Eric looked hurt. "You thought all men—"

"Not you, baby." Hillary wrapped her arm around his waist. "You're a prince...who only ribbits occasionally."

As we laughed, Eric grumbled, pulling away and heading for the counter. "I need something to drink. I'm parched from all the ribbitting."

Hillary came over and hooked her arm through mine. "I want to get to know this friend you're not dating. Let's all go out sometime. Me, Eric, you, and your *friend*."

"I swear, we're not dating, Hillary. He just wants to sleep with me. That's it. He has no interest in dating me at all."

"Then he's a moron."

"No, he's not. He doesn't date. Just like I don't date."

"Are you guys sleeping together?"

"No! We're just two people who hang out and have no desire to date each other or anyone else."

She studied me for a second, looking for any sign I was lying, I guess. "Bummer. In addition to wanting you to break out of this man-hating phase you're in, I like having another couple to do stuff with. Like say...go out for drinks after the opening of that new gallery on Third."

"I wish." Aside from it being humungous, the gallery would focus exclusively on art using recycled or repurposed materials. "You need an impossible-to-get invitation to go to the opening."

"Do you?" Hillary asked with feigned surprise. "Well then, aren't I lucky that Eric just happened to get *four* of them?"

"Seriously?" Hillary knew I couldn't wait to see it, and it wasn't open to the public for another two weeks. Since you had to be really well known to show there, I didn't bother dreaming about that. But aside from seeing the gallery itself, getting even one of those buyers to look at my stuff could catapult my entire career. I grabbed her by the arms. "Oh my god, Hills, I'll be the best third wheel you've ever had."

"But I have four tickets, and I really wanted to go with another couple. Even if they aren't actually a couple."

"If you weren't smiling right now, I'd be so pissed at you." I sighed.

"Please?" She put her hands together and begged. "Even if you aren't dating him, you're spending time with him, right? Then as your best friend and the person you were hiding him from, it's imperative I make sure whatever you're giving him is appropriate."

"Time. That's all I'm giving him."

"Great. Then give him some time on Wednesday night."

"I'll mention it to him but there's probably a two-percent chance he'll go. Or less."

The ticket was mine with or without Carson, but eventually I'd have to introduce him to Hillary. Plus, I might need someone to keep me calm at the gallery.

The next time I saw him was Saturday, for what Carson referred to as his 'Getting Handy' class, but which was actually a chance for him to make a huge mess in my shop while I tried to get some work done. He did his part while I spent the entire time distracted by how to bring up the gallery opening.

I stared at him across the worktable, trying to work out what to say.

"Why do I get the feeling you're about to tell me

something terrible?" He didn't look up from the project he was varnishing. He'd given up on brushes and neatness and was now happily finger painting.

"It's not terrible, but..."

"It's not good, either."

"I need to ask you for something that...might be construed as being against our...Code of Conduct. But I don't mean it like that. It's just..." I slumped back into my chair in disgust. It was just a gallery opening. "Never mind. Forget I said anything."

"Okay."

I felt a sudden wave of courage hit me and sat up straight. "What would you say if I asked you—" Courage gone. Mouth snapped shut.

He looked up slowly. "I'd probably say yes if the word 'sex' was in the last part of that sentence, but if there was mention of other men, hookers, or animals of any kind, I'd say no. And then I'd ask if I could watch." He paused for a second, studying me. "What are you afraid of?"

I thought of all sorts of words: 'rejection,' 'humiliation,' 'men,' 'love.' But all I could do was shrug. A stupid question had suddenly turned into a need for emotional catharsis.

He leaned towards me. "Lane, everyone has damage. The trick is learning how to deal with it. When that doesn't work, you need to figure out how to push it down really deep so you can forget about it. To help you with that, I brought a couple pieces of fruit for my favorite teacher...along with a nice bottle of tequila and some salt." A bag I hadn't noticed was near his feet. Amusing since, for whatever reason, he didn't drink in public.

"Yeah, that would probably help."

"Or...you could just say it. I'm not sure you know this, but I have a lot of money and come from a family some people have heard of. Having a lot of money and coming from a family some people have heard of means that some of those people ask me for shit. Occasionally I say yes, but more often

I say no because people ask for very strange things. But no matter how bizarre the request, I've never ordered someone's head chopped off for asking. Not even once.

"So I'm pretty sure, no matter what you're about to say, you'll still be alive five minutes from now."

"My roommate Hillary dangled a ticket for a gallery opening in front of me and I really, really want to go."

He let out a breath. "I thought you were going to ask me to make an honest woman out of you. Although"—he cocked his head—"that would mean I'd get to make a *dis*honest woman out of you first. But I don't get why that was so hard to say."

"Because she has four tickets. One for her, one for her boyfriend, one for me, and..." I waited for him to acknowledge he understood. It didn't take long. But he didn't look angry, just a bit wary. "Obviously, I'm not seeing anyone, but after she found out about you, she, of course, assumed we're dating and she wants to go to this thing on, like, a double date."

"And you told her...?"

"That in order to double date, you have to be single dating which we aren't doing. Now or ever."

He nodded. "Good answer. But I'll go if you want me to."

"What?"

"Not as your date because I don't do that with anyone, even with you and your roommate."

"And her boyfriend."

"All the more reason—if it was just the three of us, at least I could pretend the night was going to end really well for me. But if you want me to go somewhere, I will. And I'll only ask for one thing in return."

I laughed, trying to clean up some of the mess he'd created. "You're evil, you know that? I could just see her face if I told her I slept with you to make her happy."

"I'd like to think sleeping with me would make *you* happy."

"I'm sure it would." Probably too happy.

"Lane, you know that I'd really like that, right?"

"Yes, Carson, you've been pretty clear about it."

"And you know that I get a perverse amount of pleasure reminding and teasing you about it, right?"

"That's also clear, yes."

"And you know that if it's ever too much, you should tell me so I can immediately stop, right?" He stood up, putting his project under the worktable and tossing his gloves into the garbage can. "I mean it."

"Clear."

"So should I?"

I walked away from him. When he followed I laughed. "I have an incredibly attractive, interesting man literally following me around and telling me how much he wants me. And even though I keep saying no or ignoring him completely, he doesn't give up. Do you have any idea what a stroke to the ego that is?"

He slipped his arm around my waist and pulled me back against him, his breath warming my neck, his hand resting low on my belly and holding me still. "He doesn't give up because there's an incredibly attractive, interesting woman right in front of him who will eventually say yes because she wants me to stroke things besides her ego."

Being with him was torture. It was much easier to say no when he was joking around. But when our bodies touched and he spoke with a voice that went straight to my core, it was nearly impossible to keep my hips from pressing against his growing erection. We stayed in that position for a very tense couple of seconds. Or maybe it was hours. Both of us coiled so tightly, if either of us moved, there would be no turning back.

"I can't. Not yet." It was more of a plea than anything else—begging him to release me. After a deep sigh, he did.

"Until then, he gets to tease her mercilessly and enjoy being incredibly sexually frustrated." He went into the small storage space connected to the shop area and got a beer out of the mini-fridge/freezer he'd bought me. I mean *him*. I was allowed to use it as long as I didn't drink the last beer. If I did, I would be punished in a way he couldn't discuss but that made him smile in a very wicked way.

"You're not sleeping with anyone?" I asked.

"I don't have time to. I spend all of it trying to sleep with you."

I'd be lying if I said it didn't take a huge burden off my chest. But it was completely unfair, illogical, and irrational to expect him—someone very upfront about his sexual dos and don'ts—to be saving himself for a woman who couldn't make up her mind.

I'd assumed he'd been sleeping with people while I'd been trying not to imagine him sleeping with people. But when I actually thought about it, we really were spending a lot of time together. He worked all week, met me for coffee every night, and spent at least one weekend day with me, usually both.

He sat back down at the worktable. "So are we having this foursome or not?"

"I don't know when I'll be ready. Before we do it, I have to know I won't feel anything. I mean anything *emotional* because that would really be sad if I didn't feel *anything*."

"We're not talking about your roommate anymore, are we?"

I shook my head. "I don't want to be a tease, and I really want to. Like, *really* want to. But not if it screws me up." Sex always screwed me up—as if the second the deed was done, my ring finger started itching. And Carson was so amazing, I wasn't sure I could keep my promise to myself and to him. "So if you want to take a break from trying to get in my pants or if you want to stop completely, I totally understand."

He paused. "I'm glad you said that because I think you needed to. It's good practice for you and was a nice offer. But honestly... I don't actually give a shit. I am a selfish prick, Lane. If I wanted to be somewhere else with someone else, I would be. If and when I decide I want to, I'll let you know and then I'll do it. Because I'm a selfish prick. But for right now, the only pants I want to get into are yours, and the time I choose to devote to the cause is up to me. The only decisions you get to make are when—note I didn't say 'if'—*when* you say yes and when—again notice the absence of the word 'if'—*when* you want me to go away."

I sighed. "I love your honesty. I really do."

"Well, I love your breasts, so we're even." His smile disappeared faster than it showed up. "Oh fuck. Does that mean we're in love?" Amazingly, he kept a straight face until I hit him. "Oww. I need a drink to ease the pain."

Before I could stop him, he used one of my very sharp, very expensive chisels to split a lime open.

"No, Carson, the blade!" I yanked it out of his hand and ran to the sink to rinse the acidic juice off the steel. "Lime juice will dull it."

"Wow, speaking of dull... I hope you're more fun when you're drunk because, as soon as I find a tool I'm allowed to touch, it's going to happen. I didn't bring a shot glass though, so you may have to whittle one."

Thankfully, I woke up in my own bed. Alone. Although I really could've done without my head feeling like a condemned building being torn down by a huge iron ball. I reeked of tequila and when I wiped my neck, I felt something grainy like sand. Nope, not sand. Salt. I had salt on my neck from where Carson's...

Oh shit. His tongue. The heat of his mouth running up my neck, his lips lingering just behind my ear.

"Yes, that really happened." Then with a whole new kind of pain in my head, I remembered us staring at each other while I took my time sucking every last grain of salt off his finger.

Even more vaguely, I remember him getting us a cab and dropping me off here. I'm pretty sure we didn't have sex. Almost sure. Plus, I'm pretty sure it's impossible to forget having sex with someone. If I remembered sucking on his finger, I'd have remembered if any other parts of his body went into mine. Oh god.

I wondered what he felt like right now. Hopefully worse than I did, seeing how it was totally his fault. After a long, life-sustaining shower and putting on some clean clothes, I'd call Carson. Then I'd have to go find out if my shop looked as bad as *I* did.

Hillary came out of the kitchen, smiling and horrifically cheery. "I haven't seen you in forever."

"I've been working a lot."

"All night long?" she smirked.

"Maybe."

"Is it that guy?"

I brushed hair off my face. "Yes, but it's not something to goofy-grin about. Really."

"When's the last time you were here?" Hillary followed me through the apartment, stepping over the bag I'd dropped in the middle of the living room at some point. I'd get it later.

"I'm here every night," I said.

"Not when I go to bed." She totally didn't believe me. I needed to either stop caring or start sticking to a curfew.

"What do you mean? I watched TV with you for three hours the other night."

"Yeah. On Thursday. Today's Monday."

How was that possible? There's no way I spent the last three nights hanging out with Carson. No way. If for no other reason than he probably kept track and had a limit of how many nights he could spend with a woman before he went into estrogen shock.

"Are you sure?"

"Yes," Hillary said, amused at my obvious expense. "I know how to keep my days straight because I don't have the kind of job I do seven days a week, and I don't have the kind of boyfriend I sleep with every night. Because *that* would be more like living with someone, which *I* don't do. I have a normal job with normal hours and a boyfriend who takes me out to dinner every Friday night. Then we go to his house and have sex and go to sleep. Then we spend Saturday together and on Saturday night we have sex again."

"I really appreciate you telling me this." I turned the shower on, praying the water wouldn't take too long to heat up.

"Then, like many, many other normal people, Eric and I spend Sunday watching TV and vegging on the couch. On Sunday night I come back here and sleep in my own bed for the next five nights before doing it all over again. But one thing I *don't* do is see my roommate anymore. So are you really going to keep telling me this guy isn't your boyfriend?"

"No, I've given up on you." I shooed her out of the room. "But he's not my boyfriend, and I don't live with him. I live here, with *you*. And I'm not having sex with either one of you." I blinked, my hand ready to close the bathroom door.

"By the way, you should consider trying to liven things up with Eric because that sounds hellishly boring. People our age shouldn't already be hellishly boring." People our age should probably not do shots with someone they're trying very hard not to sleep with, either.

I called him as soon as I got out of the shower and felt mildly human again. "Did we have sex last night?"

"Of course not."

Hallelujah.

"No, last night we made sweet, sweet love." He didn't stop laughing for about ten minutes. "I promise, Lane, when we have sex, you will be completely sober, awake, and begging for it."

"Has a woman ever actually needed to beg you for sex?"

"No. But I'm playing hard to get with you, so you're going to have to beg. On your knees. While you're—"

"Shut up! I'm begging you." Then it was my turn to laugh.

CHAPTER 8 - LANEY

Unfortunately, I didn't realize that my wardrobe was completely unacceptable for the gallery opening until the day of the event. My clothes consisted mainly of jeans and shirts because cute tops aren't so cute when your bra is filled with sawdust or the sleeves are splattered with varnish. And in a fit of 'I'm never dating again, so I don't need going-out clothes' frustration, I'd tossed a lot of reminders of my old self.

After Kevin had shown me the error of my loyal and trusting ways and I'd finally wised up, I didn't want to look sexy—I was purposefully trying *not* to attract anyone. And every outfit reminded me of a man. It was actually pathetic—I could remember when and with whom I wore every attractive outfit I had.

They were souvenirs of the delusion I'd lived with since I agreed to go to junior prom with Michael Buckley and he celebrated by sticking his tongue in my mouth. Worst kisser ever, although I didn't know that at the time because he was my first. My first everything—kiss, love, lover. Worst *everything* ever, actually. For his sake, I hope he's gotten better.

Tonight was special, though. I didn't need to look sexy but

jeans weren't going to cut it. There would be potential clients for my business and, more importantly, for my art. I needed to go shopping.

Carson called just as I got to the department store. "What are you doing?"

"Shopping for a dress I can't afford. What are you doing?"

"Leaving work. Are you almost done buying a dress you can't afford? I thought we could have a drink before you drag me to this horrible thing tonight."

I heard the smile in his voice. Doing what he did and being who he was, Carson probably went to this kind of thing all the time. Then his offer sunk in—he'd just asked me to have a drink a few hours before an event it would take me hours to get ready for.

"Oh my god, it's true—you've *never* gone out on a date, have you?"

"What'd I miss?"

"I'm a woman." I pulled dresses off the racks, cringing every time I saw a price tag. So I stopped looking at them— they were all more than I could afford. Hopefully I wouldn't discover I could buy the dress I wanted or pay my rent, but couldn't do both. "I have two hours to find a dress, go home, shower, do my hair and makeup, and get to the gallery. Yet the guy I'm not dating is asking me to meet him for a drink."

"And he still doesn't know why you can't."

"Because I've already been to two stores and haven't found a single dress I like. If Nordstrom doesn't have anything, I'll probably have to go in the dress I wore to my high school prom."

"Dear god, I hope you're kidding. Just pick one. You'll look good in whatever it is. Except your prom dress. Don't do that to me…unless you went to the prom in a cheerleading uniform."

I held the phone between my shoulder and my ear as the

stack of dresses grew. "This is important, Carson. I can't go there looking like crap." A saleswoman took pity on me and brought the stack to a dressing room.

"You won't look like crap. You'll look great. I'll make sure of it. See you soon." He hung up before I could ask him what he meant. I jogged after the big pile of options, crossing my fingers that one of them would work.

Ten dresses—mostly black, in two different sizes—and I still had nothing. How could I possibly be the only woman in the world to have boobs and a butt? Evidently, I was only allowed to have one or the other. Just as I slipped dress number eleven, i.e. the last one, over my head, a long royal blue dress came sailing over the top of the dressing room door.

"Try this one." It was a man's voice, not the saleswoman's.

"Carson?"

"Hurry up and try it on. I only have two hours to go home, get dressed, do my hair, and meet the woman I'm not dating for a drink I'm not going to drink."

I felt the fabric of the dress he'd picked out and immediately knew it was out of my price range. Then I looked at myself in the mirror. The dress I already had on was perfect...for someone else. On me, it gaped near the arms and pulled across my chest.

"Hurry up," he called.

I took the last failure off and slipped on the dress Carson had tossed me. It was perfect. For me.

When I opened the door, he let out his breath. "You look...the complete opposite of crap."

"Thank you." That was probably as close to a compliment as I was going to get. "How'd you know it would fit so perfectly?"

"Because I do nothing but stare at your body when we're together." Just like he was doing now, his eyes running the length of my body, covetous. And it wasn't of the dress. "Take it off and let's go."

"I wish. I'm about ninety-nine-point-nine percent sure it's

out of my price range." I couldn't find the tag until I looked at him and saw it in his hand. "Why do you have that?"

"You're gonna owe me a lot more Getting Handy lessons." Then he walked away. "Get dressed. We need to go."

"Carson, wait! You can't buy it for me." It was so pretty, though, perfectly snug on the top, draping gorgeousness on the bottom. He'd already made up his mind and nothing I said would change it. Plus, I would never, ever be able to afford it and it was so beautiful and it fit me so well and...

No. "Carson!"

I ran back into the dressing room to grab my purse, carefully taking the dress off and yanking my own clothes back on, not bothering with shoes. When I got to him, the saleswoman asked him if he wanted his receipt emailed to him.

"I can't let you do that," I said.

"It's just an email, Lane," he said without turning. "I think I can handle it."

The saleswoman laughed, taking the dress from me and wrapping it up. "Do you need shoes? Nylons?"

I said no at the same time Carson said yes.

"No, thank you. I have shoes." Not nice enough for this dress, but I had a pair.

As we walked through the store, I held onto the box as if it was the most valuable thing I'd ever owned, which it may have been.

"You shouldn't have done that, but thank you." It felt so inadequate, but what else could I do?

"Don't think you're getting it for free," he said as we cut through the men's department. "You're buying me a drink at this thing tonight."

"I think it's an open bar."

"Then you're buying me a few drinks at this thing tonight."

"If I get you drunk, will you let me take advantage of you?" I teased.

"Alright, that's it," he growled. He took the dress box from me, picked me up, plopped my ass on a display of jeans, and nudged my knees apart so he could stand between them. "I tried to be patient. I really did, but this friend thing sucks."

"Umm..." I took a quick breath when he put his hands on my thighs. "You know we're in public, right?"

"So?" He was really close, looking intense and amused and completely focused on me.

"So people are staring."

"The place is practically empty."

"But not completely." I looked over his shoulder, seeing the stares of a few customers but no employees. "There are three guys and—"

"Any women?"

"One, but her mortification only lasted as long as a quick glance. Men are slower."

"True, but we're also better at prioritizing." He moved a tiny bit closer. At least, I think he was the one who moved. Either way, I was in trouble. "Why do you think they're staring?"

"Probably because some nutcase has a girl on a display case in the middle of a store."

"You're wrong. They're staring because they wish they were exactly where I am right now, with their hands exactly where mine are." He ran them up to my hips. "Since the poor guys aren't that lucky, I figure letting them stare isn't a big deal."

My heart was pounding so hard, it would be a miracle if he didn't hear it.

"Next thing," he said. "I'm now going to try a less subtle approach to convince you a sexual relationship doesn't have to come with a romantic one. I'm assuming you know the reason behind this."

"You haven't exactly been vague." Is it possible to die of nervousness? "But I don't think this is that kind of store."

"You're right. Let's go somewhere more appropriate." He yanked me by the hand, giving me just enough time to grab my new dress. When he pulled me into the dressing room area, I finally started wondering why I was letting him do whatever this was. He glanced around, took a credit card out of his wallet, and fiddled with the lock to one of the rooms.

"What are you—?"

"You don't really think this is my first time sneaking into a women's dressing room, do you?" The lock clicked open. "It's either this or the bathroom. And trust me, bathroom stalls aren't made for two people who aren't...intimately connected, if you get my meaning." His meaning was gotten and imagined and wanted. But not like this—not here, not now. "I'll take you there as soon as I can. Promise."

"You know, a place where we're actually *allowed* to go might be even better."

"Those are all too far away. I'll try to make it quick—the discussion, not what I hope the discussion will lead to." He yanked me inside the small space and locked the door.

I pressed my back to the wall as if that would actually do anything. The door was behind him, and even *I* didn't want him to open it yet.

"Tell me all the components of a romantic relationship," he said. "Even the little ones. Pretend I don't know any of them...'cause I don't."

"Um... You have to like the person."

"Simple start, okay. Do you like me?"

"Yes."

"Bummer," he said, smiling. "What else?"

"Attraction."

"You're insanely attracted to me, so that makes another point not in my favor. Keep going."

I was throwing out anything I could think of. I didn't know how to define a romantic relationship. "Sex."

"Well, that's the grand prize, but only if the other issues are taken care of. Next."

"Chemistry?"

"Shit," he grumbled, but there was humor in his tone. "This

isn't looking good for me. It may have been a bad idea to bring it up. We'll see soon enough. Next."

I was running out of answers. "A spark?"

"Okay, in my opinion, this one and the last two aren't exclusive to a romantic relationship, so let's hold off judgment until later. Next."

"Some kind of romantic feeling, I guess."

"You guessing isn't actually that helpful. What we need is—" Damn, his smile was wicked. "I have an idea." He stepped in close to me, held my face between his hands and brushed his lips over mine. Soft, then a little harder but still gently, taking his time. I opened my mouth to his tongue, my hands sliding up his chest. I didn't know how this was going to prove anything other than he'd basically perfected the art of kissing, but I went with it. Because...well, because he'd basically perfected the art of kissing.

Then, without warning, he pulled away and whistled. "Wow, okay. Yeah, okay. Damn it." He rested his forehead against mine and took a deep breath. "I need you to be completely honest with me right now. Okay?"

I swallowed, knowing it was a bad idea but ready to say yes. To anything.

"Lane?" He tipped my chin up so I was looking directly at him. "Did you just fall in love with me?"

I shoved him back when he started laughing. "You're such a shithead! Stop making fun of me when you're even weirder than I am."

"Re-do then." Before I understood what that meant, what any of this meant, he kissed me again. Still slowly, but way more deeply. I wrapped my arms around his neck as he pulled me into him. I rose onto my tiptoes when he squeezed my ass, holding onto the fabric of my jeans to get me closer. It was like in the stairwell but even better because we knew each other now, understood the other's likes and—

Oh my god, I liked this. So much, I would happily stay here and do this for the next few years.

He finally pulled away, wiping my lower lip with his thumb and leaving his hands cradling my face. "Fuck." Nothing in his expression held humor. "I don't know what I'm going to do if this doesn't work, Lane."

I didn't either. This much stress couldn't be good for my heart.

After a moment of silence, he leaned against the wall, creating a little bit of space between us. "We've confirmed that we like each other, are attracted to each other, and the chemistry and spark are definitely there. If they weren't, I wouldn't want to rip your clothes off so fucking badly right now. We've also done something that's traditionally a romantic thing to do—the kiss, not sneaking into a dressing room. So, do you?"

"I..." I wouldn't have stopped him. If he hadn't pulled away, I would've let him take my clothes off and I would've taken off his. I would have run my lips over all the skin I constantly caught myself imagining the taste of, and then wrapped my legs around his waist. I would've fucked him against the wall of Nordstrom's dressing room even if it screwed up everything between us and turned me into the weak, weeping lunatic I'd been six months ago.

"Please tell me I can I have you without it messing with your head," he said, adjusting himself.

I didn't know. I wouldn't know how I'd feel until it happened. That was the problem. If he wasn't so gorgeous and great, things would be a lot easier. Of course, if he wasn't so great, I wouldn't want him so badly, either. Damn him. This was totally his fault.

He looked a little nervous. "What are you thinking?"

"I'm still thinking you're a shithead."

"Excellent," he said, laughing. "Then I really think you should consider letting this shithead have his way with you. But I'd suggest it happen somewhere you can lie down after you've come so hard you can't stand up anymore."

He was the devil.

Someone pounded on the door. "If you don't come out immediately, I'm calling security."

"Have you ever been arrested?" he asked. When he opened the door, an older woman was glaring at us, one hand on her hip.

"Sorry, ma'am," he said with sincerity. "We didn't mean to cause any trouble. She and I are just friends, but I really want to be more. So I have to take every opportunity I can to convince her how great we'd be together."

The woman's face softened and she glanced back and forth between us. Her reaction might have been different if she knew what kind of 'more' Carson wanted.

He spoke to the woman, but his eyes never left mine. "Have you ever wanted someone so badly that using common sense doesn't make sense anymore?"

"Once. A very long time ago." She sighed. "If you want to impress her, you should take her somewhere nicer than a dressing room, though." As we passed, she touched my arm. "You never know what you might get until you try. But if you *don't* try, you're sure to get nothing."

My mouth dropped open. Was she kidding? "Did he pay you to say that?"

Carson thanked her and pulled me away. "She seemed awfully wise, didn't she? Maybe even psychic. Although, I know *exactly* what you'll get when you try. And you're going to love it." He winked. "But not *that* kind of love."

CHAPTER 9 - CARSON

I unhappily said goodbye to Lane. Did it actually take two hours to put on a dress and twist her hair into a pile on the top of her head? I've had a fair amount of experience helping a woman take off her clothes and let her hair down, and it never took longer than thirty seconds. A minute if we were drawing it out. But I let her go do her thing and planned to meet her at the gallery so her roommate didn't think we were actually together. Because evidently, her roommate wasn't smart enough to understand the words: *We're not together.*

Unfortunately for Lane, her nervousness about that gave me an idea. She needed a lesson in not caring about what other people thought of her. I wasn't planning on embarrassing her publicly, because this event involved her art. I knew how to be subtle. It just seemed like too much work most of the time.

She called just as I pulled up to the valet. "We're waiting in the lobby. Where are you?" Yep. Definitely nervous.

"I'm still doing my hair. Probably won't be there for another half hour."

"Are you serious?"

"No. I'm around the corner. I'll meet you inside at the bar."

I tossed my keys to a covetous kid who was probably already

planning to have a really hard time finding a spot to park my ride and would need to take it around the block a few times to find one.

"Don't fuck it up," I said to the valet.

"What?" Lane asked.

"Nothing. Just talking to my dick." I went up the steps, stopping as soon as I saw her through the window. Nice choice on the dress. However many pennies it had cost me, it was worth all of them. "When I get there, I expect you to have a drink ready for me. Nothing with an umbrella."

"We have the invitation. How will you get in?"

"Do you seriously think I don't know how to crash a party? I'll see you at the bar." Before she could say anything else, I hung up. She made a face at the phone before putting it into her purse and saying something to Eric and a woman who had to be Hillary.

I'm not sure why I hesitated. Just to gawk at her uninterrupted, or to see how many eyes she drew as she walked through the crowd? She had no fucking clue how many heads turned. It was sweet and naïve, but screamed insecurity. Probably a gift from the assholes she'd dated. They weren't frogs, they were idiots.

I took a deep breath before heading in. It was the first time I'd been near a bar since that night I hated thinking about. Fortunately, the chance of someone throwing a punch while wearing Armani and looking at recycled hippie art was slim.

On second thought...

That chance skyrocketed when I saw my wicked stepsister on the arm of a guy I'd never seen before. Anna looked great, like always. No one could ever say she lacked fashion sense or didn't know how to spend someone else's money. She also looked bored as hell. Not a good sign, considering the evening was only starting, but Anna didn't excite easily. When our eyes met, hers opened wider but she made no move to come over or call me to the group she was standing with. I gave her a little nod before heading inside.

I was one-hundred percent okay pretending we didn't know each other. I'd be one-hundred percent okay with doing it one-hundred percent of the time, too. The only thing that stuck in my throat was who she was with. Was that the new boyfriend she mentioned and, if so, how much of an asshole was he?

Fuck it, I was here for someone else. If Anna wanted to screw her life up, there wasn't anything I could do about it. Lane stood next to the bar with Eric and Hillary, her back to me. The closer I got, the wider Hillary's eyes became. At least I assumed it was Hillary. She looked a little familiar, but the only Hillary I'd ever met gave me a damn good blowjob after a—

Oh shit.

That was only a couple months ago, definitely less than Lane said her roommate and Eric had been dating. Unless I was getting my blowjobs mixed up. Well, this should be fun. I'd have to try not to laugh too loudly.

She whispered something into Eric's ear and he nodded. Obviously it was about me, but since her boyfriend's forehead barely wrinkled, it probably wasn't a confession. Another thing I didn't care about. Too bad for Eric, but not my problem.

I held my finger to my lips until I was right behind Lane. "Hi, honey. Sorry I'm late."

She spun around and stopped. Her drink kept moving— most of it landing on my jacket. She attacked it with a cocktail napkin apologizing and mumbling obscenities under her breath about what I'd said.

"Quit grumbling. I'm only about ten minutes late." I stopped her and took off my jacket, handing it to the bartender to toss in back somewhere.

"That's not what I'm grumbling about."

After setting her empty glass down, she turned to her friends. "This very cruel man who I am not dating and who is about to promise never to call me 'honey' again is Carson."

"I promise to never call you or anyone else 'honey' ever again, muffin." When I caught Hillary's eye, she stepped back, her lips tight. And while I couldn't give a shit if Hillary could take a joke or not, Lane did. "Alright, fine. I won't call her or anyone else muffin again either. Oh, and we're not dating."

"Or sleeping together," Lane added quickly.

I turned towards her and mouthed, "Yet."

"Laney, help me find the bathroom," Hillary said, looking at me.

"I'll be right back." Lane let herself be dragged off, shrugging her shoulders. As soon as she turned, Hillary bent in close and started whispering.

"Do you think women really think they're fooling us when they do that?" I asked. "Why don't they just say, 'We're going to go talk shit about you'?"

"Not sure. But then again, how often have you said, 'I'm gonna be over here with my friend talking about your ass,' to a woman?"

"Point. You think they're talking about me or you?"

Eric chuckled. "Hillary and I have been together a long time—the whispered conversations stop long before the two-year mark. So it's definitely about you."

"Two years." Minus the night my cock was in her mouth. I could've been wrong about the timing, though. Or the mouth. "Think they're talking about my ass?"

"Maybe."

"Lane was really worried Hillary might get the wrong idea about us. Know what that's about?"

"Hillary wants her to be happy and to find a guy who isn't like any of the assholes she's dated before. They call them frogs."

"Yeah. Well, you can let Hillary know that her dream has become a reality. I'm definitely not like any of the assholes she's dated. I'm a totally different kind of asshole. But dating isn't on the table." And at this point, neither was sex.

Suddenly Lane was heading towards us, stomping really, her jaw tight and her eyes wary. Hillary was right behind her, with the same expression.

"I don't think they were talking about your ass, man," Eric said.

"You"—Lane pointed at me—"come with me."

"Do you need help finding the bathroom?" I went with her because my only other option was to stand around with Eric and his grumpy, cheating girlfriend. "What's up?"

She didn't say anything until we were in the lobby. "You didn't recognize Hillary at all, did you?"

"She looked familiar."

"You slept with her."

"Did she actually say that? Because I don't think we had sex. I could be wrong, though."

She threw up her hands. "What does that even mean? How do you remember someone but not know if you had sex with them?"

"Come on, how am I supposed to remember someone I slept with two years ago?"

"It wasn't two years ago. It was four months ago. She and Eric broke up for a few weeks."

Okay, so my timing was right. But I still didn't remember the sex. "I'm not sure how to take that. One night with me and she gets back together with her boyfriend. Does that mean I was so good or so bad?"

"She said you were amazing. Right up until you said goodbye and left. Well, she actually told me you said, 'Sayonara, baby,' and then slammed the door on your way out, but I'm going to give you the benefit of the doubt considering how pissed off she is right now. You don't really say 'Sayonara, baby,' do you?"

I shook my head. "I don't slam doors either, especially after I come. I'm usually pretty happy at that point."

"I was there, you know." She spoke so quietly, it took my brain a second to figure out what she'd said. "In the apartment.

I didn't see you, but I—" She looked away. "I heard you guys, like, you know…during..."

"Well, isn't that awkward?"

"And she talked about you the next day. The whole fucking day. She didn't stop once."

I almost made a joke, but we'd already talked about this a hundred times more than I wanted to. And Lane didn't look ready to laugh.

"Hillary told me no one had ever made her feel as special as you did. I think she used the word: worshipped. Please tell me how it's possible to *worship* someone and then not remember her."

I blew out a breath. "I remember her mouth. She has a very nice mouth."

Lane's lips slammed together.

"And her face looked familiar." I shrugged. "What do you want from me here? We fucked, that's it. If that made her feel special, or whatever word she wants to use, then maybe she needs to reevaluate her sex life, because while what I remember was good, there was nothing overly special about it."

She stared at me as if I'd done something wrong.

"Jesus, Lane, it probably won't be the last time we'll be in a room with someone I've screwed around with. And chances are I won't remember some of them, either. So what do you want me to do about that? Should I go?"

"No," she said quietly. "I just don't want things to be horribly awkward between my best friend and—"

"The guy you're not dating. Got it. I'll try not to piss her off more. Although, in all fairness, she has no reason to be mad at me. I'm always clear about what I want."

"I've noticed."

"And also to be clear: yes, I remember somebody being on their knees, but it wasn't me and it wasn't to propose."

She groaned. "Please don't say anything like that around her. Or me, actually. I don't need that visual."

"Does Eric know?"

She shook her head. "She's going to tell him, but not now."

"Great. I'm tired of talking. Show me some fucking art."

We walked through the gallery and I tried to keep my mouth shut. Art should be either beautiful or *deliberately* ugly. Most of these looked like something *I*'d make in one of my Getting Handy classes.

"I'm pretty sure this one is made from the recycled hairballs of feral cats," I said. "It's..." Fuck it. This shit was scarring my retinas. "Can we leave now?"

"If you want to leave, then leave."

"If I wanted to leave, I'd be across town by now. But I want to leave with *you*."

"I can't yet. I need to network, start a conversation with someone from the gallery or someone else important."

"Then why are we looking at the crappy art? You want to meet someone important, you go to the middle of the room or you go to the bar. No one from the gallery will be looking at the art—they'll be looking at the *people* looking at the art."

"I hate it when you make sense." She turned around and scanned the room. "Do you think the guy in the red jacket is the gallery owner?"

"No way. He's sweating and keeps glancing at that wreck of a— I don't even know what the fuck that is. Anyway, he's probably the—Do I *have* to call him an artist?"

"How do you know this stuff?"

"My parents threw a lot of parties. I've never been a good sleeper, so I'd sneak into the kitchen and snag a bottle of champagne."

"How old were you?"

I thought about it, but not for too long because I didn't have many memories that didn't make me want to throw up. "Hayden, my brother, wasn't there—they'd already shipped him off to boarding school. It was a few years before my dad croaked, and I had to have been old enough to know how to open a bottle of champagne, so I guess I was around ten."

"You were stealing champagne when you were ten?"

I shrugged. "It has bubbles. Like soda."

"Oh my god, that's horrible!" She covered her mouth. "I shouldn't laugh, but I can't help it. It explains so much."

"Shut up. We're here to get you noticed, not giggle about the drunk ten-year-old."

Laney's laugh cut off and her body stiffened. "Twice in one night? What are the chances?" I followed her line of sight and saw why. A common reaction to seeing Anna. Laughter ceases to be around anyone from my family. We are the black holes of happiness.

My stepsister was standing next to the guy she came with and talking to a man who was either one of the obscenely untalented artists showing their crap tonight or the horribly tasteless gallery owner.

"Anna likes to be ignored at things like this, so don't worry about her." As if that was possible. We were surrounded by drama—artists, an irritable stepsister, and a pissed-off woman with a talented mouth. "You look like I need a drink. Don't move. I'll be right back. I'll get you one, too."

She clutched my arm. "Don't you dare leave me to deal with all your women, Carson."

"My women?" I laughed. "I swear, none of them are, or ever have been, my women. I'll be two minutes, and I promise not to get into any trouble."

Ninety seconds. It couldn't have been longer than ninety seconds. And I hadn't gotten into any trouble—I'd walked away and left Lane to it. That minute and a half had been enough time for Anna to come over and make Lane feel like shit. She wasn't crying or anything, because my girl is tough as hell, but there was a distinct look of triumph on Anna's face.

I glared at her as I came up to them, handing Lane both drinks. She needed them more than I did. "One and then the other. Come on. You can do it."

"I'm fine." She rolled her eyes but downed the first drink

and didn't hand back the second. "Anna was just telling me how surprised she was to see you at an event like this. Because you don't usually take your 'playthings' out."

I turned to my wicked stepsister. "I'm *her* plaything, actually. Lane's an artist. That's why we're here."

"Oh?" She looked around the room. "Which piece is yours?"

"I'm not showing here."

"Yet," I added. "That guy you were talking to, he owns the gallery, right?" As poisonous as Anna could be, she might also be able to help.

"Richard? Yes. It's next to impossible for new artists to show here, unless they're amazingly talented." When the corners of her mouth curled, I knew what was going to happen next. "Or if they have an inside track—Richard always helps his friends. He's wonderful that way." And that's where she shut up.

"Then since Lane is amazingly talented, he'll love her." I tried to keep my voice down because I'd just finished promising I wouldn't cause any trouble, but all I wanted to do was permanently tape my stepsister's fucking mouth shut. "I think I heard him calling you—you should go see what he wants."

She ignored me. "I love your dress, Laney."

"Thank you." She glanced at me, blushing. "It was a gift."

"From you, Carson?" Anna asked loudly. "So you *do* have some taste. In women's clothing, at least. You still need some work on the women who wear it though."

"What the fuck is wrong with you?" It happened so fast, I wasn't sure if Lane's gasp was because of Anna's insult or the volume of my response. "Isn't your boyfriend giving you enough attention?" I tried to lower my voice. Not sure it worked, though. "I'm with who I want to be with. So either apologize and play nice or apologize and leave us the hell alone. Understand?"

All conversation had stopped, making my voice seem even

louder and more pissed off. I knew I'd embarrassed Lane and might have ruined her chance of ever getting some of her art in here, but fuck if I was going to let Anna get away with that shit.

"It's okay." Lane put her hand on my arm. "A friend of my parents used to be like that. Until her family had her committed. So with the right meds, I'm sure Anna will be fine."

I wanted to kiss her. Stopped myself right before it happened, actually. She was so damn impressive.

Anna cleared her throat. "You two enjoy your evening."

"You forgot something," I said loudly. I had no problem embarrassing her to get what I wanted.

"Are you serious?"

"Yep."

She glanced around at the other guests. They were all staring, her date glaring at us from across the room. "Fine. I shouldn't have said that, Laney." She looked at me to see if that was enough, then sighed and got the rest out as quickly as she could. "You really do look beautiful in the dress and that comeback about your parent's friend was good." She threw her hands up. "Happy now?"

"Happy now?" I asked Lane.

"No. But I want her to go away and for everyone to stop looking at us. So…"

Anna took the hint and headed back to people who liked her, or at least pretended to.

"I'm going, too," Lane said. "You can stay if you want."

"Why the fuck would I want to do that?"

Conversations started back up before we'd made it out of the main room, only to be silenced when a woman stepped up onto a pedestal and let her robe fall to the floor.

"Finally, some actual art." That put a hurdle in my way out the door.

Lane grumbled something about the predictability of men. I wasn't going to argue.

A guy tied ribbons that hung from the ceiling around the nude woman's wrists and ankles.

"Please let me do that to you," I whispered. "Please, Lane. I'm begging you."

Then the guy pulled a screen up from the ground so all we could see was the woman's silhouette as she moved awkwardly, like she was a puppet or something. *And* there went the kind of art I enjoy. What a waste.

"Never mind." I grabbed Lane's hand and dragged her out to the street. We didn't speak until we got in the car.

"I may have handled that wrong." I was supposed to be there just as a ticket in and I'd not only screwed her friend, I'd screwed her entire night just by being there.

She shook her head slowly. "*Anna* handled it wrong."

"You'd think people like her don't exist outside of high school movies, but they do. She's actually gotten better with age. Like vinegar."

"Do you know what she said when I told her what I do for a living? She asked me if refinishing furniture was code for something in"—she did air quotes—"the business. You know, screw and nail and drill. Why is she such a bitch?"

"Anna loves competition almost as much as she loves attention. This is the first time she's ever seen me with anyone. I think she was in shock."

"How long have you known her?"

"Since we were in high school. With breaks, most of them not nearly long enough." Out of the corner of my eye, I saw her grimace. "She and I have a very odd relationship. One day she hates me, every day I hate her, sometimes we don't talk, all the other times we talk more than I want to, that sort of thing. But after what she pulled in there... You don't ever need to worry about Anna. Okay?"

She nodded. "At least I got noticed. It would've been nice if it had been in any *useful* way, but that kind of thing takes time." What followed was the longest train of silence we'd ever had.

"Carson? Let's promise never to do this kind of thing again."

"Okay." Too bad, though. Parts of it had been fun.

Chapter 10 - Laney

It started as soon as I got home from the gallery opening and didn't stop until Hillary packed her bag and went to Eric's for the weekend. She didn't miss a single opportunity to tell me what an asshole Carson was. She'd been very vulnerable after breaking up with Eric, and Carson had somehow used that to get her into bed. I wasn't sure how he was supposed to have known how vulnerable she was feeling, but he should have. Of course, the truth was that he wouldn't have been listening even if she *had* told him.

I wasn't sure what I believed. When I met him, he was pretty damn straightforward and, now that I knew him, it was hard to imagine him manipulating someone into bed. It was hard to imagine him *needing* to manipulate someone into bed. Although, yeah, he might have said something moderately rude before he left. Not to be mean, just because he doesn't think about stuff like that.

It was the other thing that freaked me out more. I remembered the morning after they slept together and thinking what a mistake Hillary had made. Not for the sex, but for the way she talked about the mysterious guy she'd been with. As if he'd actually cared about her. I was right—four months later, he didn't even remember being with her. He didn't care about her or want to make her feel special. All he wanted was to make her feel good while he made himself feel good. Hillary was a smart woman, a realist in almost everything, but she'd turned one night of sex into something more than it was and then had gotten upset when she found out she was wrong.

After a night with Carson, would I do the same thing? Would he?

Saturday morning, I decided to take the whole day off and do absolutely nothing. Since Hillary was off having another unexciting weekend with Eric, I didn't even bother getting out of my pajamas.

When Carson called, I flipped the TV off and stretched out on the couch. "What do you want?"

"You know what I want, Lane. But that's actually not why I called. I screwed up and forgot to send someone for that coffee table. The auction is tonight, and Eric's photos of your table were sent out in the catalogue."

I'd completely forgotten, my mind on all the wrong things, even with a very full workload. "Should I bring it to you?"

"I don't want to mess up whatever you planned to do today. Well, I need to mess up enough of it for you to be at your shop when the guy comes by. What time's good for you?"

"Give me an hour to jump in the shower and get down there."

"What are you doing later?"

"I'll be at the shop anyway, so I'll probably work for a little while. Why?"

"I take back my earlier comment. It was too polite. I've already ruined your plans for this morning, so it's only right that I ruin them for the whole day." His voice never changed inflection or speed. "And since it's my birthday, you should give me a present. Guess what I want."

"Is it really your birthday or are you just saying that because you want a present?"

"It's really my birthday and I *told* you because I want a present. But you haven't guessed what I want yet."

I laughed. "I don't need to guess. I know what your answer will be and you're not getting it." Yet. He wasn't getting it *yet*. Or if Hillary had her way—ever.

"Oh, you thought I wanted you wrapped up in nothing but a big bow, didn't you? Eww, gross. No. Ewww." I could practically see his face twisted up with feigned disgust. "No, I want you to take me out for a birthday dinner and then go to the auction with me."

I bit my lip. "I don't think that's a good idea. We just agreed we weren't going to do things that were too…"

"Date night-ish? Yeah, I considered that. But as long as you don't have any other roommates I could've slept with, we both know it's not a date, and you wear more than a big bow, I don't think it'll be a problem. Don't you want to see your piece go to the highest bidder?"

"Yeah, but…" Would it work if I promised myself I wouldn't do anything lame like pretend we were actually on a date?

"I have to spend my birthday with a bunch of people I don't like, Lane. The only way I'm gonna get through it is if I have someone to harass and grope under the table."

Well, that made it far less of a date night, didn't it? "No hand-holding."

"Fuck no! Are you kidding me?"

"No whispering secrets in my ear."

"Unless it's something seedy or morally questionable that will make you blush."

"No getting my jacket for me. Or walking me to my door after."

"Does that stuff really still happen? In this century?"

"Not as much as I wish it did, actually."

"I swear I'll be nothing but rude to you the whole night," he said. "In fact, I might accidentally forget that I brought you and you'll have to find your own way home. You should bring some cab money just in case."

"Okay," I said on a sigh, trying not to sound as excited as I was.

In true Carson-style, he called me from his car and told me he was in front of my building. I thanked him for his rudeness, but he was going to have to wait because I wasn't ready yet. So he grudgingly decided to come upstairs.

I was still doing my makeup when I heard the door open. I never left it unlocked, so—

"Lane?" he called loudly. "Help! She needs emotional support. Stat."

I ran into the living room with no idea what he was talking about.

He looked panicked, Hillary's keys in one hand, his other pointing to her. Her face was hidden in his chest, her shoulders shaking and the sound of weeping muffled by Carson's jacket.

He mouthed, 'Help me!'

"Are you okay, Hills?" I put my arms around her and led her to the couch.

"That's not my fault." He backed all the way to the opposite wall and leaned against it, sliding his hands over his suit. Carson in a suit was the second of the two most amazing things I'd ever seen. The first had been him, too, but he'd been wearing something different. My eyes lingered for only a second before redirecting to where they should be—on my sobbing friend.

"What happened?"

Hillary just shrugged, her lips trembling.

"Lane?" Carson asked. "Can I talk to you for a second?" When I nodded, he flicked his head towards the kitchen.

"Are you going to be okay?" I asked Hillary as I stood. All

I got was a whimper, but it seemed like an affirmative whimper. "I'll be right back."

When I got to the kitchen, Carson was opening a bottle of wine. "You don't have anything stronger than this, do you? I'm not sure wine is gonna cut it."

"What are you doing?"

"She needs empathy and since I'm not very good at that, I'm going to give her booze. And then I'm going to give myself booze to ease the scarring of what just happened."

"Which was..?" I asked quietly.

"I have no fucking idea." He took down three wine glasses and filled all of them to the rim. "I was minding my own business, waiting for the elevator and grumbling about how rude it was for you to keep me waiting for our not-date. Then, out of nowhere, she comes stumbling up. She didn't actually start crying until the doors closed and we were trapped together in a fairly tight space. I figured, worst case, she'd want to discuss my memory lapse of her. Awkward but nothing I couldn't ignore. But when the tears started..." He shivered. "It was like a volcano erupted out of her eyes."

He handed me one of the glasses and leaned against the counter after taking a big sip of his. "I could only make out a few words, but I think it was boyfriend stuff which we *both* know I'm not equipped to handle."

I wasn't hugely surprised Hillary and Eric had fought—it seemed like they were doing that more and more often. But I'd never seen this reaction before. Hillary wasn't a crier—she was a shouter, an arguer. So something big must have happened. Maybe she'd told him about Carson.

"You know this means I'm going to have to stay with her, right?"

"But it's my birthday," he whined.

"I know. Happy birthday, Carson." I went to kiss him on the cheek at the same time he turned. When our mouths met, his was already open, probably about to say something rude. It had to have been an accident because no one could have anticipated my movement that well, but Carson knew how to take advantage of an opportunity when he saw one. The next thing I knew, we'd both turned so our lips could connect all the way, and his hand was at my neck. I couldn't have pulled away even if I'd wanted to. Since I *didn't* want to, his hold on me just made me want him all the more, a hint as to how strong he was and how incredible he could make me feel. His kiss was hard and demanding, but his fingertips were light as he carefully traced my collarbone and down my chest between my breasts. He cupped me as if I was built to fit into his hand perfectly and brushed his thumb across my nipple. I moaned into his mouth.

He shoved me backwards against the counter, not allowing any space between our bodies. I felt his erection, his abs tightening as he ground himself against me. My entire body could do nothing but react to his—I wasn't breathing, that was for sure.

The only thing keeping either of us from forgetting all about...everything...anywhere...at any time was the increased volume of Hillary's crying.

I put my hand on his chest and pushed him back, finally getting a full breath. "Wait, we can't."

He groaned my name and said, "Please," allowing the space but not releasing his grip of my hair. He kissed my forehead, his lips still touching my skin as he spoke. "I need more."

So did I. But even though I thought about it constantly, my mind was still flopping back and forth, doubly so ever since finding out Carson was the mysterious guy Hillary had slept with months ago. This wasn't the kind of thing I should let my hormones decide for me. Or my lips. Or my hips. Or any part of his body.

"We can't."

"For my birthday, Lane. One more for my birthday. Just a kiss. Maybe some tongue. No, definitely some tongue. Please."

"Hillary?" I called out, unable to take my eyes off him. "Do you want wine or Kahlua and ice cream?"

A mumbled, teary "ice cream" came from the living room. "I'll be right there!" Then I lowered my voice. "Only because it's your birthday." And because I couldn't help myself.

I wrapped my arms around his neck, pressing the full length of my body against his. He pulled me higher to catch my lips with his, sliding one of his hands down to lift me up on the counter. I squirmed, lifting my dress up and widening my legs, so he could be between them. I lost track of whose hands were where, but if I said, "everywhere," I would've been *almost* right. There were a few places on each of our bodies we hadn't gotten to yet.

No! A few places we *wouldn't* get to...tonight.

I gripped the waistband of his pants to keep myself from going farther down. He still had one hand in my hair, but his other was on my thigh, fingers denting my bare skin. He was having just as hard a time not touching me as I was not touching him.

Maybe I was wrong, but I thought somehow we both understood how fragile the line we were pushing was. We merged for another few minutes, until it was either stop or find ourselves in territory we didn't have the time for and I wasn't ready to deal with yet.

"More," he groaned.

"I just gave you more."

"Not enough."

"Rain check." I grabbed his hand to keep it from creeping higher on my thigh. "Wait."

"Laney," Hillary wailed.

"Carson, we can't."

"Shit." He backed up and adjusted his pants, his clenched jaw expressing everything he was feeling. "Expect me to be inside you about four seconds after you say yes. And don't make any plans for the rest of that week." There was a seriousness in his tone that I hadn't expected. Lustful, yes. His normal *joie de vivre*, nothing-really-matters attitude, yeah. But there was a fire in him I'd never felt before.

He tossed back the rest of his wine without taking his eyes off me and then refilled both our glasses. "You should probably start resting up now because once it's on, you're not getting any sleep for a very long time."

"Okay," I said weakly, not having anything to add because air wasn't something I had enough of and, honestly, it sounded perfect. While I tried to focus on ice cream and Kahlua—heavy on the Kahlua—Carson just watched me, his arms crossed over his chest. Simmering.

When Hillary whined my name again, he laughed sadly. "Better go help your friend."

"Carso—"

"Go help your friend."

I may have grumbled something before picking up the ice cream and my wine and heading for the living room.

"Hey," he called, grabbing my arm to stop me.

"Jesus, Carson!" I almost lost hold of everything and covered his fancy suit with ice cream, Kahlua, and Pinot Noir. "What? You tell me to go and now I'm supposed to stay. Can you please just make up your mind?" The words were snapped, not because I was mad but because I was frustrated. Nothing was wrong, but nothing was right, either.

"I made up my mind the first time I kissed you. It's only gotten clearer since then. The part I don't get is why you can't."

Because of the look on his face. A hurt and confused look that made me want him to be mine. That made me want to do whatever I could to take it away and turn it back into a smile. Even if I knew I'd lose in the end.

"I have issues," I said quietly.

"Ya think?" The corner of his mouth rose.

I rolled my eyes. "As if I'm the only one in this room with issues."

He looked around himself and then back at me. "The only one *I* see." He sighed. "One of these days you're going to be in my bed, Lane. I'm not giving up until it happens."

"Why not?" It seemed kind of a stupid question to only be thinking of now. But why *was* he being so patient? "I'm sure you've been with prettier women with better bodies and less issues. Or maybe the same amount of issues but ones that weren't in your face all the time and didn't keep them from having sex with you. Shit, even the woman weeping on the couch right now got over her issues long enough to sleep with you."

He took a while to answer. "I'm gonna skip the whole 'women with better bodies' thing because it'll come off like a compliment and that will negate what I'm about to say." His volume dropped momentarily. "I find you highly, *highly* attractive and want to fuck you more than I've wanted to fuck anyone in my entire life, by the way. So I don't ever want to hear you compare yourself to another woman again. Got it?"

He sighed. "And now for the good news—I can be a real dick. Almost all the time, actually. Sometimes it's a good thing, but most of the time, for me, it's a really bad thing. I've done a lot of stupid shit, hurt a lot of people, and never made it up to anyone. The foundation is the way I pretend I'm not as much of a prick as I am. *You* are a way I can pretend being selfish isn't a bad thing. Because in your case, it isn't. You need to be more selfish, and I want to teach you how to not let dicks like me and your exes treat you less than the way you deserve."

"They're frogs."

"Right," he said smiling. "Frogs."

"But you're not a frog."

"Well, I sure as hell am not a prince." We stared at each other for a few more seconds and then he said, "Go help your friend." He followed slowly.

Hillary took the bowl from me before I sat down, but she just chopped the ice cream up and mixed it into the large pool of Kahlua.

"Did you tell Eric about…how you know Carson?" I tried to be as delicate as I could be, not wanting her to start fighting with Carson on top of everything else.

She swallowed, setting down the bowl. "Eric and I… We've been together forever and have been talking about moving in with each other for a long time. But we're *so* boring. You were right, Laney. Do you know what we did today? Nothing. Do you know what we did last night? Nothing. We spend two nights out of seven together and he was too tired to have sex. A man too tired to have sex. I didn't even think that was possible."

I didn't either. "Maybe he had a bad week or wasn't feeling well."

"He's a man. It doesn't matter how bad he's feeling."

"I'm sure he had a good reason. Like…"

Over Hillary's shoulder, Carson shook his head. He stopped when Hillary sat up and looked at him.

"You wouldn't have, would you, Carson?" she asked. "If a woman wanted to."

"Uh…" He glanced at me for help but I was too busy holding in my laughter at his expression and the guilt I felt for finding anything funny when my friend was obviously hurting. "I'm different, Hillary. You shouldn't use me as a marker for all men. Eric loves you, right? So…yeah, he probably wasn't feeling well."

"If he wasn't feeling well, he could've told me that instead of falling asleep without a word."

"True. You know what's also true? I'm the worst possible person in the world to get relationship advice from. So I'm going to… I should probably go."

He took his empty wine glass into the kitchen. Coward. He couldn't escape through there. He had to come back through the living room to leave. Obviously Hillary hadn't given him a thorough tour of the apartment when she had him over.

"What exactly did you say to Eric?" I asked.

"That we were turning into old people and I was tired of doing old people stuff and having old people sex and—"

"You said that?" Carson yelled from the kitchen. He came in, bringing the wine but no glass. "Damn...um...yeah, that's not gonna go over well with a guy. Even an old guy. Old people sex. I'm not even sure what that is. I'm not even sure I *want* to know what that is." His brows furrowed. "Seriously, though, is that an actual thing?"

Neither of us answered him. Hillary went back to crying and I went back to telling her it would all be okay.

"You and Eric are great together," I said. "This is just a bump in the road." Eric treated her really well and was with her for all the right reasons. She hadn't changed who she was to be with him, like I always had when I was with someone. "You guys have the healthiest relationship I've ever seen."

"You don't believe in relationships, Laney. Or love. So what do you know?"

"Not much. But he makes you happy and you guys love each other just the way you are." If there was such a thing as love, that's what it would be like. Two people wanting to be with each other, knowing they each came into the relationship with their own full set of issues and working together to make sure those issues don't overwhelm one or both of them. "No two people are going to always have the same needs, but the kind of trust you guys have is so much more than I ever had with any of the frogs, even before I turned them into frogs."

"Do you think he's cheating?" She hadn't asked me. She'd asked Carson.

"Well, Eric and I aren't fucking each other, if that's what you're asking. If you want to know if he's sleeping with anyone *other* than me, you're gonna have to ask him."

Hillary pulled away from me and leaned towards him. "You're a guy and I need to know what Eric's thinking, so be totally honest." She was going to regret saying that.

"You're really upset right now, right?" Carson asked. "This isn't just a cry for attention." My mouth dropped open, but Hillary didn't seem offended at all.

"Okay." He sighed, set the bottle on the coffee table, and slid into an armchair. "Me and love aren't that well acquainted, but I've known a lot of guys who say they are. So does Lane, so she can back me up. The bottom line is that most of them are pretty good at forgetting all about love when there's a chance of getting laid."

"Carson!"

He shrugged. "She told me to be honest, so I'm being honest. But let me finish. I don't think Eric is like most of us. First off, when I made a joke about sleeping with his woman, before I actually knew I *had* slept with his woman, he laughed. If he was cheating, he wouldn't have laughed—he would've assumed you were cheating, too."

That actually made a lot of sense. I motioned for him to continue as I reached for my wine, only then realizing that I had to put down Hillary's empty bowl of alcoholic ice cream before I picked up my drink. Oops. Thankfully, she didn't seem to have noticed either.

"Second," Carson said, "from what I've seen, most guys can forget about their women, but not all of them can. And not all those who forget will actually go for a quick lay. Do you know what the largest deciding factor is?"

Both of us shook our heads.

"The woman he's in love with. If she teaches him that's how he can treat her, he'll do it. Why not, right? She told him it was okay." He paused. "Lastly, sitting here whining isn't doing fuck-all for any of us. If Eric's not cheating, you're condemning an innocent man. If he *is* cheating, he's at home thinking he got away with it and will get away with it again. So if it were me, I'd get him on the phone and ask him instead of spraying my tears all over everybody else."

When neither of us said anything, he pulled his phone out of his pocket. "What's his number?"

"What are you going to do?"

He stood, growling. "What you should've done while I

took the woman I'm not dating or fucking out to a party that might've made her happy and excited enough to let me get her naked."

Hillary looked at what I was wearing. "You guys were supposed to go out?"

Before I could say anything, Carson did. "In a non-dating manner, yes."

"Sorry."

"It's okay," I said. "I already gave him his birthday present while we were in the kitchen, so he'll live. And complain a lot."

"Damn straight I will. And now that the mood is completely lost, it's my turn to cry. Right after I yell at Eric for ruining my night."

After a quick glance to me, Hillary gave him Eric's number.

Carson put the phone up to his ear and slumped onto the sofa, right next to me. "Hey, Eric? It's Carson. Yeah, listen, be straight with me. Are you fucking around on Hillary or what?" He jerked his head away from the phone when Eric yelled. "Whoa! There's nothing kinky going on, if for no other reason than Lane's here with us. And the way things are going, that woman is never going to let me take her panties off. Plus, your girl is all sobby about you." He paused. "Yeah, well...you guys need to sort that shit out.

He paused again, listening. "Uh huh... Not if I can help it."

"What's he saying?" Hillary whispered, reaching across me to pull on Carson's arm.

He shook her off, still talking to Eric but staring at me. Then he turned away. "If I knew that, I'd be a much happier man right now... It's not like that. Anyway, you and your girl need to be the ones talking. I'm the one who needs to be leaving. Yeah. Good luck."

Hillary took the phone from him and put it to her ear. In the next thirty seconds, Eric must have said exactly the right thing because whatever it was made her make a half-giggle, half-sob sound and run into her room.

"That's my phone!" Carson yelled.

Hillary opened her door just long enough to toss him the phone and say a quick, "Thanks, Carson," before slamming it again.

"Well, that was exhausting," Carson mumbled.

"It was really nice of you."

"I didn't do anything. Those two have a good thing going. They belong together." He leaned back on the couch and pulled me into his side. The position felt uncomfortably good, like something I'd want to spend a lot of time doing.

"I had no idea you were such a romantic."

When he laughed, I felt his breath move my hair. "I believe in love. I just don't *do* it."

"Why not?"

"You know as well as I do that some people just aren't good at it. Or maybe they know they'll never be able to do it right."

We were those people, both of us. So why couldn't I stop wondering if we would always be those people? It's hard to let go of things you've believed for your entire life. If you're attracted to someone and like who they are, you date. When you date someone you're attracted to and like, you have sex. When you have sex with someone you're attracted to and like, you fall for each other. Isn't that the way everyone did it? Everyone other than Carson?

And me. Why was I always forgetting about me?

"I can't go with you tonight," I said quietly.

"Thought you might say that."

"I know I told you that I would, but—"

"Not a big deal, Lane. I'll make it without you. Promise." There was humor in his voice, so I believed him. I always believed him. Before he stood, he kissed my forehead. "Thanks for the birthday present. I loved it."

"Me too."

Right before he shut the door, I heard him say, "Can't wait to find out what you're getting me next year."

CHAPTER 11 - LANEY

It had been days since we'd spoken, which seemed odd even though we hadn't known each other that long. Carson had become part of my everyday. A habit I didn't want to shake. But the night of the auction and dealing with Hillary had ended so strangely, I was a little afraid of what would happen the next time we were together. Of course, *not* being together didn't really solve the problem.

As soon as I found an excuse to call him, I did. "Hey! Hillary's doing the Bennett Foundation's Walk for a Cure on Sunday."

"Tell her she can't come unless she's stopped crying."

"She invited me to go with her. So...um...I was thinking about it."

"Great."

"Really?"

"Yeah." There was a slight question in his tone. "What am I supposed to say now, Lane?"

"I wasn't sure if you wanted me to be there because you didn't tell me about it and we haven't talked in a couple days."

"I've been busy with last minute Walk stuff—advertising and media crap." He paused. "And I didn't mention it to you because my mother is going to be there. Whenever I'm within three miles of my mother, I get grumpy. I'm not fun to be around when I'm grumpy, and my mother is *never* fun to be around. But I have nothing against you going."

"Okay, then I'll go. Can I say hello if I see you? I don't want to make things awkward for you. I know how you like to divide the personal and professional things."

"As long as you don't finally take me up on my offer in the middle of the crowd, I think it'll be okay. We're friends, right?"

My lip ached from gnawing on it. "Right."

"Then I'll see you there. It'll be loud, so carry your phone in your hand or you'll miss my call." Why did it make me smile to know he was going to call? "Say thanks to Hillary for me." He hung up, leaving me lots of time to wonder what he wanted to thank Hillary for.

"You're thinking way too much." And my mild obsession with remembering everything Hillary had told me about the guy she'd slept with four months ago wasn't helping.

I didn't need to read between the lines with Carson. I knew exactly what he wanted and didn't want because he told me. So either he was happy we were going to be there to support the cause or he was happy because of that and because Hillary had invited me to come along. I didn't need to worry that I was missing something or should react in a certain way. As the idea settled into my brain, I felt an enormous amount of peace. I'd try to hold onto it whether the sex happened or not.

Who was I kidding? I'd try to hold onto it even after the sex happened. Because it was the only thing that would keep me from doing exactly what Hillary had done for most of Saturday night. Which was the same thing she'd done four months ago, after one night with Carson.

The Walk was utter chaos and since Hillary and Eric had given each other the flu and were both sick in bed, I was alone.

The group I was supposed to walk with wasn't where I thought we were all supposed to meet. So I started wandering through the crowd, looking for faces I recognized, not finding a single one.

When my phone rang, I didn't hear it, but I felt the vibration because I'd taken Carson's advice to hold it.

"What are you wearing?"

I laughed. "Nothing too exciting, promise."

"Let me guess—a red bra and a matching thong." His voice was deep and heated, and I had to press the phone to my head because there was so much noise around me.

"Wrong."

"Wait a minute. I'm not done. Tight black—what are they called?—yoga pants? That are a true gift to mankind because you have a fantastic ass."

I looked down at my pants—a good guess, or was he nearby?

"A white and blue shirt that should be tighter because you have fantastic breasts, too. And I'm guessing you're blushing like crazy right now. Am I warm?"

Yes. And so was I.

"Turn to your three o'clock, beautiful."

I did, seeing him about twenty feet away, standing near a large group of people who were all wearing bright yellow team shirts. "They can't hear what you said, I hope."

He shook his head.

I shouldn't. I really shouldn't. But I was going to anyway. Turning my back to him, I cocked out one hip. "So you like my pants?"

He laughed. "If you *have* to wear pants, then yeah, those are a good choice."

"My bra and panties are black, not red. But you were right—they match and it's a thong. I probably should've worn something more practical though, because it's a long walk and this pair rubs my—"

"Okay, joke's over." Suddenly his entire tone changed to

irritation. "Hanging up now."

"Wait! What's wrong?" I turned towards him. His jaw was tight and his eyes were searing.

"You're making me hard." When he adjusted his pants, I had to laugh. Served him right. "Get those pants over here and say hi, Lane. Now." He tucked his phone into the pocket of his jeans and waited for me to come over.

I scoured the group for someone fitting the image I had in my mind of what Carson's mom would look like. Tall, thin, pretty, mid-fifties probably.

"If you're looking for someone better looking than me, you're not gonna find anyone. I had all of them thrown out about a half hour ago."

"As if."

"Anna hasn't woken up this early since she was in high school, if then, so she's not here. My brother is out of town. My dad's dead. And if it's my mother you're so anxious to see, she's mingling with the important people—the donors who come to have their pictures taken." He shrugged. "Which I'm more than fine with, considering how much they're paying for the privilege. Where's the team you're walking with?"

"I'm not sure. Hillary's sick and I don't know where they're meeting but I'll probably—"

"Walk with me."

"Are you sure? I don't have to."

"I need someone to carry me for the last few miles. Think you can handle it?"

"I don't want to make things awkward between you and your mom."

"She never walks. You might have to meet her at the end, though. I'll try to shove you out of the way before that happens. Come on. Amuse me for a few miles before I have to deal with her."

He went over to the registration table, slipping a bill into one of the donation envelopes and exchanging it for a t-shirt.

"Put this on. You'll be less distracting because it's specially designed to hide every curve of your body."

"You don't have to—"

"Shut up. We've known each other long enough for you to know how often I do something I don't want to do. I try to limit it to one thing per week, and having lunch with my mother is taking up three or four months' worth of things I don't want to do."

He introduced me to the people we'd be walking with— women from the foundation's office and the families of some children they were helping. Eventually he gave up because there were just too many of them. His team made up half the event.

During the walk itself, he stayed close but left space in between us, never touching me, joking with me whenever he wasn't talking to a parent or someone else. My respect for him quadrupled because he treated everyone the same way—as if every single one of them was special.

He was nice, really nice. And he was attractive, really attractive. But no matter how long I stared at him or how many times I saw him pick up a child or do something extraordinarily sweet that normally would've had me rolling over and begging for his attention, the gooey feelings weren't showing up. Lots of holy-crap-that's-sweet but no gooey-ness.

Hopefully, that meant my brain had completely accepted that love wasn't an option, especially with Carson, so it had chucked out all the parts that sent those deluded messages. Oh my god, I might be cured. Of course, it didn't cure me of being terrified to try. Because I could also be completely wrong and the second we crossed the line, I could start feeling more than just the physical, and everything would be over. Then the only time I would see him would be if he happened to be at the café at the same time I was.

He bumped into me and slowly pushed me to the side of the mass of people walking. He kept looking straight ahead but his hand curled around my hipbone, pulled me to a stop, and then was gone. Four fingers on a few inches of my body brought back every hormone that had been released when I gave him his birthday present.

"Go ahead," he called to the group. "I need to tie my shoelace."

I looked down at his two neatly tied laces.

"You gonna tattle on me?" he whispered, bending down and pretending to retie them. He stayed there until the main mob of walkers had passed us. "Follow me." Without another word, he turned into the alcove of a nightclub that wouldn't be open for hours. Evidently I was moving too slowly for his liking because he grabbed my hand and yanked me into a corner not visible from the sidewalk.

"Hi." He was really close and his gaze was on my lips. All of my smart decision-making skills slipped away.

"Hi."

"This whole just-being-friends thing isn't working for me anymore."

I flinched. "Cars—"

"I want to mess around, get you so hot you can't stop yourself from ripping my clothes off, and then fuck you for the next twenty-four hours straight."

I was having some trouble breathing. "How is that different from what you wanted yesterday?"

"It's not. But I'm less patient today. Not helped by the fact I've been staring at your ass so hard, I think I've developed x-ray vision because I swear I can see a black thong through the black fabric of your pants. So what's it gonna be, Lane? I'm still not going to give up if you say no, because sleeping with you is a cause I truly believe in. But I need a status report."

I wasn't sure, because I tried not to think about it. I failed miserably, but I tried. Crap, I wasn't trying—I was obsessed. Yes's and no's kept spinning in my mind and the wheel didn't seem like it was going to stop anytime soon. Because the whole thing was so confusing, awkward, and overwhelming.

What if I went right back to a time I didn't want to remember? To when I'd been a person I never wanted to be again? I didn't want to go back. If Carson was overestimating my ability to separate love and sex *or* if he was underestimating his appeal, I was screwed. Literally and figuratively.

Before I could decide what to say, someone called his name.

"Shit," he mumbled. "We have another mile or so to go. I don't want to pressure you...more than I usually do. But I want you really fucking badly, and I need to know what's going on in that beautiful head of yours. Think you can you figure it out by the time we reach the finish line?"

"I'll try."

He nodded. "Try not to walk in front of me, too. A hard-on at a work event qualifies as an awkward blend of my personal and professional lives."

Carson and I walked side by side the rest of the way, but we barely spoke, each left to our own thoughts. I was doing the should-I-shouldn't-I thing while he was probably thinking of something completely different. Although, I was thinking about sex and *he* was a man, so actually, we were probably thinking about exactly the same thing.

We could hear the blare of a live band—a sign that the end was near. He expected me to have an answer and I couldn't come up with one. Only two choices, and I couldn't pick one.

You are a sad, sad excuse for a woman, Laney.

"Oh shit." He made a quick turn towards a water station and handed me a bottle. "Time to make a choice, Lane."

I swallowed. "Right now? That's not fair. You said I had until the end of the walk, and there's at least another forty feet to go."

"You can either stay here for a few minutes to avoid an awkward conversation with my mother, or you can act as a human shield for me. If you opt for the human shield, I guarantee she'll assume we're dating. And since I've never introduced her to a girl and I haven't introduced her to a friend since I was fourteen, I have no idea what she'll say to you."

"Why don't you just tell her you're gay so she won't think you're hiding women from her?"

"Ideas like that are exactly why I need to keep you around. It's perfect. I'm going to come out of the closet during lunch. I may need some moral support. Interested?"

I wasn't sure what to say. Part of me couldn't wait to meet the woman who raised him, but another part flashed back to all the other times I'd met a guy's parents. Meeting a guy's family signified a big step in a relationship. The kind of relationship Carson and I didn't have.

"Stop thinking, Lane."

"I wasn't. I haven't done that since I was fourteen."

"Liar. Renee is probably a lot different than anyone you've ever met, but she's still human." He cocked his head. "I think."

"You call your mother Renee?"

"I call her a lot of things, but Renee's the only polite one. I'm asking you along because I'll need an excuse to leave early. So when I kick you under the table, pretend you're going to throw up and run out of the restaurant. I'll have to skip dessert to go help you, of course, because I'm your considerate gay friend." Not even Carson could say that without laughing. "No pressure, though. Especially when you compare it to the pressure I'm putting on you to sleep with me."

"Especially that."

"Oh shit. When you don't make a choice, the choice is made for you. Hey, Renee," he said over my shoulder. "This is my friend Lane. I invited her to lunch."

I turned around and saw Mrs. Bennett. Tall, fifty-something, expensive-looking, gorgeous.

"It's Laney, actually." I liked Carson being the only one to shorten it. "Nice to meet you." I started to say that Carson had told me all about her, but I had a feeling she would know I was lying.

"What a pleasure. Carson so rarely introduces me to his *friends*."

Friends. A simple word that can mean so many things. What Carson calls a friend is a sexual partner. What Renee calls a friend is obviously a girlfriend. And what I call a friend is...a friend.

"Of course I don't mind Laney joining us for lunch," Renee said, smiling politely.

I immediately noticed the discrepancy between what Carson had said and what Renee had—he hadn't asked permission to bring me along, and we all knew it. I shook Renee's hand, feeling the hard press of metal rings against my palm. One quick look at the multitude of sparkles on every one of the woman's fingers blinded me.

"I need to talk to a few people before we go," Carson said. "Lane, wanna help?"

Renee took my arm. "I need someone to keep me company, honey." She looked at me. "I rarely get up to Northern California these days, so I'm afraid I don't know many people."

"You know everyone, Renee."

"Not anyone who matters. Laney and I will be fine. Go finish up what you have to. We'll wait here."

Carson tightened his jaw. "No, I—"

"We'll be fine," I said. Nothing could possibly be more uncomfortable than the three of us standing here staring at each other. "Besides, I need a chance to ask your mom for pictures of your awkward and embarrassing teen years. I'm dying to see those."

"You sure?" He shook his head in warning.

I nodded, not sure at all.

"I'll hurry."

"So," Renee started, "have you and Carson been dating

long?" Wow, she'd timed that perfectly. Carson must have been about three seconds out of earshot.

"We're not dating."

"Why not?"

"Um...because neither of us is interested in dating right now." Geez, that sounded awful. And it was the truth, which meant it was also the wrong thing to say to his mother. "I'm gay."

"Oh. Oh, I'm sorry—I didn't mean to pry. I just worry he's too busy to find someone."

"I wouldn't worry. He's not in a rush to settle down."

"That's usually the time love finds you, isn't it?"

"Is it? I wouldn't know." I immediately jumped into the monotony of small talk—exactly the kind of thing I hate, but *anything* was better than discussing Carson's love life.

He came back a few minutes later, slightly winded, as if he'd been running from person to person, shaking hands and thanking them before moving to the next. "The Windhams and the Curtises are meeting us at the restaurant."

"I'd thought..." Renee looked disappointed for a second before shaking it off and smiling. "I'll let the restaurant know."

As soon as she reached into her bag, Carson grabbed my hand and pulled me away. "We'll see you there."

I had to power-walk to keep up with him. "Does she have a car?"

"And driver. She'll be fine. So, on a scale of one to wanting to stab yourself in the eye, how terrible was it?"

"I've met worse. She wanted to know if you were dating anyone."

"And you said...?"

"That you were happy being single, and that I'm gay."

"Shit, you stole my excuse! What am I going to tell her now?"

"We can both be gay." I followed him to his car, having taken the bus to get there this morning. Before we left, he gave me one more chance to back out, but I didn't take it. His mother wasn't evil and seemed to genuinely care about her son. I wanted to know why Carson didn't reciprocate those feelings.

"Your mom seemed so..."

"Whatever the next word you pick is, it'll probably be wrong." His tone had its normal depth and ease, but each word was clipped, as if he was struggling to control them. "Renee knows how to play a crowd. She's graceful, well educated, and great with everyone she isn't attracted or related to."

"Why don't you like her?" I asked.

He took a deep breath. "It's a long, complicated, bummer of a story, but the short version is she made some really bad choices while I was growing up, and she's still making them." His hands tightened on the wheel as he spoke. "It's hard to watch someone do that to themselves, and it was even harder to live through it as a kid."

I wanted to know what kind of choices he was talking about. But Carson was the most open book I'd ever know—if he didn't offer information, he didn't *want* to offer information, so I wouldn't ask. Yet.

CHAPTER 12 - CARSON

I felt Lane's stress-level jump as soon as we pulled up to the valet.

"I should've opted out," she said. "This place is *really* nice, and I'm basically wearing sweats."

"You could take them off," I said, smirking. "You look fine. Great, in fact." I took the ticket from the valet and waited for her to come around the car.

"I have five dollars and my bus pass tucked into my bra," she whispered when she was next to me. "Do you think that will get me more than a glass of water?"

"Don't talk about what you have in your bra, Lane. Pulling off being your gay best friend is going to be a lot tougher if I keep staring at your breasts and adjusting my hard-on." I slipped my arm around her waist as we went inside, staying close enough to whisper in her ear. "By the way, I'm buying, so feel free to order some bread to go with that water."

"Good thing you're my gay best friend and not someone who's trying to get in my pants. Because bread wouldn't pop open the first button."

"Good thing your pants don't have buttons then."

I loved it when she tried to hide her smile by putting her

lip between her teeth. Could watch her do that all day. But unfortunately, today was not that day. Today I'd be lucky if could walk out of here without biting my own tongue off.

As soon as I saw the Windhams in the lobby, I put on my work-mask, one of the only useful skills Renee had taught me. They were longtime friends of the family. Longtime friends who were nice enough people to believe Renee was equally nice. Plus, they had good-sized pockets and were big supporters of the foundation.

"You got here fast." I shook hands with Michael and introduced him and Nina to Lane, who'd never looked more uncomfortable. She was fidgeting and angling her body to hide what she was wearing. She had no idea that she'd be the most beautiful thing in the place even if she was wearing a tablecloth. We sat down and ordered drinks while we waited for Renee and the Curtises.

As I watched Lane struggle through the small talk, I felt a tinge of regret for bringing her. It was a completely selfish thing to do—use her as a buffer between Renee and me. But she could have refused and she hadn't. She needed to learn how to say what she wanted instead of pretending she was fine with every decision someone else made for her.

Fate and frogs—the two things she liked to think existed, maybe even *needed* to think existed. Not as if I didn't have my own pathetic issues with both of those things. What she called fate, I called heredity—nature and nurture. I couldn't actually beat it, but I could manipulate it. Like pointing a gun at someone: You can hope and pray it won't fire as much as you want, but if you keep your finger on the trigger, chances are it's going to go off eventually.

So as long as I kept my finger and all my other parts away from the trigger, I could enjoy her. I was fine with being a frog. I just didn't want to be the poisonous kind. Because to hurt the woman sitting next to me—her hands gripping the fabric of her pants, her lips stuck in the fakest looking smile I'd ever seen—to hurt her would mean I'd lost. I wasn't ready to say goodbye to her, for a bunch of reasons—some good, others idiotic. But it wasn't really a choice at this point.

Why was I doing this to myself? Every time we kissed or she did her "yes" look, it got worse. She was the one who was supposed to be working through shit. Not me. I was just supposed to be around to fuck. Damn, I hoped that happened soon.

Instead, it had turned into a test of both our limits. A long test with only one right answer.

I leaned towards her, peeling her fingers off her pants and whispering, "It'll be okay. Whenever you want to leave, squeeze"—I couldn't help myself—"my cock."

She gasped and looked at me with a horror-filled but slightly amused expression. What was it about her that made me want to tease her so mercilessly? She could take it, for one. I wanted to make sure she remembered how badly I wanted her, for two.

"Do you play golf, Michael?" she asked Windham. "Because Carson absolutely *loves* golf, but he never has anyone to play with." And she could throw it right back at me, for three. "Right?" She looked at me so innocently. Only the subtle curl of her mouth gave her away.

"I would never have pegged you for a golf lover, Carson," Michael said. "I'd love to meet you for a game sometime. You don't play, Laney?"

"With Carson? No, I don't play with him. In fact, most of the time he just plays with himself." She took a sip of water to hide her smile.

"Don't think there won't be repercussions for that," I mumbled.

All enjoyment disappeared when Renee and the Curtises came in. I was almost fast enough to hold out one of the chairs on the opposite side of the table for Renee, so she'd be as far from me as possible. But the Curtises were quicker, and I ended up holding out the chair next to my own for Renee.

When she ordered a bottle of champagne, I instantly tasted

bile and knew something really bad was about to happen. Under the table, Lane put her hand on my thigh and, without saying a word, asked me if I was okay.

No. No, I wasn't. I could fake it for a little while, but I was never okay around Renee. Every time I saw her, the last thirteen years suddenly disappeared and I was just a clueless, terrified kid looking up at my beautiful mother, afraid of asking her why.

"Carson," Lane whispered, her lips barely moving, "what's wrong?" She'd probably seen me tense, just like anyone else at the table who'd been looking at me would have. My mother definitely saw. And my mother definitely did nothing, which didn't surprise me at all.

I took a deep breath, focusing on making it through lunch, knowing that once it was over, I wouldn't have to see her for another year.

When the other people at the table asked what was going on, Renee smiled, giggling like someone thirty years younger.

"What's the big secret, Renee?" Michael asked.

I'd never been more tempted. Fuck, I'd *love* to tell everyone what Renee's big secret was. Fucking love it. In my head, I could actually hear my voice say the words, watching Windham's jaw drop, his wife's eyes widen. Gasps and whispers, my mother's hurried list of denials.

So tempting. And such a bad idea.

"What's the champagne for, Mother?" I used the title for the donors' benefit, not because she'd ever done anything to deserve it.

"I'll tell you when it gets here." For two of the longest minutes of my life, I waited. Once everyone had a glass of champagne in their hand, Renee blew out a breath, smiled, and held up her glass. "I thought it was fitting to announce this on a day that celebrates my late husband's legacy."

Fuck. This was going to be bad. When I downed my champagne, all eyes turned towards me. "Oh, I thought you were done." I refilled my glass. "Sorry, Mother. Please continue."

"When Carson started the Bennett Foundation, I wasn't sure it was the right decision. But it has turned into something I'm very proud of him for." She looked at me lovingly and I felt the eyes of everyone at the table again, but this time they were probably thinking what an amazing relationship she and I shared. Envied it even.

All I could think about was how she'd reacted when I told her what I was going to do with my half of Dad's estate that he'd split between my brother and me. Six years after he croaked, as soon as I turned eighteen, I'd used every penny to start and fund the foundation. The look on Renee's face was something I should've taken a picture of.

She'd been horrified. Initially it was because, after putting up with the man for over two decades, the asshole had only left her a *small* fortune, the entirety of which she went through in the first couple years. And then that I had "blown it all" on something for people outside our family...? That was inexcusable. She was so pissed, she couldn't bring even herself to speak to me. It was probably the best year of my whole fucking life.

I wouldn't have touched my father's money even if I was homeless and lived in a shopping cart. It was blood money, tainted by the bastard it belonged to. Now it was helping a lot of kids who my father would've— Well, who my father would have treated a lot better than he did his own.

Because he didn't *love* those other kids. Which meant he didn't hate them, either.

Ironically, a year later my aunt, the poor woman who'd grown up in the same house as my old man, died and left everything to her nephews. She'd had more cash than my dad had.

"Carson's father would've been proud of him, too," Renee said, calling up a few of those fake tears she had an endless supply of. I doubted she could even make the real ones anymore. "He'd want both of us to be happy, which is why, in just over a month from now, I'm getting married to a wonderful man."

And there it was. My abs clenched, shooting the breath out of me but not letting any back in. Another marriage. Another asshole. Another chance for Renee to ruin her life. Good for her, but I wasn't going to fucking watch it happen again.

As the other people at the table congratulated her, all I could be thankful for was that I hadn't eaten anything. I pushed my chair back from the table and stood, not caring how it looked or what anyone thought. I walked blindly for the exit, hearing someone call my name. She was next to me before I knew who it was.

"What just happened?" Lane asked. "I thought *I* was the one who was supposed to pretend to throw up."

"Let's get out of here."

"But"—she motioned back to the dining room—"you don't want to say…anything to them?"

"No." I wasn't nearly as good at faking it as Renee was.

The woman had always been gifted at that. Smiling without wincing even when under her expertly applied makeup was a split lip. Coming up with new lies every time she couldn't hide the damage my dad or any of her other asshole husbands did to her.

And to me.

Now she was heading back in for more. I didn't need to meet the guy to know exactly what he was. Renee would never be with someone who didn't treat her like shit. I shouldn't have been surprised, either—the last one had thrown her out over a year ago. And a year was way too long for her to go without being smacked around.

"Carson." Renee's voice was piercing. Even though it never rose in volume, I could always hear it from fifty feet away. Every lie she told, every emotion she faked, every excuse she gave.

"I don't want to talk to you." Now or ever.

"You will talk to me because I am your mother and I

deserve respect." She was only a few feet away now.

"Respect? For what exactly? Name one thing you've ever done that deserves my respect." My mind was on a train to totally-fucking-useless-ville and picking up speed. She wouldn't answer and she'd never change, but I couldn't keep my mouth shut anymore. "Why should I be the only one? *You* don't. None of your ex-husbands did, so I'm pretty sure your newest fiancé doesn't either—why break the loser streak, right?"

"If you have a problem with me, then we can discuss it." She glanced back towards the dining room and then at Lane. I guess to remind me I needed to lie. "But not in public, not in front of people we know."

"How well do they know you if they don't know you like being hit?"

"Carson, stop right now!"

"Isn't that kind of a fundamental part of you?" We spoke over each other without raising our voices in the slightest. If anybody was looking at us, they'd be able to tell our conversation was heated, but wouldn't hear a single word.

"Why are you ruining what should be a wonderful day, Carson?"

"Not in a kinky way, though. Renee can't go very long before she needs it. Like a drug. She's an addict."

"How dare you call me names? Tell awful lies about me?"

"Lies, right."

Lane stepped backwards, practically cowering. The look on her face quelled the fire in me, made me regret an argument that had never really started because it would never really end.

"Whatever ridiculous things you might think about me, they are wrong. Situations misconstrued by the perceptions of a child."

"You're right—I was just a child." It had never mattered that we lived in the same houses and felt the same fists. Because no two people ever punish themselves in the same way.

I handed Lane the valet slip. "Can you get the car while I finish congratulating Renee on her good news?"

Lane was silent for a minute, staring up at me. "Are you sure you don't want to come with me?"

"I'll be right there." As soon as she was out the door, I turned back to Renee, but my anger was gone. I even followed her when she stepped into a small alcove where no one would be able to overhear proof of our familial dysfunction. "Who's replacing Dad this time?" Hopefully she was smart enough not to marry a boxer.

"You have no idea what you're talking about, Carson. You never did. I loved your father with all my heart."

"I know that. Every time we left him, you told me. I know you loved him because what other possible reason could you have had for dragging your son back for more?"

She turned on the tears like turning on a fucking faucet.

"And I guess you've loved every man who's hit you since. Because what possible other reason could you have for continually picking them? You've got some kind of radar, Renee. Or maybe it's a magnetic pull to any man with good enough fists."

She slapped me across the face, and all I could do was laugh. She reacted with violence. Understandable, but still surprising. She'd never hit me before, maybe because she always made sure someone else was there to do it for her.

Obviously, all that experience being on the receiving end had taught her something. I rubbed my cheek and jaw to lessen the sting and get the blood moving. "It hurts even more than the hit does, but if you rub the area right away, you don't get as much bruising." My next words were soft. "My mother taught me that."

"Carson, I'm—"

I stopped her by putting my hands up at two and ten. Three words, when put in the right order, have the power to maim or to heal. Same words, same order. The only difference is what's behind them—truth or bullshit.

I couldn't count how many times I'd heard them.

"I am sorry."

The only thing I could count was how many times it was the truth.

As for those other three words—the really famous ones—well... I'd heard them countless times, and I knew they were true. Just like I knew the pain of the beating that came with them.

"I'm probably not going to make the wedding, but I'll try to send you something." I didn't ask her if she would keep cashing my checks, because it wasn't about money. It had never been about money. Or about self-respect or protecting her kid or finding someone who could show me the right way to be a man.

"Good luck, Renee."

"Do you mean that?" she asked.

"Yeah, I do. Because whoever the fuck this guy is, you're going to need it."

When she moved to slap me again, I reacted instinctually. I caught her wrist, stopping her hand a few inches from my cheek.

"Stop it," she hissed. "You're hurting me. Let go of me right now."

"What did you say?" I'd heard every word, and they'd stung so much more than if her hand had actually made contact. Because she'd told me to stop. She'd told a man to stop hurting her, probably for the first time in her life.

But the part that didn't let go of me was that *I* was the man she was talking to, the one whose fingers were digging into her flesh, whose entire body was tense with the potential for violence, who couldn't find a way to release her, whose hands were both fisted—one at my side and the other around her thin wrist.

I focused on relaxing, letting her go, coming back from a place I knew I'd end up if I ever let myself get too close.

I left Renee standing there. It wouldn't be long before she

wiped her eyes and went back to the table to lie about why I'd left. She'd probably go with something like me being upset that my father didn't have a chance to see me succeed in something so worthwhile. She'd used that one before and, from what I'd heard, it worked pretty damn well.

The next time I saw the Curtises or Windhams, they'd tell me how proud my dad would've been of me. And I would be silent, unable to say anything to keep up the farce but knowing I had to. Not for myself. Not for my family, either. I kept my mouth shut for families who had all the reason in the world to be screwed up, but who actually loved and took care of each other.

If people found out about my parents or any of my mother's rich, powerful, and abusive ex-husbands, it would probably suck for a while, but we'd live. The problem was that no one would donate money to a nonprofit named after an abusive husband and father. Run by his fucked-up kid. I hadn't realized it until the name was too much a part of the foundation. If I changed it now, donations would plummet and people would want to know why Bennett's kid didn't want his name attached to it anymore. They'd find out why because people care about that kind of shit. It's entertaining.

So I'd pay people to keep quiet about my fuck-ups and I'd keep my mouth closed until I found somewhere to get drunk and get laid and forget everything for a little while. All things I was good at. The only things I was good at.

Since Lane was in the driver's seat, I got in the passenger side. "I shouldn't have brought you."

She shrugged. "Aside from not knowing what I was actually getting into or understanding whatever just happened between you and your mom, I thought it was great. I had some fancy water and a piece of bread. And..." She waited until I stopped staring at my hands and looked at her.

"And what?"

"That champagne was really, really good," she said. "Thanks."

I should've thanked *her*. "We left before the check came, so it was someone else's treat." Although, knowing Renee, she'd talk the restaurant into sending me a bill.

"What now?" she asked.

"Normally after I spend time with Renee, I get loaded and fuck someone to take my mind off it. You interested in doing either or both of those things with me?"

"Let's start with the drink."

"I guess I'm coming out of the closet today after all. Take me to the nearest bar." This was the first time I didn't want to get her naked. Renee would taint it somehow, and even though sex with Lane wouldn't be emotional, I didn't want to use her to forget something shitty. I wanted to remember her for something great.

CHAPTER 13 - LANEY

Carson ordered whiskey for both of us, ignoring my pleas for something tamer. "Okay, fine. Jesus. The lady wants a beer to go with her whiskey. Make it a double, though." We took our drinks to one of the many empty bar tables.

I let him lead the topics of conversation, knowing that if he wanted to vent or share, he would. We didn't talk about his mother or what he'd said at all. After I forced down the whiskey and he'd had another, I stopped drinking, knowing one of us should be thinking clearly or both of us would be in trouble.

"One night when I was about eight," he said after I came back to the table with a glass of water, "my dad dragged me out of bed by the ankle. Scared the shit out of me, but I knew it would only be worse if I cried. When he took me into the garage, I think I stopped breathing."

I think I did, too. And I almost started crying, imagining Carson as a child, terrified of his own father. The argument between Carson and Renee had been impossible to follow, but I picked up enough to understand a little about why Carson was the way he was.

"There are a lot of tools in a garage. Metal and wood tools, you know?"

I nodded, knowing I should stop him, so he wouldn't regret opening up to me once he was completely sober. But I wanted to know. I wanted to believe he was choosing to trust me with something he'd probably only told a few other people. So I didn't stop him.

"When he told me to get into the car, I was just confused. Scared too, but that was more of a perpetual thing, so it wasn't that big a deal. We drove two hours to the boarding school my brother Hayden went to." He looked at me. "You'd like Hayden. He's a good guy. Quiet, though. Needs to relax, misbehave a little. Kind of like you."

He pushed his drink away and pointed to my glass. "Can I have some of that?"

"How about I get you one of your very own?" Before I'd even stood up all the way, he'd taken my glass and drank half of it. "Carson!"

"I only have so much patience," he said, smiling.

When I came back, he started talking as if he hadn't stopped. "Dad told whoever was on duty in Hayden's dorm that there'd been an emergency, so he could take Hayden out. Want to know why?"

Thank god the question was rhetorical because honestly, I couldn't decide if I wanted to know or not.

"All so the motherfucker could take us fishing. Fishing. Something he'd probably never done in his life. He didn't even know how to put the worm on the hook. Hayden and I had to teach him. That part was kinda nice—teaching him something. We sat on that fucking dock all day long. Probably the only time in history anyone had their fishing trip catered, but my old man didn't know another way to be. Nature and nurture."

He picked up his drink and took a sip. "I still don't know why he did that. Maybe he knew he was dying and wanted to give us one good memory before he croaked. The next day, shit went back to the way it'd always been, as if that night had never happened. Don't talk about the good shit 'cause then somebody might accidentally mention the bad shit, too."

I took the glass out of his hand. "I thought you didn't drink in public. Something about hiding your shame."

"That's a recent development."

"Why'd you stop?

He paused. "Because the last time I got drunk, I hurt someone pretty bad. More than pretty bad, I guess. I don't actually remember what happened, so I figured it was time to go into hiding until I could figure out why I'd done it. But that's not going to happen here or now, so let's stop talking about it."

Sometimes I felt like there was a hundred times more I didn't know about Carson than I did. I was probably right.

He held my eyes with his for a second longer than was comfortable before he spoke. "I'm gonna ask you something, but you're not allowed to get weird about it."

"Um... I'll try my best."

"Why did you go out with so many frogs?"

"They weren't frogs when I started going out with them."

"Yeah, they were."

"Yeah, they were," I repeated. I knew I wasn't the reason they'd changed, it just seemed like it. I sighed, wondering if he'd open up more if I started. "My parents were high school sweethearts, love at first sight, fated to be together. After high school, my mom left everything she knew to go to California with him. I must have heard their story a thousand times growing up. I figured it would be the same for me—I would know from the moment we met that he was the one. I was wrong once in high school and have been wrong another four times since then."

"And now you don't believe in love?"

"Nope."

"Do your parents still?"

"Yeah," I said quietly. "I guess they do. But they're both good people, so being together is just something they don't think about anymore. Something they've believed for so long, it's turned into a habit they'll never break."

"You mean a habit like how deeply I believe you need to get laid? I'm going to need your help to break that one." I laughed. "I think you'll make it."

Over the course of a few hours, he'd calmed down, sobered up, and found his *joie de vivre* again. I knew this because he started making more frequent passes at me.

When I came back from a bathroom run, he was in the hallway, waiting for me. "Can I help you with something?" I stepped to the side, but he didn't let me pass. "Are you okay?"

"I need to repay you for the hell I put you through today. You and I are going to play a game."

Why was I suddenly so nervous? "What game?"

"I haven't named it yet. Let's call it 'Something for Nothing,' at least for now." He grabbed me by the waist and turned us so we both faced the bar area with him behind me. His hands stayed put, and he bent down so he could whisper in my ear. "The goal is to get as many drinks as you can out of a guy I choose for you. You don't have to drink them all— you just have to get him to pay for them. Give them away, dump them in the plants, whatever."

"This sounds like a truly terrible idea."

"No, it's a great idea. As in all games, there are rules," he said seriously. "Under no circumstances can you take the guy's number. If he asks you for yours, you can't give it to him, not even a fake one. That's cheating."

"What exactly is the point of this game?"

"To be open and honest and say what you want and don't want. Practice getting something for nothing. Because believe me—I know this from experience—the guy is going to be trying to do the exact same thing. He'll have a lot more practice and motivation than you will, so don't think you can half-ass it."

"I don't know."

"It's just for fun, Lane. No one's gonna get hurt. You're not forcing him to do anything. You need practice not worrying about other people's needs more than your own."

That was true. "I guess I could try. But you're not allowed to laugh if I fail miserably."

"I swear I'll only laugh if you fail any other way. Now, who's the lucky guy gonna be?" He walked me into the crowd, saying, "Eeny-meeny-miny-moe."

Just before I could say I wasn't going to do it, so he was free to laugh at me all he wanted, he shoved me sideways into a tall, good-looking guy about our age. When I looked back, he mouthed, 'No cheating,' and went to go sit at a table near the back of the bar—with a perfect view of me.

"Sorry," I mumbled, trying to squeeze around the guy. "I was just trying to get to the bar."

He smiled down at me. "No problem. Let me help. What are you drinking?"

Seriously? That was way too easy. I guessed it wouldn't hurt to get one. Then Carson wouldn't be able to laugh as hard. "Vodka tonic. Thanks."

He reached over a few people and tapped the bar to get the bartender's attention. A minute later he handed me a drink and invited me to sit down. I saw Carson switch to a table by the door to have a better view. The prick.

CHAPTER 14 - CARSON

The game was hysterical to watch until I saw Lane lean in close to the guy and whisper something. Then he said something back and she laughed. Why'd she laugh? The guy couldn't possibly be funny. I'd picked him because he seemed like the type who'd appreciate some attention from a woman who looks as good as Lane does, and I figured she'd get a boost to her self-esteem. It was supposed to have been my good deed of the year.

Now it looked like they were actually having a good time. I fell against the back of my chair when Lane licked her lips. What the fuck? It was a game. Games are fun.

This wasn't fun.

Someone stopped right in front of me and blocked my sightline. "Pick a direction and keep moving in it."

"Is 'down' one of the choices?" A blonde slipped into the chair across from me, smirking. "I really enjoy going down."

"That's quite a coincidence." My view just got a lot better. She was pretty much as different from Lane as you could get. Fake blonde, fake tan, fake tits. All the things women think men shouldn't like, for whatever reason. Her lips might have even been fake, but I have firsthand knowledge that silicone has no effect on how well a woman can use them.

I bought her a drink. She told me about her job. I pretended to care. We both knew I didn't. Every once in a while, I felt like I could hear Lane's voice. In this loud room of strangers, her laugh came through, taunting me.

I started to get antsy. Every time I looked around whatever-her-name-was's shoulder, I saw Lane smiling and the table fill with more empty glasses. This was her first time out, so she needed to take it easy. I should've warned her about that.

When I saw the guy run his hand up the back of her neck and pull her in, I shot out of my chair.

The blonde stood, too. "Are you okay?"

"No! Obviously not!" I took her by the arm to scoot her to the side so I could see, although I wasn't sure if I should look. As if I could stop myself.

Lane's eyes were huge—focusing on me, then the blonde, then me, the blonde, down to her drink, and finally on that stupid fucking guy she was with.

"Do you want to leave?" the blonde asked.

"God, yes." Then I understood she meant with *her*. "No. No, I can't leave my friend." I slumped down in my chair and put my head in my hands. This had to be the worst fucking idea I'd ever had.

I didn't notice the blonde had gone until I heard Lane's voice. "I thought you were going to leave with her."

The guy wasn't around. Thank fuck.

"I couldn't. I had to stay and make sure you didn't get yourself in trouble."

She smiled as if she knew something I didn't and turned towards the door.

"What?"

"I won your game, Carson. I kicked ass."

It was nice to be able to breathe. Doubly nice to be able to leave. With her. "You must have cheated."

"You're a terrible loser. But you're also right."

"Wait." I caught up with her. "What does that mean? You

gave him your number? A fake one, right?"

"No."

"What do you mean no?" What the fuck? "You actually gave him your number?"

"No."

"Oh." I cleared my throat. "Cool. So how'd you cheat then?"

"I asked him if he could buy me a few drinks and hang out with me for a while. Because I needed his help to make you jealous."

"Nicely played, Lane." It completely fucking worked.

CHAPTER 15 - LANEY

Two days later, Carson and I met for lunch and spent the next four hours talking about things that couldn't possibly have taken four hours to talk about. Time didn't seem to work the same around Carson as it did around everyone else.

Since his place was between the restaurant and mine, he made me walk him home.

"I get a little nervous walking home alone in the daylight," he said, getting up and tossing some cash on the table.

"At—what are you—six-foot-one, I can see why. You're so weak and frail. Don't worry—if anything happens, just hide behind me."

Thankfully nothing bad happened, and I delivered him to his building without a scratch.

"Come up for a second." He held the door open. "I promise to behave." He let go and then caught it just before it smacked me in the face. "Mostly."

I had purposefully avoided his apartment when we were together, which all of a sudden was a lot. I hadn't invited him up to my place, either. I was well aware people can have sex in places other than a bed, but it was easier to keep my thoughts clean in public.

As soon as I decided I could do it—separate sex and love— it wouldn't matter. I would finally be able to do something that I pretty much filled my days imagining. But, unfortunately, another fantasy appeared out of nowhere recently—that I was the one to tame him, make him change his ways, want to be with me and me alone. Ugh. If I knew how to give myself a partial lobotomy and knew where my delusion center was, I'd be picking out a drill bit.

Maybe it was because now I knew about his childhood, and the maternal, girlie side of me was triggered by the pain in his voice. I didn't know. And he wouldn't care.

The longer it lasted, the more dangerous it was. Carson would walk away if he even *smelled* anything that moronic on me. His senses were heightened when it came to recognizing monogamy pheromones.

He'd been more than clear about what he could give me— sex. And no matter how amazing it was, he was also clear about what would happen afterward—nothing. He didn't do long term. We both knew how risky it was, how quickly things could go bad. Neither of us wanted it to happen until I was one-hundred percent sure I wouldn't attach a whole bunch of strings to him.

When I walked into his place, the first thing I saw was my driftwood table. The table that was supposed to raise money for his foundation, not be here.

"What the hell is that?"

He turned to see what I was freaking out about. "That is a three-year-old piece of art. It's not strong enough to hold strippers though, so you'll have to use one of the others for that."

I stomped over to it and then spun around to face him. "I thought it was for the auction."

"Oh shit." He laughed. "You don't really think all of that was a ploy to get it for free, do you?"

"I hadn't gotten that far—my thinking is still stuck in confusion." Sighing, I stepped back a little to see it better because, honestly, it looked really great with the rest of his furniture and I was kind of proud. "Why is it here?"

"Do you like it?" He came up behind me and put his hands on my waist, his body barely touching mine. "I'm told the artist has others, if you want one. But be aware: they're not cheap."

"You bought it at the auction?"

"Yep."

"If I knew you wanted it, I would've given it to you."

"That would have been a poor business decision. Instead, you did a really good thing by giving it to the Bennett Foundation, and you should soon be getting a thank you letter that doubles as proof of the tax deduction." He let go of me. "Um... Promise me something. Just say yes. It's not illegal."

"Is it about sex?"

"No, but I'd be happy to throw that in."

"I'm not going to promise you anything without knowing what it is." I wasn't sure what he was hesitant to say. He didn't get hesitant or uncomfortable—that was *my* department.

"I swear it has nothing to do with sex or any of the depraved things I want to do to you. Please?"

Oh hell, I wasn't signing anything in blood. "Fine, I promise."

"Cash the check."

"What do you—?" Shit. I sighed and crossed my arms over my chest. "It's in with the thank you letter?" When I opened that envelope, I knew I'd find a check with his name on it, written out for fifteen-hundred dollars.

"I saw your website, Lane. I almost started crying. Seriously, cash the check."

"How much did you pay for it at the auction?"

"Six."

Six made sense. "That's pretty good. I didn't actually expect anyone to pay fifteen-hundred dollars, but gallery owners are more likely to show your—"

"Thousand."

My arms dropped to my sides, and I was silent for a second. Then I shouted, "Six *thousand*? Oh my god, you paid *six thousand dollars* for my table?"

"*My* table. I was almost outbid by some guy who didn't deserve it—he'd probably put his feet up on it or use it for strippers. So I swooped in and took what was rightfully mine. I got mad skills with an auction paddle." He raised his hand quickly as if he were pulling a gun and then dropped it just as quickly. "I'm kidding—it was a silent auction. But I'd be happy to show you my skill with a paddle. *Really* happy to show you."

"Six thousand dollars." The figure was doing circles in my mind. Even if Carson puffed up the price, it still meant other people would've paid something close to that. Six thousand dollars for a piece I made. All told, Carson had paid seventy-five hundred. For a piece of my art.

"I wish you'd been there to see the guy's face when he realized he was a loser." He drew out the word, belittling something that made me feel more supported than I ever had by anyone, including my parents.

"Did that really happen?" I asked quietly. "Was there really a guy you had to outbid?"

"No. There were two guys and three women I had to outbid." He straightened and looked at me with a furrowed brow. "What's wrong? Six thousand dollars is going to families who need it, and I love my new table. Why are you upset about it?"

Because even though money didn't mean anything to him, and he'd refuse to believe he had done anything special, he'd validated my art and my dream and made me feel like I could do this. But I couldn't tell him that because I'd probably start crying and getting all girlie.

"I'm not upset." I shook it off before I scared him. "I'm in shock—a happy kind of shock."

"I'm in a happy kind of shock *for* you. The bidding was tight. I didn't want to tell you because then you'd be working more instead of paying attention to me." He winked. "But your phone number might have accidentally slipped into a few of their hands. I would've given them your website address if yours wasn't so humiliating. Which brings us back to... Cash the check."

"It's not a donation if you pay me."

"Then call it something else. Or *give* me something else." His gaze flew around my body. "Do you even have anything? I guess this will have to do." He reached to my waist, yanked me towards him, and started undoing my belt.

"Carson, stop!" I backed up quickly, pushing him away. But he'd already gotten the buckle undone, and it stayed in his hand. "What are you doing?" I shoved him as hard as I could.

Time froze. He stood perfectly still, staring at the belt running from his hand to the last loop of my jeans. We both watched it come loose and fall.

"Buying your belt." His voice was raspy and deeper than normal. Not like his real one at all. There was something so accepting about the look on his face. Like he'd been expecting something like this, known it was coming. But he'd misunderstood—I wasn't afraid of him.

"For fifteen-hundred dollars," he said. "It was lovely doing business with you." He rolled it around his hand and walked towards the kitchen. "Want a drink?"

It wasn't as if I thought he was going to do anything horrible. "Don't be like this. I just thought—"

"I know what you thought," he called. "Let's leave it at that."

"Carson!" I stood there for a second, frustrated, before hurrying into the kitchen. "I didn't mean anything by it."

"You thought I was trying to take off your clothes without your permission." He shrugged. "Your reaction was exactly what it should've been."

"Yeah, but I know you would never—"

"You didn't think those guys would ever lie to you, cheat on you, or treat you like shit, either."

"You would never hurt me like that."

"No. Not like *that*." He held out his hand, my belt wrapped around it multiple times. Tight. "But there are a lot of ways to hurt someone." His eyes stayed on the belt for another moment before rising to meet mine.

I took his hand, slowly unwrapping the leather from around his fist and wrist. Once I had all of it, I put it in his open palm and curled his fingers around it, wanting more than anything to make him stop looking like he knew it was just a matter of time before one of us hurt the other. How had everything changed so quickly?

"Don't you think fifteen-hundred dollars is a little too much for a belt?" I asked, smiling in the hopes he would too. "I'm sure you have something better than me—"

He squinted for a moment. "Better than you?"

"To spend your money on. You can't buy a crappy belt for fifteen-hundred dollars."

"I have a lot of money in a bank account with my name on it. That means I get to decide how I spend it and you don't."

This wasn't how I wanted things to be—awkward and stiff.

"Hey." I smacked him on the arm. "I just didn't understand what you were doing."

He nodded. "It's okay."

I paused, wondering if that was even a little bit true, knowing there wasn't anything I could actually do about it. "You know what's totally *not* okay? That you gave me crap for my business sense when you just paid fifteen-hundred dollars for a twenty-dollar belt."

I waited for his eyes to go back to playful mode because then I'd know it really was okay. It didn't take long. He was so good at pushing away anything he didn't want to deal with, including himself.

"Yeah well, I got a great deal on a table recently, so I figure I'm about even." He took out a bottle of wine. "Do you want something to drink or not?"

After a second of indecision, I hiked up my jeans and reached for two glasses. "I like that belt. I should've charged you more."

My wine glass was half-empty again when he tossed me something. As soon as my hand closed around it, I knew what it was.

"It's just a key, so don't be all girlie and read girlie things into it," he said, flopping down on the couch. "I need you to keep an eye on my place. I get to go to Los Angeles tonight. Very exciting, because there's nowhere I'd rather be trapped for a week than in a room full of lawyers, financial advisors, and Renee. Except with her fiancé and a wedding planner. Gee, I hope I get to do that, too."

"Sounds horrible. But you realize you're giving a key to someone you haven't actually known all that long, right?"

"I'm gonna let you in on a little secret—you're the most trustworthy person I know. By miles. If I asked any of my guy friends, the place would be completely trashed when I got home. If I gave it to any woman besides you, she'd read into it somehow."

"What about Anna?"

He paused. "I don't trust Anna."

"Then I guess I'm the best person for the job. I'll do it"— I tucked the key into my pocket—"but only if I get to take a bath in your tub." He had literally the biggest bathtub I'd ever seen. Jets, a waterproof remote for the TV on the wall, Bluetooth speakers everywhere, built in cushions to lay your head on. All I had to do was not think of the women who'd used it with him.

"Great," he muttered. "Now I'm going to spend a week in L.A. picturing you naked in my tub."

"I'm sure you'll find something to keep you entertained." But nothing I wanted to think too much about.

"Do you know how to turn it on?"

After I shook my head, he headed into the bathroom, explaining where things were and what I shouldn't touch. When hot water started pouring in, I couldn't get the stupid grin off my face. Like I'd never seen running water before. But even when it was completely full, the bathtub in my apartment was only about eight inches deep and I could barely straighten my legs.

"I'm going to live in it," I said. "Become a big prune. You'll still be my friend if I look like a wrinkly old lady when you get back, won't you?"

"Um...no," he said. "But while I have your full attention, check this out." When the water got high enough, he punched a button to turn on the jets.

My squeal wasn't that loud, but he acted as if it was.

"You're such a girl."

When I reached down to feel the pressure of the jets, my other hand slipped off the edge and I fell forward, screaming. Carson grabbed me, only catching my leg. If the tub had been completely filled, my entire upper body would already be under. Although, between the depth of the water and the splash as I fell, I was still soaked. He tugged on my leg, but was laughing so hard he couldn't lift me up.

"Stop laughing and get me out of here, you jerk!"

"Guess how badly I want to let go right now." If he did, even just to get a better grip, I'd go in. Thankfully, he put hand over hand, climbing up my leg, over my knee, going higher. When his hand reached my inner thigh, he let go with his other to get more leverage, then once he had me he adjusted his other hand.

Even though at this point he could've easily pulled me out, he didn't move. "Hmm..." Now I knew why—because of what he was holding onto. One hand was on my ass and the other holding the side of my breast. It was awkward and I was drenched, but part of me wanted to fall in and pull him in with me. Stop caring so much about limits and rules and dos and don'ts. Just enjoy getting messy for a little while.

He cleared his throat and asked, "You ready?"

God, yes. I got a little wet and all the wondering and worrying about what to do had become completely moot. My body made the decision for me. No thinking and no planning.

Thankfully, I stopped myself before I screamed out 'yes,' opting for something a little more vague just in case I came to my senses in the next few seconds.

"Probably."

CHAPTER 16 - CARSON

Probably?

I knew Lane had misunderstood me because her lips parted and she didn't take her eyes off my mouth, other than a brief glance at my cock. But she was still pretty horizontal, and if I didn't pull her up soon, the laws of physics were going to kick in, and we'd both go into the water.

Probably. What did that mean? I should *probably* kiss her. If I was really lucky, it would *probably* go further. Hopefully all the way to where I *definitely* wanted to be. Or was it just that I should *probably* get her out of the bath before we both fell in?

Then, even if I begged for more, would the 'probably' turn back into a 'no'?

Fuck, 'probably' could mean anything. I straightened, keeping her in my arms, as close as I could even though she was sopping wet. I watched her expression, recognized it because I'd seen it on a lot of women's faces.

But Lane's was different—it was hers. And I wanted to make sure I saw it constantly because knowing she trusted me was... I'm not sure anyone had ever trusted me before, not in the way she did. And it made me feel—

Drop the sap and stick to what I'm good at.

I shook off the weird connective element and focused on the physical. That's what I wanted. Just the physical. I moved slowly, knowing she could balk at any moment, and I'd have to take my hands off her. I'd gotten hard the second I grabbed her ass, and I was only getting harder. She *had* to feel me. And she stayed in my arms long after she had to.

"Are you ready for this?" I asked again, knowing she'd understand and praying she'd say—

"Yes."

My lips were on hers instantly, my hand moving lower on her ass and pulling her tighter to me. I'd stop if she said stop but I was going to go for as long as she let me. I'd never wanted a woman even close to this much before. *Probably* because she'd made me wait so damn long. Her hands went around my neck, and she moaned into my mouth. So I took the opportunity to deepen the kiss.

Wait. Maybe I should slow down. I didn't want to slow down. Honestly, I was torn. If I didn't say anything, we could be together now and all the damage would come out later. And later was *really* far from now. But if I said what I should say, she might want to stop.

Shit. I didn't want to, but if we didn't make things clear right now, it was never going to happen. Any second my brain would turn off and let my cock take over.

Not *too* slow, just enough to be able to speak in between swipes of lips or tongue.

"How you doing?" I asked.

She made a noise I'd never actually heard before. Something in between what she sounded like when she ate chocolate and the sigh she made whenever the couple finally got together in one of those horrible movies she made me watch.

God, she felt good. Everywhere, every part of her that was in contact with any part of me felt so fucking good.

"Lane, tell me you're doing okay." Both of us were in

uncharted territory. She'd never handed herself over to an idiot she didn't have feelings for, and I'd never been this close to sleeping with someone I knew even moderately well and liked a hell of a lot.

In my experience, there was a point when the flirting and conversation went on too long, crossing from "I really want to get you under me" territory into the "I really want to get to know you" zone. Lane and I were way past that point. I was counting on us being so far beyond that point that things had looped around again. But that was somewhere I'd never dared go.

She still hadn't answered.

I pulled away from her, catching her chin in my hand to hold her back. "Talk to me. No emotions, right?"

"Right." Is there anything sexier than a breathless woman? "Am I not allowed to like you, either?"

"You can like me all you want, as long as you remember this is nothing more than two people who can make each other feel good."

"You keep saying that, but I have yet to see any proof you can actually do it."

"Oooh, you have no idea what you're in for."

Her eyes flashed wide, and her fists went limp and fell from my collar. "We'll go slowly, right?"

"Yeah." I caught her hands and put them back around my neck where they belonged, waiting until she understood their place before I let go. "As long as we're going in the right direction, we can go as slowly as you want. What's my stopping point gonna be?"

"No sex. Not now, and later..."

"No sex now. Got it. We'll figure out later when it comes."

"I'm all wet." That's hot.

When her arms slid off my shoulders again, I cursed, the word drawn out until I understood what she was doing.

She pulled up her soaking shirt, exposing her smooth, curvy, feminine belly and waist. When the shirt got stuck on her shoulders and she couldn't get it over her head, I helped. Her pants were next. I helped with those too. Shoes came off with them.

Beautiful.

"Not yet, okay?"

"Huh?" I yanked my eyes away from her body. "Sorry, lost focus there for a minute."

"Sex. Not right away. Is that okay with you?"

"It's your call, Lane. I'll take whatever's offered." Was my look of disappointment as bad as I thought it was? "We'd better stay away from the bed and the couch though." I was only so strong, and lying on top of her would pretty much negate all of it.

"And the shower."

I loved her mind. I really did. "Okay, that means we could go table or counter or wall. Lots of possibilities here, Lane. Pick one."

"Whatever's closest."

Deep breath. "You said slow, right? If I forget, just smack me." I scooped her up into my arms and carried her to the door, my feet momentarily getting wrapped up in the pile of her wet clothes.

When we got to the doorway, she shouted. "Carson, stop! The bath!"

"Shit." I turned around just as the water crested the edge of the tub and poured down the sides. I looked at the woman in my arms with regret for another second before cursing, putting her down, and running to turn off the faucet.

"Okay, where were we?" Just about to get to the good stuff.

"We need to clean up all the water."

"No. No, we—" Yeah, we did. *Fuck.*

Instead of doing what we *should've* been doing, we spent the rest of the evening sponging water off the floor, making sure it hadn't gone down into the apartment below mine, and doing all sorts of other shit I didn't want to do.

And then my time ran out. "I need to leave for the airport."

Yet another episode of my mother ruining my life. I'd put off the trip as long as possible and booked the last flight of the day. I would've blown it off completely if the trip was just to spend time with Renee. But I also had to talk to a few of the Foundation's board members to discuss my fuck-up in the bar.

"Don't worry about the water, Lane, we got most of it. The rest will dry eventually."

"I want to use the tub." She was on her hands and knees using a towel to mop up the last of the water, wearing a t-shirt I'd loaned her until her stuff dried. "And I don't want you to be able to blame the water damage on *my* bath instead of your distractibility."

How the fuck did she expect me not to be distracted? It would be so easy to get on my knees behind her and forget all about taking things slowly.

I was so tempted to ask her to come to L.A. with me. While I was talking to people I disliked, she could visit her parents in San Diego, as long as she was back in the hotel room and naked by the time I escaped. But unfortunately, Lane had work to do and her own life to live. Not to mention that going out of town together was way over the "This is getting serious" limit.

"Come here." I fucking loved that she did it without question. Everything masculine and alpha in me eating it up. It wasn't a big deal, but it was a sign of trust, and that's why we were doing this, right? I grabbed her and kissed her for a good couple of minutes—too long and not long enough.

"I'm going to fantasize about you in that tub for a week, and we're going to revisit this as soon as I get back."

A shadow of fear passed over her face.

"Stop thinking," I grumbled. "That's the kind of shit that gets you in trouble." And the kind of thing that would make me have to back off, which I didn't want to do.

"I'm going to revisit these, too," I said, taking one last taste of her lips. We could have a good thing together, a really good thing. Something I'd never tried before because I'd never had anyone I liked enough to try it with. But only if she played by the rules—no attachment, no expectations, no commitment, no feelings.

I hoped she could do it.

She pushed on my chest to separate us. "Go away, or you're going to miss your flight."

"Yeah, okay." I kissed her again because I couldn't stop myself.

"Go away." She shoved me backwards, laughing.

"I'll see you soon, beautiful." One last kiss—a small one— and then I was out of there.

Oh fuck. Maybe she wasn't the one I should be worried about.

CHAPTER 17 - LANEY

I stayed at Carson's place a lot more than I should have. Being there was like a vacation—no roommate, an incredible bathtub, and total quiet.

He didn't call but he texted dirty messages a few times, begging me to take pictures of myself in the tub. So he could make sure I hadn't broken it. No pictures were taken but there was a message returned, letting him know just how well I was taking care of his tub. The new soap I'd bought made bubbles that wouldn't ruin the jets, so the bath and I were both very, very clean.

His response came in multiple texts over the next hour, as if he couldn't stop thinking about it.

The first was, 'Stop torturing me.'

The second—'Keep torturing me. Tell me you've been touching yourself in my bathtub. If you haven't, do it immediately and get back to me.'

The third—'There better be enough soap left when I get back because you and I are going to get *really* dirty.'

And the fourth—'You know I'm kidding and not kidding, right?'

I did. That was the best part of all. He was a massive flirt who would back it up the second he could, but who somehow knew that if he pushed me too hard into something I wasn't ready for, we'd both lose.

I held the phone between my shoulder and my ear while I flicked the lights off and locked up my shop. It was just starting to get dark, the time I'd normally have gone to the café to see Carson. Normally? I wasn't sure how much normal there was in this situation.

"When are you coming back?" God help me, I missed him.

"I wish I didn't have to say Saturday, but I do."

So I had a few more days before he got back to town and wouldn't have 24/7 access to his bathtub anymore. Not that he would say no if I even hinted at it, especially because I'd be naked.

"Unless some kind of divine intervention happens and Renee's fiancé calls the wedding off. Maybe he'll finally realize she's been lying to him about being a decent person. Or found someone who was with him for a healthy reason."

"What do you mean by healthy?"

"How the fuck should I know?" he said, laughing. "The only reason I've ever been with anyone is sex. Although, if you're doing it right, sex is exercise, and exercise is healthy. So I guess that means I'm a health nut. You and I should start exercising together."

"I don't think that's what they mean."

"I was kidding. Not about sex being healthy—I totally believe that. But about sex being the only reason I'd ever be with anyone. Look at you and me."

"Right. The only reason you're with me is because you *want* to have sex with me."

"Come on, you know that's not true." His voice changed— got lower, more serious.

"Yeah, I know."

"I'm with you because I want to have a *lot* of sex with

you."

"Should've seen that one coming." The pedestrians I passed looked at me oddly because I'd rolled my eyes so dramatically.

"Until then, I guess I'll have to enjoy your company," he grumbled. "You'll let me know when I don't have to do that anymore though, right?"

"You'll be the first person I tell, promise."

The volume of his voice dropped again. "It would be a mistake, you know."

"What would?"

"To fall for me."

"I'm not." I didn't want to, either. What I wanted was to understand him and to know that he trusted me enough to feel like he could tell me anything. Because I was pretty sure he didn't have anyone else he could tell.

"The only thing I love about you is your bathtub. But just out of curiosity, why do you think it would be such a mistake?"

"Because I can't give that back to you. It would have to end, and you'd be worse off than before we met. That would be my fault. I wasn't kidding about being a selfish bastard. If I wasn't one, I would tell you to walk away."

"And then I would say, 'Why don't you go fuck yourself because I don't want to go away?'"

The smile was back in his tone. "At which point I would probably say, 'Since, unfortunately, it's not physically possible to fuck myself, why don't I fuck you instead?'"

"And I would say, 'Okay.'"

"What?" he said on an inhalation. The kind of inhalation I was having trouble doing. I'd surprised myself as much as him by saying it, but I didn't want to take it back. I was more comfortable with him than I'd ever been with anyone, probably in my entire life. All the worry and fear I'd always felt while I was with a guy wasn't there because I knew Carson wouldn't judge me. He knew who I was better than anyone and he liked me anyway.

"Say it again, Lane."

"Okay." Because it *was* okay, and I wasn't afraid. Carson wouldn't let me be afraid. It had nothing to do with love—it was better than that. He would protect me, even from myself, because that's who he was, whether he admitted it or not. He would help me deal with this just like he'd helped me deal with everything leading up to this—with a joke, a stupid comment, or just by listening.

"Seriously?" It was whispered.

"Seriously."

"Damn it," he whined at full volume. "You couldn't have waited to tell me that? I'm stuck here for a few more days, and I'm going to be hard the whole time."

I laughed. "Flattering, but I'm not that irresistible."

"Pretty damn close. Listen, I gotta go. But... I don't want you to regret anything. So until I'm inside you, you're allowed to change your mind. Even after I'm inside you, you're allowed, although you might have to use small words and lots of hand gestures to get me to focus."

After he's inside me. That was going to be playing on repeat in my mind for a while.

"Think about it, but don't overthink it, until I get back," he said. "In the three longest days of my life from now."

Over the next two days, thinking about him and what was going to happen took more of my time than anything else. I'd made a commitment, but only to sex. Does that qualify as a commitment?

The night before he was supposed to come back, I went to his place after work and took a long bath. So long that it was dark by the time I got out, so I decided to crash at his place instead of walking home.

He had lots of extra rooms, but none of them were set up as a guest room, an absence that screamed 'don't get too comfortable here 'cause you won't be staying long.'

I could've slept on the couch. But I didn't.

Instead, I climbed into his gigantic bed, trying not to think too hard about why I wanted to try it out, ignoring my body's Pavlovian reaction to being there. He'd told me that when he slept without sleeping with someone, he went to her place so he could go home afterwards. Because he can't sleep with anyone in his bed, so this might be my only chance to spend an entire night with his scent surrounding me.

He'd probably be fine with me crashing here—Carson wasn't attached to things or territory, or people for that matter. The worst and inevitable thing that would happen is he'd tease me about it. Maybe I shouldn't tell him at all and just make sure his bed looked exactly the same as he'd left it. I'd have to give myself plenty of time to get it to look that chaotic.

I woke up when the bed dipped and someone got under the covers.

"Go back to sleep," Carson whispered.

It was absolutely idiotic for me to be sleeping here, but I *had* and he'd caught me. I didn't turn around. "You aren't supposed to be here."

"Neither are you."

"I..."

"I don't mind. Actually, it's kind of nice to find a beautiful woman in my bed after going a whole week without seeing her."

As great as he was for my ego, I wasn't supposed to sleep over. That was a rule from the first conversation we'd had.

I slid to the side of the bed, slower than normal because I still wasn't fully awake. "I'm gonna—"

"Stay." His hand was hot on my skin as he slipped it around my waist and dragged me backwards into him.

At least I was wearing a tank top and underwear because it would be all *sorts* of weird if he found me naked in his bed when he wasn't supposed to be home yet. I knew he was wearing something but it didn't blunt the feel of his erection pressing against my ass.

I was just as stiff, beyond uncomfortable and embarrassed, so I tried scooting away. He didn't let me. "Carson, I—"

"I'm not going to step out of line, okay? It doesn't mean anything other than you feel really good next to me. I'll calm down eventually." After mumbling something I couldn't understand, his hand moved down my side, his touch light. When he reached my hipbone, he curled his fingers around it and used it to pull me closer. My back arched at the same moment, pressing my ass harder against him.

"Unless you keep doing that."

Then he stopped speaking and the only sound was the occasional deep sigh or a whimper I couldn't stifle. Every time I felt his lips touch my shoulder, my neck, that spot just behind my ear that sent a sharp bolt of delicious directly to my core, breathing got more difficult.

"Do you want me to stop?"

"God no."

His hand kept moving, over my shoulder to my neck, pushing my hair out of his way before continuing its torturous path. Down the outside of my arm, up on the inside, the back of his fingers brushing my breast and stopping, as if he couldn't decide which direction he should go.

I turned slightly to encourage him to touch my chest, but he was already moving back down my arm. His gentle caress continued onto my hip, down my leg, then back up as close to as much of my ass as he could touch with our bodies pressed so tightly together. Back to my hip and then down onto my belly. Inching closer to the edge of my panties. One finger went under. Then multiple. My breath caught.

"I want to make you come so bad," he whispered, his breath warming the side of my neck. "Just my hand. Is that okay?"

I couldn't speak, and I wasn't sure if I wanted it to just be his hand. "Uh huh." The truth was I could probably come from all the tension built up over the last few weeks. Actually, I'd come plenty of times fantasizing about something really similar to what he was doing right now.

I rolled onto my back, wincing as he yanked my panties down hard.

"Sorry." He waited for me to lift my legs and then pulled them the rest of the way off.

"No, you're not."

"No, I'm not." His unshaven cheek scraped my skin when I turned my head to find his lips. He rested on one elbow and his hand snaked behind my neck, controlling the angle of my head and forcing my mouth open for his tongue. He tasted so male—so Carson. Honest, no holds barred, putting everything he was into this amazing collision that had started out as a simple kiss. One that wasn't supposed to be happening because neither of us were supposed to be in this place at this moment. But we were, and I wouldn't have given it up for anything.

His other hand kept moving, doing something I couldn't focus on because the pleasure was systemic. All insecurity about the other women he'd been with disappeared. I wanted to thank each and every one of them for giving him the practice. He knew exactly where to be gentle, when I needed more pressure, even when to free me from the kiss so I could get more air.

I ran my fingers through his hair, tore at his shoulders, grasping any part of him I could as he stroked and filled me.

"Fuck," he groaned. "I think I could come just hearing you moan like that." Had I been loud? I didn't know, couldn't tell, couldn't remember, and didn't care.

When I slid my hand down his side to the crest of his hip, fingertips under the band of his boxer-briefs, his hand disappeared, reappearing to stop me before I could grab his cock or climb on top of him.

I whined, "Don't stop. Please, Carson. Don't stop."

He pushed my leg off him, moved my arms back onto his shoulders, and then finally put his hand back exactly where I needed him to be. "If you move your hands again, I'll leave."

"Why?"

"Because you just woke up, and I need your complete focus for our first time together. I shouldn't even be doing this. There's a limit to how much I'm going to use you when you're not completely aware of what's happening."

"I want you to use me for everything."

He groaned. "You need to shut up now. The only thing I want coming out of your mouth is a lot more moaning. And the only thing I want your body to do is what it's already doing." He didn't let me agree or disagree, silencing any protestation with another kiss and a deeper stroke of his fingers.

Oh god. I tried moving on top of him again, not on purpose but just because I couldn't help myself. He grumbled and moved me where he wanted me and told me to knock it off. After that, if he really wanted me to shut up and take it, he got exactly what he wanted.

To not have to think or anticipate what someone else needed, to have all his attention on me, on what I was feeling, being controlled by what he was doing, was—

"Soooo good!" I said through my teeth, every muscle tightening, fighting not to roll over and slide onto his cock. I'd never wanted anything or anyone more. He slipped his leg over mine, pinning me to the bed somehow.

"Shut up, Lane."

I think I'd been begging, if not in words, in tone, whimpering, asking him to take me completely. My hips raised off the bed, forcing him to go deeper, harder, faster.

His lips moved to my neck and he mumbled, "I said just my hand, didn't I? That was stupid."

It was too late anyway. I was so close, my back arching, my nails digging into him. I was making desperate sounding noises that I knew I'd be embarrassed about later. Not now, though. Now I felt too good to be embarrassed or worried about anything.

"Damn it, I can't wait to be inside you."

Then why *was* he? With his breath hot against my skin, the last piece fell into place and I went over, screaming a release that had been building ever since we met. It went on forever, my entire body tensing and my back jerking off the bed with each aftershock.

My body was dead, gone, over, completely useless. "That was..."

"The most beautiful fucking thing I've ever heard," he said, still caressing me gently even though he was breathing almost as hard as I was.

"You mean I didn't scream out someone else's name?" My laugh increased the feeling and then immediately sent it over to the too-sensitive side.

"Nope, it was mine." He kissed me, increasing the pressure of his fingers. "Again." It wasn't an offer—it was a demand.

I pushed him away. "God, no. I can't." As much as I wanted to. "I can't." But *he* could...if he didn't stop me from touching him again. "Don't you want to—?"

"I'm good."

Not nearly as good as I was right now. "But I want—"

"Shut up and go to sleep." He pulled me close to his chest, and I could hear his heart pounding. "You'd better believe we're going to discuss it tomorrow, but for now, just go to sleep."

Well into the exhausted, post-orgasmic preamble to deep, deep slumber, I wished he was in it with me. And I'd be happy to help him get there. But out of everyone I knew, Carson was the one who'd never be shy about telling me exactly what he wanted. So, if for whatever reason he gave a little while ago, he didn't want to, maybe I'd...sleep. And then when we...

CHAPTER 18 - CARSON

When I woke up, I still had a raging hard-on. Not at all helped by Lane's leg being on top of mine, her thigh far too close to my cock. Plus, since I'd been the one to take them off her, I knew for a fact she wasn't wearing any panties. If I moved a little to my left—

No. I wasn't going to move to the left, because that would be *highly* stupid.

I'd fucked things up *really* nicely last night. I wouldn't have kicked her out of my bed in the middle of the night, but I had a couch for fuck's sake. I didn't have to slide into bed with her, press myself against her as I listened to her come, and then sleep with her wrapped around me.

I'd slept. Shit. I'd actually slept. Before I stopped bringing women to my place completely, I'd tried to sleep with one of them in my bed a couple times. I couldn't send a woman out onto the street at two in the morning just because the party was over. But eventually I always had to give up and go into another room.

Except with Lane. I'd crawled into bed with her because I couldn't stop myself. And pulling her closer, feeling her body, making her come, and tasting her on my fingers after she crashed—all of those were things I couldn't stop myself from doing. And I would do whatever it took to do them again. But I wouldn't kiss her. Kissing was great—I was all for kissing—but not after a night like the last. Not when I'd made a hundred different bad decisions within twenty minutes of seeing her in my bed. If I wasn't careful, I'd screw it up or make her think something was there that wasn't. I couldn't afford to make any more mistakes. I wasn't worried about myself, but she wasn't used to the kind of relationship we could have.

She stretched, her face squishing up before she opened her eyes and saw me. "Oh shit."

I laughed. "Good morning to you too, Lane. How was your week? Mine was no fun at all but it's picking up rapidly. Thanks for asking."

She sat up, her cheeks on fire for a reason I didn't understand. It was the morning-after-very-little-happening. Great stuff but definitely nothing to be embarrassed about.

"Thanks," she mumbled. "For the...um..."

"The what?" I got it when her blush darkened. There's something innately wrong about thanking the person you're in bed with for giving you an orgasm. Like it was a big surprise or a special gift. What the fuck other reason would you be there for?

"I made you come because I wanted to, not because I wanted your gratitude. Or payback." I smirked. "Although I'm not opposed to the idea. But not now. Maybe later." Damn, I wanted to kiss her. A lot. "You know what's worse than a woman giving you a hand job because she feels obligated to?"

"What?"

"Her not giving you a hand job at all. I'm just kidding." I smiled, pushed out of bed, and went into the kitchen to cool off with some scalding hot coffee. "We agreed to talk about where things stood when I got back. I can be patient a little longer." Look how long it had been already.

It was going to happen, I knew that. She'd finally said it would, but more than with anyone I'd ever been with before, things had to be clear between Lane and me. Or she'd get hurt, and I'd feel like the biggest asshole on the face of the earth.

"It would be helpful if you weren't so nice about all this," she called.

Was I being nice? No. I was being horny and selfish and a little bit desperate.

"Nope, all of this is me being a selfish prick. I'm only being your friend for self-serving reasons." Anything that kept us in the same room would get me where I wanted to be sooner. And honestly, if I could only hear one thing for the rest of my life, I wanted it to be her screaming my name.

"You're so full of shit. When's the last time you worked this hard to get a girl to sleep with you?"

"Never." Ever, ever. Nothing even close to this. "But you're helping me test out something new. To me, at least. The theory is: the more the sexual tension builds up, the bigger the explosion will be when it finally happens. This is all foreplay."

"I'm not sure I can live up to that kind of expectation."

If last night was any indication, then yeah, she definitely would. My anticipation was so high, I'd been like a teenager touching a woman for the very first time. Unless I'd kept a certain amount of pressure on her, she would've felt my hand shake. Luckily, once *she'd* started shaking it wasn't a problem anymore.

She jumped in the shower while I made coffee. I'd already poured two cups when I realized I'd never made coffee for a woman before. That had to be some kind of record. My rep was a lot more exciting than my reality, but I would still need a lot more hands to count the number of women I'd slept with. I needed less than one to count the number I'd cared about.

That I knew exactly how she took it—grotesquely sweet with lots of cream—didn't bother me at all, though. We'd spent a lot of time at coffee shops. Her choice of locations where we couldn't get horizontal wasn't lost on me. It showed a certain cute naïveté that she didn't realize I wanted to take her vertically just as badly.

I'd just given up my search for milk that wasn't chunky when I heard her come into the kitchen.

"I only have sugar and—"

Her body pressed against my back, molding into me. She hadn't put anything on after her shower, not even a towel. This was very good. She was fully awake and taking things into her own hands. Hopefully into some of her other parts too. As long as she wasn't doing it out of guilt. Or payback. A payback orgasm seemed an awful lot like a pity-fuck, and that was never going to happen. I was horny as fuck, but I still had some pride.

I already knew that once wasn't going to be close to enough with her, and I didn't want us to stop hanging out together. Lines couldn't be crossed haphazardly if I wanted to keep all of that.

She reached around me and ran her hand down my abs, past the waistband of my boxers.

"This is because you wanna feel good, right? Not because of any dangerous, emotional, female reason?" My voice was like sandpaper as I not only *felt* her fingers curl around my quickly hardening cock, I also saw them. *Fuuuuck.*

"You don't know anything about women, do you?"

I knew how their bodies worked but right now that was only one of the things that I needed to be paying attention to.

"Don't ask me *why* I want it," she said. "Just give it to me."

Yeah, I think I could do that. When she started moving her hand, stroking my cock, I groaned. Coffee forgotten. Time and space gone.

As tight as her grip was and as fucking great as it felt, it wasn't going to be enough. I needed to feel her come again, this time around my cock.

"If I turn around now things are going to escalate, Lane." I spoke with my eyes closed, my hands clutching the countertop. "So what would you say if I asked you how far you wanted to go with this?"

"I'd say, 'Why are you asking me questions when you should be fucking me?'"

With a quick breath that might have to hold me for a while, I spun around and lifted her into my arms, unable to keep my mouth off her. Lips, jaw, neck, collarbone—anything I could reach.

I'd been imagining this happening since day one, but had to struggle to remember I wanted it to last. That meant I shouldn't lay her down on the kitchen table or put her on the counter or even the couch. Making sure it was done right meant we needed a bed. First time, anyway.

Holy shit, I was finally going to get to put my mouth everywhere I wanted to.

It was easy to know how her body was doing—I'd been watching her for weeks, noticing every time she looked happy or satisfied or horny. Plus, she was so fucking expressive vocally. Her gasps and moans acted like a goddamn GPS. If I touched her the right way, she made one sound. If I did something she didn't like as much, she made another.

I tried to remember to check on her from time to time just to make sure she was doing okay and that no feelings were where they shouldn't be, but I kept getting distracted by everything else that was going on. And even though I wanted to feel every inch of her with my hands and tongue, I knew the theory was right—after weeks of foreplay, shit was about to combust.

She was just as hungry as I was, as if I'd opened a cage door and was now face to face with a wild animal. It was an actual possibility that if we ever found my boxers, they'd be in shreds.

Inside. I had to be inside her. Or I wasn't going to make it until tomorrow. Focus. Okay, what did I need? Besides her, of course. Besides her legs apart which was only making my focus weaker. Jesus, her skin was so soft. Concentrate. There was something I—

"Condom," she gasped.

Right! Right, a condom. Get to the drawer. Focus on getting to the drawer. Open it. Maybe I wasn't getting enough oxygen. But at least I got the condom. We fumbled a little—a lot—in our need to connect, hurrying to make up for all that wasted time.

Everything was absolutely amazing. A bit chaotic but in a good way, in a things-are-incredible-and-are-only-getting-better way. With me, *to* me, to *her* and then—

"Holy fuck!"

—inside of her.

"Oh my god, Carson. Oh my god."

I stayed still because her GPS told me very clearly that she needed a second. I needed a second too. I'd never looked into the eyes of someone I cared about and seen exactly the same surprise on her face that I felt.

I kissed her, knowing this was exactly where we were supposed to be.

Oh shit. "You feel... God, Lane. You feel...perfect."

She was *so* worth waiting for.

CHAPTER 19 - LANEY

What I'd always *thought* was sex, wasn't. Because *this* sex made me want more before Carson even started moving. Even calling those other times sex was like calling a paddleboat a yacht. So this was pretty much the best day of my entire life, and I wanted to beat my head against the wall for putting it off for so long.

All the air came out of my lungs the first time he pressed into me.

"Lane, stop. You can't do that."

"Do what?" What did I do wrong?

"If you keep it up I'm going to come. I don't want to come yet. And you don't want me to come yet. So switch from my name to 'oh god' or something."

I busted out laughing, making him groan when my muscles tightened around him. "If I forget, are you going to gag me? Please?"

"Fuck!" He whistled on an inhale. "Don't say shit like that."

"Or tie me up."

"Stop it," he growled.

"Or spank me."

"Well, *that* was going to happen whether you mentioned it or not." Then he was laughing too, and cursing, and blaming me for whatever was going to happen and whatever he had to do to make sure it did.

When he started moving, both of us stopped laughing. I couldn't do anything but feel and press into every thrust. It was almost eerily quiet, other than the occasional gasp or groan. Okay, a lot of gasping and groaning, but I couldn't help it. Especially when he started thrusting faster, going deeper and harder.

We watched each other and, while I didn't know what he was seeing, I saw everything. In his eyes and his mouth, the way his expression changed right before it got too intense and he had to kiss me or change position to break the tension. But he always went back to looking at me, as if he couldn't help himself, as if he were trying to tell me something that he couldn't say. I didn't know what it could possibly be or even if I was right about something being there. It was just a feeling, a powerful one, almost as powerful as the pleasure.

His kiss made everything almost too good, too beautiful and intimate, way more than I could've ever dreamt of.

Then the opportunity to think passed. "I'm gonna—" Oh god. I was losing it, trying to hold it back because it was all-consuming, too dangerous. I couldn't stop it, though. When the dam broke, what I wanted or didn't want or thought or didn't think made no difference anymore.

He groaned as if he was experiencing it alongside me. But he couldn't have because he was still moving, rocking deeper into me, and he wouldn't have been able to do that if he'd felt the same thing I did. My orgasm went on and on, lengthened by his intensity as he started really driving into me.

He said my name quietly, reverently. "It wasn't supposed to feel like this." Before I had a chance to consider what he said or respond, he pressed deep inside me and let go.

Aside from kissing a lot more, separating, a quick trip to the bathroom, and getting under the covers, neither of us had moved in about an hour. Neither of us had gone to sleep, either. We just stared up at the ceiling, absorbed in our own thoughts.

Every once in a while I'd glance at him out of the corner of my eye, but I didn't think he looked at me once. A little paranoia set in—even though that was by far the most incredible sexual experience of my life, there was a chance he would've given it a five out of ten. What had he said about Hillary? The parts he remembered were good, but it wasn't overly special. *Nothing* about me was overly special, but somehow I'd convinced myself it would be different for us.

Maybe he was staring at the ceiling, trying to figure out a way to tell me to leave. Oh my god. Of course he was. He just didn't want to seem rude. Not that I actually imagined Carson would have a problem being rude, but what did I know? I opened my mouth, but he spoke first, still not looking at me.

"I need to know something." His voice was flat, without any of its usual humor or sarcasm. "When you were with a frog you loved, before he became a frog, is that what it felt like?"

"I was just thinking about that." And just thinking how they hadn't compared, not even a little. "Um…no, it never felt like that."

He let out a breath, and his body relaxed a little. Then he scooted me closer. "How are you feeling?"

"Really good." That wasn't even close to an accurate description, but it was the best I could come up with. "I'm still tingling."

"Glad to hear that," he said on a laugh. "What about the other stuff—the…*feelings* stuff?"

"Well, I really like you and that was a fantastic way to start the day, but I'm not going to turn you into a frog."

"I already *am* a frog, so that doesn't help."

"No, you're not." And I wouldn't make him one. "I feel

exactly the same way I felt yesterday except a little more tired and a lot more satisfied."

"Great answer." He finally turned his head towards me and studied me for a moment. I started to get fidgety, not knowing what to do.

"Should I leave now?"

"Not if you don't have to."

"I don't." So I curled up under his arm a little more and pulled the blanket down so I could trace his abs with my finger. None of the frogs had a body even close to Carson's, nor were their sides as ticklish.

"Quit it." He swiped my hand away and then flipped onto his side to face me, looking at me seriously. "Can we do this again? I mean on a different day because I've already decided we're doing it a few more times today. In fact, I'm going to take you in a *very* long shower as soon as you answer the question."

"Yes," I said immediately. "Yes, we can do this again."

And we did. Repeatedly.

I'd spent most of my free time with Carson *before* we started having sex. After? After, we were practically inseparable. Still friends, still hanging out, but the minute he decided he wanted to get me alone, he did. Wherever we were.

It was going so much better than I ever imagined it would. Even though Carson was amazing in bed and out of it, somehow knowing there was no possibility of a future negated all the crap that used to get me in trouble. We had all the good parts of a relationship and none of the bad.

I was finally able to be with someone without expectations or resentment, insecurity or subtext. Because those were all things that didn't exist in Carson's world. If he wanted something, he asked for it...or demanded it...or just took it. And when *I* wanted something—I couldn't ask for anything more than this.

Whenever Carson asked me something, I answered without hesitation, not worrying how it would make him feel or if he would judge me. Every once in a while, my mind would flash back to one of the frogs and I'd instantly feel my shoulders lift and self-consciousness set in. That didn't happen with Carson. It didn't happen because we both knew there was no forever for us, nothing to protect or plan.

Knowing what I wanted and being able to say it made my time with him easy and stress-free. In a million years, I would never have thought things could be so perfect. I'd always believed love was what I wanted. I was wrong. I'd wanted to like myself and be with someone who did, too.

Love wasn't real, but *this* was. And I wasn't going to let myself ruin it.

CHAPTER 20 - CARSON

Why the hell had I waited so long to do this? Oh right, because I never imagined I could get along with anyone this well. Someone I liked hanging out with who I could also strip, screw, and shower with. Without the clingy, needy thing I'd seen my friends suffer through—whether they knew they were suffering or not.

It wasn't as if I'd never slept with the same woman twice, but I'd never had a regular, couple-nights-in-a-row kind of thing. Too risky. Hook-ups were spread out, no less than two weeks apart. No one could get overly comfortable that way.

But this thing with Lane was different. It just worked. I didn't question why because it didn't matter. It worked, I was getting well-laid, she seemed to be enjoying herself, and there was no drama.

If I'd thought the sex was amazing when we started... There's a lot to be said for spending some time learning someone's body and finding out exactly how to make them happy.

And I was. *Very* happy.

After the first time, I'd had a second of 'this was a huge fucking mistake.' For a minute—or an hour—I actually thought *I* was the one who was going to screw things up by liking her a little too much. But now I know my initial reaction was due to a really great orgasm with a very impressive woman and being greedy enough to not want to share her with anybody. I'm better now. Even though that's all still true.

As long as Lane was good with the arrangement and didn't get girlie, my life was golden. Other than the occasional tough day at work or anything to do with my family or lawyers. But knowing I would be spending the night with her mouth on me made the nine-to-five stressors a lot easier to handle.

From the outside it might have looked like we were dating—going out, lots of sleep-overs— but I didn't give a shit what it looked like. All I cared about was what it *was*. For both of us. And it was pretty damn close to perfect.

After seeing her website again and asking a few questions about her business that should've been easy to answer, I couldn't handle it anymore. I get that whole right brain/left brain artistic thing, but something had to be done. I liked her a lot, but I wasn't going to have her move in with me because she couldn't pay her rent.

We went to her place to get her stuff because, sure, what kind of idiot would keep their business stuff at their place of business? But I was fine with it because she really liked elevators—something about fooling around in one making her feel naughty. And who was I to stop her from that? But today, we couldn't fool around because a guy was on the elevator with us, so I settled for standing behind her and groping her ass.

Unfortunately, even if Hillary hadn't been home, Lane still had weird issues about having sex in their apartment.

"It'll just take a few minutes to get everything together," Lane said before going into her room. Leaving me with her roommate. Great. I'd hoped crying all over me when she was upset over her fight with Eric and then crying all over me after

I helped her figure out what was going on meant that we'd moved past horribly uncomfortable moments like this.

"Carson." Hillary had great posture—her back was straight, her shoulders tense, both feet on the floor. When I sat down on the other end of the couch, I couldn't help but emulate it—back, shoulders, both feet on the ground. Then I bumped it up a notch and kept my knees slightly more than shoulder-width apart just in case I had to run for it.

I bowed my head. "Hillary, good to see you again. How's Eric?"

"Fine."

"Great." Awkward silence, complete with an out-of-the-corner-of-her-eye glare.

She turned directly towards me in one motion, speaking before she'd completed the move. "Laney's been hurt before."

Wow. This was going to be that kind of conversation. The kind I'd only seen on TV. I thought I'd gotten through this minefield the other night. Helping her with Eric had obviously meant more to me than to her. Or maybe she had just as bad a memory as I did.

But okay, I could do this. "I'm not going to hurt her, Hillary."

"Then how's it going to end?" she snapped. "Let's say she meets somebody she wants to start dating, which she *won't* because she spends all her time with you. But let's just say she does. What then?"

I slumped back on the couch. I was wrong—I couldn't do this. "Okay, let's just say she does, which she *won't* because she's still dealing with all the shit from the last guy she dated. The guy I'm betting you *didn't* have this conversation with because he seemed so nice and cared about her so much. So much that he couldn't bring himself to let her know he was fucking somebody else."

Even though Hillary backed off a bit, I wasn't done. "But sure, let's just say she meets someone. If that happens, she will tell me one of two things—either she still wants to be my friend or she doesn't. Obviously I'd prefer the former and obviously, either way, I'd be unhappy things had to change."

I swallowed, not having actually thought about that possibility in a little while. 'Unhappy' didn't begin to describe how I'd feel if Lane or her new boyfriend wanted us to cut ties. I'd miss the sex and I'd miss her. "I'll never stop her from doing whatever she wants to do."

"And *when* you start sleeping with another woman, you're going to tell her so she won't get hurt, is that it?"

"Yep."

"You're an idiot."

"Well, thanks, Hillary. That means a lot." I should've stayed in the car. Consider that mistake never made again.

"Laney isn't the type who can sleep with a guy and not give a crap about him. How could you have spent this much time with her and not figure that out?"

"I know she gives a crap about me. It's just not a romantic crap. Lane's different than she used to be, mostly because she didn't like who she was." I blew out a breath. "Maybe you need to *re*-figure her out."

"You're not good for her." Hillary's intent was good, and I liked the idea that Lane had people watching her back, but *I* wasn't the one she should be worried about. Things were completely clear between Lane and me.

"Hmm… Since she's not fourteen, we're not her parents, and this isn't 1950, I think she gets to make her own decisions."

"Okay, I'm—" Lane walked into the room, stopping as soon as she saw us. "Oh shit. What's going on?"

I turned to her seriously and grabbed Hillary's hand, pulling her towards me. "Lane," I said in a low voice. "Your mother and I need to talk to you about something." Hillary ripped her hand away. "She thinks the young man you're sleeping with is no good." Then I looked at Hillary. "Right, honey?"

"You're such a jerk."

Lane looked at Hillary. "I'm not sure exactly what I missed but I'm fine, Hills. Promise. Yes, he's a jerk—"

"Hey!" I yelled.

—"but at least he's honest about it. I'm fine. Really."

"You deserve more than just a hard cock, Laney." She got up and went into her room.

Lane stared at her until she slammed the door. "Can we go now?"

I didn't say anything until we were in the elevator. "She's right."

"About you being a jerk? I know—I agreed with her."

"You deserve more than a cock."

"I don't want more than a cock right now." Without turning to me, she reached over and wrapped her hand around my package. "I'm happy with the one I have."

When I'd told her to get her financial stuff so we could see exactly how bad it was, I thought she'd bring a laptop. Nope, not Lane. It was on paper. Lots and lots of paper. She had to be the last person on earth who still used paper. For anything.

Right before I was going to give her shit about it and possibly order a "Welcome to this century" card, I got distracted. It happens.

"What?" She looked up from the worksheets she'd laid out all over the coffee table. "Why are you looking at me like that?"

Because I wanted to fuck her. All the time. "I like this a lot." My knee hit hers. "Sex with a beautiful woman almost whenever I want it and *definitely* whenever she wants it. Someone to scrub my back before I get distracted and want the sex I already mentioned. Someone to talk to without worrying she's going to be reading into every word." I nudged her knee again. "You don't, right?"

"Right."

I slipped my hand around the nape of her neck and saw my

bicep twitch because I was trying so hard not to pull her into me and open her mouth for my tongue. This might be getting to be a little much—I couldn't be next to her without needing to feel her. A little control might be nice.

"It's a tiny bit away from perfect, to be honest," I said. "But something's missing." She tensed slightly. Something about knowing she wanted perfection and thought it would be possible with me made me really fucking happy. But it wasn't good.

I pulled her forward so I could whisper. "You know what would make it perfect, Lane?"

"What?" Her voice was breathy and sexy as hell.

"If you go get me a beer." I couldn't stop myself from laughing, even when she smacked me. Even when I grabbed her by the waist and brought her onto my lap, straddling me. Then I stopped laughing and she stopped smacking me and both of us sighed as she rocked against me, making me harder.

"Were you saying something about perfection?" She didn't stop moving.

"I don't remember what I say normally, why would you think I can remember it now?"

I'd had a moment of absolute genius the other day and had bought seven boxes of condoms and put some in every room, even taking them out of the box for easy access. And when all she had to do was reach over to the side table and grab one, I thought it was probably the smartest thing I would ever do in my life.

"Weren't we supposed to work on accounting stuff?" she asked.

"I can't concentrate on numbers right now." Or anything. "I'm seriously starting to worry about myself. I'm having trouble thinking about anyone el—" I kissed her to shut myself up.

"Carson," she said after a minute, pushing me gently in the chest. "I want..." When her cheeks reddened, my mind went into overdrive trying to figure out what made it happen.

Whatever she wanted was hard for her to talk about while she was sitting on my cock with a condom in her hand. Those were three good indicators that it was something I really wanted to hear.

"Tell me." I waited until my patience ran out, which was actually only a few seconds later. "Jesus, tell me what you want, Lane."

"I want to do it up against a wall. You always see it in movies, and..."

"Are you fucking kidding me?"

She flinched. "Is that too weird?"

"Jesus, woman. Stop worrying." I slid my hands under her ass and picked her up. "Nothing is too weird. Nothing. If you want it, you got it. All you have to do is tell me."

There's a certain finesse to fucking up against a wall. It's not as simple as it seems. Well, most of it is simple, but to do it *right*, you need a good wall. A door has too much give and will thump every time you shove her back against it, and that usually distracts the woman from being totally in the moment. Probably worried about someone hearing us, as if I give a shit if anyone hears us.

But the other requirement for a woman like Lane is to have something to hold onto, which is why the door is sometimes a better option. If she didn't have a ledge or a doorframe or knob to hold onto, she was going to hold onto me. Not a bad thing at all—it's great when she holds on. But when we're vertical, holding on actually makes it harder for her to thrust back and force me that tiny bit extra into her. That tiny bit extra is worth a hell of a lot, probably more psychologically than physically, not that it matters.

But it got her involved and she enjoyed it more. Because Lane likes to fuck me back. I *love* it when Lane fucks me back.

That door got pounded so hard, it would never be the same. And we might be locked in here forever.

CHAPTER 21 - LANEY

He collapsed onto me, his arms around my waist and under my ass, the stubble on his cheek scratching my neck. I pried my fingers off the doorknob and frame.

No wonder they always do it against the wall in movies—it's fucking awesome. "I've never done anything like that before."

"Their loss. Truly." He groaned and pressed deeper when I shook my head. "Don't move. I'm going to fall over if I stand up right now, babe."

It sounded so bizarre to hear Carson call me anything other than Lane, so the four-letter pet name caught me off guard. He didn't notice.

"What'd you think?" he asked.

"I think I loved it, but I'll need more data before I submit my official response."

"Okay, but I'm gonna need a little break first." He slid out and straightened, pulling me up with him. "What is it about your neck that I love so much? It's addictive. Do you sprinkle crack there or something?" He ran his teeth across my shoulder to my neck and up to my ear.

"When I come back, we need to talk." He grumbled. "I

shouldn't have said it like that. Makes it sound like we need to have a serious conversation, which is something I never, ever want to do. It's nothing serious. Just me being greedy."

While he was in the master bathroom, I put my clothes on and stopped in the guest bathroom for a quick assessment on my way to the kitchen. My cheeks were flush and my hair was out of control. But I looked really happy. Probably because I was.

I'd just finished filling my glass when I heard him shout.

"I thought you wanted to do it again!" He was still completely naked, completely at ease with his body, which he had every reason to be. "If I had my way, I'd have it like the Japanese do. Everyone leaves their shoes at the door. Only mine would be exclusive to you, and you'd have to take off everything *but* your shoes."

I scooted onto the counter and handed him the glass when he motioned for it. "You can't get your own?"

"You owe me for not getting me a beer earlier." He smiled flawlessly, like there wasn't a single thing wrong in his world. And there probably wasn't. If there was, he'd change it.

"What did you want to talk to me about?"

"Right." He held out my empty glass before rolling his eyes dramatically and refilling it. "I need a favor. Although I'm not sure it's actually a favor and, even if it is, I'm not sure who it's for. I'll be getting a lot out of it either way but—"

"Did you know that after we have sex you don't stop talking? At all."

His smile faltered.

"I'm not complaining. Most men don't talk enough." There was something in his eyes, as if my comment made him nervous. "What's wrong?"

"I've just never heard that before."

"It's not a bad thing." I didn't understand his reaction—how could he have taken that as an insult? "It's a good thing."

"I don't... I don't talk after sex. I leave." After a few more seconds of silence and one deep breath, whatever had been

there was gone. His smile was forced, but he obviously didn't
want to go into it. At some point we'd made a silent agreement
to never talk about anything serious, but it was starting to get
to me. I liked him, cared about him. If it was a female friend,
I would feel the same way. I just wasn't sure how to ask.

"And that's an absolutely awful segue to the favor, but I'm
gonna ask anyway." He came closer and put his hands on my
knees. "I want you to make a bucket list of all the things you
haven't done and want to or *have* done and want to explore
further. Sexually speaking, obviously."

What? "Never gonna happen." Make a list of all the things
I would probably be, or already was, bad at? "Not only would
it be mortifying to put on paper, but it would mean we'd only
do things I either have no experience doing or am totally
insecure about. So I look stupid and you get to have terrible
sex."

"There *is* no terrible sex, especially not with you and me."
He pushed my knees apart so he could get closer. "Right now
I'm like a kid in a candy shop, and I want everything at once.
But since that's not physically possible, I'm happy with
whatever I get. Because it's *all* candy."

"I can't."

"Hey," he said, tipping my chin up so I'd look at him. "I've
never done anything like what we're doing either and,
honestly, it's making me feel really fucking good. I'm
thinking we need to even things out, so your needs are getting
met and I'm staying within your limits."

"So you can stay in the candy shop?"

"Exactly."

I'd assumed it would be more of a boot camp thing—
'Practice makes perfect.' Not that I minded practicing with
Carson but... "It's still mortifying. I can't do it."

"I promise not to show it to anyone, and it's not like you
have to put your name and homeroom number at the top. It
can be three things or twenty. Like the wall thing earlier and
the scene you started explaining to me the day we met that I'm

incredibly disappointed in myself for not having set up yet."

Things started flying through my mind—some I'd always wanted to try and others I fantasized about but never wanted to try in real life. Probably.

"Whatever I want?" I asked.

"Whatever you want. I promise to be gentle...unless you don't want me to be." He looked at me expectantly.

"Okay."

His expression didn't change.

"Wait, you mean right now? You want me to do it *now*?"

"Well..." He stepped back and held his palms up. "I don't have any pants on and am getting hard just imagining what you're going to write on that list, Lane. So, what do you think?"

CHAPTER 22 - CARSON

Lane kept looking up from the blank page and glaring at me. "Stop hovering. I'll show it to you when it's ready." On the top she'd written: Candy.

Shit. I put on a pair of shorts and went through my calendar for the week and tried to think of anything other than all the things I fucking prayed she put on that piece of paper. It was another brilliant idea. Maybe this much sex was helping my cognitive abilities, too—increased blood flow or something.

Writing things down would be a stepping stone to just saying what she wanted. I didn't understand why it was so hard for her to do, but it was. If she was really going to move past those assholes who screwed with her head for so many years and who made all her decisions for her, then this kind of shit was important. It was also really fucking fun.

Half an hour later, I checked on her again. She was looking out the window, chewing on the pencil.

"You done?" I called.

"Not yet."

Twenty minutes later I asked again.

"Almost." Good. She was definitely writing something.

"What number are you up to?"

"You'll find out when I'm done. But since I'm not done, go away." She was probably doing it so slowly just to drive me insane. It was working. I stared at the ceiling over my bed for fifteen incredibly long minutes.

When she finally came into the bedroom, she was waving the paper in the air. "If you laugh at any of them, I'm walking out."

"Get that fucking list and your fucking ass over here right now." And damn, I hoped that was on the list.

She shoved the paper at me and laid down right next to me with bright red cheeks and eyes that were clenched shut.

"You're not going to read them to me?" I pouted.

"Stop it." She curled into my arm, hiding her face. "I don't want to see your expression when you read a few of them."

I didn't look at the list, instead deciding to look at her for a little longer. "You mean like number seven? Oh dear god, Lane. Believe me, I'm smiling." Then I groaned, trying to keep still so she wouldn't know how badly I wanted to laugh. "Ouch, number four's gonna hurt. It might even cause some permanent damage." My abs tightened in jerks but my voice still sounded serious. "I'm not even sure it's physically possible. Are you absolutely sure you wanna try that?"

She smacked me.

When I actually looked at the list, I realized why it had taken her so long to finish. She'd used both sides of the paper...and her print was small. I cleared my throat to cover how anxious I was to start reading.

Why the fuck doesn't everybody do this? Hell, maybe they did...in relationships. I swallowed and shook it off.

"Number one," I started.

"Don't read them out loud!"

"You wrote them and we're both going to *do* them, so why can't I say them out loud? Number one..." I stopped reading and put the paper down next to me, crumpling it in my fist. "Goddamn it, Lane."

"What's wrong?" she asked quietly, nervously.

"*That* was the first thing you thought of?"

"Yeah."

Damn it. Sure, when I thought of the list idea, I knew I'd get something out of it. A lot of something. But it wasn't about what *I* got or what *I* wanted. It was so Lane would finally own up to what *she* wanted and not be embarrassed about it.

"The list is supposed to be about what *you* want," I grumbled.

"Why can't I want that?"

"You *can* but you don't. You just know *I* do. I have a good memory about important shit. And one of the very first things you ever said to me was, if I wanted to keep my dick, that shouldn't happen."

"I changed my mind."

I paused, not wanting to rush into believing her just because I'd get what I wanted to do every time her lips were around my cock. Of course, if she really *did* want it and I refused because I thought I knew better than she did, that kind of defeated the purpose of everything.

I couldn't say I wasn't anxious to try. But I couldn't get distracted until I knew for sure it was what she wanted, too. Don't get distracted. Right.

"You sure?" I asked.

She nodded. "Keep reading so we can get it over with. I'm sure there are other ones you'll freak out about. Read them quick, then you can freak out about all of them at once."

I took her hand and put it on my already hardening cock. "I'm freaking out, but in a really good way, Lane. Okay? A really good way." I lost track of the paper when we started kissing, but it didn't matter—I'd read the rest later.

"Then let's start with number one," she whispered.

"Okay." I tried not to sound as fucking eager as I was but patience had never been my thing. I stood by the edge of the bed and pushed the hair off her face, forming most of it into a messy ponytail as she pulled my shorts down. "You really sure about this?"

"Are you worried I'm going to bite you, Carson?" Her smile disappeared when she wrapped her lips around my cock, getting it wet.

"No." I groaned and pushed deeper into her mouth, trying to go slow—not too much too fast. But holy fuck was it not easy. She reached behind her head and covered my hand with hers, pushing herself forward to take more of me, to force my cock deeper, all the way in, staring up at me with those big, beautiful eyes that I could look at forever.

"I know you won't bite me," I said, my hips slowly starting to take control, my hands sliding to the sides of her face, holding her still. "I'm just worried this will kill me and"— *oooh fuck, that feels good*—"while I'll die a very happy man, I'll never get to know what else"—*breathe, need to breathe*— "is on that list."

But that wasn't what I should be worried about. What might be happening between us could be way more dangerous.

CHAPTER 23 - CARSON

"I'll get it," Anna said.

"No, you won't. You don't live here anymore. Remember?" Although it felt like it occasionally. Ever since I started hanging out with Lane, Anna was suddenly around more. I could usually avoid her here—I wasn't at home during the day and she was unavailable to annoy me at night. Every time she showed up at the office, I put her to work. She was on the board of directors and that had some nice perks, so the least she could do was suffer through twenty minutes of stapling or punching holes into paper. Added bonuses: it was fucking hysterical to watch *and* she didn't drop by as often.

"I said I would get it, Anna."

But she got there first. As soon as she opened the door, she cursed. "He doesn't want any."

I yanked it open and saw Lane turn around to leave. "Actually, I *do* want some." When she didn't stop, I yelled her name.

"Sorry." Her eyes were wide, darting from me to Anna and back. "I should've called first."

Oh fuck! She didn't think Anna and I were—? Gross. That thought hadn't gone through my head since a few months after

Renee had married Anna's dad. An impressive feat for a fifteen-year-old, considering how focused I was on fucking anything that would let me close enough.

"I'm really sorry," Lane mumbled, her eyes starting to fill with water.

"No," I said, pushing Anna out of the way so I could get to Lane. "Don't do that." She wasn't supposed to care. She *didn't* care. So why the fuck was she about to cry if she didn't care? Why did I feel the need to make her feel better, to assure her that nothing was going on with anyone but her? That I wasn't interested in anyone but her?

"What, these?" She wiped her eyes with the sleeve of her shirt. "They're not about you, don't worry. I had a hard day."

Part of me thought it might be smart to let her keep thinking Anna was an ex-lover or whatever she assumed Anna was, to use my wicked stepsister to keep a little necessary space between us. But I hated that she looked so uncomfortable, and I didn't want anything to change.

"Go home, Anna," I said, not taking my eyes off Lane, knowing she could bolt any second.

"No, *I'll* go. I didn't mean to disturb you."

I grabbed the collar of her jacket, yanking her inside. "Go home, Anna."

She huffed, her hands on her waist, until I shot her a glare. "Fine. Call me later. After you guys are done. I need to know what you want to do about—"

I slammed the door shut, but Lane slipped around me and went for it. So I reached over her and put my hand on the door to keep it closed.

"Let me go, Carson." She was still facing the door. "I should have called. Lesson learned. But I really want to go now."

"No."

"I'm embarrassed. Okay? I'm embarrassed because I should've known you might have someone over here. I didn't think it would be Anna, but whatever. Who you sleep with isn't up to me. But I want to go."

"No." I ran my hand up her neck, her hair between my fingers. When I had enough of it, I curled it into my fist and used it to turn her around. The tension kept her face raised but her eyes wouldn't meet mine.

"I'm not fucking Anna. The only person I'm fucking is you and, like I told you before, when that changes I will let you know." I'd used the world 'when' on purpose. So both of us would remember what this was and what it wasn't. She could see other people, too. Of course, if I was in a room with any of them, I'd make it so that they physically couldn't fuck her again, but she could *see* whoever she wanted to.

"We need to clear something up." I didn't know why it hadn't dawned on me before this—it had probably been going through Lane's head from the first time they met. "Anna's my stepsister, and I'm not into that taboo crap."

She blinked and her mouth fell open a little before she had a chance to process.

"Renee married Anna's dad when I was a freshman in high school. He and Anna left when I was a junior." And he died a few weeks before Anna turned eighteen. Kind of ironic— when she could finally get out of the bastard's house, she didn't need to. "Now Anna uses me for money and enjoys bugging the crap out of me whenever she can. But that's it."

Lane let out a big breath. "You have no idea how happy that makes me." That stopped me. "Every time I saw her, I kept thinking you could find someone so much better than her."

"I already did. And now that she's done being embarrassed over something she shouldn't be embarrassed about, why doesn't she tell me why she's here?"

"It's embarrassing," she said, finally letting her beautiful smile come out.

I hadn't released her hair, so I bent her head back a bit more and kissed her. Solidifying the idea that I'd take what I wanted and she should do the same, especially when what she wanted was me.

When I broke the kiss, I said, "I wet the bed until I was nine. Does whatever you're embarrassed about top that?"

She laughed. "Not a lot could top that. And I can't believe you told me that."

"Life's too fucking short to spend any of it embarrassed or guilty. If you're going to learn how to put yourself first, you can't keep being controlled by what other people do." Something in my own words shocked me, triggered something in my brain, like a thread I couldn't hold onto until there was more to it.

I brushed it off—sometimes thinking was the last thing you should be doing. "So what is it?"

"I got a huge job." As soon as she started talking, it's like everything else was forgotten. She was practically jumping. "Like, huge. It's commissioned but she doesn't want furniture, she wants art. Art, Carson. *My* art. She saw my table, I mean your table, *the* table. She saw it at the auction and loved it. This morning, I met her at the building so we could talk in the space where she wants them. It's gigantic and open and there's a huge infinity-type pool at one end. While I was sitting there thinking about the auction and you and the water and everything else, I got this idea." She either stopped to take a breath or so I could respond.

"Are you going to tell me the idea or is it a need-to-know kind of thing?"

"Frogs."

"Not getting it."

"Methods and hurt aside, each of my frogs got me one step closer to this moment. To you. And you got me to the job that might lead me to something even bigger. So, I'm going to build seven driftwood tables in the rough shapes of lily pads leading up to the infinity pool."

"Wow, that's...an awesome idea."

"She thought so, too. And I'm totally charging her too much. Just like you told me I should."

"Congratulations. That's great, you totally deserve it, and it's not too much to charge them what you're worth. But I missed the embarrassing part."

"She gave me an advance to get the equipment and supplies I'll need, but I didn't buy new equipment." She grimaced. "Well, it's equipment but not for my shop." Blushing, she held up a nondescript black plastic bag. The kind of bag that only comes from one kind of store, the *best* kind of store.

I took it from her, peeked inside—"Damn, we'll definitely cross a few things off the list with these"—and pulled her towards the bedroom. "Let's go celebrate art."

CHAPTER 24 – CARSON

Lane still had the key I'd given her. She just refused to use it. I opened the door for her and then went right back to work.

"Can't do it, Lane. Whatever it is. Unless it's you and it's a quickie." I'd been preoccupied and occupied and probably post-occupied if I knew what that was, and I was supposed to meet a board member from the foundation later who'd hinted he wanted to step down. Problem was, he also happened to be the CEO of one of our largest sponsors. If he was out, he might take his company's money out with him. My job was now to convince him how lucky we were to have him without too much groveling.

After a few minutes Lane peeked her head into my office. "Did I leave my sunglasses here yesterday?"

"Yeah," I said, not looking up from my laptop. "I put them in your drawer."

"My what?" Her voice was sharp, surprised, and I realized how that might be misconstrued.

"The drawer you fixed." I slowly turned my chair around so I could see her. "I wasn't using it, and since you occasionally leave your crap around here, I figured I'd shove it all in one place. But since it's making you uncomfortable and that's making *me* uncomfortable, I'll leave your shit wherever I find it from now on." I waited for her to respond, somehow knowing this was one of those moments that could potentially fuck everything up. Over a drawer and a pair of sunglasses.

She took a deep breath. "I'm not sure how I feel about that."

"It's just a little bit of space people make too big a deal about. You didn't freak out when you started keeping a toothbrush over here."

"That's because you always jump on me as soon as I open my eyes—or earlier than that—and it seemed like a better alternative than morning breath."

"There's nothing that needs subtitles here, Lane. The drawer is a drawer and you can use it for drawer-type activities. Or not. Up to you."

"It just surprised me, that's all." She went into my bedroom and came back with her sunglasses. "I'm gonna leave the other stuff in there for now."

"It's your drawer and your stuff. Do whatever you want with it." I stood. "Are you gonna stick around, too?"

"Can't. I have to work. I'll call you later if I have time."

If she had time. Fuck. I felt her pull away, which meant she was thinking things she shouldn't be thinking. Dangerous things that, if they weren't dealt with now, would get bigger and more toxic.

"Come here," I said.

"I have to go to work."

"Come here."

She sighed and came over, stopping a couple feet away. I grabbed her waist and pulled her the rest of the way.

"Things changed in thirty seconds because of a drawer. Can you explain that to me, please?"

"It's normally a big step in a relationship, and we don't have that kind of relationship. I needed a minute to remember that."

I tipped her chin up. "I love what we're doing. I like you a lot. I don't want what happened between you and your frogs to happen between you and me. So…" I didn't want to say it. "If we need to cool it for a while until you can remember what this is, that's okay. Is that what you want?"

"I don't know."

"Yes, you do. You're just afraid to say it. Don't be afraid of me, Lane. I would never deliberately do anything to hurt you, but if you don't tell me what's going on, it might happen accidentally."

"I don't want to cool down." She smiled. "I want things to stay hot."

Hallelujah. "Do you really need to work?" Like I did.

"I guess I could stay a little longer." How the hell did she keep getting more beautiful? That wasn't possible, but somehow she was doing it.

"Listen," I said, "I would put superglue on every single drawer I have to make sure things didn't change between us. Okay?"

She nodded. "Do you ever think we spend too much time together?"

"Constantly. But do I care? Not at all."

"How much time do you spend working?"

"Depends on what events are coming up, the season, shit like that." Fall was always insanely busy though—still nice outside but around the time companies start thinking about tax write-offs. "Why?"

"By my figuring, hanging out with me is like a part-time job—twenty hours a week, at least. And that's not counting sleeping time."

"What about waking-up-in-the-middle-of-the-night-and-screwing-around time?"

"I didn't count that, either." She blushed. "So when do you see your other friends?"

"Huh." I didn't. Initially, I'd stayed away from them because most of what we did together was drink and try to get laid. The drinking I could handle now, but the women? I didn't need to pick anyone up when I had the world's most perfect woman in my bed almost every night and—

Oh shit. "Yeah, I can see how that might be a problem. Maybe I'll go out tonight. I haven't done anything with a guy for a while. *Aaand* that came out totally wrong. I meant—"

"I know what you meant," she said, laughing.

"Good. Because the plan doesn't include sex with a friend or a stranger until tomorrow when you come over." Damn it. I wished I didn't feel the need to tell her that. "Then my plan is to get one of my friends naked and horny. Guess which one."

"I have absolutely no idea who you'd subject yourself to. But maybe you should walk through each step now, to make sure it will work tomorrow." She wrapped her arms around my shoulders and went up on her toes.

So I kissed her. Lightly. For now. "We're talking about the naked and horny part, right?"

"Right."

"If only I had a friend around here to try it out on. Hey, wait a second! *You're* my friend. Think you could help me out?" When she jumped, I caught her under her ass and took her into the bedroom.

"I guess I could try. If you really need the help."

"Oh yeah, I really need it." I laid her down on the bed and started to pull her jeans down while she fought with her shirt. It was halfway off, covering most of her face, showing off her breasts. When we met, I'd told her a woman should love her body at least as much as I do. Completely untrue—she couldn't possibly love hers more than I did.

It was so easy to forget about everything outside this room, outside of her. As soon as I'd shaken her out of her jeans, I moved my hands to her hips, then to her waist, then to those gorgeous breasts. I pulled the cup of her bra down so I could get my tongue on her while I helped her take her shirt all the way off.

"So far, so good," she said. "Now all you have to do is get me totally naked." As soon as I pulled her panties off, she wrapped her legs around my hips and pulled me down on top of her. "I'm glad I can help."

"Me, too. Because I really, really need it." Just like I really, really needed to keep my lips on her skin as I slid down her body.

"Carson?" She tapped me on the shoulder while I focused on her belly button.

"Uh huh?" I'd never taken the time to truly appreciate how sexy a woman's belly button was. When I kissed it, part of my lip went into the little dip, got me closer to her. Great things, belly bu—

"Carson?" She grabbed my hair and pulled until I looked her in the eyes. "I don't mean to be weird, and it's fine either way, but did you mean it about other women not being on the menu tonight?"

"What?" It took a second for her words to sink in. "Oh, yeah. No women. There's only so much a man can take. Now, can I get back to what I was doing?"

When she let go of my hair, I forgot all about her belly button and went straight to a part I liked even more.

I wish I had three hands. One would hold her still and keep her hips down, the second would stop her thighs from squeezing the shit out of my head when she's close to coming, and the third would get to join in with my mouth to do the fun parts.

As soon as I put my tongue on her, her legs flopped open and her hips pressed up. My beautiful bedmate gets a little impatient when I go down on her. She wants me to make her come right away, and that is exactly why it's so much more enjoyable to take my time. Getting her really close and then backing off a few times frustrates the crap out of her but it also makes her orgasm stronger. Even better than *that*, it makes her want to have another, preferably with me deep inside her. But I wasn't in a hurry.

"I want your cock *now*, Carson."
Fuck it. I'll take my time tomorrow.

CHAPTER 25 - LANEY

Obsessed with the idea that Hillary was right about Carson and me spending too much time together, I'd been working with an unofficial schedule. No more than three nights at his place. I chose three because it was the most I could do and still be able to say I was spending less than half the week there.

I'd stuck to it, more or less. But no city is truly safe and they're all more dangerous at night, so after it got dark, I couldn't leave. It was for my own safety. And that was the only reason. Kind of.

Okay, fine. It was a lame excuse, but sex makes me sleepy. Plus, I liked Carson's bed and while he was a terrible pillow, he was a very good blanket.

Oh shit. I was getting too comfortable.

That's why I was *almost* happy he was going out with his friends—his *other* friends, the male ones. Before I left his place, he assured me, without provocation, that he was going to get drunk but not falling-down drunk, possibly get another tattoo, and probably do something that might land him in jail. But women weren't on the menu. I wished that didn't mean as much to me as it did.

Hillary and Eric were off doing something boring together,

so I had the apartment all to myself. Not that I was doing anything exciting. Most of the evening was spent wondering what I *should* do for the evening.

It's not as if I'd never been alone. In fact, after breaking up with Kevin, I liked going solo. I'd been part of a couple pretty steadily from fifteen until a few months ago, always having to consider another person's feelings or opinions. Now I wasn't part of a couple and didn't have to worry about those things, but I had someone's body to use whenever I wanted. Except tonight.

So, while Carson was out getting drunk, I fell asleep wondering where he was and how much fun he was having. When I woke up in the morning feeling refreshed, I smiled, knowing he was at his place right now, nursing a hell of a hangover.

I got coffee and bagel sandwiches and headed over to wake his ass up and talk really loudly. Fortunately, he'd never asked for his key back and I'd never offered to give it back, so I could let myself in and make sure he truly enjoyed his hangover. He was going to be so pissed—I couldn't wait.

When I opened the door to his building, I jerked to a stop. Anna did the same thing. "Morning." And wasn't she looking smug this morning? More so than usual, anyway.

"I'm so glad to see you, Laney. I'm supposed to meet someone in twenty minutes, but can we talk a sec?"

I was always on edge when I was around her, but the sticky, feigned sweetness in her voice made the edge that much thinner.

"About what?"

Anna leaned against the wall, her head tipped in fake sympathy. "I think it's time you moved on."

"Excuse me?"

"Carson doesn't do long term." Her tone was one she might use with a child...that she didn't like.

"Yeah, I know." If my hands weren't full, I would've crossed my arms over my chest.

"Then why are you still hanging around?"

"We're fine, Anna. Thanks for your concern." I didn't have any siblings, but Anna's animosity didn't seem normal. What was she so afraid of?

"Carson has a short attention span when it comes to women. It's even shorter with women he has nothing in common with."

I lost it—Anna didn't know anything about me or what I had in common with Carson. Because Anna had never bothered to do anything but be a bitch.

"What the hell is your problem? You've treated me like trash from the second we met." Carson hadn't told me much about her, but it wasn't hard to pick up things from what he didn't say. Anna had problems—financial, personal, emotional. So, yeah, I felt bad for her. But no one was forcing her to be a bitch.

"Whatever your holding a grudge about," I said, "I didn't do it."

"I'm just trying to stop you from getting hurt—woman to woman." Yeah, right. "Believe me, I know how it feels to have the guy I'm with move on to other people."

"That's"—the word stuck in my throat but it was a lot better than any of the other ones I could've used—"nice of you. And when that happens—"

"It's already happened."

All sound stopped. "What?"

"What do you think Carson was doing last night?"

I didn't respond because Anna needed to mind her own business and stand down. After taking a deep breath and lowering my shoulders, I went around her and headed for the elevator, grinding my teeth instead of speaking. Unfortunately, I didn't do anything to slow my heartbeat.

"He told you he went out with friends, right? Friends. You're his *friend* aren't you, Laney? Carson has always been really good at making friends. But I don't think the friend he made last night will last long—his friends never do." She gasped dramatically. "Oh! I didn't mean you. I'm sure you're the exception."

I smacked the elevator call button over and over, refusing to think of how close it emulated the shaking of my body. I should take the stairs, anything to get away from Anna. But I couldn't. It was a moment of flashback—the same heat in my chest, tension in my shoulders. It was all coming back, as if the last six months hadn't existed, as if none of my wounds had healed at all.

But why did he make a point of telling me women weren't on the menu if they were?

Maybe she'd read my mind, maybe she'd read my facial expression, but she said, "He probably didn't mention it because he didn't want to hurt your feelings. But you guys are casual, right? So it's not a big deal. Not to him, at least."

Wait, this was Carson. "He's not a frog," I whispered, poking the stupid elevator call button harder. "He's not."

"Last night I saw him at a club downtown," Anna said. I didn't need to look at her to know she was smiling, enjoying the damage she was doing. "I didn't say hello though because I *hate* the girl he had up against the wall, and if I said hello to *him*, I'd have to say hello to *her*. Plus, they looked...busy. The next thing I knew both of them were gone, so it was a non-issue anyway."

He'd said he wouldn't, but it's not as if he owed me anything. We weren't even together, and I knew it would happen eventually. He'd promised he would tell me, so I'd let him tell me. I'd wait until I heard it come from his mouth. Not Anna's.

Right? Right. I took a deep breath and turned as the elevator door opened. "Thanks, Anna. It's nice to know there are sincere and caring people left in the world." Anna said something, but I'd already stopped listening. "Have a great day."

"Bitch," I said, as soon as the elevator door closed. It was all bullshit—Carson didn't even trust his stepsister, so why should I? The reasons didn't matter and I refused to let Anna's lies get to me. I came here to mess with Carson, and mess with him, I would.

He wasn't in his room. "Carson?" Or his bathroom or in the living room or kitchen or any other room.

"Carson?" I called louder, knowing there was nowhere I hadn't already checked. What Anna said flashed through my mind, but Carson said he wasn't going to. He didn't even know how to lie. Plus, he never spent the night with a woman because he couldn't sleep and hated awkward morning afters. And the only reason he liked it when *I* stayed over was because our morning afters were as good as our night befores.

Did I actually think I was the only exception? There was nothing overly special about me. Carson and I had sex—that was it.

I pushed the paranoid thoughts away and replaced them with a bunch of possible reasons he wasn't home, none of which involved a woman. But the tension in my body wasn't as easy to release because I couldn't make Anna's voice go away.

He would tell me. The next time I saw him, he would tell me, and I'd deal. Because he'd be honest.

I left the coffee and bagel on his kitchen counter with a note.

'Call me. I need to talk to you about something.' Then I added, *'Hope you had fun last night.'* Maybe since I'd written it down, I'd believe it.

CHAPTER 26 - CARSON

There was no tension on my key as I turned it. I knew I'd locked it before going out last night, and I'd only ever given one person a key. Which meant I just might find Lane in my bed like I had when I got back from L.A. But this time she'd be naked.

Excellent. I headed straight for my bedroom, flinching when I saw her walking out of the kitchen doorway, completely dressed and looking as if she was leaving. That wasn't going to happen anytime soon. After the horror of last night, I needed a warm body to remind me there was still good in the world. *Her* warm body.

"Is that for me?" I nodded to the coffee and bag she held.

"Yours is on the counter." She stood to the side so I could pass.

"Much appreciated. And much necessary."

"How was last night?" she asked quietly.

"Meh. The place was really loud and overcrowded. I'm already getting too old for that kind of shit." I leaned against the counter and took the cover off my coffee to blow on it. "It's sad actually. I think Hillary may have done some kind of voodoo spell on me because the best moment of the night was when I left the place."

"You left early?"

That's when I noticed the tension in her voice, the discomfort in her body. It was so obvious, I was surprised I hadn't noticed before.

"Is something going on that I should know about?" I asked.

"No. I'm just curious."

"Okay," I said slowly, having a tough time believing that. "Yeah, I left a little early. I'm not sure how it happened, but Marcus got so wasted he could barely stand. I had to hold his hand and listen to him whine about his ex all the way to his place." God help me if I ever got that stupid over a woman. "I crashed on his couch."

"Oh."

I watched her for a minute, not understanding why she was being so weird. Only one way I was going to find out:

"Why are you being so weird?"

"I'm not," she said quickly, trying to move her arms into a defensive position that was thwarted by the stuff she held.

"Yeah, you are. And I can't help feeling like it has something to do with me which doesn't make sense because that's not what we do."

"What do we do, Carson?" she snapped. "We fuck, we talk, we hang out. But evidently we aren't as honest as I thought we were."

Whoa. She'd completely lost me. "We *are* honest with each other. Aren't we?"

"Well...you were honest when you said you were a prick and selfish and didn't commit to anyone. But you also told me you weren't a liar."

I drew back, confused. Where the fuck was this coming from? "What are you talking about?"

"You're just as bad as the rest of them."

"Yeah." What the fuck happened in the last twelve hours? "I told you I was. The first time we met, I told you who I am."

"You also told me that you couldn't sleep with anyone in

your bed and that you didn't apologize or open doors or a bunch of other things."

"I wasn't lying *then*. I didn't do any of that stuff." And I hadn't really thought too much about why I was doing all of it now. Frustration filled my voice, something that happens when you find yourself in a fight about something you're not privy to.

"How am I supposed to know which ones are true and which ones aren't?" She tossed her bag onto the counter and threw up her hand. "I don't know about you, but I can't keep track of it all."

"Tell me what the fuck you think I lied about, Lane. Right now."

Since when did I care more about what she thought of me than my pride? And why was I so fucking angry right now? If anyone else yelled at me like that...

"What the fuck is going on?"

"You said if we were going to sleep with someone else, we would tell the other person." When her eyes filled with water, she looked away. "Because that was fair. That's what you said. Because you knew...you knew how scared I was it would happen again. Why did you lie? I thought we were good for each other."

"We *are* good for each other. And I didn't— I'm not sleeping with anyone else. I didn't lie. Jesus, Lane. I didn't lie." I backed up a few steps, needing the space.

That was all bullshit. She wasn't upset because I lied— which I *didn't*—she was upset because she thought I'd screwed someone else. And that upset her because she didn't want me to be with anyone else. Just like I didn't want her to be with anyone else. Just like I didn't want anyone other than her in my bed and my mind and my life.

Oh fuck. I needed to get out of this. Right now. But I couldn't, not while she looked so hurt, so damaged by something she thought I did. I couldn't leave her just like all the other assholes had, especially because it wasn't true.

"Lane, I didn't—"

"Stop lying to me!" She threw her cup into the sink. The top came off and coffee splashed everywhere, but she didn't even flinch. She put her hands on her hips, as if that gave her more strength. More strength to do what? "I heard what you were doing at the club last night."

"What? What was I doing at the club?" I'd spent the night leaning on a table, milking a beer, listening to Marcus bitch about his ex, and watching my other friends talk to women they didn't give a shit about and whose names they would forget in less than forty-eight hours. Probably a lot less. Just like I used to do.

"It's not about you fucking someone else, Carson. It's that you lied. Lying is disrespectful—like you think I'm too stupid to catch on." She threw her hands up in the air. "Shit, maybe I am. Maybe I *am* too stupid. I mean I've fallen for it lots of other times. But I thought...this was different. I thought *you* were different and I was safe because you wouldn't lie to me. But you're exactly the same."

No. No, I wasn't. "Stop comparing me to those other guys!" Even though I'd done it myself a minute ago, it had suddenly become very important that she not group me with the other assholes she'd been with. "I don't lie to you, Lane. Ever."

"Maybe you didn't use to but—" Her mouth stayed open while she backed up a step. "Oh my god, I did it again. I turned you into a frog."

"Enough with the stupid frog thing. I'm not another one of your frogs, and I'm not lying. I don't know where you're getting your info but it's wrong." Shit. I shut my eyes. There was only one person I knew who could and would lie that well. "It was Anna, wasn't it? Anna told you whatever she told you, and you decided to believe *her* instead of me."

"It's happened so many times, Carson." Her tears came on so fast, she couldn't catch them until they were at her jaw. "You don't know how humiliating it is. I just started to trust my own judgment again. *Please*"—her jaw was shaking, softening her voice, weakening it—"if you are, then just please tell me the truth. I won't be mad. I promise."

When I saw the disappointment and doubt on her face, it felt like I'd been stabbed in the gut. I'd done that. By bringing Anna into her life, by making Lane trust me, I'd made her feel like that. So I was the one who had to stop her from feeling like that.

"I am not sleeping with anyone else, Lane." Each word was clipped, severe, and totally fucking honest. "I won't lie to you. I won't." Most of the room was still between us, her pulling away and me not being brave enough to move forward.

It felt like shit that she believed Anna more than me. Lane knew me better than anyone, so if *she* didn't trust me, what other good did I have? I didn't know that meant anything to me until now.

I gathered up enough courage to take one step. "Please stop doubting someone who respects the fuck out of you and who couldn't—not wouldn't—*couldn't* do that to you. Ever. Because I would rather see the moon fall than see you cry."

Her arms were crossed, and she wouldn't look at me. How could I convince her I was telling the truth?

I swallowed, my throat dry and tight. "Think about it— why would I lie? Why would I *need* to lie? We've talked about it and we're not together, so how could I possibly benefit by lying? Why would I risk a really fucking good thing to lie about something I didn't need to lie about?"

I didn't tell her that I was having the best sex I'd ever had, so I didn't want to go anywhere else. A one-night hook up with someone who didn't know what I liked, might be a disaster in the sack, and who I'd want to get away from as soon as we both came. Versus someone I knew was incredible in bed, I actually liked talking to, and I could have in the middle of the night and the next morning if she was up to it.

Did she think I was a moron?

"Anna's messed up—her dad was even worse than mine." She'd never said anything, but I was pretty sure the asshole used more than his fists on her. Fucking pervert. "It's not an excuse, but it's a reason. She's worried"—and scared shitless—"I won't be there to catch her next time she fucks something up or someone fucks her up. She lied so this would happen. This exact thing we're doing right now. You know how she is—you've seen her try to screw with us before."

"I'm not her, Lane. I don't want to screw this up." I was practically shaking, waiting for her to say something like 'I believe you' or 'I trust you' or 'You're not a horrible person for bringing this into my life.'

She shrugged, hopefully a sign I was getting through to her, past the bullshit Anna had piled onto a woman who deserved so much better than me and my fucked-up family. But who I didn't want to let go of yet.

"*Nothing* is worth fucking this up for," I said. "So have a little faith. Please."

She studied me for a while without moving. Maybe even without breathing. I was jittery as hell, amped up by anger, betrayal, and anxiety.

"I'll try," she said quietly. "But if you…"

"Yes. Yes, I will tell you. *Before* anything happens. And you'll do the same." I took a deep breath to let go of some of my unease. It didn't work. "So you believe me?"

"Yeah."

"Then we're done talking about it." I stared at her for a long couple of minutes, trying to figure out what to do. "I'm really fucking pissed off right now, Lane."

"I know."

"I'm pissed off and I want you. Hard. You got a problem with that?"

She shook her head.

"Then take off your fucking clothes."

CHAPTER 27 - CARSON

"Anna!" My fist pounded against her door. I knew she was home because I saw her car out front. The car I'd bought for her. Was this her way of paying me back? "Whose life were you trying to screw up, Anna? Hers or mine?"

Whatever she'd said almost fucked up the best thing I'd ever had. The expression on Lane's face...

I couldn't get it out of my mind. I'd never had make-up sex because I'd never fought with anyone I was fucking. Yeah, it was phenomenal, but not enough to ever want it to happen again. Nothing would ever put things back the way they were. One well-placed lie had changed everything. Lane wasn't as trusting as she'd been. I could tell she was more protective, had lost that freedom we both got to enjoy. And it was one person's fault.

"You have no idea what you did to her!" I screamed at the door. "You wanna fuck with me then fuck with me. But leave her alone. She has nothing to do with any of this." I didn't care why Anna did it. I just wanted to make sure she never did it again. "Open the fucking door!"

As soon as she did, I pushed past her and stormed into the living room, surprised my footsteps weren't leaving skid marks on the wood floor.

"If you ever—" I saw it as soon as she came into the room—a cut on her cheekbone and a busted lip. "Damn it, Anna." In the time it took to say her name, my voice dropped to a whisper and my anger disappeared. No. It didn't disappear—it redirected. "Who did it?"

She looked at me with dead eyes, expressionless. No pain, no life, no emotion. No words either.

"Who did it?" The longer she was silent, the more frustrated I got. Until my heart was pounding faster than it had been on the way over here.

"No one you know." She always said that, and I never knew if it was the truth or not. All I knew is that if she told me his name or I recognized his face, he'd be bleeding, too.

"It's not that bad." She winced when she touched it. Fresh.

"Why didn't you call me?"

"I figured you'd be too busy with your girlfriend."

I didn't correct her because it didn't seem to matter anymore. Plus, after the little stunt she'd pulled, she probably thought Lane was long gone.

"Let me see it," I said. She tried to turn away. "Knock it off. I need to see it." I smoothed the hair off her face and tucked it behind her ear, then took her chin and gently turned her face to one side and then the other. Split lip. Cheekbone bruised not broken. Swollen but didn't need stitches. Both areas meant it had been more than one hit. More than one hit meant it wasn't accidental.

Probably no more than a few hours old, so it must have happened pretty soon after she messed with Lane. Coincidental or deliberate self-punishment?

"Why didn't you ice it?" I went into her kitchen and grabbed the ice pack out of her freezer and a towel off the stove handle. It wasn't normal to always have an ice pack ready to go for when you got hit. And it wasn't normal for your stepbrother to know where it was because you waited until he got here to use it.

It wasn't infrequent, either.

When I put the ice pack on her cheek, she flinched and then put her hand over mine. "I'm sorry about what I told your girlfriend."

I ignored her apology and focused on her injury, making sure she was holding the ice pack before I slid my hand away. "You okay?"

"Never better." Bitterness ruined her laugh.

"Tell me what happened."

"I said I was sorry. It won't happen again."

"What won't happen again, Anna? He won't hit you? You won't go back to him? You won't just move on to another loser? What?"

She bit her lower lip, gasping when her teeth touched the cut. She didn't lower her hand as she spoke. Hiding. "Why don't I stay out of your life and you stay out of mine?"

"We already tried that. Didn't work out so well."

"I'm sorry, Carson. Okay? I'm sorry ten thousand times over. If I could go back in time, I would do everything differently. But I can't. Your mom can't. And our...fathers can't either." She sat down on the edge of the sofa.

"This isn't about the two fuckers in the ground." We both knew how wrong that was—*everything* was about them.

"Did you know that, despite everything, you're one of the least screwed up people I know?" That was depressing. She needed new friends.

"I'm completely fucked up." Just ask the guy I kicked the shit out of. "You think I don't have to try? That I don't think about who I could turn into if I stop trying? I do. All the fucking time. But with you...it's like you don't even see that anything's wrong. This"—I motioned to her face—"it isn't normal. You don't have to keep doing it."

"It's not like I try. Somehow they always seem to find me."

"Okay, but how long do you stay with the guy after the first hit? How many second chances does he get?"

Her body tensed, but she didn't look at me. "You have a

life now and it seems like a good one, so why don't you just go home and live it?" She turned her back to me and walked towards her room. "Now that you have someone else to take care of, you can forget I even exist."

I followed disgustedly. Her manipulation was usually subtler. Why did I bother? She never heard a word I said. She just wanted… I didn't know what she wanted. And I was done caring.

"Because you're unhappy, I should be too, right?" I grabbed the top of the doorframe and stayed just outside her room. "If you want to fuck up your own life, go for it. But you don't get to fuck up the best thing I have just because you need more attention."

She spun around. "Get out!"

I knew she was hurting. I was the only one she had, who knew what her dad did to her without her having to admit it. I'd tried to get her out, to stay with Renee and me, even though we were just moving on to another asshole. I'd tried but I'd failed.

So I spent the last eight years trying to make it up to her. I couldn't. Not then, not now. Especially not at the cost of someone who was completely innocent of all the shit Anna and I had dealt with. Not that either of us had dealt with it well. But Lane didn't deserve to be involved in our dysfunction. I wasn't ready to give her up yet.

"Take care of yourself, okay?" I asked quietly.

"Are you really going to leave?" She looked at me through her lashes and lowered her chin—her damsel-in-distress mask.

I ran my hand through my hair. Every fucking time. "Yeah, I'm gonna go." But I'd be back. Because I always came back. No matter how many times, how many different ways I said the same things and she gave the same fucking excuses, I always came back. On the off chance that someday things would be different. I wanted to be there on the day she realized she was worth more than she'd always thought she was and she didn't have to manipulate me to get me to care about her. Because I already did.

"I'll call you later. I wish…" I sighed, knowing it didn't matter. She'd go back for more, probably to that guy at the gallery opening…who I wanted to kill. "Do you have any idea how bad I wish you'd look back on the past few years and see how many times you made the wrong choice even when you knew it was wrong?"

"What the hell does that mean?" She chucked the ice pack at me. Not even close. I would've made a joke if I wasn't so goddamn frustrated with her.

"If I can see the carbon copy of your dad in every guy you've been with from fifty feet away, then you should be able to see it when he's close enough to hit you."

"Fuck you!" She came at me fast. "You don't get to judge me, Carson. You don't get to."

I dug my fingers into the doorframe when she hit me in the chest. Harder the second time she did it. And when she started shouting that she didn't need me and hated me and that I didn't matter or care, all I could do was stand there and take it, ride it out until she was done, understanding that it was the only way she knew how to hurt.

If it wasn't me then it would be someone else, so I made sure it was me.

"Do you know why I lied to your girlfriend?" she asked, her voice all broken up. "Do you?"

I shook my head, part of me wanting to punish her, tell her a hard truth that she would never stop being able to hear.

She beat me to it. "Will you bring Laney ice, too? Tell her it won't happen again?"

I shoved backwards, but the words had done what she'd wanted them to do. I'd never unhear them. The thing I could never get away from no matter how far or how fast I went. Because you can't outrun something that's a part of you.

"I'm not going to hurt her." Because I didn't let her come close enough. I wouldn't hurt her because I didn't love her. I didn't love anyone.

She shrugged. "Yeah well, I used to think I'd never be with anyone like my dad."

"No fucking around, do you really think I could be like him?" I could've been talking about her dad or mine—same asshole, different packaging.

We'd never even been *close* to talking about this before. I never knew I needed to. But her opinion mattered more than anyone else's. Because she'd been there, lived through a lot of it with me. She knew a part of my life I never wanted Lane to know about.

Anna knew me before I even realized most people didn't live like I did, like she did. That most men didn't tell their family they loved them *while* they were beating the shit out of them. That most moms didn't tell their kid the same thing while washing the blood off them and then bringing them back to the man who'd caused it.

"Do you honestly think I could do that?"

"You're far from perfect, Carson." She crossed her arms and shrugged, a smug look on her face. "You act like you have it all together, but you're not perfect."

Motherfucker. She was fucking with my head to prove a point. "Is that what this is about? Proving you're better than me? Is that what this is?" I couldn't breathe. "You are, Anna. Congratulations, you win. Okay? Can you stop now? Can we both please just stop doing this now?"

I wasn't talking about this moment or this conversation. All I wanted was to move on, for both of us to stop doing this to ourselves and to each other. For everything to just stop.

"Yes," she whispered after a long pause.

I sighed. Thank god. One word didn't actually prove anything but it was a start and—

"Yes, I think you could be like him. Like all of them."

"What?" I shut my eyes, my stomach tightening so quickly I thought I was going to puke. The idea wasn't new to me—it was the reason I lived the way I did and was the way I was.

But to know for sure that someone who'd lived part of it with me thought the same thing was...indescribable.

"So does the guy you put in the hospital," she said. "You don't actually believe that was an accident, do you? Being drunk was an excuse. My dad used it all the time. Did yours?"

Yeah, but not a lot. My dad preferred to be sober, so he could make sure I knew he was doing it for my own good. Because he loved me.

"We are who we are, Carson."

I'd known. I'd always known. But I'd never had the balls to say it out loud. Turns out I didn't have the balls to hear it, either. I slumped against the wall without thinking. When there's no solution, no way out, what the fuck is there left to think about?

"Carson?" Her voice was sharp and demanded attention, so I opened my eyes and looked at her. When I saw the look of triumph on her face, I felt even sicker. Because I finally understood who she was. Whether or not she was lying didn't matter. She'd said it to...to what? To destroy. Yeah, she'd won and she knew it. Now she was just gloating.

I still didn't know what to say, but I knew what to do. What I should've done a long time ago.

"Where are you going?" she asked when I walked away.

"I'm done picking you up, Anna. Done." With all of her bullshit, her lies, her manipulation. "Go find someone who hasn't had to do it for a decade. Because I'm too fucking tired to do it anymore. I have my own shit to wade through and now, thanks to you, I have more."

"Carson, wait."

"For what?" I spun around, watching her shift from one leg to another.

"Don't go." She looked younger, a girl dressed up to look like a woman. Unsure of herself and in pain.

"I'm the only one who hasn't hit you, and I'm the only one you hit. I take it, and I don't hurt you back. So why would you use that against me? Because I can finally be alone with someone for longer than an hour without worrying I'm going to do it? Jesus, Anna, why *that*?"

"I…" After a minute, she lowered her head and whispered an apology that was too late and too little and always would be.

About halfway home, I noticed how white my knuckles were and how sore my jaw was. I pulled over to the side of the road, put my forehead on top of my hands, and closed my eyes. If I was lucky, maybe someone would rear-end my car. And end me.

After a few minutes, I sat up. After a few more, I peeled one hand off the wheel and grabbed my phone. Because I knew I needed her. Because she was the only thing that made me feel right.

"Hi," Lane said quietly. "Why did you leave so fa—?"

"Where are you?"

"Home."

"Can I come get you?"

"I think I should stay here tonight."

"Please, Lane. Can I come get you?" I leaned my head back and stared at the roof while I waited for her to answer. "Please," I whispered.

She sighed. "I'll meet you out front."

"Thanks."

"Is everything okay, Carson?"

I shook my head. "I'll be there in a few."

CHAPTER 28 - LANEY

The entire day had been a complete and total mess. Horrible run-in with Anna, big fight with Carson, completely insane make-up sex, and then he gets up and leaves without telling me where he's going. But at no point in any of that did he sound as upset as he just had on the phone.

If I thought he only wanted to hang out or have sex again, I'd have said no. Because I was in a lot of trouble and needed to figure stuff out. After Anna tried to mess things up, I was okay. When Carson came home, I was okay. But as soon as I accused him of lying to me, everything started to collapse. By the time I knew what had happened, it was too late to make it better or go back to the way it had been.

How many times did I say it had nothing to do with him sleeping with someone else and I was only mad because he lied? At least five. I started to see a problem around the second time. By the fourth, I knew it was total bullshit. It *was* about him sleeping with someone else. I was lying while accusing *him* of doing it. Then everything got so confused—what I was saying and feeling—that I stopped being able to think.

When he told me to take off my clothes, it would have been really, really smart to walk away, but I didn't. Or couldn't, whichever it was. Because I knew I wasn't going to get many more chances to be with him before he figured it out, if he hadn't already. Seriously, it takes a special kind of stupid to be that blind to yourself.

It had taken me this long to figure out something so incredibly obvious, I should have it tattooed on my ass as a warning to all: *If you're close enough to read this, you should run away as fast as you can.*

I couldn't separate sex from love. The emotions showed up whether I wanted them to or not. It was embarrassing that I hadn't noticed until now, because my feelings for Carson were way stronger than they'd been for any of the frogs, and this wasn't even love. So if this was just the beginning and there was more to come, I was in deep shit. Because I was just stupid enough to want them. To want *more* of them. Right now they felt unfinished—the emotional equivalent to what I always felt after having sex with the frogs and never felt after being with Carson.

It wasn't fair to him to pretend things weren't what they were. I should get out before everything got any worse.

And, of course, I was standing in front of my building, waiting for the last person on earth I should be waiting for. Maybe if he hadn't sounded so upset I could've said no. Maybe. Probably. Maybe.

Shit.

He pulled up and opened my door from the inside. I tossed my bag in the back, slid in, and focused on my seatbelt, keeping my mouth shut. The car didn't move. When I looked up, he was staring at me. What had happened to him in the last hour? He was just as gorgeous, but he was paler. There was an innocence to his expression, a pained innocence. However confused I was suddenly seemed trivial. All I wanted to do was throttle whatever had put that look on his face.

I touched his cheek. "Can you tell me what's wrong?"

He took my hand and used it to pull me forward, leaning closer at the same time, until we met. A gentle brush of lips, then he was kissing me. Not the usual, hot, pre-ripping our clothes off kissing—this was careful, gentle, asking not demanding. Because I didn't understand what was going on, I stayed where he needed me, was gentle in return, and waited until he trusted me with more.

His hand became a more insistent pull at the back of my neck, his mouth opening mine wider, his tongue delving deeper. I'm pretty sure I moaned before I could stop myself.

He pulled away but kept his hand on me. "I wanna take you home. Can you stay over?"

I just nodded.

"You don't have to, Lane. If you don't want to, I'll—"

"I want to." Too much and maybe for some of the wrong reasons, I wanted to.

He looked down, maybe in embarrassment, maybe something else. I didn't know. All of this was new to me—I never worried about Carson. Carson didn't need or want anyone's concern and things didn't bother him the way they bothered everyone else.

But right now he seemed to be struggling for the right words. "Thanks." He let me go and straightened so he could drive.

"No problem." Another lie.

We didn't get halfway up the first flight of stairs in his building before he pushed me against the wall, kissed me, and grinded his hips against mine. A breath later, he stepped back, took my hand again and started walking. It happened two more times before we got to his door. His hands had been everywhere on me, always releasing me a minute after he started, as if he couldn't decide what to do. As if he wanted to use my body to stop thinking about whatever the hell was going on.

That was the way Carson communicated. His emotions were encapsulated in his touch, the way he moved his body, the intensity of his kiss. I knew him well enough to understand he needed me, but I didn't know him well enough to know why.

Inside his apartment, he started taking off my clothes, more methodically than he ever had before. Shirt and bra were easy. He slid to his knees to unzip my boots and take them off, followed by my pants, his lips slowly trailing over my naked skin. His thumbs hooked through each side of my panties and pulled them down slowly, his mouth just behind the cotton. Soft kisses and caresses on my belly, my hips, his eyes staying closed.

His touch was as amazing as it always was, but this wasn't sexual. This was a need beyond the physical, for companionship, or...

Love. As much as he didn't want it, he needed it more. But it wasn't the same thing as what I was feeling, and this wasn't the time to deal with my shit. It was the time to give him whatever he needed from me. Not to bring more drama in.

I ran my hands through his hair as he pressed his cheek to my belly and wrapped his arms around my legs.

"Stand up for me," I whispered, afraid of speaking louder. He did what I asked and stood still while I undressed him, kissing his chest, rising onto my toes to kiss his lips. Holding his hands, I walked backwards into the bedroom, never breaking eye contact, stopping when I bumped into the bed.

"There's a lot you don't know about me," he said with the same calm and quiet I had, lowering his chin and looking at our feet. "I've never lied to you. I wouldn't do that. But I haven't told you about all the bad shit in me."

"There's nothing bad in you." I brushed his hair back.

"Yeah, there is. And I should've told you about it."

"It doesn't matter."

"It matters." He shook his head but didn't lift it to look at me. "I shouldn't have brought you here and I shouldn't have taken your clothes off." He spoke faster, his shoulders shrugging the tiniest bit, his hands fidgety and unsure until I stilled them with my own. "Because I think... I think I should let you go. I think I should've done that a long time ago, but I didn't. So I think I should probably do that now because if you're here then you're not where someone good can find you. Where someone good can *love* you." He swallowed. "That's what you should have—someone good who can love you." Then he looked into my eyes. "I want you to have that."

"Well..." I sighed, fighting back tears that he would probably misunderstand. That might make him feel worse, as if he'd done something to me. He needed me to be strong. "You might be right. But I'm naked now, and it's cold, so I was hoping I could borrow some of your covers for a little while."

As small as his grin was, it was beautiful. I sat down on the bed and scooted higher, motioning for him to join me. He crawled up to me. "I know you probably want to jump on top of me like you always do, but I was thinking we could wait a little while." Just that would've been a big indicator. We were in bed and naked, and he wanted to wait.

He laid down on his side and pulled me into him, my back to his chest, kissing my neck lightly. We were both quiet for a long time, and then he squeezed me just a little tighter.

"If it could be anyone," he whispered, "it would be you."

I wasn't fast enough to hold in the whimper, stop the motion of my stomach as it clenched. At least he couldn't see my tears. I forced my breath to be steady, my body to stay relaxed even though all I wanted to do was curl up and sob.

"I shouldn't have said that." Whispering the words didn't make them sting any less.

"S'okay," was all I could manage.

Oh my god. Oh my god. Oh my god. I hadn't known. Not really, not for sure. I hadn't known until that moment. I'd thought I knew what it felt like, because I'd been through it before. A few times. But it turned out I hadn't, not even close, never like this. Everything before now hadn't been real. It had felt real at the time, and I'd spent the last six months convincing myself it didn't exist. That it was all fake, something people talked themselves into believing.

But I wouldn't have talked myself into this because I didn't want it. Because it was going to ruin everything. How fucking ironic—I'd been looking for love for the last eight years. And when I finally stopped wanting and believing in it, it found me.

I didn't have feelings for Carson—I was in love with him.

And what's worse than falling in love when you don't want to? Falling in love with someone who can't love you back.

CHAPTER 29 – CARSON

I held her, knowing how wrong it was, how fucking selfish I was being, but I couldn't let go. It would be too cold if she weren't pressed against me, too empty if she was somewhere I couldn't reach her. So I kept my arms around her all night long, running my lips across her shoulder, harder each time I felt her body jerk as she pretended she wasn't crying. Pretended I hadn't made her cry.

When her breathing slowed and evened out, I knew she'd fallen asleep. I focused on her skin and her heat so I wouldn't think about how wrong everything had gone and how fast it had happened and how many lives besides my own I was fucking up.

"I'm sorry." I don't know if I'd whispered it or just moved my lips. It didn't matter—either way I'd made sure she couldn't hear it. Coward.

When I woke up, she was using my chest as a pillow and my arm was around her, holding her like I was afraid she'd slip away while I was sleeping. Her eyes were open, and I knew she'd been up a while, just like I knew I'd fucked everything up for both of us.

Her eyes were wide and sad and ashamed. She didn't cry but her voice cracked when she spoke. "I don't think I can make it stop."

I looked away, knowing and fearing what she meant. I didn't want to let go of her when she sat up. I wanted to pull her down and tuck her back into my arm, so I wouldn't have to see her expression. As if that could make things like they'd been before...before she became the only thing that made me happy and feel whole. Before I brought her into my fucked-up life.

"Carson, I'm—"

"Don't say it." I shook my head, avoiding her eyes. "Don't think it. Don't feel it. It's not real, right? It's just your mind playing with you."

"I know you didn't sign up for this, and I'm really sorry I couldn't do it. I wanted to, and for a while I thought I was, but I was wrong." She cleared her throat. "I'll go if you want me to."

Did I? No. Should I? Yes. If I let this go on any longer, I'd end up hurting her just like every other asshole had. I'd already let it go on too long, taken too much from her. But I owed her some kind of explanation, to let her know how incredible she was and that if there was any chance for us, I would take it. I just didn't know how to tell her.

I started with a deep breath. Right. I needed to do this because it wasn't fair for her not to know. "I like you a lot. A lot. More than—" Chicken-shit—I was just as afraid of telling her as I was of her not knowing. "A lot. But I can't be with you that way. You can't feel anything for me." Because I couldn't let myself feel anything for her.

"I didn't want this," she said. "I was afraid of it happening. I warned you it might but you said..." She ran her lip through her teeth, looking so miserable and confused. "Why were you so sure it wouldn't? Why are you so sure it won't work now?"

I wasn't sure of anything anymore. Except that I didn't

want this to end. To not see her anymore, not be with her? No, that couldn't happen. Maybe we could figure out a way to make her feelings stop. Maybe if she understood what I might do to her...

"Okay." I got out of bed, needing the distance before I told her. "It won't work because if we were together, I would be the worst parts of every guy you've ever dated. I would cheat and lie and make you think it was your fault. I would want all your attention and give you none of mine."

My eyes were stuck on the wall behind her because I was too weak to tell her and look at her at the same time. "And I wouldn't hide it, which would mean that everybody would see what I was doing to you, and they'd feel sorry for you. They'd talk about you as much, probably more, than they'd talk about me. Because it's easy to figure out someone is an asshole. There's not a lot to it. It would take a lot more words and wondering to understand why you let me treat you like that, why you didn't leave me, why you thought so little of yourself that you kept pretending everything was okay."

I had to tell her all of it because there's no coming back from the truth. She'd know, and it would make her stop caring about me. Maybe we could go back to the way we were and maybe we couldn't, but anything was better than this, than being this afraid of myself and what I might do to her. At least she'd be safe.

"When I was little, I was more terrified of growing up than I was of my father. I prayed I'd be like Peter Pan—never grow up and become a man, because of what they had to do. Men had to teach the people they loved how to behave. They *had* to. It was extra confusing because one day something would be forgiven with a smack to the back of the head and another day I'd be punished for it. You know, punished with...um..." I swallowed. "With whatever he could find that wouldn't break when he...um..."

My throat felt constricted, like my body knew I wasn't supposed to tell anyone about this and was trying to stop me.

I had to finish it, though. "I never understood when or why. My father always knew, though, and so did the men that followed after he died."

"And one day *I* would know. When I became a man, I would understand the requirements, and I would have to make sure the people I loved followed the rules and were good people. Or I would have to punish them. I would have to hurt them because I loved them."

I glanced at her quickly and saw pity on her face. That's not what I wanted. I wanted her to understand why I could never be with someone. Why I couldn't trust myself to love her.

"You're not getting it," I said, running a hand through my hair and starting to move. "Shit, Lane, I want to think that I wouldn't. That I *couldn't*, but who knows what the fuck they'll do in a situation they've never been in before?"

"What are you talking about?"

"What if I hit you?" I knew what would happen because I'd lived it so many times. "You'd forgive me and take me back because I'd convince you it was your fault." I slumped down on the edge of the bed and let shit come out of my mouth that I'd never told anyone. Because I'd never trusted anyone before. And all of it was going to kill that trust, smash it into little pieces like it should be. "You'd hide the bruises and try to do better, but it wouldn't work. Because it would have nothing to do with you or what you did. It would have to do with me and how fucked up I am. And no matter what you did or how hard you tried or who you were, I would keep doing it. Because I hate myself. Because picking on someone who loves me makes me feel better. Makes me feel like I'm not weak or stupid or powerless."

I took a breath, not knowing when I'd last taken one. "I would fuck it up because I don't know how *not* to."

"That's what your dad did?"

I nodded, not looking at her, not really seeing anything. But I was feeling it—everything I'd felt back then: angry, afraid, worthless. "Did you know I look just like him? And people have told me I think like him."

"You're not him."

"When someone tells you they love you so much, they have to hurt you, everything gets mixed up in your head and you don't know what's right and what's not. And when the person who's supposed to protect you tells you it wasn't that bad and sends you back in for more... That shit doesn't go away. It's part of you, changes the way you react, the way you are."

"It doesn't mean you'll do what he did."

"How do you know? *I* don't even know. But I know it's not worth the risk. *I'm* not worth the risk." I'd gone through hours and hours of therapy, but nothing stuck. Nothing could convince me it wouldn't happen. I got angry at people. I felt that pressure build up inside me. The bar fight was the worst, but it wasn't my first. I didn't even care about those people, and I couldn't walk away. If I could hurt someone I didn't care about, what would I do to someone I loved?

"What if I told you I think you *are* worth it?" she asked.

"I'd tell you you're wrong." I felt her hands slip under my arms and around my chest, the heat of her body on my back.

"What if I told you I know you care about me?"

I paused, not moving. Unable to move. "I'd tell you that you're right." It wasn't love, but it was so much more than I should have ever let it be. "I don't want to hurt you, Lane. But, if we don't stop now, I will. I know I will. And you've already been hurt too much. I can't do that to you."

Fuck. I pulled out of her grasp, wiping my hands over my face and through my hair. "You need to leave now."

"No." There was no real expression on her face—no anger, disappointment, or fear. All the things that I was feeling.

"Go away, Lane," I said tightly.

"No."

I couldn't touch her, couldn't force her out because touching her was the risk. "Please."

She shook her head and scooted back to lean against the headboard.

"Fuck, Lane. Go away. I'm trying to warn you what might happen."

"It's not going to."

"Do you actually think you know me better than I know myself? Get out. Of my bed and my life."

"No." Her body seemed unaffected but a tear gave her away. Then another that she wiped away roughly.

Proof positive. I'd hurt her. And that was just the beginning. "What do you want? To fuck with me? To make me—" Then I realized it. Recognized it. "It's deliberate. You do it on purpose."

"Do what?"

"This." I motioned back and forth from her to myself. "You're so self-destructive you put yourself into situations where you know you're gonna get hurt. Just like Renee did. Even after my dad died, she couldn't help herself. Guy after guy, all of them beat the shit out of her. I used to think my friends who didn't get beaten were the weird ones because every man I'd ever known hit my mom. And most of them hit me. But then I realized that she went into the relationships knowing what was going to happen. She chose to be with men who treated her like shit because that's all she thought she was."

"That's not why I'm here," she said, shaking her head, "and it's not what's going to happen."

"Only because I won't let it." It all seemed so obvious now. People don't change. She was just like my mom and Anna, and I almost fell for it. "If you had your way, I'd be just like the rest of your frogs. Keep me close until you think you're in love, because you know that as soon as it happens, I'll leave you. Because that's all you think you deserve."

She was openly crying now, her knees tucked up to her chest, her arms wrapped tightly around herself.

"I'm just another one, aren't I? I almost fell for it. I almost fell for you." Fuck it. I *did* fall for her. "I can't wait to see you, I smile like a shithead every time I see it's you calling, I want you to stay over every single night because I sleep better when you're next to me and the next day always seems brighter, better."

I kept talking, not knowing which of us I was hurting more. But better it happen now than when it was too late. "Being with you makes me feel like I'm more of a man, because I know without a doubt that I would do whatever it took to protect you." My voice caught. "So that's what I'm finally doing. I'm telling you to go away."

She lifted her head to say one word: "No."

CHAPTER 30 - LANEY

He moved so fast, he was on the bed before I'd even registered his reaction. He yanked me down and spread my legs open, setting his body between them.

"Do you want me to hurt you, Lane? Is that what you need from me? What you *want*?"

I shivered. His weight seemed heavier than it had ever been before, his voice lower and crueler and more intimidating.

"No," I said. But he'd been right about everything else. The truth seemed so obvious when he said it, as if the reasons only became real when they were spoken. "I don't want you to hurt me. I want you to love me."

He let out a shuddered breath. "You know I can't."

"All I know is you've never tried."

His lips crushed mine, punishing and desperate. His hand found my core, his touch commanding but not hurtful. Controlling my pleasure. He knew my body, what it needed. What it wanted. And even though I didn't understand what was happening between us, nothing could stop me from coming, crying his name halfway in and halfway out of his mouth. He kept stroking me gently, slowly letting me come down from the high. But he wasn't done. He was just giving me a chance to catch my breath before his touch became firmer, more insistent.

"Be inside me, Carson. Please, I need you inside me."

Even as he shook his head, he slipped on a condom and pushed into me, both of us moaning. Each stroke brought us closer together, like we were supposed to be.

"This is what I can give you, Lane." His thrusts got stronger. "We can do this. And it's good, right?"

"So good." Every word took air neither of us could get.

He was so deep, slamming into me so hard, it would've felt like a punishment if it didn't feel so fucking amazing. "I can give you this, but you can't ask me for more. Tell me this is enough."

Was it? I couldn't answer. Not now. Not when he was making me feel like this. Being with him was more than I'd ever wanted physically. But what about everything else? I couldn't choose until I could think.

"Yes or no, Lane. Is this enough?" As if his cock didn't feel incredible enough, he slipped his hand between us and used his thumb to stroke me with exactly the pressure I needed.

"I can't...oh...I can't think." I put my hands above my head, tensing my arms every time he pushed into me so I wouldn't be shoved into the headboard. "Don't make me choose."

For a moment a shadow passed over his face, disappointment that I didn't answer maybe. What did he want? Which answer did he really want? To let him keep me from getting too close or to force him to take me all the way in.

"I can't." I didn't know how I felt, what I wanted, or what I could handle. "This isn't fair."

"I'm sorry."

"Carson," I moaned as everything collided—physical and emotional, pleasure and hurt. He followed me over, pressing deeper and clutching me to him, groaning against my neck. A tremor went through his body as we both tried to catch our breaths.

He didn't pull out, keeping us connected. Our bodies, at least. "I can't love you, Lane. Ever." Even though the words were whispered, a tiny vibration against my skin, they thundered in my ears. "Tell me this is enough. That you don't want something I can't give you. Tell me we can have this and you won't need more. Say it."

"Okay," I lied, knowing it was already too late. Knowing that even though he would never feel the same way I did, I couldn't let him go. "It's enough."

"Yeah?" he asked, his voice so eager and hopeful.

"Yeah. Everything's gonna be fine... Like before. Nothing has to change."

I made it all the way home before I started crying.

CHAPTER 31 - CARSON

I saw my brother as soon as I walked through the door—same table in the same restaurant we always met at. Not that we met very often. I was the only guy whose sleeves were tattooed on, but the servers didn't hassle me because they knew I tipped well.

"I have to get back soon, so I ordered for both of us." Sure. Hayden's office hours were from nine am to five am the next day, even on weekends.

"Very romantic, bro, but you're not getting any."

Hayden didn't smile because Hayden never smiled because Hayden was never happy. He wore his melancholy well, though, and the only reason it was so glaringly obvious to me was because over the years we'd had a couple conversations. Not many, because our family saw emotions as something *other* people had, at least while we were sober. Even though Hayden is about the same size as I am, he's always been a lightweight.

But to someone who didn't know what a train wreck he'd lived with until Renee shipped him off to boarding school, he looked pretty damn perfect. Professional, way more socially acceptable and better behaved than I was, hardworking, and with no idea how to have a good time.

My theory was that he worked so much so he didn't have to be at home with his wife. Clare was great and *really* nice to look at, but it didn't take more than two minutes to figure out there was absolutely no connection between them. That was probably why Hayden managed to look lonely in a crowd of people.

"Why have I been summoned today, big brother?" I asked.

Hayden put his napkin on his lap. "I heard you've been giving Mom money."

"So?"

"Why?" He held up his hand. "Don't answer that. I know why and I think it's a terrible idea, not to mention incredibly unhealthy. If you don't want to have a relationship with her, fine, but don't pay her off and think that's enough."

"Why not? It seems to work pretty damn well most of the time." I rolled my eyes at his glare. "She blew all of it. Did you know that? Everything Dad left her, and everything she could get out of her other husbands. She generously donated it all to Saks and Gucci. They thanked her by giving her shit she doesn't need and only uses once or twice." Our mother was a piece. Thank goodness there was always another guy to treat her like a queen in public and a pauper at home.

"I also heard what happened after the Walk—her side at least. I'm sorry I couldn't make it, by the way." Since Hayden was one of the few board members I actually liked, I knew he wanted to be there. "Clare and I donated a little extra online."

"To pay me off?" I sighed and waited until the server left before speaking again. "She's going right back in for another round, Hayden. Doesn't that bother you? Even if there weren't a whole bunch of other tragic reasons, she wants to live a certain lifestyle, and she doesn't have the funds to do it. I wanted to give her a chance." Again and again and again. "If that means sending her a check every month, then I'll send her a check every month. Although, she's doing it anyway so it didn't work after all, did it? Unfortunately, she's not *only* the gold-digger I always thought she was. I guess she needs something other than money."

Without saying it outright—because we never did—Hayden knew exactly what I was talking about. We had the same father and had seen and felt a lot of the same things. Including, but not limited to, belts, hardcover books, and fists.

Hayden was a few years older than me and had already been out of the house for a while when our dad died, so he'd missed all the fun years after that. The years when our mother went from asshole to asshole, dragging her younger son along for the ride, keeping him close instead of sending him to boarding school like she had with Hayden. But it didn't matter who'd gotten more of it or from whom—damage is damage.

I could have run away or moved in with Hayden when he turned eighteen, but back then I'd been stupid enough to think that being with her was actually doing something to help her. He didn't know about any of the shit that was going on. Not until a lot later. When we both got shit-faced and I got chatty.

For a reason I didn't understand, Hayden had always known it wasn't normal. Maybe it was because I'd known so many of them—every man Renee picked was just like our father. So I'd grown up thinking that hurting the ones you claim to love is what a man did. I spent a lot of nights with a lot of tears, wishing I wouldn't have to do it someday.

All the assholes who said they loved my mother couldn't keep their hands off her. Some of them couldn't keep their hands off me, either. Not in a touchy-feely way. No—when I got touched, it was with a fist.

I remembered the night I found out that it wasn't normal. The look on my friend's face when I asked him what he usually got hit with. All men have their weapon of choice. But this kid's dad didn't. This kid's dad punished by grounding him or taking away the keys to his car. At the time, Renee and I had been living with Anna and her dad for about a year. His weapon of choice was leather. That fucker sure liked leather.

The next day I'd talked to Anna about something real for

the first time. She didn't talk back. She didn't say a word, even though I went after her, trying to make her understand. From that point on, I wanted to take care of her—clean her up and get her ice whenever she needed it.

"How many times have you tried to get Mom out?" Hayden asked. "How many times has she wanted your help?" He shrugged. "Unfortunately, we can't decide for her. Someday maybe, which is why I keep in touch with her, but it's up to her. It's not your responsibility, little brother. Just like it's not your fault."

People always say that. They also say, 'if you're not part of the solution, you're part of the problem,' and a whole bunch of other contradictory shit.

"I'll think about it."

"Think hard," Hayden said. "I hear you had to write a big check to someone else recently, too."

Did he mean—? "The guy from the bar fight?" I shoved back from the table. "I need to fire all those assholes. Did the whole client-confidentiality thing get thrown out while I wasn't looking?"

"They work for me too, and Scott is on the board. What you do affects the foundation, Carson."

"As if I don't know that. Yes, I paid." In coin, at least. "But no, it wasn't a big check—it was a regular-sized one. I don't think banks will cash the big cardboard ones."

He completely ignored my attempt at humor and tossed his napkin on the table. "Nothing like that can ever happen again, Carson. I don't care how good your reasons were—it can't happen again."

"It won't."

"Good. So tell me about this girl."

I groaned. "She's a friend."

"Benefits or no?"

"What the hell?" We didn't talk about this stuff. Ever. But Hayden just sat there with an expectant look on his face. "Yes. Okay, yes. There are benefits. Great benefits. Don't tell

Renee, though. It will give her an excuse to call me."

"Do you treat her well?"

I leaned back in my chair, not even pretending to eat anymore. "Yeah, I treat her well."

"Do you think it's going to turn into something?"

I paused. "No. She's great but...no. Neither of us want that."

Hayden laughed but it was a sad laugh, something deeper. "Someday it won't matter what you want. Hopefully someday, with someone, you won't have a choice. She'll come into your life and show you how wrong you've been about everything you've ever known. And you won't stand a chance against her, little brother."

For the first time, I saw life in my brother's eyes. And, as good as it was to see, it also scared the shit out of me. Because Hayden never laughed and there was never a spark in his eyes—that just wasn't who he was. And if my older, stable, logical brother was doing things he'd never done before, anything was possible. Well, *almost* anything.

"Nah," I said. "We both want to keep things just like they are."

CHAPTER 32 - LANEY

For the next few days, I made excuses about why I couldn't see Carson. They were all true—I'd been completely neglecting my business and everything else. But that had nothing to do with the real reason I didn't want to see him.

I needed time. A chance to think about what he'd said. He was wrong—I didn't want to be hurt. I wanted to be *loved*.

Idiot.

Since that was a no-win scenario, I tried remembering what a basket case I'd been a few months ago and why I'd decided love was bullshit. As each day went by, I got better and better at convincing myself I'd been wrong. It was a momentary delusion. What the hell did I know about love? I'd confused things in the past, multiple times, so in six months from now, I'd probably look back on what I was feeling and laugh at how stupid I'd been.

Love is a two-way street, right? Doesn't everyone say that? So when I took my head out of my ass, I understood that I was misinterpreting my emotions because I still hadn't completely shaken the old me. Realizing that made me glad to have Carson in my life because he was the only person who wouldn't judge me for my fuck-up, even when it involved him.

It would be okay. Nothing had to change.

Oh my god, what complete bullshit. Everything had changed, for me at least. Now it was just finding the balls to face it. I was pretty sure that wasn't going to happen for a long time. Hopefully before it did, I'd remember love was a fairytale and sex was only sex.

I was deep in the midst of my Saturday morning ritual— pajamas, coffee, and couch—when I heard a knock on the door. My mind instantly went to Carson, with something like excitement. But I still needed time before I was ready for us to go back to our old selves, to the pre-delusional-Laney times. So, I slowed down.

"Oh." I blew out a breath of disappointment. Multiple counts of disappointment. Not only was he not the man I wanted to see, he was Kevin, the last guy I'd turned into a frog. The guy who, though perfect on paper, was anything *but* in reality. I'd actually pictured myself having a future with this asshole—kids, house, dog. Back then I hadn't understood what passion was and had confused it with contentment. I'd been content with him—not happy or unhappy. Just…content.

His smile looked forced, and he was holding a white bag and a coffee carrier with two cups.

"What are you doing here?" I asked.

"I tried to call you but—"

"I changed my number." Too bad I didn't change my address, too.

"Can I come in?"

"I'm not sure. How would Brittany feel about that?"

"We're not together anymore." What a shocker.

"That's too bad, but I'm actually not interested in being your backup plan."

"That's not why I'm here." Right, of course, he was only here to apologize for being such a douche. It had nothing to do with him being dumped and feeling sad and horny. "Can we talk for a few minutes? Please."

I sighed, but stepped back and let him inside. After excusing myself, I went to put on my robe. When I came back into the living room, Kevin was sitting on the couch, and I had a flashback. He was sitting in exactly the same place, but only wearing his boxers because we'd just had sex. Okay sex. What I used to think was good sex.

He smiled at me as he leaned back, making himself at home. Even though the image was the same and *he* was the same, I wasn't. I didn't want anything from him—not even an apology. But after everything that had happened lately, I wasn't up to another argument, so I'd hear him out, pretend to be sad he screwed up his own life, and then ask him to leave.

When I heard another knock on the door, I knew it was Carson. Had to be. I still wasn't sure I was ready to see him, but at least he'd be able to get Kevin to leave with just one glare.

"Gotta get that." I practically ran to the door, opening it only to be pushed backwards by a very unhappy Carson, coffees in hand and eyes on the floor.

"I know you probably have shit to do," he said, shoving one of the cups at me and heading into the living room, "but you know how impatient I am. I wanted to—"

He got there only a half second before I did. I saw his shoulders rise by at least an inch and his entire body tense. This was something I hadn't foreseen happening.

I stepped in between them. "This is Kevin. Kevin, Carson. Carson, Kevin."

Carson's eyes went to me and then traveled down my body, his expression turning into one of understanding...something that wasn't true. Wait a minute. How'd that happen?

"Kevin was my last frog." I didn't look at Kevin when he made a what-the-hell sound. My eyes were glued to Carson's because...well, because he mattered.

"Wow." He laughed through tight lips and looked away, shaking his head slightly. "Okay. I'll go." Then he glared at

Kevin. "You fuck her over again, and I'll turn you into road kill. Understand?" He handed me the other cup of coffee without making eye contact and backed out of the room.

Kevin grumbled something or protested or did some male posturing, but I didn't pay attention. My focus stayed on Carson. Did it matter if he thought something was going on? Yes, of course it did. Especially because he'd been so clear about saying he'd let me know before he slept with someone and I should do the same. But I hadn't slept with anyone, so whatever Carson thought was an assumption *he'd* made.

That wasn't fair. "Carson, listen—"

He held up his hand. "Don't worry about it."

As if that was possible. But maybe whatever he thought had happened would keep some much-needed space between us until I was sure I was okay. No one would get their feelings hurt and we could spend time together while the emotions that shouldn't be had a chance to cool down and be put to rest.

I followed him back to the door. "Want to meet tomorrow?"

"Why?"

I grabbed his jacket so he wouldn't walk away. "Because I want to see you."

He glanced back towards the living room. "He cheated on you so you'll pay him back, is that it?"

"What? No." I scrambled for an answer, stuck in a lie I hadn't even verbalized. But I hadn't corrected him, either, told him whatever he was thinking was wrong. "Kevin just wanted to talk."

"I'm sure he did." He looked down to what I was wearing again. "I guess whatever he said worked."

"That's—"

"I know, not fair. You're right. Apology number four. You can do whatever you want. Just..." He wiped his hand across his mouth. "Just be careful. Okay?" He leaned in and kissed my forehead. "I can't meet tomorrow. Maybe later in the week sometime. I'll call you."

No, he wouldn't. Because he knew I wouldn't sleep with two men at the same time. So whatever it was that we were doing would stop because he thought Kevin and I were back together. I watched him walk down the hall, wondering how something so right could go so wrong so quickly. I'd wanted a little space, not a continent.

Instead of saying anything, I was silent. My mind was going in too many directions, and I hurt in a way I wasn't sure I had a right to hurt in. For all I knew, this was his way out. Maybe while I'd been avoiding him, he'd been avoiding me. And maybe he'd just come over here to say he was done with me.

Well, tough shit. Because I wasn't done with him.

I just needed a little time to figure out what I wanted to do. I wouldn't lie to him, but I had to understand what I felt, thought, and wanted before I could be honest with him.

"Carson," I called. "I'm coming over later."

He turned around without stopping and shrugged. "If you want to."

"I do." As soon as he was gone, I went back inside to get rid of Kevin. My conversation with Carson couldn't wait until tomorrow.

I went into the living room. "I have a busy day planned and—"

"Sure. I won't take too much of your time." He didn't get up or leave, though. If he wanted to talk, maybe I could encourage him to talk quickly, so he would *leave* quickly.

"So... How's...what was her name again?" I knew the name of my replacement because I'd spent months reliving that relationship and trying to figure out what I'd missed, what I'd done wrong, and what I should have done differently. Even though Kevin had broken my heart and I didn't want anything to do with him, I'd still obsessed about it for more time than I'd ever admit to.

"Brittany," he said. "She wants to have our marriage annulled."

"Wow." My eyes flew to his hand, stopping on the gold band he wore. "You really married her. I didn't know." It didn't mean anything was different. It just confirmed that all the months I'd spent sobbing and googling wedding announcements had been a complete waste of time.

"In August." Meaning, a month after he'd broken up with me. Tops. He looked at me expectantly, waiting for a reaction, I guess. But honestly, I couldn't think of a single reason I would care.

"Congratulations on the wedding," I said, hoping we could wrap this up quickly and he'd go away. "And sorry about the divorce. Did you try therapy?" For *any* of his issues?

"It was too fast." He shook his head and gave me what I now knew was his 'feel sorry for me and do something to make me feel better' face. That look used to make my heart clench. Now it made my stomach clench—there was a good chance I'd throw up on him. "We didn't know each other well enough."

"Really?" I couldn't hide my smile as I leaned my hip against the back of the couch. "But you guys were dating for, like, three weeks before you proposed. How could that possibly not have been enough time to get to know each other?"

"I knew you'd be bitter."

I laughed. "This isn't bitter. This is over it." The bitterness stopped once I realized how much I owed Brittany. Without her, I might be living with the bastard right now.

"I wish it would've ended differently, Laney. I want you to know that."

"See, there's proof that I'm not bitter. A few months ago I would've been pissed by the way you phrased that—'it would've ended differently'. As if you had nothing to do with it. As if you *accidentally* stuck your dick into someone else and lied about it for an entire month. Or more, I guess. I'm still unclear about the timing, but it doesn't matter. And I'm not mad. If it hadn't happened, I would still be right where I was." Afraid to be honest with someone who'd never bothered to ask what I wanted out of life. He'd never been to my shop, never even asked me about my art.

I got out of that dysfunctional relationship and now was in a much healthier, dysfunctional *non*-relationship. At least I knew Carson wanted what was best for me. Kevin never cared about that.

"We weren't good together," I said.

"Yeah, we were." He stood.

"No, we weren't. I forgot I had my own thoughts and needs, and you were okay with that. Didn't you ever wonder if I had an opinion of my own?" I was a doormat he enjoyed wiping his feet on and sleeping with. What kind of man wants someone like that? "I love being able to pick where I go for dinner, to leave a place when *I* feel like it, and to not be obligated to do what someone else wants to do." Those were things Carson didn't ask for or want to control.

"I never want to go back to that," I said. "Not because you did anything wrong, but because *I* did. I was afraid to be myself because I didn't think you would stay with me if I was, so I pretended to be someone else. Of course, the irony is that you dumped me anyway. But I'm really happy now." Happier than I'd ever been. Satisfied.

I couldn't wait to see Carson and tell him most of it was his fault. Not because he made me happy, because he *let* me be.

It took Kevin a while to respond, as if he were still weighing his chances. "Okay. We'll just be friends then."

I nodded. "That would be..." Then I stopped nodding. "No, it wouldn't. I wasn't honest with you back then because I didn't know what I wanted. I never lied to deliberately hide something from you. But you did. You lied, knowing it was lying, and you cheated, knowing it would hurt me. So no, I don't want to be friends."

"People should be allowed to have a second chance, Laney."

"You're totally right. People should be allowed to choose who they let into their lives, too. I'm a different person now and have a better life. Why would I let you into it?"

"So, that's it? That's how it's going to end?"

"Yeah, that's exactly how it's going to end." I swung my arm towards the door, a none-too-subtle hint that he should go. "There are no hard feelings, though. I hope you have a great life, Kevin. I really do."

His expression turned from forlorn to angry, and I knew that whatever he said next would be out of spite.

"You're fucking that guy, aren't you?"

It couldn't be any further from being his business, but it didn't matter. "Yep."

"He thought we'd slept together and then walked out without saying anything. Do you know what that means, Laney? When a guy doesn't give a shit about who you fuck, it means he doesn't give a shit about you. You're just something to jerk off into."

"Wow. That was classy." And an insight into how Kevin thought of me when we were together. I regretted ever saying anything. I regretted ever letting him into the apartment. I regretted ever letting him into my life.

"You need to leave now, Kevin."

He stood so quickly, I flinched backwards. "Don't be like that."

I backed up a few more steps. "Go away. Now."

He stood there staring at me, his jaw tight. "I care about you, Laney. More than he ever will. I never would've walked out."

"You *did* walk out, and now you should do it again."

"Laney, I made a mistake. I know it was a mistake."

"*A* mistake? Every time you chose to fuck someone who wasn't me was a mistake. Every time you lied to me about it was a mistake. So it was way more than 'a' mistake, and the only reason you're here admitting it is because Brittany showed you how I felt when you did it to me." Duped, betrayed, and humiliated. I wouldn't wish it on anyone, but none of it had anything to do with me.

"I said I was sorry," he spat. He'd never intimidated me before, but I'd never said no to him before, either. Was this the real him? "What do you want from me?"

"I want you to leave."

I heard a key slip into the unlocked door. Then it swung open and Hillary came in.

"You need to keep the door locked, Lan—" She stopped when she saw us, her gaze darting back and forth between me and Kevin. "Sorry. I'll just…" She sidled towards her room.

"It's fine. Kevin was about to leave me alone."

He snagged the bag of pastries and his coffee from the table and stomped out of the apartment.

"What was that?" Hillary asked.

"I have no idea." But at least it was over.

CHAPTER 33 - CARSON

I spent the morning fuming about something that I shouldn't have cared about. Pacing and bitching at myself, getting more and more agitated as I crossed off each excuse as complete bullshit. Or at least not the reason I was so fucking angry.

First reason: Lane and I were friends, and she seemed to be backsliding into a person she didn't want to be anymore. So it was only natural for me to worry about her getting back together with that fucking asshole frog.

"What the fuck did she ever see in that guy anyway?" I asked the empty room. "He looked like more of a toad than a frog."

I moved on to the next reason: Lane and I were great together. Sexually, I'd never had a better partner. "*I* know her favorite position. Why? Because I've done it with her a bunch of times, including her *first* time." I smacked the door. "Right there." Her idiot ex never even tried it with her. What kind of man sticks to one position when he's got someone who's incredible and hot and generous and adventurous and fun and—? Okay, that wasn't helping.

So I went on to another reason: Because that dickwad didn't deserve her. It was a crime against humanity that he even be allowed to touch her.

I stopped pacing, breathing, blinking, all of it.

"Holy shit, that bastard touched her." And he was going to touch her again. And again. He could touch her whenever he wanted to because she'd gone back to him.

She'd taken him back, knowing what an asshole he was and that he'd probably hurt her again. Why would she do that? She wasn't the same person she'd been—how many times had she told me that. But if she was stronger now, why go back to that dickhead?

The thought triggered something in me, a huge section of my life that I wished I could forget. People couldn't change no matter how much they wanted to or *said* they wanted to. Lane went back to her frog because that's what she thought she deserved—someone who would lie and cheat.

All the things I would never do to her. Ever.

My heart rate kicked up a few notches and my crazy mumbling started again, cursing Lane for backsliding. She was fucking tough. So much stronger than Renee ever was. I watched my mother take punch after punch, slap after slap, suck in a breath and then go right back in before the bruises were even gone. And I couldn't stop her.

When I'd finally understood how a man should behave, how he should treat the people he loved, I hated my mom. For being weak, for putting us into fucked-up situation after fucked-up situation. It was her fault as much as it was my father's or the other bastards she brought into our lives, including Anna's dad. It was her fault because it was her choice to go back and to take me with her.

My vision blurred, because it was my fault, too. I could have done something to protect her. From the men and from herself. I should've fought harder, tried to hit back, dragged my mother out of the house if I had to.

I hadn't done shit back then. I hadn't done shit when I saw Lane do the same fucking thing. Nothing ever changes. I walked away from her without saying anything, even though

I knew what she was in for with that prick, how badly she'd get hurt again. And I'd done nothing to stop it from happening.

Someone knocked on my door. I froze for a second, trying to gain control over the uncontrollable. I shouldn't open it, not when my emotions were so raw. Even if I opened it to a deliveryman, I'd probably go fucking insane on his ass. If it was—

"Carson, it's me," Lane called.

Ignoring all the danger signs, I bolted for the door, yanked it open, and dragged her inside. I slammed her against the door as soon as it shut and kissed her. Hard. Possessively.

If she remembered how good everything felt a week ago, how right, then she wouldn't go back to the frog. She wouldn't be able to. I had to stop her from making the wrong decision. Protect her. I couldn't let her turn from the person I respected most in the entire world back into a woman she had no respect for. She was worth so much more than that.

I couldn't think right. My lips were on hers and I could taste her, but everything was moving too fast. Focus. I had one goal. One thing to accomplish in my sorry excuse for a life— stop Lane from going back to him. How?

If I reminded her how we were together, how *good* we were together, she'd forget about Kevin. I made her feel good. How many times had she told me that? Kevin never made her scream or fall apart when she came. None of her frogs did.

I did. I could make her understand she didn't need him by doing the only thing I was good at. The only thing I could offer her.

As my teeth and lips moved to her neck, her nails dug into my chest and it drove me fucking insane. Lust and fear took over all my anger and guilt until I didn't think anymore. I didn't hurt anymore. I could only *do*.

I lifted her skirt and slid my hand into her panties, tugging them to the side. Fuck, her body was always ready, on fire and slick. The echo of her calling my name stopped when I took her mouth again and yanked open my jeans so I could get to my cock. She loved this position—up against the door, hard and dirty.

It wasn't the sex itself that was going to help. It was a reminder of the moments when she completely let go, stopped thinking and judging and caring about anything or anybody else.

"...can't do this!" When she shouted it, I stopped, dragging air into my lungs. I was almost inside her, my cock already lined up to take her.

Was I already too late? She was so fucking good. If she was with him, she'd only be with him. And she'd never be with me again. Never.

"Just once, Lane," I begged her quietly. "He cheated a lot, right? So you can do it just this once." With me. Please, let me be with her one more time. "Just once." I was so full of shit. I didn't want just once—I wanted just *always*.

"Stop!" Her eyes were huge and welling with tears while her entire body pressed into the door even after I stopped pushing her into it. "Please, Carson. Just stop."

Fuck. How long had she been saying that without me hearing her?

I jerked away, shoving my cock back in my pants, my hands shaking. Countless apologies pouring out of my mouth, none of them clear because they were coming out so quickly and because my mind was too confused, bouncing from understanding her fear to knowing I'd failed again. I failed really fucking well.

"I wasn't—" I stepped back, giving her room to move. To leave.

"Stop," she mumbled, not looking at me. She straightened her skirt while I stood frozen, awaiting the verdict. "You can't do that. You can't... I came here because we needed to talk, not... Jesus, Carson." She looked at me with moist, wounded eyes, eyes that reflected the part of myself I most feared. The part I most hated.

"I'm sorry. I didn't mean to hurt you. I thought—" It didn't matter what I thought. It mattered what I did and, if she hadn't said stop, I would have picked her up and slid inside her without even realizing I was forcing her. "I'm so sorry, Lane."

"Yeah well... I don't care." She yanked the door open and left, slamming it behind her.

CHAPTER 34 - LANEY

The next week was awful. Everything seemed to be going wrong in every part of my life. Why was that? Why couldn't one catastrophe happen at a time?

I was supposed to be working on the lily pad tables, but no matter how much I looked, the right size, shape, and quality of wood just wasn't there. So I ended up spending all my time looking for supplies and none of my time building or working on any of the refinishing projects I'd been hired to do. And the worst part was... Okay, there were two worst parts: none of that frustration and concentration kept my mind off Carson *and* since he wasn't around, I didn't have anyone to bitch to.

I missed him. He'd become a constant in my life, a support beam I could lean on whenever I lost my balance. I wasn't mad anymore, just confused. It all happened so fast—I went there to explain what he'd seen at my place and then suddenly my skirt was hiked up and his pants were down. But he stopped as soon as he really heard me. I knew he didn't want to hurt me. He would never hurt me. I should have stayed or at least said something better than "I don't care."

"I don't care" sounds pretty final.

Things between us had just gotten too complicated, and it

was better to reassess things before anything else could go wrong. I figured after a day or two, we'd be ready to talk. I waited for his call all week—he always called. Except this time. So maybe me walking out the door was all the goodbye he needed. And maybe I would have to live with that.

"Shit." It's not as if I couldn't call him. I kept putting it off because I was afraid. What if that really was goodbye? Maybe it should be.

When I got home, there was a letter on the floor just inside my door. My name was written in his messy scribble and was missing the 'Y.' Thank god Hillary hadn't found it or she might have thrown it away. I hadn't told her what happened, but she wasn't dumb and I'm not much of an actress. A weeklong moping session is hard to miss.

I closed the door to my room and sat on my bed before opening the letter. Carson hated paper, so it made whatever he'd written more personal. Because I knew he would never have done it for anyone but me.

Lane,

I can't do this not-talking thing anymore. I tried being patient and waiting for you to call but you didn't call and I don't have any patience.

I need to talk to you. Please. In public. I promise I won't touch you again. I just need to make sure you're okay, have a few more chances to tell you what a fuck-up I am, and say goodbye.

I'll be at the café in our regular spot from 6:30 until it closes. If you can't make it tonight, that's okay because I'll be there tomorrow night too. And the next, just in case you're busy tomorrow too. Then I'll probably take the hint and leave you alone.

I want you to know that I've done a lot of shitty stuff in my life, but I've never regretted anything as much as I regret that moment. I wish there was a way I could take it back.

If I don't see you again, was scribbled out, replaced by, *I need to see you again.*
    Carson

I thought about it until seven-thirty, the decision flipping back and forth until I got dizzy. Should I go? Or was a clean break better? All of Carson's other relationships ended that way, after far less time. It was the way all the frogs had done it, too.

Yeah, and look how much closure that gave me. Shit. Okay, I'd go. But it wouldn't be to say goodbye.

CHAPTER 35 - CARSON

I'd spent the last five days replaying what happened, where it went wrong, what I should have done, why there was no reason on earth for her to forgive me.

Everything had changed, and our relationship—if we still had one—would never be like it was. I didn't think I could miss something so much, care about anything enough, to not be able to sleep or work or focus without it. Without her. I'd fucked it up and I'd fucked it up good. Impressive.

But I didn't want her to think I was just another frog and that she was wrong to trust herself. That wasn't fair. She went into this hoping I could help her move past the damage other men had done. It was supposed to be a lesson in getting what she wanted on her terms, instead of being treated like shit on someone else's.

I'm not sure when things changed for me. When it became as much for me as it was for her, to watch her find out she deserved so much more than she'd ever gotten.

Instead, I'd blown it all into itty-bitty pieces in a fit of frustration and stupidity, of not wanting things to change and thinking I could manhandle them back to what they were. I knew better than to trust my instincts and let myself react so quickly. I knew better, and I'd done it anyway. Because it was something I couldn't control. Not now, not ever.

So I'd tell her how sorry I was, and I'd tell her how amazing she was, and I'd say goodbye. If she gave me the chance.

I stood as soon as she walked in, suddenly acting like a thirteen-year-old boy at a school dance. I forced myself to stay still even though my whole body fought me on it. There wasn't a single part of her I didn't miss. Not one.

Her hair was up the way I like it—made it easier to get to her neck. That wasn't going to happen anymore, though.

She walked over slowly, cautiously, and then pointed to the coffee cup in front of her chair. "That for me?"

"Yeah." I'd been replacing it every fifteen minutes so it would be hot when, and if, she ever came.

She came. She was here.

And I'd forgotten all the things I wanted to say.

We sat down and were silent for a few minutes. This was stupid. After I fucked something up, I was usually pretty good about making things right, so why was this so hard? Because it was going to take words, not cash.

Determined to say something, even if it wasn't what I'd planned, I leaned forward and rested my forearms on my thighs. "I don't expect you to forgive me." Because I didn't deserve it. "I know what I did—it's on repeat in my mind. All the ways I screwed up. I didn't mean to hurt you but I did, so…"

I took a breath. "I think you're fucking incredible, Lane. No, that's not right. You *are* fucking incredible, no thought necessary. The guy you choose—Kevin or somebody else"— *please*, let it be someone else—"will be the luckiest man alive. If he forgets that, if he hurts you, walk away. Run away. Whatever you have to do. Don't stay there because you think he's going to change because he's not. People can't change."

"Yes, they can. People change all the time."

I wasn't going to argue with her or discuss how wrong she

was, because I'd lost the right to be her friend. "Anyway, I just wanted you to know that it had nothing to do with you and everything to do with me. I'm really sorry." I stood up when I ran out of ways to apologize. "Just…try not to pick any more frogs."

She grabbed the bottom of my shirt as I moved to leave. "We talk about a lot of things but always avoid the important stuff. Why?"

I shook my head, knowing the answer but not knowing how to say it. It was too hard, too close, too late. If I let her all the way in… I *couldn't* let her all the way in.

"What were you trying to prove?" she asked.

"I didn't want you to go back to him. I don't want you to get hurt again and I know he'll do it. So I guess… I know it's hard to believe, but I was trying to protect you. To remind you that you were happier without him. Didn't work out so well, though."

"Yeah, I noticed that," she said, letting go of my shirt. "Kevin came by because he wanted to get back together. His wife dumped him, and he needed an idiot to listen to him whine and then screw him, so he could forget about it for a while."

I closed my eyes. She could screw whoever she wanted for whatever reason she wanted. The sex meant nothing to me. But *she* meant everything to me.

I know sex is just sex. Two bodies combining for a little while, feeling good, and then splitting apart. Except for her and me. For us, it was better than that—our bodies matched, *we* matched.

No, we *used* to match.

"But I'm not an idiot." She sighed. "Well, okay sometimes I'm an idiot. But I'm not *his* idiot anymore. So I told him to go. Nothing happened. I'm proof people can change, Carson. I'm never going back to the person I was. So sit down and talk to me."

I slowly went back to my seat and waited for her to tell me

what would happen next.

"You scared me."

"I know. If I could do it over again——"

"Don't," she said, shaking her head. "Don't ever do it again."

I looked at her, unsure of what that meant.

"After Kevin broke up with me, I swore I'd never give anyone a second chance, but I'm going to give you one. Is that a bad decision?"

"No." But a second later, I wasn't sure 'no' was the right answer. I would never screw things up this way again, but I'd screw them up some other way. Maybe a worse one. It was in my DNA to fuck up everything good. But I wanted it to be true and I would try. Really fucking hard.

"I shouldn't have assumed you were with him again."

"No, you shouldn't have, but I shouldn't have let you believe it. I could've told you right then, but I thought I needed space. I still do. Not much—I want to keep hanging out if you do, but not as often, especially not overnight. Because…it's messing with my head."

I knew the feeling. "I can do less often." I nodded even though I didn't want to. "I'm really sorry, Lane."

"You're a total liar," she said with a small grin. "You apologize all the time."

"Just to you. And only when I mean it."

"You make me happy for a bunch of reasons, not just the sex. You know that, right?"

Oh shit. I couldn't remember if I knew that or not. All I could focus on was how much I didn't *want* to know that. I should get out of this while I still could, use her need for space as the beginning of a larger one. So she'd avoid the damage I could do to her.

"That's the biggest problem," she said.

No, it wasn't. *I* was the biggest problem. She was wrong to give me a second chance. But if I told her, I'd have to walk away now and I couldn't do that. Because I was weak and stupid and selfish, just like my father. The only difference between him and me was that I hadn't hit Lane, I hadn't made her feel worthless. But I would—it was inevitable. Because I was weak and stupid and selfish.

CHAPTER 36 - LANEY

I started asking Carson to do more and more with me—mostly carrying raw wood and moving the lily pad tables to the storage area as I finished them so they wouldn't get bumped. I loved the company, though I wasn't as crazy about the mess he left behind when he finished one of his Getting Handy projects. I didn't think it was possible for someone to get *worse* the more he practiced.

But I didn't say anything because I figured the more time we spent together, the faster things would go back to the way they'd been. Unfortunately, all it accomplished was that we had more time to feel awkward and unnatural around each other. And I was sick of it.

Since a lot of our time together had been in his bed, I planned an ambush as close to it as I could get him. My drawer and his uselessness with tools were the perfect excuse.

"Can you bring me a screwdriver?" I called from inside his bedroom. "My drawer is stuck."

He came in, holding the screwdriver out, glancing at me and the bed uncomfortably. As soon as the tool was in my hand, he flipped around and started walking away.

I grabbed his arm and tugged so he would face me. "Knock

it off."

"Knock what off?"

"I don't like this, what we're doing now. I want to go back to the way we were. You haven't made a lewd comment or touched me in two weeks." And that meant he wasn't being himself. "I want you to go back to the way you were."

"But you said—"

"I don't care what I said." I stepped in close. "Kiss me."

He hesitated, his body at war with his mind. "Are you sure? I thought we weren't—"

"Kiss me."

With achingly slow movements, he put his hand on my hip, his other under my chin. His lips brushed mine so gently, so hesitantly, so not-Carson-ish. Something I never thought I'd get tired of became irritating. I wanted him to take control and be who he was, who I needed him to be.

"More," I whispered. "I want more."

"I don't want to hurt you."

"More of you won't hurt me, but you treating me as if I'm about to break any second is. Something has to change, and by 'something' I mean you."

I didn't wait for him to make a decision. I'd already made it for him. This was what I wanted, so I took it. If he had a problem with it, he'd let me know. I undid his pants and wrapped my hand around his cock, tightening my grip until his groan turned into a curse, and I felt him start to get hard.

"Lane." It was a warning. One I wouldn't listen to. This was how it all went to shit, and this was how we were going to get it back.

"Do you want me, Carson?"

He flicked his head as if the answer was so blindingly obvious, the question was insulting.

"Do you?"

"Yes." The word came from deep in his chest, an almost desperate sound. "I always want you. I want to touch you, kiss every inch of you, and hear you scream my name. I'm amazed

I get anything done because being with you is all I can think about." He put his hand over mine, stopping my gentle strokes that had already made him completely hard. "But I don't deserve it until you can trust me again."

"I wouldn't be here if I didn't."

His eyes were intensifying, his breath speeding up, his grip tightening. This was working almost too well. "Yeah, but—"

"Have you ever lied to me? Hidden anything from me?" Like I might be but didn't want to think about, especially not right now.

"No."

"Then you should shut up, and do what I want you to do." I needed this and for everything between us to be right again. I could deal with the other parts later.

That night was one of the best we'd ever had, both of us focused on one thing—letting the past and the future go. Even though our conversations were severely limited, consisting mostly of exclamations and swearing, I knew Carson was back. Tomorrow, I'd start seeing his eyes light up with desire and amusement whenever I was around. And every time I caught him looking at me and saw his smile grow, I would feel beautiful and special and wanted. For exactly who I was.

In the morning, he lifted me up and carried my useless body into the bathroom.

"What are you doing?" I whined, still seventy-five percent asleep.

"After you become a famous artist, you can lay around in bed all day. But until then, you have to lie around where I want you to, and I want you in the bathtub."

A half hour later my fingers were pruney, and I'd never cared about anything less. The tub was so comfortable that I wondered it Carson would let me move into his bathroom. The tub could be my bed and... Yeah, that was all I needed.

He adjusted himself behind me, pulling me a bit higher. If I tipped my head all the way back I could rest it on his shoulder. His fingers drew lines in the water, little trails where the bubbles didn't follow.

His lips grazed my neck. "So you didn't tell him he was doing it wrong because you didn't want to hurt his feelings?"

"Yes, but when you say it in that condescending tone, it doesn't sound as nice." I was jostled by his laughing.

"How is it nice to lie to the idiot who thinks he's doing it right? You considered staying with this guy, right? Like marriage and all that?"

"As nauseating as the idea is to me now, yeah, marriage and all the rest of it." I swept bubbles towards us, and he popped them.

"You didn't have a problem knowing for the next fifty years you were going to get sub-par head and would only orgasm when you did it yourself?"

"Well, when you say it like that..."

He laughed again. "There is no possible way I could say it to make it not sound completely stupid."

"Shut up." I swatted his knee, splashing water into my own face. "If you weren't such a selfish prick, you'd understand."

"Even if I wasn't a selfish prick, I'd still be a man. And no man thinks he's being selfish during sex, especially not when he's telling you what he wants. I guarantee that if you weren't as good as you are, Mr. Frog would've told you about it."

"Would you?"

"I'm a selfish prick, so of course I would. But in a non-pricky way because most of it is about intent. And what's worse than a woman giving you a blowjob when she'd rather be doing anything else?"

"When she actually *does* anything else?"

"You're very, very smart." He spoke into my neck, his voice gravelly, his lips torturous. "And very, very naked. And very, very sexy. And very, very, *very* about to practice giving a man detailed instructions on how to give you the best orgasm of your life."

He'd already given me the best orgasm of my life. He'd already given me every orgasm I'd put in my top *thirty*.

He pulled the drain plug. "Detailed instructions. You need to practice saying it out loud and giving orders. I'll pretend to be one of the totally clueless frogs you've slept with. Not Kevin though, 'cause I can't do that to either of us. But for this experiment, I'll *only* do what you tell me to do." He forced me to stand. "Up." He got out first so he could help me.

"I swear I can do it myself, Carson."

"Sure, and then when you slip and fall you can sue me for all I'm worth. I know what kind of woman you are." A fluffy white towel hit me in the face, blocking me from seeing his huge mocking smile.

"Sorry."

"Doubt it."

"Why are you so slow? We have work to do." He wrapped his towel around his waist, then pulled mine out of my hands and dried me off. The heat coming off him helped.

When I was kind of dry, he tossed my towel over the shower door and took my hand.

"If we have time, we can cross a few more things off your list. Come on."

I got one more quick glance at the tub before he dragged me out of the bathroom. It would've been much easier to be mad at him for making me leave if he wasn't about to make me come.

CHAPTER 37 - LANEY

I left for my shop late, determined to spend all night there if I had to. If I worked for someone else, I'd have been fired weeks ago. On the flip side, if things didn't get finished on time it would be solely my fault. And blowing my first art gig that Carson worked moderately hard to get for me would be beyond stupid.

My footsteps faltered when I saw Kevin leaning against the shop's roll-up door. How long had he been waiting? And why?

"What are you doing here?" I called without slowing down. Once he realized he couldn't push me around like he used to, he'd leave me alone.

"I wanted to smooth things out. I think we both got a little testy the last time we saw each other."

"I'm pretty sure that was just you, actually."

"Okay, I'll accept that. I shouldn't have said that stuff about that guy. He's Carson Bennett, isn't he?" I didn't respond. The last time I'd answered one of Kevin's leading questions, he'd thrown it back in my face. "Fine, don't tell me. I know he is."

"Then why did you ask?" I snapped, before I could stop

myself. The more I said to him, the longer he'd stay.

"Because no matter what happens between you and me, I want you to be happy, and I don't think Carson Bennett can make that happen."

I wasn't sure what bothered me most—that Kevin had made the effort to find out who Carson was, that he still didn't understand that *nothing* was going to happen between him and me, or that he presumed to know what could make me happy.

"Remember all those months when we didn't speak to each other or try to run each other's lives?" I walked around him, sorting through my keys. "I think we should go back to that."

He put his hand on my shoulder. "I loved you, Laney."

"No, you didn't."

"I could have."

I laughed at something that would have crushed the old me. "No, you couldn't have." Because he would always think of me as the girl whose only goal in life was to marry a doctor and keep him happy. "You could never have treated me the way I deserve to be treated."

"Oh, and Bennett does?" he spat, yanking his hand away from me as if I'd be sad to see it go. "The guy who helped you figure out how you want to be fucked? How to give a great blowjob?"

I groaned. What a dickhead. Maybe he was pissed because he thought Carson was now the recipient of all the subservience *he* used to enjoy.

"Sure, he loves you, Laney. He loves how you give head and how you spread your legs." Unbelievable. Kevin was used to getting what he wanted, but this was more than that. This was a spoiled brat wanting something that he'd thrown away months ago only because someone else had taken it out of the trash and fixed it.

"If that's the way you 'deserve to be treated,'" he said, "then I'm in. I'll even take turns with him, so he can have a couple nights off you during the week."

Wow. I looked at him, disgusted. This wasn't the guy I'd

known or been with. Even when he'd broken my heart, he hadn't deliberately tried to be cruel.

"Go away," I said slowly. "And don't come back." I opened the shop door and went inside, but he stopped the door from closing. "I'm not listening to any more of your shit, Kevin. Go away!" I pushed against him, slowly realizing his anger wasn't just manifesting in what he said. Even when I put my entire weight against the door, not caring if it cut off one of his fingers when it slammed, it didn't budge.

"I shouldn't have said that. Damn it, Laney! Come on, I just want to talk." He was stronger and angrier and more unpredictable than me. And each second I fought to shut the door made me more nervous.

"You don't understand, Laney. I want us to give it another try. We owe it to each other."

I didn't owe him anything, but I didn't want to argue. All I wanted was for him to leave me alone. "Kevin, enough. That's enough." If I let go for even a second, he'd be able to come inside, and then where would I go? "You need to leave now."

"Brittany was cheating on me," he whined. "The whole time."

Why did he think I cared? "I'm sorry to hear that, but it's not my fault. You're starting to scare me, Kevin, and I know you don't want to do that. So you need to let go of the door and walk away."

"She was cheating on me while I was cheating on you. When we got married, I stopped but she didn't."

"Let go of the door."

"And then I realized what I'd done to you. How I made you feel, and it's not okay. It's not okay, Laney. I'm not that kind of person. I was... I don't know... I was confused, and Brittany screwed with my head." So it was Brittany's fault now. "I want to make it right. I screwed up and now I want to make it right. I didn't know what I had when I was with you. Laney, you're the only one I have. Please, talk to me."

He was delusional if he thought he 'had' me. And he was insane if he thought I was going to let him into my shop to talk about it.

"I can do better. I can *be* better. Better than Bennett. I'll treat you so much better than he does. One more chance, Laney. Please."

"Kevin, leave me alone!"

"Goddamn it, Laney! Just give me a fucking chance!" There was no more apology in his tone, no desire to redeem himself in my eyes or in his own.

"Go—" The door slammed into my face and sent me tumbling onto my back, my head smacking on the cement floor. Disoriented, I saw him come inside, reach down, and haul me up to my feet.

"Damn it. You're bleeding, Laney. Your nose. Shit, are you okay?"

Everything was so blurry, so confusing. I started crying because I didn't know what to do to make my nose and head stop hurting so much and make him go away. I didn't know... Oh god. I couldn't find my balance, so how was I supposed to protect myself? I shouldn't have had to. I didn't do anything wrong.

"That wasn't my fault," he said. "You know that, right? All I wanted was a chance to talk to you. If you hadn't been right behind the door, it wouldn't have hit you. I didn't—"

"Kevin, you can't do this. I can't concentrate right now. Please, just leave." As my eyes refocused, tears dripped off my chin and onto my shirt. They were red. I needed help, but not his. "Go away."

"Stop crying. You're fine. It's not broken. Let me see it." He wiped my face, only causing more pain because he wasn't careful—he was desperate and cruel, as if he could wipe away what he'd done if he got rid of my tears. "Quit fighting me, so I can look at it."

I swiped at his hands and pushed at his chest, and it did nothing. It didn't stop his hands or the asinine words coming out of his mouth that had nothing to do with me and everything to do with him. He caught both my hands with one of his and held them to keep me still. When I turned my head, he yanked me frontwards again and I cried out.

"It's not that bad. Shut up for a second and stay still."

Maybe it would be better if I just let him check it out. "Then you'll leave?"

"No, we need to talk."

How did he not understand that I didn't want to talk to him or see him or let him touch me? Did it matter? I relaxed and nodded slightly.

As soon as he released my hands, I ran. If I kept some furniture between us, he wouldn't be able to reach me.

I wasn't even fast enough to get over the first coffee table. He caught me by the back of my shirt and hauled me backwards. As I fell off the table, I heard the rip of fabric and felt it give as it tore off my body.

"Let's start over." He righted me and spun me towards him, his hands now locked onto my biceps. "Okay? We'll get you all cleaned up and then sit down to clear things up."

"No!"

"Jesus, Laney! Calm down! I can't talk to you when you're like this." I was a distraction or an outlet to him, not a person, not a person he claimed he could love. I was a person he could use and hurt and then walk away from…again. All things he'd accomplished in the last three minutes, except the walking away part. The one part I *really* wanted him to do.

"Leave me alone!" I pushed him away from me the best I could, ignoring the tearing sounds, the fact that my shirt was almost completely shredded now. He adjusted his grip, hanging onto the waistband of my pants. "Stop! Please, stop!"

CHAPTER 38 - CARSON

When I turned the corner, I saw the door to Lane's shop open. She was way too smart to leave that door open. My heart did that half-jump thing it does when it knows something your brain hasn't figured out yet. I broke into a jog, pretty sure I was completely overreacting.

Then I heard her yell, "Stop!"

Adrenaline lengthened my strides, preparing me to fight.

Whatever made her scream like that was going to die.

I only saw the guy's back at first, but I heard her crying. I pulled the bastard off her and flung him onto the floor, spending half a second, tops, looking at the asshole before I turned to make sure Lane was alright. Her fucking shirt was hanging off her, only attached by a strip of fabric going around her waist.

The fucker was going to wish his balls had never dropped.

But as soon as I saw Lane's face—blood covering her nose, running onto her lips, drips of it on her chest, I—

"He fucking hit you?"

Her expression changed, grew even more shocked. She shook her head and reached out for me. She knew before I did.

I'd just lost every bit of control I'd ever had. As if a switch had turned on, the dial had been cranked all the way up, and there was no coming down. I spun towards the motherfucker who'd done it—made her hurt and cry and scream.

His turn now.

"Wait, Carson!"

Her ex, the fucking toad, was slowly climbing to his feet, until his face was just high enough for me to put my knee into. Then the asshole wasn't standing anymore. He was bleeding, holding his nose, cursing. But I couldn't stop there. The fucker had hurt her and that was bad enough. But that he'd come back and hurt her again, *this* way, was something I couldn't let slide. Even if I *could have* stopped myself.

"She loved you, asshole!" I kicked him, sending him sprawling backwards, skidding on the cement. I wasn't done. "She loved you, and this is how you pay her back for it?" Shit started pouring out of my mouth so fast, my brain couldn't keep up. My fists couldn't keep up. "Why'd you come back? Because she might have had enough time to get over you? She might actually be happy or have found someone who would treat her like she should be treated?"

Everything faded except my enemy and my fists, occasionally my boot, as if they didn't exist until they were in contact with his body. "Someone who actually understands how amazing she is? What the fuck is wrong with you? She's not weak, and she's not going to take your shit. I'm not going to let her."

I didn't even see his face anymore—it had blurred out a few seconds ago. Fifteen years gone as if they'd never passed. I was gone. I was nothing but rage and violence. The emotional and physical feeding off one another, combining into something I couldn't control. Didn't *want* to control. I wanted to hurt, to punish, to make him stop.

This time I could. I was strong enough and brave enough now—I could make him stop hurting her and me and Hayden. "We don't need you." We could leave him and not come back. We could be like everyone else. Be a family. I could be normal. Not afraid of him or myself anymore. I—

In the distance, someone screamed, pulled on a body that didn't feel like mine anymore.

"I'm not done with him yet," I growled. I couldn't stop until I'd made sure this bastard never hurt any of us again. I felt another tug as somebody tried to drag me away. "I'm not done!" I spun and open-handed the person to get them to back off.

They fell onto one of the tables littering the place, and I heard my name. "He's not your dad, Carson. I'm not your enemy. Please, just stop."

And then reality returned. And she came into focus. Crying, holding the side of her face.

Where I'd hit her.

I fell backwards onto my ass and scrambled away from her, knowing she wasn't cowering from Kevin, she was cowering from me.

"Lane." Her name emptied my lungs of air, and I wished they wouldn't fill again. So I would be punished for what I'd done and who I was and what I was capable of. But they *did* fill, and my heart kept beating, and I lived. Even though I shouldn't.

CHAPTER 39 - LANEY

I touched my cheek where Carson had hit me, but my mind wasn't on that or the pain or how much I was bleeding. Everything just out of my vision seemed to be moving faster than what I was looking at. *Who* I was looking at.

"Carson," I whispered.

A screeching noise redirected my attention. Kevin climbed to his feet slowly, knocking over a desk, one hand putting pressure on his ribcage. His face was a bloody mess. He staggered towards the door and then turned to look at me with nothing but venom in his eyes. "I hope you're not with him for his money, Laney. Because that's all going to be gone soon." The voice I used to be in love with was now ugly and nasal. I hoped like fuck that his nose was broken, and he'd speak like that for the rest of his life.

"When did you turn into such an asshole?" I shouted, stepping between him and Carson. "This was all your fault."

He craned his neck to look at Carson behind me. "You should find out more about the people you're fucking. This isn't the first time Bennett has beaten someone for no reason. I saw the guy he fought, set some of his bones. Bennett's people paid him so he wouldn't go to the cops." He spit out blood and wiped his lip.

I didn't know what he was talking about, but it made sense, explained a few of the things Carson had said. I didn't care, though. Carson wouldn't hurt anyone without a damn good reason. Asking him would have to wait, though, because I couldn't turn my back on Kevin.

"How much do you think he's worth?" Kevin asked. He talked about Carson as if he wasn't there. As if he meant nothing. "Since this is the second time he's done this, I should get double what the other guy got, don't you think? Bennett is pretty important, right? Helps sick kids or some bullshit like that. Great. Now he gets to help me."

"Don't start anything, Kevin."

"It started the second he touched me."

"You have just as much to lose as he does."

"I have nothing to lose, Laney. Nothing."

Everyone has something to lose. The question is what you'll do to keep it.

As he turned, he shoved a chair sideways, breaking it and a few other pieces I'd been working on. He didn't say anything as he left, leaving me with Carson.

At least, it *looked* like Carson. He had his arms wrapped tightly around his knees, curled into himself, his head low. He was looking at me but I wasn't sure if he could even see through all the water welling in his eyes.

I was afraid to touch him, afraid even my fingertips would shatter him. We stared at each other in silence for a while, long enough for my heartbeat and breath to slow down. I don't think his did at all.

"Carson?" I moved slowly, talking to him. "I'm fine. I'm okay now."

He flinched when I reached out to him but I didn't stop until I was right in front of him.

"It's okay," I whispered, running my hand across his face. I pulled my hand away when he grimaced. I knew his reaction wasn't just about me or even mostly about me. This was years of pent-up fear coming to the surface because of one accidental slap. Kevin had hurt me far more than Carson did, but Carson was the one paying for it, maybe for everything.

"Carson, what should I do?"

He met my eyes and spoke slowly. "Run."

"Well..." I swallowed. "I'm not going to do that. So what else can I do?"

"Stop loving me."

I inhaled sharply. The word neither one of us had ever used, the admission I was too afraid to make, spoken in the worst possible moment.

"I told you..." he said. " I told you I would hurt you. Now do you believe me?"

"No. It was an accident. I don't—"

"It doesn't matter if it was an accident or not. It happened. Because I couldn't control myself." His voice dropped to almost a whimper. "I couldn't stop it from happening, Lane. I tried so hard, but I couldn't stop it. I'm sorry."

"There's no reason to be."

He pushed away from me and stood, clearing his throat. "The reason never matters. Excuses never matter. What happens does. And what happened is that I hit you. I hurt you. I never wanted to hurt you."

I didn't know what to say, knowing that anything I said would be wrong—emotions were running too high for an actual conversation. Yes, he'd hurt me. And he'd saved me. How did he miss that part?

It was an accident. Heat of the moment, eyes seeing nothing but red. The stuff he was shouting wasn't about me or even Kevin. He'd been somewhere completely different until the moment he'd started seeing again, the moment he'd realized it was me.

He went into the storage area. I followed part of the way but stopped in the hallway, hearing him open the mini-fridge and slam drawers and mumble to himself. I leaned against the wall and tilted my head back.

He jolted to a stop when he came barreling into the hallway, almost running into me. He held a plastic garbage bag of ice and a clean rag. "Don't put your head back—you'll swallow the blood." He came close, checking my face, gently touching me, caressing my jaw.

"You're so beautiful," he whispered.

"I seriously doubt that." My voice sounded different, changed by damage that was all Kevin's fault.

"I wasn't talking about the way you look." He cleared his throat, stood straighter. "But you'll be beautiful that way too, once the swelling goes down." His tone was timid, lifeless—so unlike Carson. "You're going to bruise a lot, but I don't think your nose is broken. Lean forward a little. It's going to hurt but you need to pinch it to make it stop bleeding."

With my back still to the wall, I did what he said until my nose stopped bleeding and the throbbing was numbed by the ice pack. The whole time he stood two feet from me, leaning against the other wall, watching and waiting with his arms crossed over his chest, expressionless.

"I'm sorry," he said quietly. "I didn't want this to happen."

I saw where this was going, what he was thinking, from the guilt in his eyes. "Stop it. *He* did this to me, not you."

He let out a single bitter-sounding chuckle. "I hit you, Lane. Me."

"It was an accident."

"What about next time? Are you going to say that again next time? Am I going to say it to you?"

"There won't be a next time. It was an accident for shit's sake." I reached out but he yanked his arm away before I could touch him. "How can you not see what I see in you?"

He backed up a step. "You keep hoping I'm someone else. Trying to pretend I'm something I'm not. I'm a frog, Lane. I've always been a frog and I always will be one. If you don't get away from me now, I'll kill the life you have in you right now." His hand lifted up as if he was going to touch me but then stopped. "I love the life you have in you, Lane. But I'll end up taking it away, destroying it, turning you into a person you don't want to be."

"That's bullshit." I shook my head. "You keep telling yourself it could never be good, it could never be *great*. Well, guess what. It is. You are. You're great and you're not broken and you won't hurt me. The only person you're hurting is yourself. Over and over in some stupid, useless kind of penance. And it will never end because you'll never let it. You'll punish yourself until there's nothing left to punish. For something that's never been yours to pay for. You aren't your father."

His lip curled in distaste, probably because someone was finally throwing the truth in his face and he couldn't avoid it, ignore it, or find something to distract him from dealing with it this time.

Why is someone else's pain so much worse than your own sometimes? To see someone you love punish themselves and think they deserve it?

"You shouldn't have given me a second chance." When he straightened and ran his fingers through his hair, I knew he'd stopped listening.

"If I hadn't, I would be sobbing on the floor because you wouldn't have been there to stop Kevin. And no one would be here for me, taking care of me and letting me know I'll be okay." My body tightened as I tried to hold it together long enough to say what I had to say. "And no one would be breaking my heart because they won't believe they'll be okay, too. Because we can make sure you are."

He shook his head. I swear, if his prick of a father wasn't already dead, I would have given the bastard a prize. If his goal had been to truly fuck up his son's thinking, he'd won.

"Damn it, Carson!" I shouted. "I'll give you a second chance and a third and as many as it takes. Because you're not a frog. You've never been one and never will be. Stop punishing yourself before there's nothing left of you. Because then there will be nothing left for me to love. And I want to love you." I paused and took a breath that softened what I asked for next. "Please let me love you."

His whole body trembled, fought itself, maybe because he couldn't decide which way to go. I didn't know what else to say, how to convince him that he wasn't who he thought he was. He'd saved me and I wanted to return the favor. I just didn't know how. So I waited for him to do something, anything that would tell me where he stood, where I stood, where *we* stood.

I wasn't leaving. But *he* was.

"I can't," he said, pushing off the wall and heading for the door. "I'm sorry, Lane. I'm really, really sorry. Lock the door behind me. Make sure you call the police and get a restraining order against your ex."

I knew I'd watch him walk away eventually, but I didn't think it would be like this. "Carson, please. Don't—" My last word was severed by the slamming of the door. I stood there, undecided, unsure. A minute later, I flipped the deadbolt. There was a much bigger chance that Kevin would come back than that Carson ever would.

I found my phone under a workbench, slumped into a chair, and called the police. But what Kevin had said kept ringing in my ears.

Carson *did* have a lot more to lose than he did. How could I hurt the person who'd done so much to help me? I hung up after the first ring.

And then I cried more than I've ever cried before.

I was in love and it hurt and it wasn't going to stop. Because I would never give it up. Because he was worth everything.

CHAPTER 40 - CARSON

My misery didn't want company. It wanted time and attention and things to consume. So I let it. Finally, I'd proven myself to be just as much a bastard as I'd always known I was, just as much as my father and all the fuckers that came after him.

One problem, though. I couldn't get Lane out of my mind. I couldn't stop seeing her, tasting her, remembering how soft her skin was. I could've sworn I heard her voice, saying things I wished were true. I even went shopping for a new bed because mine was too big and too empty and I couldn't sleep. But mattress salesmen aren't very sympathetic to guys who almost lose it in their showroom. Good to know.

I couldn't even *look* at my bathtub because all I saw was her smile, and all I thought about was how happy that stupid fucking porcelain bowl made her.

So I let myself suffer, knowing how much I'd let her down. I don't know if it was ironic or poetic, but as bad as that hit was, as much as I hated myself for it, that wasn't even the worst thing I'd done. The one before this was the thing that set everything in motion. Biggest fuck-up ever. What I'd been able to deny until now.

I let her love me. I *wanted* her to love me, and I hadn't

done enough to make her see what was going to happen. Because I was a selfish prick and didn't want to stop seeing that look in her eyes or feeling her intensity. I didn't want to give up knowing she'd be there whenever I needed her. So I kept telling myself she could handle it. I even convinced myself it was a good test for her—a new skill pushed to its limit.

What a fucking idiot.

Even though there wasn't enough money in the world to make up for all the bad I'd done to the most beautiful person I'd ever met, maybe it could help her get one step closer to the life she should have.

I almost started crying when I saw her website—it looked phenomenal. Nothing like it did the last time I checked. It was nice to know she was keeping herself busy instead of just blundering around uselessly like I was. She really was better off without me. That's what I wanted, wasn't it?

Kudos to Eric on the pictures—they were crazy good and showed off Lane's talent and—

"Shit." I had to stop thinking about her. I took a deep breath before I picked up my phone so I didn't sound like a whiny four-year-old when the foundation's office manager answered.

I ignored the 'are you alright?' and 'why haven't you come in or answered your phone for the last week?' portion of the conversation and skipped straight to the favor.

I gave her Lane's website address. "Buy what you can, but don't negotiate. Give her whatever she's asking for each piece, and then add all of it to the fall auction catalogue." I set the budget at more than I guessed Lane made in a year, way more than she'd gotten for her lily pad tables, but she was still undercharging. She deserved the money, and the exposure from the auction might put her art in front of the right person. And the foundation would probably raise more than I paid from people who had too much money and better-than-average taste. Win-win for everyone. Almost everyone.

A few days later, some friends who didn't understand anything—or maybe they just didn't think I was capable of so much sap—dragged me to Vegas. We ended up at a club it was hard *not* to get laid in. Tonight, I saw at least three women who, if I was sane, I would have taken home. Three chances to forget about Lane for a little while.

Fuck, what was stopping me? I'd never felt more lonely in my entire life. Since I was really good at not letting anyone get too comfortable, I never thought I *could* be lonely. She'd ruined me, made me want things I shouldn't want. Made me need things I couldn't have. And now I was a fucking mess.

None of these women would do that to me. I'd make one of them feel good and she'd make me feel good and then a couple hours later, we'd both walk away. Simple, straightforward, easy.

The brunette had a great body, a short skirt, and moved in a way appreciated by every guy in the place. A few months ago, I'd have been on that before she'd checked me out once, let alone the four times she had.

Why was I even hesitating? I didn't owe Lane anything, didn't love her or even plan to see her ever again. So what was my fucking problem? If this brunette took me to her place, there would be no memories there. For a little while I could pretend I was my old self. I considered it. I considered it while I had three more drinks than I'd planned on having.

Then I stopped thinking. Well, I stopped thinking *clearly*. And I started thinking with my dick, the way I used to. Before all the danger started, before Lane showed up and everything got turned upside-down. I was kind of happy back then. Well, I wasn't miserable.

My brain woke up when we stepped onto the sidewalk outside the club. Something about fresh air, I guess.

"Wait a sec." The woman wasn't Lane. Why was I with someone else? I didn't want to be with someone else. Not tonight, not tomorrow, not next year. This woman whose name I didn't remember might have been really fun, but I didn't care. I'd already felt more for someone, had already been with the most amazing woman in the world, and everyone else would be a step down.

However good the sex was, it wouldn't measure up, and I would never be able to sleep with anyone else in my bed. So I apologized, took her back into the bar, and bought her a drink. When she was set, I said goodbye and took a cab to the hotel. Alone.

Just to punish myself, I got into the bathtub, closed my eyes, and deliberately remembered her. I would start to forget soon—I was really good at forgetting and denying and pretending. Everything other than feeling and loving and believing I'd ever find anything as great as what I'd almost had.

CHAPTER 41 - LANEY

If my life wasn't complete shit, it would have been perfect. A few months ago, I would've thought it was. I'd gotten calls from five different people who'd seen or heard about my work. Then, the owner of the Third Street Gallery wanted to meet me and see my portfolio. No promises, just a meeting in two weeks from now, but...

"Oh my god! He wants to meet me!"

Once my parents heard the dollar amounts—ones I never would've had the balls to ask for if it wasn't for Carson—and explained to them what a gallery showing could do for me, they realized that my "hobby" was actually turning into something. That their daughter was an artist. I cried when I heard the pride in my mom's voice when she said it.

Then again, I cried about pretty much everything these days. Ironic because I had everything I wanted. Except for the person I wished I didn't want.

Other than to finish the lily pad tables and meet a few new clients, I hadn't left the house. Even though I had repair work to finish, I didn't do anything but sit on the couch and eat take-out. I hadn't cleaned up the mess the fight had caused, just the thought of it made me tear up like an idiot. But it wasn't because of the mess or the violence. I didn't want a reminder that I wouldn't be seeing Carson anymore. He wouldn't be coming for his Getting Handy lessons, or to talk, or to sneak up behind me and start taking off my clothes while I was trying to concentrate.

Moving on.

"Laney?" Hillary called from the kitchen. She'd been awesome. I'd had to tell her about Kevin after she saw what he'd done to my face, but I didn't say much about Carson. Since I wasn't with him anymore and I was a total wreck, she must have known something was going on, but the title of "Man Hillary Most Wished Dead" went to Kevin now.

I didn't waste any time thinking about Kevin because I was too busy obsessing about the other crappy things that had happened. All of this was my doing—not the Kevin parts, those were all him—but the broken heart thing was all me. Carson had never lied or cheated or done anything wrong. He'd never wanted me to be someone I wasn't—*I* had. I'd wanted him to be someone who could love me. And saying, 'Oops, my bad,' didn't cut it.

"Didn't you hear the knock, Laney?" Oh, that's why she looked so freaked out. I didn't answer the door anymore, just in case it was Kevin. I couldn't file a restraining order because then I'd have to explain why I needed one. I didn't look up until I heard her open the door and mumble to someone. Then she came into the living room with...

Carson. I stopped breathing, afraid to move because I knew I'd do or say something stupid and he'd bolt again.

When Hillary stepped out of the way and I could see all of him, my mind couldn't bend around the idea that Carson had cut his hair, put on a business suit, and somehow got the incredibly frustrating and gorgeous smirk off his face.

"I'm Hayden Bennett. You know my brother."

"Oh shit." What a moron. I'd spent enough time looking at Carson to know better. "Of course you are. Sorry." I blamed it on the fact that I hadn't eaten a vegetable in over a week. I wiped my hands off and shook his. "I'm Laney. Is Carson okay?"

"From what I know, he's..." He looked around for a place to sit, difficult because I'd practically moved into the room—mine didn't have a TV in it. I shoved some crap out of the way so he could have a chair. "Vegas is an easy place to be for someone who doesn't want to be found. He switched hotels, so no one's seen him for a few days." He must have seen my look of panic. "But I hired someone to find him, and I'm told he's fine. Carson does what Carson wants to do, but he's not stupid. He did something like this after our father died. He ran away and then two days later he was back, acting as if it had only been two hours."

"Sounds super healthy."

Hayden smiled sadly. "I'm sure he's told you enough to know we've never had a particularly healthy family." We talked for a few minutes, which was something I was pretty proud of because not *once* did I ask him if Carson had told him about us. Hurray for me.

But I wasn't actually sure why Hayden came here. To shoot the shit with someone who was no longer an issue? "Is there something you need me to do?"

"In a way." He relaxed slightly, now that I'd let him out of small talk about how screwed up his family was. "A man—your ex-boyfriend, I believe—approached me."

Oh shit. "I'm so sorry. We broke up a long time ago, back when he wasn't crazy. Believe me, it was an unpleasant surprise for everyone when he showed up." I rambled for a bit longer, until I had to stop and catch my breath. That was when I realized he didn't care about all that stuff. He cared about his little brother.

"Did Kevin ask you for money?"

"Ask? No, there was no asking involved, but I wouldn't have expected there to be any. He did bring up a past incident involving Carson, though, something we all thought was done."

"Kevin mentioned it to me, too." I just didn't think he had the balls or lack of intelligence to use it.

"That's why you didn't go to the police?"

"I love your brother, so I don't want him to get—" Both of us stopped. "I shouldn't have said that. It was a poor word choice. I just meant I care a lot about him." If I hadn't seen Carson's 'you actually expect me to believe that' face about a billion times, I wouldn't have recognized Hayden's.

"The bar fight was over a woman," he said.

"Oh. I didn't know that." I smiled to cover a grimace. I didn't want to think about Carson and I *really* didn't want to think about him with someone else. "Well, Carson has questionable taste in women."

He looked at me oddly. "I highly doubt that, but it's not what I meant. The fight happened in the parking lot outside the club. Evidently the man was angry that his girlfriend was flirting with my brother, so he dragged her outside. Carson followed and when he saw the man hit her… Well, you can guess what he did then."

I blinked. Carson stopped her from being beaten. With maybe more violence than necessary, but it didn't mean he was unpredictable or dangerous to anyone other than someone who deserved it.

"I don't think that's how he remembers it," I said.

"I doubt he remembers it at all. I only know because I heard the story from multiple sources, am a fairly good judge of character, and I know my brother. He wouldn't have done it for any other reason."

"He needs to know what really happened. You need to tell him that he did the same thing for that other woman as he did for me. He saved her."

Hayden didn't ask me what happened, like that would be invading my privacy. Much appreciated. Although it wasn't privacy I was holding onto, it was my sanity. If I really started talking about it to someone who had the same jerk of a father Carson had, I'd lose it.

"I should go," he said after a quick glance to his watch. "My plane leaves in an hour." Then he answered the question I didn't ask. "Vegas. Only to pick him up, though—I'm not a gambler." He stood and handed me his card. "It was a pleasure, Laney. I hope things work out for you, and I hope my brother realizes what an idiot he is."

Since I wasn't sure what to say to that, I didn't say anything. As soon as I closed the door, I regretted not asking if there was anything I could do to help. Other than not talking to anyone but him or Carson's lawyer. I went back to the couch, flicking Hayden's card onto the table. I wasn't going to call. I was moving on with my life. Plus, I was chicken-shit.

When the order came in, I thought it was a scam—who would buy everything on my website for full price? I ignored it until the online payment company verified and transferred funds. Then I asked a friend of a friend of a friend who was good with computers to check it out for me, because it couldn't be true. A gallery owner wouldn't buy them and, not that I'd knock anyone who liked my work that much, but is someone bought it all for their house, the place would look a little cluttered.

I admit to sweaty palms and a thumping heart when the computer genius called. Hillary stood right next to me, as if we were waiting for news we'd won the lottery. Which this would qualify as, if it was true. Drum roll please...

"It's legit," Andi said.

"How is that even possible?"

"How's *what* even possible?" Hillary asked, tugging at my phone.

"I could tell you what I did," she said, "and where I looked, but—"

"Yeah, that would be completely useless." I put the phone on speaker so Hillary would stop glaring and pantomiming. "My brain doesn't work like that."

"And mine doesn't work like yours. I can't even doodle."

"Can you repeat what you just told me before my roommate has a seizure?"

"Um...okay," Andi said slowly. "The sale is legit."

Hillary screamed, and I laughed. Oh my god! This was even bigger than the lily pad project. I needed to call Carson. He'd be just as happy as—

Right. I couldn't do that anymore. My excitement took a tumble. It took another when Hillary's expression suddenly looked nervous and what Andi was saying registered in my mind.

"The pictures are already up on the Bennett Foundation's auction page. Just two, though, probably as a teaser since the auction is so far..." She kept talking but I'd heard enough.

The Bennett Foundation. "That bastard." Was it his way of apologizing or his way of taking pity on me? I didn't want either. I wanted him in front of me, looking me in the eyes and talking to me without the bullshit qualifications or denials.

"What?" Andi asked.

"Her old...friend works there," Hilary said, reaching for the phone as if I was going to chuck it against the wall and— Well, would you look at that: my arm was raised and prepped to throw.

Big breath. Relax muscles. Promise Andi a favor whenever she needs it, thank her profusely, and hang up.

Hillary took the phone out of my hand. "It doesn't matter who bought them, Laney. You should be just as happy as you were a minute ago."

I couldn't be. "How could he think that buying my stuff makes everything okay? Or that I even want his money?"

"You do want his money. At least, you *should* want his money. Because that's a big number." Yeah, it was a huge amount, more than I thought my bank account could hold, but it was guilt money.

"I'm not going to take it. He's paying me off like he paid off his mom and stepsister. So he doesn't have to speak to them." As if money could replace him.

"Maybe." Hillary flopped down onto my bed. "Or...he's buying your work because he knows how much you're worth and this is the only way he can tell you he cares about you."

I spun my chair around. "By writing a check?" I didn't mean to shout at her, but it came out sounding angry and bitter. Hillary didn't seem put off at all.

"He might be screwed up about relationships, but he's not an idiot. If he can't be with you—for whatever reason, true or not—but he loves you—"

"He doesn't love me."

She paused for a quick eye roll. "Right. Okay, so if he can't be with you but he has a lot of something you don't—money—and if he gives it to you—someone he *likes* a lot—and it'll improve your life, how does that make him insensitive?"

"That's the point. He *isn't* insensitive." I didn't have a legitimate reason to be mad at him, and that made it even worse. "He's amazing but refuses to see it. Like the only things he has that anyone wants are his wallet and his ass."

"I don't remember what his wallet looks like, but I remember his ass. And it's pretty damn nice, so it's not hard to see how he might get that impression."

"Hillary!" I shouted as my friend busted up laughing. She was the last person I'd expect to take Carson's side.

"Am I telling you something you don't know? After all that time you guys spent in bed? I was with him once and hated him for months, but that beautiful image is branded on my eyelids." Her expression changed, and she came over to me and hugged me. Only then did I realize I was crying again. Again? "Oh, honey. I didn't mean anything by it. I was just trying to make a joke."

"It's not that." I wiped my face. "I wish I could *do* something for him. He keeps giving me things like the money and the lily pad gig."

"You got that job because you're talented. Carson just

pointed someone in your direction."

"Maybe, but I'm happier than I've ever been."

"Yeah, looks like it," she said, handing me a tissue.

"Shut up. I mean I like knowing what I want and not being afraid of admitting it. *He* did that. He helped me understand myself. He saved me."

I tried not to think about what might have happened if Carson hadn't shown up at my shop that day. I never would have imagined Kevin was capable of what he did, so how could I possibly know where he would've stopped?

"I've never done anything for him," I said. "I take that back—I've made his life worse. He liked his life before I came along, and now…"

"Look, I have my issues with him, but he was right about you—you've changed. When you broke up with Kevin and started hating men, that wasn't a healthy change. When you met Carson, you changed again, but in a good way, like you transformed into who you were meant to be."

"Great, so I screwed his life up while he made mine better."

"Knock it off, Laney. If *I* can get over my issues with him, you need to get over yours. You didn't screw up his life. How can loving him possibly screw up his life? He's not married, he's just confused."

"He won't ever let anyone love him."

"Can anyone control who loves them and who doesn't?" Hillary asked matter-of-factly. "We can barely control our own emotions, let alone someone else's. If you need proof of that, just think of how many boxes of tissues and pints of ice cream you've gone through."

After staring at my bank balance on the computer screen for another half an hour, I changed my mind. I would take it, all of it. Even if I paid my rent for the rest of the year and bought a shitload of new tools, I'd still have more than enough to do the other thing I needed to do. With the person I needed to do it with.

CHAPTER 42 - CARSON

"Guess why the little sign says 'Do Not Disturb!'" I yelled at the door Hayden had been pounding on for, like, ten minutes. "I'll give you one shot at it."

"I'd prefer not to talk about this in the hallway. If you don't open the door in the next thirty seconds, I have to assume you've drowned in the hot tub and get the hotel's manager to open it up."

"He's already been warned to stay away." And paid. We were moving onto Day I'm-Not-Sure of not answering the door or the phone, so you'd think people would get the hint. My friends had all gone home days ago. They had things and people to go back for.

"Carson! Stop being such a baby and open the goddamn door. Things are getting serious, and you need to do something about it."

About what? I climbed out of bed to find out what the fuck had happened while I'd been in isolation. That's when I noticed the legal-sized envelopes that had been slipped under my door, despite all the money I'd paid the staff to keep people away from me. So the paperwork, plus Hayden taking time out of his workday to fly to Vegas, meant... Hell if I knew.

I flicked the deadbolt and cracked the door open on my way down to grab them, scooting back just in time to avoid getting smacked in the head as Hayden burst in.

"You have no idea what's going on, do you?" He didn't give me a chance to answer, probably understanding from my expression how clueless I was. Or maybe it was because I looked like someone who hadn't gotten out of bed in the last…

"What day is it?" I asked, scratching my unshaven jaw.

"You're in deep shit, little brother." He pushed me backwards and shut the door behind him.

"What'd I do?"

"Well, if I believe Laney's ex-boyfriend, i.e. the person most likely to have answered my phone calls, you attacked him for no reason."

Shit. That shook me out of the fog. "That's what the bastard said happened?" I regretted that day more than any other, but not because of what I did to Kevin. "He deserved everything he got. He should be happy he could still walk away."

"And that kind of comment won't help your case. He's threatening to go to the police and tell them that he almost *didn't* walk away."

"So? Lane already talked to them."

"She didn't go to the police."

"What?" I straightened. "Why the fuck not?"

"Because if she had, they would've questioned Kevin, and he would've told the police what he told everyone who wasn't holed up in a hotel room drinking their meals. Kevin O'Leary is doing his medical residency at UCSF. He was the physician who worked on the man from the bar fight."

"That guy signed a nondisclosure agreement."

Hayden nodded. "That didn't cover everything he'd already told the physician who worked on him before he signed it. When *said* physician got his ass handed to him by the same goddamn idiot his ex-patient did, he knew exactly where to hit to cause the most damage."

My lungs stayed on 'empty.' "Lane?"

"No." Hayden pantomimed smacking me on the back of the head. "Your pockets. *Our* name." Hayden gave as much a shit about our family's honor as I did, so I knew he was talking about the foundation. Exactly the same reason I'd agreed to pay the other guy off—so my screw-up wouldn't hurt other people. Shit. Not one but *two* victims of my anger issues would flush donations down the toilet. Probably get me arrested, too.

"The guy in the bar, yeah, that was on me. But Kevin..." I slumped onto the couch. "He was hurting her, Hay. I couldn't let him hurt her."

He sat down next to me and blew out a breath. "He wants money. Lots of money. But unless you've given it all to Renee or spent it all on cards, booze, and expensive hookers, you can afford it. He also wants an apology with all the sincerity you can fake. You give him what he wants, he signs some paperwork, and we all move on."

"I write a check, so I don't have to deal with it anymore." Just like I did with Renee and Anna. What I'd done with Lane. So I could pretend I was doing the right thing. Then I'd apologize to someone who deserved as much punishment as I did.

Fuck that. I stood. "No."

"Carson, think about it. Even if O'Leary doesn't go to the police, he'll still tell the media, skew what happened into something that works in his favor. And he has just enough facts to make it look true. No one roots for the rich kid, little brother. If he talks, things will only get worse for everyone—Laney included."

"I don't care about the money. If he doesn't talk, he can have however much he wants." Because his lies would hurt good families who were hurting too much as it was.

"I have to do something about my shit, Hayden. I can't

keep telling myself it's not affecting anyone." How long had I been pretending the first eighteen years of my life didn't exist? "I'll need some help with the board, though."

He raised an eyebrow. "You've got it. What about the apology?"

"Yeah, the bastard will get a fucking apology I don't mean and he doesn't deserve. But on one condition." I thought about it. "Make that two conditions: You wake Anna up to tell her about an emergency meeting of the board."

"Really, Carson? You know what I do for a living and approximately how much money I get for doing it. And you want me to make a wake-up call?"

"You never lived with her, so you've never had to deal with her in the morning. Trust me, it'll be one of the most unpleasant things you've ever had to do. And I'm not even going to ask you to break it to her that she's finally getting a real job. Because I love you too much to put you through that."

I didn't trust my wicked stepsister to be responsible for anything hugely important. But she was beautiful, smart, and manipulative—all things appreciated by wealthy men from every nation on earth. She might as well start using her powers for good.

"Oh, and make sure she understands that she doesn't have to be there in person, so she shouldn't worry too much about her hair." Expecting her to show up would be stupid, even if I *wanted* to ever see her again. Plus, not all the board members were local, so we'd have to set up the teleconference anyway.

"Is the second condition as terrifying?" Hayden grumbled.

"No. The second condition is simple: Kevin signs an agreement that says he'll stay the fuck away from Lane for the rest of his life." Just like I had to.

CHAPTER 43 - LANEY

It wasn't hard to track Renee down. The wealthy can afford more security, but privacy can't be bought. The next day I was on a plane to Los Angeles with an address and a whole lot of anxiety. There was a chance the address could be wrong, or she might have gone to Vegas, opted for the complete Elvis wedding package, and was already living with her new husband. But Renee didn't seem the type to do anything that normal.

I pulled the rental car up to the security gate and told the guard who I was here to see. If Renee refused to see me, I'd move on to Plan B. Hopefully it wouldn't come to that, because my Plan B sucked and involved acting skills I didn't have. After the guard made a call, presumably to Renee, he opened the gate and waved me through.

Renee's house was bigger than the entire neighborhood I grew up in—manicured lawn, no chips in the sidewalk. Even the house number painted on the curb out front was flawless.

My confidence turned into nausea until I reminded myself that I had absolutely nothing to lose. I'd already lost him. And, even if everything went perfectly, I didn't expect that to change. I just hoped *he* would.

Carson would never open himself back up to me—that was something I'd have to live with—but maybe he could to the woman who gave birth to him, who'd been there while the damage was being done.

The door opened before I even knocked.

"Is Carson alright?" Renee asked, looking as if she'd hike up to San Francisco in heels if she had to. That gave me hope—the woman wanted what was best for her son, she probably just didn't know what that was.

"Yeah, he's fine," I said quickly. "I mean, I think so. Mostly. Have you spoken to Hayden lately?"

"Neither of my boys tell me much of anything. The little I know about Carson's predicament is due to the tirade of phone calls from lawyers asking if I know where he is."

"I don't know much more than you, then. The last time I saw him he was healthy...physically"—I dropped the volume of my voice—"but otherwise he was kind of a mess."

"Come in."

I kept things simple but honest—about my relationship with Carson, how it had started and how it had ended. Renee was silent throughout the entire explanation, sipping her tea whenever it seemed like she wanted to stop herself from saying something.

Finally, I gave up. "You need to fix things with him because he won't listen to me."

When Renee put her teacup and saucer on the table, I understood why she hadn't let go of it since we'd started speaking. Her hands were shaking. "I don't know if it would be any different for me. You saw how he feels about me, how angry he was when I announced my engagement."

"He wouldn't have gotten that angry if he didn't care about you."

"I was the cause of a lot of hardship when Carson was younger. I don't know what I could ever do to make up for that time in his life."

"You don't have to make up any time. Regardless of

whatever happened between you and your late husband or any other man, you're the only chance Carson has to start over. He needs to start over, Renee."

"I've spent the last seven years trying to find a way to help him do that. I'm still looking."

Obviously she hadn't looked in a mirror. She couldn't change him, just like she couldn't change any of her exes. Just like I didn't change any of mine into frogs. Just like they hadn't changed me. I changed myself, once I finally understood who I was.

Renee smoothed her skirt, and I saw her bare finger—the huge engagement rock was gone. When she caught me gawking, she looked at her hand.

"You noticed," she said.

"It's hard not to—your finger was really shiny last time we met." I felt myself tense. I didn't come here to talk about jewelry.

"Yes, it was." Renee's smile was tight as she moved to pick up her teacup. Then she stopped and put her hands in her lap, her right covering her left. "I actually forget it's not there from time to time."

My impatience disappeared, replaced with blatant curiosity. Carson said Renee hated being alone. So what had happened?

"Why aren't you getting married?" I asked.

"That's none of your business."

"Normally I'd completely agree with you." Deep breath. "But normally I'm not in love with someone who will never be able to love me back. Because he's afraid that if he does, he'll turn into the kind of man his father was. The kind of man his stepfathers were. Men *you* chose to bring into your son's life."

My curiosity turned into angry frustration. "I'm not here to blame you or make you feel guilty, or even to bring you and Carson closer together. I'm here to tell you that you're the only one who can help your son understand that he's not like any of the men you chose. Honestly, I don't give a shit about your personal life. All I care about is how it affects Carson. Because whether he wants it or not, Carson is my business, and therefore, why you're not getting married to another reminder of his father is also my business."

I expected Renee to respond with an equal amount of anger or intensity, but she seemed to have sunk into herself, become smaller, less of a presence. Maybe this was the real Renee— the one not hiding behind image and position, the one who'd taken the abuse as if she'd earned it.

"Men can be charismatic." She started removing her rings one by one, placing them onto the coffee table. "They can tell you it will never happen again, and how sorry they are, in a way that makes it impossible to doubt."

My mind flashed to a moment with Carson, when he told me he didn't believe in apologies. This was why—because he'd seen how little they often meant.

"Every argument has two sides." She reached into the drawer next to her and took out a small bottle of expensive hand lotion. "So it's easy to believe you're as much at fault as he is. Maybe *entirely* at fault, because you pushed him too hard or because he feels so much passion towards you that it makes him unable to think. You want to believe it's true. You want to believe that he loves you so much, he has to fight to control himself. Because those things make you feel desired and loved. They make you feel powerful, even when you know it will only last a moment."

I grabbed a box of tissues from a side table and dropped them onto the coffee table between us, but I didn't think Renee would need one. The calm and tragic way she talked about something horrible was something I'd never seen before. Grief and vulnerability held in check by acceptance.

"Do you know how many people I've spoken to openly about this, Laney? None. Ever. Not even Carson. But I love him, and I believe you love him, as well. So you asked why I'm not getting married." She took a deep breath. "Because until that day in the restaurant, Carson and I had never spoken about his father or the other men. So I'd been able to convince myself that the only person I'd hurt was myself and that my son had no right to be angry at me. Not after I'd gone through so much to make sure he'd have the future he deserved.

"After you both left, I went back to the table and picked up my champagne for another toast. For the first time in my life, it was too difficult for me to pretend. I couldn't stop seeing the fear in his eyes, the disappointment in his voice. To know I disappointed my child, hurt him, was worse than anything his father could have ever done to me."

She covered her mouth with her hand for a minute. "I took the first flight back here. When I told my fiancé what Carson had said and how hurt I was, he agreed that I had every right to be upset. Then I told him I couldn't marry him if things continued as they were. Instead of agreeing, he slapped me. And then he struck me again and I realized it didn't matter what I said or did—he wanted to hurt me, and so he did. And until that moment, I had let him. Just like I had let my first husband hurt my children."

She looked down to her finger again and then opened and closed her hand. "The ring my fiancé had given me was too heavy for me to carry anymore, so I gave it back to him."

I nodded. "With a little time and rest, I'm sure your hand will be stronger than ever."

"I hope so." I knew Renee had used up all her energy telling her story. To help me understand. I'm not sure how well it worked, though. I wasn't her, I wasn't there, and I was seriously biased when it came to her son. But I wasn't the one she needed to convince.

"If you never tell him, he'll never know," I said. "He'll never understand."

"Carson has every right to hate me. I put him through so much, some of the worst things a man can ever do." She lowered her eyes and took another breath. "If I knew how to take it all back, I would. But it's too late. He doesn't trust me, and rightfully so, because I've given him so many reasons not to. He would never listen to me."

"You stood in front of the man who beat you and told him the truth, so you can stand in front of your son and tell him the truth, too. Because Carson would never hurt you, and he still wants to love you because he's amazing and kind and special and in an incredible amount of pain."

It took her a while to nod. "I'm glad he has you in his life, Laney."

"I'm not—" I wasn't in his life anymore. "You can't tell him it was my idea. Honestly, none of this has ever really been any of my business."

"Why not?"

"It's not what either of us wanted. Things just got a little confused for a while." Actually *I'd* gotten confused and had dragged him into something he never wanted.

"Then you should unconfuse them as soon as possible, don't you think?"

"Some things are the way they are for a reason." I shrugged. "It's better for both of us to move on."

Renee looked at me silently for another moment before she stood. "I suppose I should pack a bag, then. You're welcome to stay until you need to go to the airport."

"Thanks, but I don't get down here very often. I'm probably going to visit some old friends." It was a lie, but a harmless one. I didn't want to hang out with her, and she probably didn't want to hang out with me.

She walked me to the door. "When are you going back to San Francisco?"

I didn't answer. Instead, I wished her good luck.

"Any advice?" she asked.

"Um... Don't give up even if he's being stupid. He'll try to change the subject when something hits too close, but don't let him. And tell him—" I held up my hand. "Bye."

I left the housing community as fast as I could and pulled into the first parking lot I came to. Breathe. Just breathe. What

I'd done was a good thing. I should be happy. It didn't matter that Carson would be mad at me for butting into his life because he could be sure it would never happen again.

After a while I'd be back to my old self, kind of. Maybe I'd be better. Probably not, but I couldn't *possibly* keep crying this much, so that was something.

I'd never be the person I used to be—pre or post frogs. Because real love isn't as easy to get over as the pretend kind. Especially when you can't be angry or blame the other person. Somehow, knowing it didn't work out because some things never would was worse than being cheated on or lied to.

I couldn't blame Carson—he'd never promised me anything more than a good time. And he'd given me a *ton* of them. It was my own fault that I'd made it into something he hadn't wanted and wasn't capable of. He'd warned me. Repeatedly.

He helped me figure out what I wanted. It wasn't his fault that what I wanted was *him*.

I spent the rest of the day driving around the city, trying to get a feel for where I'd want to live. That was a perk of my business and my art that I'd never thought about—I could do it from anywhere. It would do me good to shake things up. Hillary was probably going to move in with Eric soon, I could still show at the gallery even if I wasn't in the city, and if I lived closer to San Diego, my parents would be thrilled. Career-wise, Los Angeles might actually be better for me. I could start over, make some new memories—less painful ones.

My plane ticket back to S.F. was for Monday, so I had all weekend to explore and figure out what was next for me. No men, that was for damn sure. The last thing I needed was a reminder that my useless little brain couldn't separate sex from love. Huge fail on that one, despite Carson's heroic efforts.

"Oh my god." When reality hit me, it came from multiple directions.

I'd always been so sure the physical and the emotional came as a package—sex and the delusion of love. But everything I'd believed was total bullshit. Everything.

I *could* have sex without love. I'd *always* had sex without love. Because until now, I'd never actually been in love.

And the man who'd done his best to convince me I could separate one from the other was the only one who'd ever helped me put them together.

CHAPTER 44 – CARSON

"Hold the door for me, Carson." Anna brushed past me, flicking her hair over her shoulder. She probably didn't mean to smack me with it, but Anna has always been capable of far more than she thinks she is.

"I'm pretty sure I paid for your cell phone through this month. So why are you here?"

"Because I was told to come by your smarter and hotter older brother," she grumbled.

"I'm way hotter than he is." I'd give him smarter though. Well, *normally* I'd give him smarter, but not right now. Because I distinctly remembered telling him Anna didn't need to be here for this. I didn't want drama. I wanted this to be as pain-free as possible, and pain-free was an impossibility around both Anna and my mother, in a bunch of different ways.

Hayden peeked out of the conference room. "The only two who don't have somewhere else to be are the two holding everyone up. Do you mind?"

Right, but I couldn't help mouthing off as I headed for the room. "Not true, Hayden. Anna's probably supposed to be getting a facial or hair thing done right now. Or was it a facial hair thing? I always forget."

I let Anna go in first—not because I was feeling polite, but because before I could move my feet, I had to remove my brother's hand from my shirt.

"Is there a problem?" I asked quietly.

The board members were all standing, showing the kind of chivalry my stepsister only expected from men she barely knew.

"You don't have to do this," Hayden said. "We can handle O'Leary, and nothing has to change."

"*I* have to change, bro. Me. I can't pull anyone else down while I'm trying to figure out how." I shook his hand off. "Wish me luck."

"It's a bad idea, Carson."

"Then you shouldn't be surprised I had it. Bad ideas are the only kind I have." Damn it, my laugh sounded sadder than if I was actually crying.

"What are you going to do after this? You think you're unnecessary and that people only need your money, but you're wrong. You get as much from this place as the families do."

"You're right," I whispered as I went inside the room. "That's why I can't fuck it up." The truth—and something I tried not to think too much about because it was depressing as shit—was that I was never gonna have a normal family and I was never gonna have kids of my own. And this place, the families it helped, well...they were as close as I was ever going to get.

"Wow," I said to the crowd. "You're all pretty intimidating for a bunch of rich white guys and my stepsister." Anna seemed preoccupied with her phone. A few of the others grinned, but not for long. They didn't know why I'd gotten everyone together, but they knew it wouldn't be good news.

Before I could inflate my balls enough to say what I needed to say, Hayden started talking.

"We all know my brother's proclivity towards screwing up, but what he is too stupid to understand is that he isn't the only one. Nor does he understand that his current situation isn't *his* screw-up."

"How about you let the rest of us know what's going on?" Scott asked.

"Yeah," I said. "How about you let *me* know what's going on, too? But give me a second—I'm still trying to figure out if that was a compliment or an insult."

"A bit of both, but I'd say it definitely leaned more towards an insult," Hayden said before addressing the people he was nice to. "All Kevin O'Leary wants is Carson's apology and a check. Unfortunately—"

"Wait! Who are we talking about?" Anna asked, finally raising her head and feigning interest. Hayden sighed and quickly filled her in on what had happened while she'd been playing tackle football with an asshole, or whatever she did with her time nowadays.

He talked and she listened without moving, not even her eyes.

And fuck if I didn't start thinking Hayden had slipped something in my coffee, because suddenly I couldn't breathe. It had been years since I'd seen that look on Anna's face, not since her dad left Renee, and I'd watched him drag Anna off like a suitcase, knowing what she was in for now that all her dad's attention would be on her.

Neither one of us had said anything back then. Neither one of us said anything now.

When Hayden finally finished, Anna scooted back in her chair.

Even though she spoke quietly and everyone else was practically yelling, her voice was the only one I heard. Because it was the most sincere I'd ever heard it. "So now you're going to leave?"

I shook my head. "Not leave, step down, so I can't—"

"Help those people. You can't leave, Carson. They need you. *I* need you." She bit her lip, tears welling in her eyes, completely ignoring everyone around us. "I am sorry."

Three words that could mean everything or nothing, depending on what was behind them. This time, they meant a shitload. Because I finally believed them.

"For so many things," she said. The others stopped speaking. "She's really talented, you know... Laney, I mean. I told some of my friends and they all want something by her now. And I asked Third Street Gallery's owner to take a look at her stuff. I can't make him take her on, but after what I did to you...to her, I thought—"

"Thanks. She deserves a shot at something great."

She nodded. "So do you."

"I had my shot at something *more* than great, and I blew it, multiple times. All I want to do now is keep everybody away from the wreckage."

"What does her ex want?" she asked.

Hayden explained again, irritatedly, because he was repeating everything he'd said a few minutes ago when she hadn't been listening. Until he got to Kevin's threat.

"He what?" she snapped.

Hayden sighed. "He'll claim that Carson attacked him and Laney out of jealousy, if Carson doesn't—"

She waved him off. Not a lot of people get away with waving Hayden Bennett off.

"The rest doesn't matter," she said, shaking her head. I'd never seen her look so intent, so infuriated. "Nuh-uh. He doesn't get paid for hurting Laney and then threatening to lie about it. We're talking about Carson here. He would never hurt her. He would never hurt anyone. So that guy can go screw himself if he thinks any member of our fucked-up family is going to shut up and take it."

"We're not rewarding him," Hayden said. "We're protecting the foundation, Anna. In the long term—"

"Oh my god." She turned back to me. "Carson, you of all people... No, you can't do that. I won't let you."

There was nothing funny about what she was saying, nothing at all, but I laughed anyway. I don't know—stress, depression, relief that Anna might have finally woken up... It could've been a million different reasons.

She went on, asking questions about which hospital Kevin worked in, which department. Then she excused herself to go make a phone call. I followed her into the lobby.

"Hey," I called. "If you're going to do anything crazy or stupid, I want to know about it. As someone who's had a lot more experience than you have, I may have some pointers."

"Do you know what I'm good at?" She didn't let me respond, which was kind of her. Because I was still trying to think of an answer. "I can keep a secret. And a lot of people in this city have secrets, including one of the people in charge of UCSF's medical residency program. It's nothing terrible, but he definitely wouldn't want it to get out."

I shook my head. "The whole point of me doing this is so other people aren't involved and don't get hurt."

"I would never break his confidence," she said. "And I would never threaten him. He trusts me. So I'm sure he'd be happy to take me out for a drink and be agreeable to inviting Kevin along. Then, while enjoying an evening out with a friend, I will wink at the asshole who's trying to mess with my family and continually mention my amazing stepbrother and the charitable foundation he runs."

"But you're not planning to say anything that he could take as an outright threat?" Hayden asked, coming up behind me.

"Of course not." She rolled her eyes. "I'm a woman—our unspoken threats are ten times more intimidating than the spoken ones. You're married, Hayden, you should already know that." She turned and put her phone up to her ear.

"I think Kevin's going to regret screwing with our little stepsister, don't you, Hayden?"

"I think Kevin's going to regret a lot of things really soon."

"Good."

I should've been happy. Or at least not so fucking

depressing to be around. I'd expected the board to say, 'Great, then get the hell out,' when I told them I'd be taking a permanent sabbatical from the foundation. But I don't think I said more than four words.

My brother and my stepsister suddenly decided they cared about me, or some shit. I don't know. I wish I'd been at the meeting Anna set up with her secretive friend and Kevin, though. I would have shoved money into the prick's pockets myself if I could've seen his face when Anna winked at him. Who knew a frog would set off something in Anna, a good something, a healthy something, a non-retail-related something.

So I should have been happy. But I wasn't.

I laid in bed, staring at the ceiling. It wouldn't be as pathetic if I was actually thinking about something instead of trying really hard not to. If I thought about anything other than how many beers were in the fridge or what game I was going to watch this weekend, other shit came with it. I couldn't even look at the goddamn tile in the bathroom anymore. It was blue. Like her eyes. Like her toenails were painted one day when we took a bath together and—

"Damn it!"

In my entire life, I'd only cared about three women, and the one I was never going to see again was the one I couldn't stop thinking about and wanting and missing. I'd had her for months, right in front of me. She wanted me, and I chickened out because I couldn't let the other stuff go.

I ignored the knock on the door the first time. And the second. When the third one came, I gave up and went to tell whoever it was to go to hell.

"Hello, Carson." Both of Renee's hands clenched the strap of her purse as she held it in front of herself like an overpriced leather shield. I guess she'd left the arrogant posturing, the pretense of being one-hundred percent perfect every minute of every fucking day, in her other bag. There were no bruises that I could see. No ring on the special finger either—

engagement or wedding.

I stood there silently, not having spoken to anyone but myself since leaving the board meeting. The only person I wanted to talk to was living her life somewhere else, hopefully dealing better than I was.

"Can I come in?" Renee asked.

I didn't want to fight. It just wasn't in me anymore. So I nodded and stepped back. Renee had never been to my place, but I hoped she wasn't expecting a tour. She wandered, chatting nervously about the kitchen and the furniture.

"Not there!" I shouted before she put her bag on Lane's table. I couldn't get rid of it—not yet, maybe not ever—but I didn't want to see it, so I'd covered it with a sheet. Eventually I'd donate it somewhere it could be admired and not be a constant reminder of what a fuck-up I was. Eventually...but not now.

"I'll get my checkbook." I was already on my way. Just sign the bottom and leave the rest blank, then shove her out.

"I didn't come here for money, Carson." She sat on the edge of the couch, her hands resting in her lap. Her knuckles were white, something the people she conned wouldn't have noticed. Something I didn't want to see, because it meant that whatever she was here to say made her uncomfortable. And that made *me* uncomfortable.

"What do you want?"

"To apologize." She let out a breath, smoothed her skirt. "I need to apologize, because even if you never want anything to do with me again, I want you to be happy."

"Cool." Thumbs up for her. "Thanks for stopping by." I hadn't sat down, so it was a quick trip to the door, hinting she should leave.

She didn't move. "I could tell you I didn't know how much it affected you, and that each time we went back to him, I thought things would be different. And that would all be true...but it would also be an excuse."

Shit. Why now? Why was she doing this now? Was today

the twenty-year anniversary of my first smackdown? Or maybe seven years ago today, I gave up on her and got the fuck out of her latest husband's house.

Should I pretend I didn't know what she was talking about? Or would agreeing get her out of here faster? I had tile to replace.

"It's fine," I said. "Water under a bridge or whatever."

"Your father loved us, Carson. I gave him too many chances because I loved him just as much. He used to tell me he'd stop and we would be happy. He also used to tell me that I'd be nothing if I left him and that I wouldn't be able to feed you or give you a home. You and your brother would be less than you could be because I selfishly took the life we had away from you."

"I said it's fine, Renee." I didn't want to hear any more. She needed to go away before my headache got worse and all civility was gone. "And I meant it's fine."

"You couldn't be more different than him. Can you imagine him doing any of the good you have? When you gave away your entire inheritance, I was afraid you'd given away your chance at a good life, the life your father promised me you'd have."

"Good to know," was all I could manage, my tone flat, my need to be alone fucking enormous.

"I stopped trusting myself a long time ago, so I thought everything I did was wrong. But if I'd known what it was doing to you, what it's *still* doing to you…" Blinking, she sat up taller. "I've spent most of my life believing things that weren't true, that I deserved no more than I was given. And because of that, you've done the same—"

"Stop talking!" If my hands weren't squeezing the sides of my head, I swear it would've exploded. "I don't want this. I don't want you here. You have no idea what I feel or what I've done, so don't pretend. I can see through it, Renee. I've always been able to see through it."

She was quiet for a moment, watching her hands tighten

around each other before standing and picking up her purse. "I understand. Maybe another day. Whenever you're ready. I'm trying to change, Carson. I am. And in order to do that, I can't be dependent on other people." She took an envelope out of her purse and set it down on the coffee table. Her name and address in my handwriting on the outside, the checks I'd sent her inside. "It's not all of them. I intend to pay you back as soon as I can."

Huh. "That's why checks aren't used anymore—nobody knows how to balance a checkbook." Especially me. I'd thought they were all been cashed. *Assumed* they'd been, because it was the only thing I'd ever offered her, the only connection we had. "Keep them." I picked up the envelope and held it out. "If you're really going to change things, then think of it like a business investment. There are always start-up costs."

"I can't."

"It's my money. I get to decide who I spend it on."

She hesitated before taking the checks and putting them back into her purse. "Thank you."

I could tell she was trying, that she wasn't here to argue or spout more excuses about what she'd done. It was something—she hadn't cashed the checks, she'd tried to give them back, and she was here when she'd obviously rather be anywhere else. That was something...I guess.

"Laney came to Los Angeles to talk to me."

And *that* stopped any positive feelings that had shown up in the last few minutes. "Don't." I didn't want to know Lane was still thinking about me, caring about me. She was supposed to be moving on to someone better.

"She asked me not to tell you that, but I'm not going to lie to my sons anymore."

"I don't want to talk about her."

"She came because she knew how badly you were hurting."

"Don't," I said through clenched teeth. "Please."

"She loves you."

"Stop! Just stop!" I waited until the reverb of my yell had completely gone away. "I can't...do this right now. It's too much. I need to process it a little but maybe... Is your phone number the same?" Did I say that because I cared or because it might get her to leave?

She nodded quickly, encouraged by a few words spoken with a broken spirit. "I'm going to go see Anna."

"That's good." Maybe they could help each other. "She has more going on now, and she needs somebody."

"You do, too."

"I'm fine."

"Are you?"

I was silent for as long as I could manage, not wanting anyone to see how weak I was. Especially not her.

"Are you, Carson?"

"No."

She stepped forward slowly. "I want to help you. Tell me what I should do. Anything, please."

"Why didn't you send me away like you did with Hayden?" I stood there stunned that I'd actually said it. Why now? After all this time, I finally had the balls to ask her. I'd always been too afraid of her answer to say the words. Now I guess I didn't have anything left to lose. I couldn't feel any more than I was already feeling. "Why did you make sure he was safe, but not me?"

Her purse fell to the floor, tears welling in her eyes, her shoulders sagging. "Because I needed my baby boy with me. Your father would have killed Hayden. He almost did. But you were so beautiful and sweet, and you could make him laugh."

"When he wasn't beating the shit out of me. Didn't stop him from doing that, did it? Didn't stop the ones after him, either." I heard her inhale quickly, as if she was barely holding it together. Good. "But in all fairness, I wasn't so beautiful and sweet by then."

"Yes, you were." She lifted her head slowly. "You still are. I know how wrong it was, but back then I needed you to take care of me. Like you've always done for Anna and like you'd do for Laney if you let yourself get close enough. But she doesn't need you to protect her—she needs you to love her. And you need her to love you."

"I can't—"

"Please don't let your father be the reason you lose something else."

I didn't look at her or stop her from coming closer. Or from wrapping her arms around me while she cried. I didn't stop myself, either.

CHAPTER 45 - LANEY

I dumped cream and sugar in my coffee and headed straight for the door, stirring as I moved. Despite what I'd always believed, apparently you *can* get jetlag flying from L.A. to San Francisco. My brain was screwed up, but still able to cause excruciating pain around my temples. Although, it had felt like that even before I went to L.A.

My weekend of regrouping and coming up with a plan for the rest of my life had turned into a weekend of sitting in a hotel room and crying over commercials. Not even sappy commercials. Paper towels shouldn't make people cry, they just shouldn't.

Now that I was back in S.F. and had my coffee, I needed to start packing. My apartment would be easy, my shop much less so. At least I didn't have to worry about all the pieces the Bennett Foundation bought. I'd wrap them tomorrow, so they'd be ready to go for the delivery guys on Tuesday. With so many pieces going, I wanted to be there to make sure they were handled properly. But no way would I get within two-hundred feet of the foundation, not with the chance I'd see Carson again.

It would take me a week to get through all the refinishing

projects I'd already been paid for, and that was if I worked eighteen-hour days. Long days would actually work really well, though. If my focus was on anything other than what I was doing, I'd end up chiseling a finger off or leaving fingerprints in urethane and having to completely start over.

I saw Carson before he saw me, but only by a few seconds—enough time to start jogging for the other exit.

"Lane," he called loudly. "Wait up! A minute, thirty seconds, whatever I can get. Please!"

I stopped. A minute of my life wasn't too much to ask, was it? Plus, like an idiot, I wanted to talk to him. As hurtful as I knew it would be, I couldn't help wanting to see him again.

He looked tired, as if he'd been working too much. Or not sleeping enough. I didn't want to read into the shallowness of his breath or how wide open his eyes were or how his fingers tapped his thighs rapidly. It didn't mean anything. With Carson, there was no reading between the lines. Because Carson didn't have lines.

He had walls.

"Thanks for..." He stayed a few feet away, his hands in his pockets. "How are you?"

Really? How did he think I was? "Been better." This was a terrible idea.

"Can we talk somewhere for a couple minutes? No strings."

"You get me to agree to a minute and now you want a *couple*?" I joked. "Seems a little greedy, doesn't it?" But I'd give it to him. It was too hard not to.

You never walk away from someone just once. Sure, the big dramatic one is important, but it's all the little ones before and after that really matter. Walking out a door and slamming it behind you is easy. Getting someone out of your mind and your soul... That's the hard part.

Every time you avoid going somewhere, so you won't see him and every time you run away if you do. Every time you switch the song that's playing because it reminds you of him.

Every time you walk into a room and know exactly why everyone is staring. Every choice you make to keep yourself from thinking about him. *Those* are the things that wear you down.

"What do you want, Carson?"

"Not here. We can talk at my place."

"No." I couldn't even get a single word out without my voice faltering. "I don't think that's a good idea."

He wiped his hand over his mouth, rubbing the stubble on his cheek. "I want you to take your coffee table back. And get all the stuff out of your drawer."

God, I was pathetic. Did I really think he was going to suddenly say all the things I wanted him to, or even thank me and tell me how much our time together had changed him? Unfortunately, yes, that's what I'd been hoping. But nope, he just wanted to get my crap out of his life.

"I'll send someone—"

"I want it out *now*. Not tomorrow or three hours from now. This second, I want it gone."

"Fine," I snapped. I'd dump the table in the trash, because I didn't want it either. And the stuff in my—*his*—drawer? I didn't even remember what was in there. It had become so normal so fast, and it hadn't meant anything for him to give it to me. Not like now. Now I guess it meant a lot to him. Fine, he didn't want reminders of me around his place? Well, I didn't want him to be reminded of me. So I'd take my crap and throw it away somewhere, and he'd never have to see it again.

He walked a step behind me as I stomped to his place, taking the stairs because I wouldn't be able to handle standing in an elevator with him for thirty seconds. As soon as we were one flight up, I realized my mistake. This was where everything had started—and continued. I couldn't do this. Just before I turned around to tell him he should throw all my stuff out his fucking window if he wanted, I felt his hand on my waist.

"Don't touch me." My voice reflected the mess I was emotionally—weak, confused, scared as shit that this was going to make me hurt more or make the pain last longer. "You can't touch me."

His hand disappeared, but I still couldn't turn around. If I did he'd be right there, and I'd have to look into his eyes, and I just couldn't do that again. So I kept moving forward, away from him but towards his apartment, trapped on both sides by something I wanted but couldn't have.

I waited for him to unlock the door, standing back with my arms crossed. When I followed him in, I noticed he'd moved the coffee table and covered it with a sheet. It stung. He didn't even want to look at a part of me, and I was so easy to put out of his life. But mostly it was because all I could think about was him bringing some woman back here and not wanting anything around that reminded him of the last girl he fucked. The last one he—

"My mother came by," he said, stopping and blocking my way. Why couldn't he just let me do what I came here for and then let me leave? "She said some good stuff."

"That's nice," I mumbled when it seemed like he expected me to respond.

"I was thinking of going down to Southern Cal for a few days. Probably rent a car and go to San Diego after spending some time with her. We're trying to start over."

"That's great." It was what I wanted, why I'd gone to see Renee. Sadly, I didn't feel very successful right now.

"Your parents still live in San Diego, right? So you probably know all the best places to go." He finally let me step around him, but I didn't get far. "What would you say if I asked you to go with me?"

Was he serious? "I'd say no." Did he think that I could just forget how I felt and we'd go back to sleeping together? Take a trip to San Diego so we could fuck on the beach maybe? I practically ran to his dresser and pulled out my cosmetic's bag, a pair of underwear, a piece of paper that—

Oh my god, it was the list, the list of things I'd wanted to try, with him. I crumpled it in my hand and dropped it back in the drawer, on top of the black bag of toys. What was I supposed to do with those?

Fuck it. He could deal with them, because I sure as hell couldn't.

"Lane? I know you're still mad at me, and you have every right to be." Even across the room he was still too close, his voice was too soft and sad, and I didn't want to be here anymore because I was just getting more confused.

"I need to go." Stuff started falling out of my hands. I bent down to pick it all up, hiding my face. "Just...um...put the table in the trash or maybe call Goodwill or something. I think they'll—"

"I'm keeping the table. It was just an excuse to get you up here."

"Why would you do that?" I looked at him and stood, ignoring everything but him. "Fuck you, Carson! I'm not... I can't go backwards." I couldn't pretend I didn't feel the way I felt or miss him or want him. It was becoming hard to breathe without crying. "I have to go."

"You can't. I know you're mad at me, but give me a chance to talk to you."

Wanna see a grown man jump out of the way so fast he hurts himself? Five simple words will do it. As long as they're the right ones.

"I'm in love with you," I shouted at him, hating every word because I knew they were poison to him. "I'm in love with you. I didn't want it to happen, but it did. And not saying it out loud doesn't make it any less true." But it sure made it harder to look him in the eyes. "I can't be your friend any more, Carson. It's too hard, because I'm too screwed up.

"I'm not mad at you," I continued. "I've never been mad at you, because you didn't do anything wrong and you've never been anything but honest. I'm disappointed in myself because I couldn't stop it from happening. I couldn't turn it off or even slow it down once it started, and I didn't tell you because I knew you'd leave. It was unfair and selfish. I knew it was the whole time, but I did it anyway because I wanted to be with you for as long as I could. So…I'm sorry." I wiped my face with my sleeve. "Now, if you don't mind, I'd really like to go. Because this hurts."

"It doesn't have to."

"Actually, I think it does." If there was a way around it, I'd sure like to know what it was. But I deserved this. I'd practically begged for it to happen.

"Tell me what you want, Lane."

"I don't know," I whispered.

"Yeah, you do. You're just afraid to say it because you don't want to hurt anyone's feelings. *My* feelings. I can handle it, so just fucking say it."

"I want *you.*"

"You already have me." He stepped towards me. "I'm right here."

I shook my head. "I want more than you just being there. I want all of you. I don't want you to hold yourself back."

"Okay."

"No, you don't understand. What I want is for you to accept the way I feel about you and be okay with it. Then—" I laughed, even though it didn't sound like a laugh because it wasn't funny—it was stupid. "Then I want you to tell me you feel the same, and I want it to be the truth. But it doesn't matter what I want because I can't have it. It's not anybody's fault and admitting it doesn't change anything. So, in terms of things I want that are possible, I guess…I guess I want you to be okay."

"That's a lot of things."

"You asked. I answered."

"How would you answer if I told you I want to open doors for you and pull out your chair and bring you breakfast in bed and spend hours getting pruney in the tub watching that shit you call television, just as long as my arms are around you?"

"I'd probably say, 'As incredible as that sounds'"—my next breath was broken—"'it's not enough.'" A relationship would never work with as much inequality as we had. I'd always want more, and I'd always be disappointed.

"Then I'd say, 'Shut up, Lane, because I'm not done. Because I want to wake up next to you every morning and make love to you every night. I want to protect you and make you understand that you're the most amazing person I've ever met.' I've known you were ever since you told me to fuck off in the coffee shop, but I was afraid to say it. Because if I said it out loud, you might realize I was right and that you could do so much better than me, you *deserved* so much better than me and what I could offer."

"Cars—"

"Then I'd tell you to shut up again, because there's some stuff I need to say, and if I stop talking now I'll chicken out. Stuff like how, at first, it was easy not to tell you how I felt because I'd never felt it before and didn't know what it was or what to call it. Then it was *hard* not to tell you because you deserved the truth even if it made you run for the hills. So that means I *did* do something wrong and I haven't always been honest. And for that I'm sorry. What would you say then?"

"I...I don't know what I would say."

"Then I guess I would have to come up with something to cover the awkward silence. And even though I'd really want to fill it by kissing you, I'd probably feel like that was a bit presumptuous after all the horrible things I've done to you. So I might try something else."

"Like what?"

"Like maybe telling you that—" He took a step towards me. "Can I touch you, Lane? Just...just...your arm or your shoulder or...your cheek?"

I wanted to say yes so badly, but I knew one touch would turn into something neither of us could control. We'd end up in bed with nothing solved or different, and it would keep happening. And a month from now, I would wake up knowing that sleeping with someone you love is a terrible thing to do when that love isn't returned.

"It's okay," he said, nodding, understanding what my silence meant. "It's okay, Lane. You don't owe me anything." When I moved to go around him, he deliberately stepped in front of me, his hands tucked in his back pockets. "But I'm going to take it anyway because I'm still a selfish prick, and I can't let you walk out that door."

I stood there like an idiot, tears running down my face, not knowing what to do because it had taken all my strength just to *start* walking. And now all that strength and the little bit of momentum I'd had was gone, so I was stuck standing there in front of him, waiting for...for something that would never happen. "Can you please just let me leave?"

"No, not like this. Not yet." Staring straight at me, he mumbled something. He said it again, a little louder this time, his head bowed forward. "Because I haven't worked up enough courage to tell you I'm in love with you yet."

"What?"

He blew out a breath and ran his hand through his hair. "I'm in love with you, Lane. And it feels— Well, I can't honestly say it feels good right now because I'm really nervous about how you're gonna react. But it feels right, and I don't want it to stop."

"Do you really mean that?"

"I don't say things I don't mean." So quiet, so still.

I didn't want to move before he did but nothing could stop my heart from pounding even faster and a warmth filling every part of me. Just like nothing could stop the stupid amount of tears that were sliding down my cheeks or the sudden peace I felt knowing I wasn't going to hurt anymore, because we would be okay.

I could tell he was afraid to look at me and couldn't stop his body from trembling. "Come here." My heart skipped when he obeyed me, something he'd never been particularly good at. He stopped about two feet in front of me. "Closer."

Again he obeyed. "Look at me." He swallowed, raising his head, his eyes shy and unsure. "Now say it again."

"Aw, come on."

"Say it again, Carson."

He let out his breath really slowly, maybe to give himself time. "I love you. Every part of you, not just the parts I've already told you I love. I need you to be in my life, Lane. Permanently."

It took me a minute to speak because I'd never, ever expected this moment. So I had to think about what it meant and what would happen. After I did, I smiled. Because I wasn't afraid. I didn't need to be, not anymore.

"Then you'd better be really, really good to me."

"I can do that." He kissed me gently, only our lips touching.

If we were both waiting for the other to make a move, we were going to be here all day. I cradled his face in both of my hands and deepened the kiss, felt him respond, relax, and then want more. As good as kissing him had always been, it felt even better than I remembered, as if he'd stopped holding back the last tiny bit of himself.

"You really love me?" I asked, lifting my chin so he could reach my neck more easily.

"Yeah, I really do."

"Show me how much."

He picked me up and walked across the bedroom, pulling my sandals off along the way. "I can't believe I almost screwed this up, Lane." But instead of lying me down on the bed, he kept walking. "I can't believe it."

I jolted when I felt him set me down on my feet inside the bathtub and turn the faucet on. "What are you doing?" Without answering, he got in and started pulling off my clothes. It became a race to move faster than the water level raised. When we were in our underwear, he sat down and yanked me onto his lap, wrapping my legs around his waist.

After another kiss, he said, "Your lips will be on mine for

the foreseeable future, so if you have anything to say, say it now."

"Does this mean I get to use your bathtub whenever I want to?"

He laughed. "*Our* bathtub. And only if you leave me a little room."

"Doable. I want another drawer."

"I'll give you four, but no more than that. 'Cause that's all I have."

"I could probably be convinced to share." I swallowed. "I don't want to separate sex and love."

"Good. Because you'll never need to." He ran his fingertips along my jaw, stopping to cup my chin so I couldn't turn away. "When I tell you that you're beautiful and I love you and you're my world, it's because it's true."

"Thank you." My lips brushed his. "When I tell you to go get me a drink, it's because you need to get me a drink."

"Okay, that's it—no more talking for you."

We stopped laughing, only because it kept us from kissing. And feeling. And loving.

Once Upon a Time...there was a woman who, though not stunningly beautiful, thought herself to be. Because she was in love with a man who made her feel that way. And despite himself, he was in love with her.

After all of the princes who'd turned into frogs and had damaged the woman's heart, it took a man who was not a prince to mend it. And in return, she mended his. For even though he'd long believed himself the lowest of creatures, he wasn't. His heart was locked away, deep inside of him, and he had never allowed anyone in for fear they would discover how truly ugly it was.

But what he didn't know was that his heart was pure and beautiful and strong. And all he needed was the right woman to unlock it and set him free...with a kiss.

The End

NONE OF US ARE ALONE

According to the CDC, an average of 24 people *per minute* are victims of rape, physical violence, or stalking *by their partner*, in the US alone. That's over 12 million women and men per year. More than 1 in 3 women (35.6%) and 1 in 4 men (28.5%) will experience this type of violence in their lifetime.

If you are involved in an abusive relationship, there are *so* many people who want to help you. But they can't help if they don't know. You *have* to tell someone. You *have* to ask for help. You aren't alone.

Call the National Domestic Violence Hotline,
or the hotline in your country
1.800.799.SAFE (7233)
www.thehotline.org

Virtually Impossible
Once & Forever   2

Once and Forever will be a series of at least seven stand-alone novels. Each story uses a theme or symbol from a fairytale, but only as a starting point. Because while fairytales aren't real, love *is*.

Virtually Impossible is Hayden's story,
and this how his fairytale begins:

Once Upon a Time...there was a woman who made the mistake of trusting the wrong man. And that mistake led to another. And another and another, each more damaging than the last. But the woman was as ignorant of her mistakes as she was of the damage they caused. Until she was punished for them. But because all knew she'd acted out of youth and naiveté, imagined love and true stupidity, her punishment was not grave.

However the woman believed she had not paid enough for what she'd done and how stupid she had been. So the punishment she gave herself was far, far more severe. She locked herself behind glass, only coming out from behind it when she was forced to, which wasn't often. And the longer she stayed behind the glass, the safer she fel,t until she didn't see it as a prison at all. Until she loved it for its beauty and depended on it for its clarity.

For you see, her cage was made from one-way glass and the mirror faced out, so the woman never had to look upon her own reflection. And when she saw the world beyond the glass, things were clear and simple and fair, for she was not part of the world but separate from it. And from behind the glass, there was nothing hidden from her and everything to hide behind.

Day after day she toiled, working hard to repay the wrong she'd unwittingly done and the people she'd unwittingly hurt. And thus she was so focused that she didn't notice how the glass pressed in on her, how stagnant and lifeless the air became. And when she finally realized, it didn't matter anymore, for she knew the tiny box was what she justly deserved for believing the lies told to her. So of her own volition, she remained behind the glass, knowing that one day she would have no more mistakes to make, no one left to hurt, no more sins to pay for, and no more air to breathe.

ABOUT LAUREN STEWART

Lauren Stewart lives in Northern California with two of the most amazing children that the world has ever seen. She reads almost every genre so, naturally, her writing reflects that. With every book, every story, you'll find elements of other genres—fantasy, mystery, romance, paranormal, suspense, YA, women's literature, all with a touch of humor because what doesn't kill us should make us laugh.

CONTACT LAUREN

Sign up for my newsletter to get:
A FREE COPY OF MY PARANORMAL NOVELLA,
SECOND BITE
As well as
Behind the Scenes Looks at Your Favorite Characters
Updates about Coming Soon and New Releases
News about Contests and Giveaways
Teasers and Sneak Peaks
Book Signings, Conventions, and Appearances
It's really easy to sign up. Just go to:
www.ReadLaurenS.com

Find me at:
www.facebook.com/LaurenStewartAuthor
Twitter: @ReadLaurenS
ReadLaurenS@gmail.com

OTHER TITLES BY LAUREN STEWART

Unseen, The Heights Vol. 1
Hyde, an Urban Fantasy
Jekyll, Hyde Book II
Strange Case, Hyde Book III
The Complete Hyde Series Box Set
No Experience Required, a Summer Rains Novel
Second Bite